Also by Vladimír Páral
From Catbird Press

The Four Sonyas (in cloth)

CATAPULT

A Timetable of Rail, Sea, and Air Ways to Paradise

By Vladimír Páral

translated from the Czech by William Harkins

CATBIRD PRESS ✳ *A Garrigue Book*

Translation of *Katapult* © 1967 Vladimír Páral.

The translator acknowledges his indebtedness to the late
Dr. Miroslav Rensky, who helped him greatly in matters of
contemporary colloquial language, slang, and technical jargon.
The publisher acknowledges the help of Ellen McGoldrick in
developing the concept of the bookmark. The translation that
appeared in Catbird's hardcover edition has been edited and
corrected for this paperback edition.

Library of Congress Cataloging-in-Publication Data

Páral, Vladimír, 1932-
    Catapult: a timetable of rail, sea, and air ways
to paradise.

    Translation of: Katapult.
    "A Garrigue book."
    I. Title.
PG5039.26.A7K313 1989   891.8'635   88-34053
ISBN 0-945774-17-6 (paper) 04-4 (cloth)

Characters and Pronunciation

This page and the next contain the names and nicknames of the major characters, as well as the pronunciation of their names and of the places they live. If you like to be able to say what you read, this will help a lot. Also, the nicknames will protect you from Russian-novel syndrome (Czech nomenclature is, however, much more simple, based primarily on diminutives).

This page can be used as a bookmark, for easier reference. Simply cut along the line, or fold the page each way a couple of times and rip the bookmark out.

If this book is yours, don't hesitate to mutilate it, no matter what your teachers said. If it's a library's, please leave the bookmark where it is so that others can use it.

The pronunciations are approximate, as close as possible without lengthy explanation.

JACEK JOST *Yahts'-ek Yohsht* (hero, lives in Usti nad Labem *Oos'-tee nahd Lahb'-aim,* or Usti on the Elbe)
Jaromir *Yahrr'-oh-meer* (formal name)
Jacinek *Yahts'-ee-nek* (Lenka's special name for him)
Jastrun *Yahs'-trroon* (Hanicka's name for him)

LENKA JOSTOVA *Lain'-kah Yohsht'-oh-vah* (Jacek's wife)
Lenunka *Lain'-oon-kah* (Jacek's special name for her)

LENICKA *Lain'-each-kah* (Jacek and Lenka's daughter)

TROST *Trrohsht* (Jacek's across-the-way neighbor and alter ego)

NADA HOUSKOVA *Nah'-dah Hohs'-koh-vah* (Jacek's first lover, lives in Decin *Dyeh'-cheen*)
Nadenka *Nah'-dyain-kah* (nickname)
Nadezda *Nah'-dyehzh-dah* (nickname; Russian)
Speranza (an Italian word with same meaning as her Czech name—hope—and name of Yugoslav hotel)

VLASTA *Vlahs'-tah* (Nada's friend on train)

PETRIK HURT *Payt'-rzheek Hort* (Jacek's boss)

VERKA HURTOVA *Vyairr'-kah Hort'-oh-vah* (Petrik's wife)

VITENKA BALVIN *Vee'-tyain-kah Bahl'-veen* (Jacek's co-worker, originator of the Balvin experiment)
Vitezslav *Vee'-tyehz-slahv* (his formal name)
Vitak *Vee'-tahk* (another nickname)

MILADA BALVINOVA *Meel'-ah-dah Bahl'-vee-noh-vah* (Vitenka's wife and Jacek's doctor)

JAROMIR MESTEK *Yahrr'-oh-meer Myehs'-tehk* (Jacek's across-the-hall neighbor)
Jarda *Yahrr'-dah* (nickname)
ALOIS KLECANDA *Ahl'-oh-ees Klets'-ahn-dah* (Jacek's old co-worker who's now a rock star; **Candy**)

FRANTA DOCEKAL *Frahn'-tah Doh'-check-ahl*
(Jacek's old co-worker who's now the boss
in Brno *Bare'-noh*, Czechoslovakia's second
largest city)

BENEDIKT SMRCEK *Behn'-eh-deekt Smairr'-check*
(Jacek's old co-worker who's now head of
the research institute in Brno)

ANNA BROMOVA *Ahn'-nah Brrohm'-oh-vah*
(Jacek's woman in Prague, scientist)
Anci *Ahn'-tsi* (nickname)

HANICKA KOHOUTKOVA *Hahn'-each-kah*
Koh'-hote-koh-vah (Jacek's woman in
Pardubice *Pahr'-doo-beets-eh*, teacher)

LIDA ADALSKA *Leed'-ah Ahd'-ahl-skah* (Jacek's
woman in Ceska Trebova *Chess'-kah*
Trzhay'-boh-vah, forest ranger's widow)

JANICKA *Yahn'-each-kah* and **ARNOSTEK** *Ahrn'-*
oh-shtek (Lida's children)

TANICKA RAMBOUSKOVA *Tahn'-each-kah*
Rahm'-bohs-koh-vah (Jacek's woman in Svitavy
Sveet'-ah-vee, bookkeeper and poet)

MOJMIRA STRATILOVA *Moy'-meer-ah Strraht'-*
ee-loh-vah (Jacek's woman in Brno, translator)
Mojenda *Moy'-ehn-dah* (nickname)

TINA VLACHOVA *Teen'-ah Vlak'-oh-vah* (Jacek's
woman in Bohosudov *Bow'-hoh-soo-dohv*,
barmaid; **Tina de Modigliani**)

MR. STEFACEK *Shtaif'-ah-check* (runs the
storage room at Jacek's plant)

NORBERT HRADNIK *Nohr'-bairt Hrrahd'-neek*
(Jacek's first attempt at replacing himself;
nahradnik means substitute)
Nora *Nor'-ah* (nickname)

TOMAS ROLL *Toe'-mahsh Rrohl* (Jacek's second
attempt at replacing himself; **Tom**)

VLADIMÍR PÁRAL *Vlah'-de-meer Pahh'-ral*
(author of this novel)

THE FIRST HALF OF THE GAME

Not to dare is fatal. —René Crevel

Part I — Chances and Dreams — one

Late, as usual, Express No. 7 from Bucharest, Budapest, and Bratislava was just pulling into Platform One at Brno Main Station. It was Wednesday, April 1, and there was the usual confused rush of travelers who lacked reservations but were trying, as a matter of principle, to board the middle cars of the train, even though these cars were intended (likewise as a matter of principle) for those who had reservations. In the midst of this rush Jacek Jost (33/5'9", oval face, brown eyes and hair, no special markings) took in the always unexpected sequence of numbers on the middle cars until, sufficiently amused, he finally caught sight of his own car, No. 52, hooked up between Nos. 34 and 38.

In compartment E two unpleasant surprises: First, Jacek's seat, No. 63, the second from the window, was just being occupied. Second, and even more unpleasant, its occupant was that loathsome Trost, like himself from Usti, in fact from the apartment house opposite his own. In the window seats, Nos. 61 and 62, two women stopped talking, as if scandalized by the two newcomers actually venturing to sit down in an otherwise empty compartment, right next to them.

"I've got No. 63," Jacek Jost declared, his ticket in his hand as evidence to the women and a challenge to Trost.

"I'd like to sleep and I don't want to be awakened by somebody trying to claim my seat."

"So just sit across from me on No. 64," said Trost. "It's mine. No one'll disturb you."

Jacek shrugged his shoulders, carefully placed his large black satchel with brass fittings into the baggage net above seat No. 64, hung up his raincoat, and the train pulled quietly out.

"Twenty-two minutes late," said Jacek.

"We'll have to look lively in Prague to catch the 4:45 to Berlin," said Trost.

"I've never missed it yet."

"You make the trip often, don't you?"

"Quite often. And you?"

"Not so much. The weather's nice, isn't it?"

"It is now."

The women by the window began to talk again, they leaned so close together they hid the view, the compartment was overheated as always, and already Trost had taken shelter behind his dangling coat. Jacek spread his own out in front of himself, and in the darkness behind it he closed his eyes.

It was getting harder and harder to reach an agreement with the higher-ups in Brno, three days of exhausting negotiations and we still won't get any ethyl acetate this year either—better not to think about next year—where have the days gone when you could save something from your travel budget , Lenka will be pleased with the Dutch cocoa, we can sprinkle it on our hot cereal, milk dishes sit best in a stomach queasy from six hours on a train, that's what Lenka says, they're the cheapest too and quickest to make, if I don't miss the 4:45 to Berlin we'll find Lenicka still awake and the water pistol will amuse her, but for how long?—ten minutes, no more, the blow-up squirrel would have been better, of course she'll spray the water pistol all over the place, when she gets fed up with it we'll build a play house out of mattresses and then an obstacle course, but that might be too much jumping around and then she won't feel like going to sleep and she'll keep calling from her crib, our sweet little beastie, Daddy come and tell the story again about the enchanted prince, you know, the one who had to ride the train through eleven black tunnels until the golden aurochs taught him which one the princess had been walled up in—it's aurochs, my sweetie, you're saying auwochs, yes, it's a great big hairy cow, this big.

"...and when Joe told her about the bidet, she bought him a bathroom brush."

"What?!"

"A pink one, made of nylon—" the women next to the window were making each other laugh and to Jacek's distaste his neighbor pushed her hip farther and farther across the border between seats Nos. 62 and 64, into Jacek's territory. From the expropriated No. 63 across from him, Trost's pig-like snoring had already begun.

First class was still authorized for trips over 150 miles, the seats had armrests, and you could still save something out of your travel budget , but what would it be like five years from now or ten? Lenka probably had some Dutch cocoa left from last time, Lenicka would probably have gotten tired of the squirrel as well, if only the girl were older, no, if only she could be a two-year-old again, how she's growing, soon she'll be coming home just to eat and sleep as if to a hotel, what would it be like ten years from now or twenty?—only on a train, it seemed, could a man get at Gauguin's WHERE DO WE COME FROM—WHO ARE WE—WHERE ARE WE GOING, once Lenka and I used to go through it almost every evening, but surprisingly the answer kept getting harder to come by—better not to think about some things—but Lenka's a good wife and we do have a darling, clever little girl, we both earn good salaries and we've got a first-category apartment, the first year each of us in different dorms, the second year each of us in different rooms, the third year at last a little attic room together, but Lenicka had already come by then, entire nights by her bed, carrying water from the cellar and heating it on our hotplate in the sink, if only it could be settled all at once, the fourth year a comfortable co-op at last, but another down payment to make, a loan to negotiate, furniture, rugs, a refrigerator, a television set, enough cares, if only it could be settled all at once, the best five years of your life suddenly gone, not very happy years at that, but now it was all settled and fulfilled, even that final wish, THE SEA—

—crowded on his right by his intrusive neighbor, baked from below by the uncontrollable heating system, tossed rhythmically and knocked on the head by the stiff imitation leather of the headrest, struck on his left by the draft from the door and tickled on his face by his hanging coat, to the snoring of Trost, the slob, and the prattle of those women by the window, in the tension of the ever narrowing time span linking the delay of the Bucharest express to the departure of the 4:45 to Berlin—

—alone with the sun in a blue, blue hemisphere, outside time, naked, free, only desire, will, body, sex—all that makes a man a man—blissful, Jacek was swimming toward Africa.

Half an hour must have passed already, hurriedly he turned, quickly back toward the shark net, he tore his trunks free of the wire (Lenka had knitted them from an old sweater), swiftly back toward the rocky coast of Istria with its dozens of tiny terraced beaches separated by rocks, up to ours, the highest above the sea (and farthest from it), swiftly into his red beach chair alongside Lenka's red one: "You're always going off someplace," Lenka says, and Lenicka wants him to play bunny-rabbit.

From the highest section of the tiered beaches of our hotel, the Residence, beach is visible to the south as far as the narrow channel on the horizon—a day's sail off in that direction is the coast of Africa. Right behind Lenicka's little white knees, one level down, lies Mrs. Vanda (she kisses in the elevator), she keeps drawing into her mouth and then letting slide from her lips a huge, dark red, swollen oval grape. On the tiny concrete square by the Pension Jeannette the freckled artist presses his chin to his knees (he had offered to paint Jacek in the nude). On the rocks at the Belvedere handsome Yugoslav boys open black mussels with a knife, swallowing the contents and rubbing the remnants on their chests and thighs. On the tiny beach of the Hotel Palma that magnificent black-haired French-woman (before breakfast she too went swimming without a suit), with her palm she slowly wipes her moist, shiny hip. High up on a cliff, gazing toward the horizon, sits the bearded Swedish pastor (he keeps trying, in his absolutely incomprehensible language, to attract Jacek's attention to something or the other). Lenicka's gone to sleep in our arms. "Where are you rushing off to again?" Lenka asks.

Jacek swam southward toward the freckled painter at the Jeannette and got a piece of chocolate from him, but what were Lenka and Lenicka up to—in order to see, Jacek made his way through the bushes up to the rail of the promenade—everything's fine, Lenicka's asleep and Lenka's talking to the Mareceks, Jacek swam off toward the beach of the Hotel Palma, the dark Frenchwoman spoke fluent German with a husky laugh, suddenly he noticed her watch, he jumped up and ran out to the rail of the promenade—everything's fine, Lenka's talking to the Janeceks and Lenicka's still asleep, and Jacek swam along the beach of the Stefanie (where they make those fried sardines) and the Kvarner (where the redhead is lying) toward the cliff with the bearded Swede, his childish, trust-ing blue eyes and the warmth of his unknown language, suddenly Jacek stopped short, and now he was leaping over the rocks and up to the rail of the promenade—everything's fine, Lenicka's splashing with some kids and Lenka's talking to the Mareceks again, and greedily Jacek swam along the beaches of the Naiad, the Speranza, and the Miramar, toward the south, suddenly, in order to see, he struck out toward the east—the red trapezoid of his empty beach chair between Lenka and Lenicka was like an insistent outcry, and nervously Jacek turned and swam quickly back, through the warm green waves that washed the welcoming stairs of the Miramar, the Speranza, the Naiad, the Kvarner, the Stefanie, the Palma, the Jeannette, and the Belvedere, to the stairs of our Residence and straight back to his place, with Lenicka's head propped against his shoulder and Lenka's fingers clasping his wrist.

Mrs. Vanda had struck up a conversation with the bald butcher from Chomutov, and before long her leg was lying across his fat hip. The freckled artist swam over to the rocks of the Belvedere and handed out chocolate, and soon he was posing a skinny boy. The waiter from Lovosice lay down near the dark Frenchwoman and soon they were kissing under her beach umbrella. The Swede on his cliff was saying something to two children and pointing to something on the horizon.

But on the stones at the Kvarner the redhead is still alone, she's lying on her stomach again and untying the back of her top, floating onto the warm green waves are rafts with girls stretched out on them as if for love-making, on the bottom of a metal boat a half-naked sun-browned blonde, and calling out along the shore toward the south a strip of radiant sea stretching all the way to Africa.

"Time to go," says Lenka, never with anyone else but her, she has a touch of sunstroke, Lenicka throws up on a rock, she must have a fever, it's all from the sun, my darlings, tomorrow we'll spend a nice long day at home and pull down the blinds, with a smile Lenka clasps one handle of our enormous bag full of towels, bits of uneaten food, rags, baby oil, talcum powder, and a thermos, she takes both handles in one hand and the exhausted Lenicka by the other, "Time to go—" the strip calls to the south, never with anyone else but Lenka, an open road of green waves all the way to Africa, at an unheard command the higher-ups take their positions on the cliffs by their mine throwers, Lenka sprinkles Dutch cocoa on the sidewalk in front of the apartment house, this week we're on clean-up duty, and from bed, with a shriek, Lenicka fires a pistol full of burning ethyl acetate, the blow-up squirrel would definitely have been better, pull off Lenka's constraining shorts and in a frantic crawl swim from the stairs of the Residence, warm green waves to the stairs of the Belvedere, the Jeannette, the Palma, the Stefanie, the Kvarner, the Naiad, the Speranza, and the Miramar, to Africa—

Thrown violently out of his seat, Jacek Jost flew across the space between the odd and even numbers and fell full force between Trost and his neighbor by the window, with a screech Trost pushed him roughly away with his shoulders and his knee, with his arms thrown out in desperation Jacek grabbed the shoulders and breasts of woman No. 61, fell kneeling to the floor, his face in her lap, and then, when he set his right cheek on her thigh and looked up, he saw the girl smile and saw his pale hands on her black sweater. The train had come to a stop.

No. 61 might be a bit over twenty, blonde and good-looking. Jacek's neighbor, No. 62, some ten years older, grinned and rubbed her stomach, which had struck against the small folding table under the window. It might have been the emergency brake—we lost something or ran over someone. The express soon started up again, on the main east-west line a train passes every four minutes, so each delay must be held to a minimum. Irritably, Trost hid behind his coat and Jacek spread his own out in front of himself, the theater last night had cut the irreducible minimum of eight hours of sleep to a mere six, they still hadn't reached Ceska Trebova and we always sleep as far as Pardubice.

No. 61 happened to be pretty, a pleasant sight, how charmingly she had protested that he didn't need to apologize, Trost had bleated something or other and crawled behind his coat, she was in such good shape, Lenka should start exercising again.

"...and then I wouldn't take it from him anymore."

"But Nada, really..." the voices of the women next to the window.

No. 61 is called Nada, Nadenka, Nadezda, she's really very pretty, we hadn't even noticed whether she was wearing a ring or not—of course she is. We've still got half a tin of Dutch cocoa at home and a whole one, too, we bought it when the general director came on board, what things he said then and what he's doing now.

"I haven't met a man like that so far," said Nada.

"How about Jirka?" said No. 62.

"He was very kind, pleasant, and an absolute zero."

"You used to talk differently about him."

To put that water pistol into Lenicka's hand would mean an immediate call to workmen to repaint the apartment, that's what happens when you buy gifts on the way to the station, what year was it when we interrupted a trip so that Lenka could have an umbrella from Ceska Trebova, a local specialty, then she left it behind somewhere.

"I wanted to believe it... I would again, too, but about someone very different...," Nada was saying.

"Do I know him?" whispered No. 62.

"I don't yet myself. I may run an ad for him: 'Slim 23-year-old blonde with her own apartment looking for a man. Key word: MAN!'"

"Speak softer, or those two..."

"They're snoring again. Do you think I'd catch anybody that way?"

"Sure, mostly with that bit about 'her own apartment'—"

"I'd take him home for the night, for a test run in bed!"

"Don't shout so, Nada..."

"Seriously, if I liked him... But if he didn't like me, then I wouldn't chase after him. You know, the way you did that time with Milan Renc."

"Yeah, that was almost it..."

"It was wonderful, wasn't it—" Nada said loudly. No. 62 just giggled.

Lenka is on her way home from work now, she hasn't forgotten the milk for his hot cereal or to stop by the school for Lenicka, this week we have clean-up duty in front of the apartment house, it's a lot for her, Lenka is a good wife, and if he's going to make up those two lost hours—eight hours a day keeps neurosis away—he has to go to sleep at once, counting off the order of the hotels on the Adriatic: the Residence, the Belvedere, the Jeannette, the Palma, the Stefanie, the Kvarner, the Naiad, the Speranza, Speranza in Italian is the same as Nadezda in Russian: *hope*—

"It *was* wonderful, wasn't it—" Nada said loudly, she almost shouted it, she's beautiful, with a smile she had bent over the face in her lap and had tolerated the touch of his pale hands on her black sweater, she almost called it out as a challenge, yet he stayed behind his coat, he ought to ask her where she was going...

"I stay behind this coat," Trost's beery voice suddenly thundered forth, "and I don't even know where we're at. Was that Ceska Trebova? Good God! We're really making time, aren't we? And where are you ladies going?" He was trying to make an ordinary and quite vulgar pickup.

Jacek was suffocating behind his wrinkled old raincoat, why didn't we take the new iridescent, it was just like that pot-bellied Trost, the idiot, the way he sticks his muzzle out of the window every day, with our windows right opposite, 100% visibility, as soon as he gets home he strips to his shorts and sniffs in the pantry and the oven (the two apartments are identical in their lay-out and appliances), gobbles down roast pork right out of the pan and washes it down with a slug of beer straight from the bottle, then he brings a pillow to the windowsill and starts to gape from window to window until TV comes on for the evening, then he gapes at that, pisses and snores, and that's the entire zoological profile of Mr. Trost.

"You don't say, really? Then we're practically from the same town!" Trost was master of the whole compartment, he wooed and pursued the poor women by the window, Nada of course soon stopped answering, but No. 62—"why don't you call me Vlasta"—had taken the bait and was giggling more and more, Trost wooed and pursued her, and Vlasta, already taking up half of Jacek's No. 64, twisted her backside, Jacek, rubbed and shoved by her hip, was rhythmically gyrated, slapped on the back of his head by the headrest, rubbed and burned by the imitation leather underneath him, annoyed to the point of pain, and then tenacious efforts to fall asleep, to sleep, back to the warm green waves and the stairs of the Belvedere, the Jeannette, the Palma, the dark Frenchwoman stroking her moist hip under the parasol, the Stefanie, the redhead is descending the stairs of the Kvarner and raising her hands to the shoulder straps of her bathing suit, at the Naiad the girls are rocking, stretched out on their rafts as if for lovemaking, and floating out from the Speranza is the sun-browned blonde spread out in the bottom of a glass-bottomed boat, Speranza is Italian for hope and the Miramar is just a dream, Mrs. Vanda kisses the huge swollen red grape, and on the rocks the handsome Yugoslav boys with their smeared chests and thighs, a seaside amphitheater of clamoring naked spectators, and the rhythmic beat of the waves insistently pressing against the rocky cliffs.

Jacek Jost pushed his raincoat aside and stood up, stared at Nada's inquisitive face, and went out of the compartment into the corridor, where, badly shaken, he staggered and clutched at doors and walls, locked himself in the little room at the end of the car, and looked at himself in a quivering mirror.

Lenka is on her way to school now to pick up Lenicka, in her bag a bottle of milk and on her palm calluses from that eternal bag, even on Sundays she doesn't get enough sleep, she never leaves anything undone, a wife a hundred times better than we deserve, so loving, never with anyone else but you, and she's a perfect mother to our clever, pretty little girl, Sunday mornings we take her into bed with us and after lunch we go to the zoo. It's true, in our civilized age the life of a father doesn't offer many experiences that are particularly exciting, in fact it doesn't offer any, however, instead of that—but five years of married life without the least shadow of infidelity aren't worth spoiling now for the sake of that.

Jacek Jost washed his hands and face with cold water and went back along the vibrating corridor to compartment E, he stopped short in the door—Trost was lounging on his seat, No. 64, alongside Vlasta on No. 62, he had even dared to take his coat with him and to hang Jacek's opposite, above No. 63, "Excuse me," he blared with his hand already resting on the shoulder of his new neighbor, Vlasta, "but in Brno you said that you wanted to sit there, and anyway that's the seat you've got a reservation for!"

"We worked it out this way," Vlasta giggled.

"Of course, only if you don't mind...," Nada added sweetly from the window, Jacek shrugged his shoulders and settled down very close to her on the green imitation leather seat. To be thrown out of your seat three times is obviously good luck on purpose, all the more when all flights have the same direction—when catapulted, there's nothing to do but fly.

The train sped smoothly over the remaining hundred kilometers, no one else would come in now. Opposite the mutual and constantly growing admiration of Trost and his already "darling" Vlasta, Jacek and Nada sat together on the settee designated for them, Nos. 61/63, and in the rocking rhythm of the warm green waves of the imitation leather seats they swam out toward the sun. The eleventh and final tunnel came just before Prague. Even before, Trost was panting heavily on darling Vlasta's neck, the golden aurochs had already fulfilled its fairy-tale destiny, and in the glowing eleventh tunnel the happy prince, no longer bewitched, kissed his laughing princess, now at last released from her wall.

When they got out at Prague the other two disappeared, and Jacek and Nada easily caught the 4:45 to Berlin.

"All my life I've never gone any farther on this train…," Jacek whispered as it pulled into the station at Usti, and Nada grinned. Fine nylon lines twitched painfully on his wrists and ankles and around his body, the sensation of tugging straps with felt lining, like a horse's harness, and the train pulled silently out along the shore and down the springtime river, but then Decin is only twenty minutes from Usti and the next stop on the express.

I — two

A feeling of vertigo on leaving the Decin station, the stream of passengers quickly poured into buses and streetcars, all going by the shortest route to their Lenickas and Lenkas…. Jacek Jost was suddenly left alone on the empty sidewalk with Nada.

"What sort of program do you propose, my lord?" she said.

"Dinner with champagne, dancing, two cognacs, and the longest way home to your place…."

"Hmm, I've read that somewhere. How about a swim?"

"Now?!—"

"Why not? I don't have hot water at home and the baths are only a few steps away. But we've got to hurry."

"But I don't have any trunks and...."

"Leave it to me."

They seemed to be closing up the baths, but Nada had no problemarranging things, laughing she picked out a large pair of canvas trunks for Jacek. As for Nada, she had her own, the warm glow of golden brown flesh in stiff white nylon, "How do you like me?"

"Very much," said Jacek, self-consciously drawing together the excess folds of his bathing suit, "you don't have to give your opinion of me."

"Except for the fabric, you'll do," laughed Nada, she pushed Jacek off the edge into the pool, he swallowed a lot of chlorinated water and as soon as, sputtering, he could see again, he grabbed her legs and pulled her in with him, they dunked and pushed each other around, she taught him the proper way to dunk and he taught her how to make a star, and in the glow of floodlights they swam together in the warm green waves.

"And now for dinner!" Nada cried on the dark, now silent street illuminated by the flickering light of TV sets in the homes they passed.

"What's the best you've got here?"

"The Grand, I suppose, but you can't smoke there and there's a lot of unnecessary hoity-toity. I know a great place, even if it is third-category."

"Whatever you want, but..."

Nada's third-category didn't look too bad, no more than ten tables with checkered tablecloths, bright landscapes in thick frames of stained wood, and above a copper counter a stag's antlers with fourteen points, Jacek sat with his back to it, wondering whether the place would have champagne.

"Boy am I thirsty," said Nada. "Two beers, Mrs. Vasata."

On the menu the only stand-out was something called

Belgrade cutlet, otherwise just some humdrum dishes, and chocolate pudding.

"Two Belgrades—" was the order Jacek gave to Mrs. Vasata.

"Jacek, I'd much rather have the Slovak sausage... Don't you like it?"

"Very much, but after all..."

"So, two helpings of the Slovak with bacon... And a heap of peppers in oil!"

It was a wonderful meal, the beer was smooth and light, in the corner by the cast-iron stove sat a group of boys singing along with a guitar, their heads turned up toward the low ceiling:

> *Blue mists on the lake*
> *Vanished like far-off desire*

"You're wonderful, Nada, really, and I..."

"Oh shush! Listen to those kids instead."

"No, really... I just wanted to let you know... You see, I'm really not used to... There are circumstances which... which..."

"You want to tell me something about yourself?"

"Look, Nada, I don't have to tell you again, really... that... well... Of course..."

"Will you tell me without lying?"

"No, Nada, look, I only thought..."

"You won't. Then don't tell me anything."

> *Oo, oo, the song of the Manitou.*

"You're really such a special girl, that really..."

"Oh shush with that, I know when it's April Fools' Day. Tell me something more about Opatije in Yugoslavia. I may go there this summer."

"You tell something, you do it better..."

Jacek ran his fingers along the ridge of his hand and, really quite involuntarily, he looked at his watch: 10:07. Lenicka has been asleep for a long time with her thumb in her mouth, while Lenka, worried, has put the bottle of milk away in the refrigerator and she'll stay up until the arrival of the night express, he ran his fingers along his wrist and looked straight into Nada's expectant face.

> There the redskins stood,
> Wild horses flew,
> Oo, oo, the song of the Manitou.

Suddenly he stood up. "Let's go—" Nada was already on her feet.

The restless gray of TV screens flickered out onto the dark, empty street. "I live over there," Nada pointed, it was hardly more than a hundred and fifty feet away, and: "We really stuffed ourselves, didn't we?" she said, and then she stopped. She wasn't making it any too easy, what could you talk about in the course of a hundred and fifty feet, and to kiss in front of a restaurant—

"Isn't there a park over there?" Jacek pointed at random.

"In the opposite direction. Why?"

"Nothing, I just thought... You know what, we could have those two cognacs now."

"I'd prefer Egyptian brandy... But that's awfully expensive."

"So let's have six of them!"

"OK, Jacek dear, I've already come to realize that you're the rich señor from Rio, but—"

"From Usti nad Labem, and I make 1,800 a month, but—"

"—but what do you really care for most? No pretending."

"Nadenka..."

"You see. So come on."

Quickly they traversed those hundred and fifty feet in silence, and inside the lobby Jacek tried to at least pinch her, but Nada pushed him away: "I smell sauerkraut, phooey—" she laughed quietly, and she pushed him toward the stairs.

Nada's room wasn't very big, a couple of pieces of light-colored furniture and a cream-colored kitchen chair, a large bay window looking out on the harbor, and beside it a drafting board on a stand. Jacek played with the jointed weight-beam, tried out the T square, and managed to recall a couple of drafting techniques.

"You look as if you knew something about that sort of thing."

"At technical school I majored in construction."

"I thought you said you were a chemist."

"After high school I wanted to study architecture, but that was the year they transferred the school away from Brno, so I had to take chemistry instead."

"Which they'd just transferred to Brno."

"No, they had it there already."

"Then why didn't you start with it?"

"Because I wanted to be an architect."

"But why didn't you become one?"

"Because they transferred the... For whom does everything turn out the way he wants..."

"For me, for instance. And how did you get from Brno to Usti?"

"Laugh if you must, but they transferred me."

"That *is* something to laugh about. And what, really, do you do in the chemical factory there?"

"It's actually a textile mill, you know, for cotton... But I don't have much to do with it, I travel mostly, our main office is in Brno."

"That's not something to laugh about—Jacek, Jacek, you can build houses and concoct explosives, and you're a traveling man in textiles..."

"You know, I didn't have things easy and there was the pressure of circumstances which... which..."

"...which kept pushing you somewhere, or there was a vacuum which kept sucking you somewhere— Like me from the train here."

"But I really did want to come with you..."

"So you only had to wait for the pushing and the sucking to work."

"Life often…"

"Don't be silly."

OK, sure, laugh all you want, but why really?, and then
in an animated tone carry on your pre-rutting conversation, why really?, still Jacek stubbornly tried to talk, but in
silence Nada looked into his eyes with ever growing
derision, finally she yawned, without even putting her
hand over her mouth, and heedlessly interrupted Jacek in
the middle of a sentence: "I think you're sleepy too."

"Nadenka…"

"Wouldn't you rather get some sleep… before…?"

Jacek got up quickly and embraced her, no easy task
since she remained seated in her chair, still he tried, he
hunched his shoulders, bent over, attempted different
approaches, knelt down, sat on the floor for a moment and
then got up again, just cooperate a little for God's sake—
how could one cope with the difference in height, bend one
leg at the knee and spread the other far out in back, that
might do it, a little more, on the edge of the sole and now
on tiptoe—but everything suddenly gave way with thunder and the cracking of wood, everything landed on the
floor, and behind the overturned chair Nada was shrieking
with laughter.

He'd had it up to here with these April Fools' jokes, he
stepped over the legs and seat of the chair and as if storm-
ing a trench he attacked Nada from behind, an open cuff
link cut him on the wrist, let's hope it isn't an artery, on,
on with hand-to-hand combat, but hell, how does that
unbutton, how many years has it been now since Lenka
and I, Nada was laughing again, they make them without
buttons now, sure, but howdo you—

"I haven't got the stamina for this," Nada finally said,
and she got up and went to the door. "But never fear, I'll
be back."

Sure, enough reasons to clear out of here for good, but when wasted opportunities pain you so much later on, and then come depression and neurosis—if it weren't for fear of them, we'd have long ago been at home in bed—what a joy it will be to find out how little is left when forbidden pleasures have been realized and then we'll be glad to get home again, sure, meanwhile why not make the bed, and Jacek, as he was accustomed to do at home, spread out the sheet, tucked it in neatly at the corners and smoothed it out, put the plumped-up pillow at the head, and carefully turned down the blanket, then he stood a while admiring his decorating efforts. "You don't want coffee now, do you?" came from behind the door, "No," he called, as was expected of him, he turned off the light, undressed, and climbed into bed.

Nada came back in a black bathrobe and turned the light back on. "I knew you wanted to sleep."

"No, no I..."

"So let's get some sleep, all right? Do you have anything against making love in the morning?"

"OK, Nadenka, I've come to realize that you're the un-conventional girl in a Swedish movie, but—"

"Look at him, he's almost turned into a man in that bed. OK, I'll take charge now. Get up— oh, I see..." Nada took a nightgown out of a drawer, threw it to Jacek, and again went out, while Jacek put on the gown Nada pushed the other kitchen chair into the room, placed the two chairs opposite each other, sat down on one of them and said, "Come and sit across from me."

"Still the Swedish film?"

"No, it's a game now."

"What's it called?"

"Train. Let's start at the beginning. Come here."

Before Jacek could sit down, she'd brought in his coat over her arm, a hammer under her arm, and a nail in her teeth, she pounded the nail into the wall above his chair and sat down on her own across from him.

"Your ticket says seat No. 63, but you're sitting in No. 64," she said. "You'd like to sleep and you don't want to be awakened by somebody trying to claim your seat. Oo—oo—we're pulling out of Brno, ch-ch-ch-ch—so far you've never missed the 4:45 to Berlin. By six you'll be home in Usti. Now throw the coat in front of yourself and close your eyes. Ch-ch-ch-ch—"

Jacek shrugged his shoulders under the open-work nightgown with a bow, still April Fools', but at least the masquerade would come to an end now, he hung his wrinkled old raincoat on the nail and threw it in front of himself, why didn't we take the new iridescent, he closed his eyes.

"Repeat after me: ch-ch-ch-ch," Nada whispered.

"Ch-ch-ch-ch," Jacek whispered diligently behind his coat.

"Ch-ch-ch—I liked you the first time I saw you—ch-ch-ch-ch—I wanted to get to know you—ch-ch-ch-ch—you didn't pay any attention to me—ch-ch-ch-ch—so I'll wait until you get a little sleep—ch-ch—repeat after me: ch-ch."

"Ch-ch-ch-ch."

"Ch-ch-ch-ch—now you've been sleeping for an hour—ch-ch-ch-ch—if you'd only go to the dining car to eat—ch-ch-ch-ch—but what to do with that stupid Vlasta—ch-ch-ch-ch—let's wait till Trebova and by then we'll think of something—ch-ch. And here we are at last, bang—smash! The trains crash and Jacek is flying toward me—"

Nada stamped her foot, Jacek jumped up from his chair and came to rest on Nada, then he grabbed her shoulders and breasts, fell kneeling to the floor, his face in her lap, and then, when he set his right cheek on her thigh and looked up, he saw the girl smile and saw his pale hands on her black bathrobe.

"Dear Jacek...," Nada said tenderly, and with warm

hands she pressed his hands to her, the magic of the eleventh tunnel returned and quickly grew.

"I like you, Nadenka..."

"Don't tell lies, go back and sit down again. Crawl behind your coat, sleep some more and repeat after me: ch-ch-ch-ch."

"Ch-ch—but I didn't go to sleep after that—ch-ch-ch-ch."

"Ch-ch—I'm glad of that—ch-ch—but what were you doing behind that coat—ch-ch-ch-ch."

"I was thinking of you—ch-ch-ch-ch—I was remembering what you looked like—ch-ch-ch-ch—I was longing for you—"

"And you didn't even open your eyes, my sleepy man—ch-ch-ch-ch—I always wanted a man like you—ch-ch-ch-ch—slim 23-year-old blonde looking for a man—"

"Ch-ch—number sixty-one is called Nada, Nadezda—ch-ch-ch-ch."

"I never knew a man like you—ch-ch-ch-ch—I always wanted to have one—ch-ch-ch-ch."

"Ch-ch-ch-ch—the Residence, the Belvedere, the Jeannette, the Palma, the Stefanie, the Kvarner, the Naiad, the Speranza, and Speranza is the same as Nadezda! Nada, I love you—"

"Don't tell lies, you've hardly known me two hours and you've slept away a hundred minutes of that—ch-ch-ch-ch—it'll be wonderful—"

"Ch-ch-ch-ch—with you on the warm green waves—ch-ch-ch-ch—kissing you under a beach umbrella—"

"It'll be wonderful—"

"Your moist hip lying on a raft ready for love-making—"

"I want you, Jacek, so much—"

"Stretched out in a glass-bottomed boat, a swollen red grape, well-smeared boys on the rocks, and the roar of the amphitheater—"

"So much—Terribly much!—" Nada screamed, her arms

around his neck, pick her up, she isn't laughing anymore, and carry her the couple of steps.

At the sound of a siren from the harbor, the sun on his face, Jacek slowly awoke and still half asleep he turned toward Nada, lightly placed her hand over his shoulder, and tenderly ran his hand over to the other one, that's the way it's done, and the tousled Nada wriggled, turned over, and finally sat up, she rubbed her eyes with her fists and then an enormous yawn, which is always contagious, Jacek too opened his mouth like a hippo.

"But you're still asleep," laughed Nada, and she yawned again. "It doesn't matter, I am too." And she rapped Jacek across the knuckles.

"Do you have anything against making love in the morning?" he quoted her with a grin.

"OK, Jacek, I've already come to realize that you're an athletic boy. But how about stretching a bit first? And then a cold shower!"

She went to open the window, in the current of fresh air the two gymnasts stood opposite one another in front of the drafting table, "Follow my lead," she commanded. Jacek made a few timid movements and stood with his arms modestly crossed on his chest.

"I used to do exercises every day by the window, but then—"

"Then they transferred the window on you!" Nada burst out as she did a remarkable toestand.

"Lenka—she's a girl I used to know, you see, she always made fun of me... And in my new apartment, a pre-fab, it would wake up the neighbors and their children..."

"You, my boy, are so considerate, not to mention house-broken, and then there's the way you put things—" Nada stated her opinions while doing push-ups, and Jacek, feverishly recalling his military exercises, stubbornly kept trying to keep up. Two people can get under a shower, Lenka is too modest, only cold water in the morning gives you that feeling of the world at your feet, and how many lost mornings have there been now without it...

"What can I make for breakfast?" asked Jacek.

"What do you eat for breakfast?" asked Nada.

"Cookies and instant coffee."

"You like that?"

"Not so much, but... There just isn't any time."

"I always make time for breakfast."

"OK. So what have you got?"

"Kippers, honey, bitter chocolate, pickled mushrooms, and—cookies!"

"How about some of those pickled mushrooms."

"All right. But you know what I'd really like? Imagine hot tripe soup with lots of pepper, two crackling fresh poppyseed rolls..."

"And herring with onions..."

"So let's go."

At Nada's third-category they had everything, even the herring, Jacek's favorite dish.

"Then why didn't you order it last night?" Nada said in surprise.

"I didn't consider it a suitable prelude to... You know, the onions..."

"That's just what I expected you to say. But at home you could have it every day."

"There's no time in the morning..."

"You could buy a big can."

"I hadn't thought of that."

"And so for years you've been having cookies and instant coffee."

"Sometimes a person— But you're right. I'll buy a can."

Outside it was a magnificent morning. "It's a magnificent morning," said Jacek and: "How about an outing somewhere...," he suggested timidly.

"I'd go, but even Swedish girls have to work sometime.

You know that drawing I have on the board, I've got to finish it by Friday."

"So go finish it, I'll disappear..."

"So disappear if you want to. Am I keeping you on a leash?"

"No, I mean I wouldn't bother you if I could only..."

"Then don't disappear if you don't want to! It's clear that you'll bother me, but if you want to—or don't want to—good God, who can tell, forchristssakegoodgoddamn-carambahombrededioshimmelherrgott!"

"You're *recht*. I love you."

The sun was drawing golden trapezoids in the room overlooking the harbor, Jacek looked over Nada's shoulder, she stuck out her tongue and waved her hand back and forth, she rolled up her tracing paper and sat down to her calculations. "What are you up to, fella?"

"I could figure it out for you on a slide rule..."

"No, you're too good at that. Wait—" and Nada spread a clean sheet of tracing paper out on the board, explained what he had to do, and sat down with her papers again. "Now not a peep out of you for an hour."

Jacek took off his coat, rolled up his sleeves, and took his position at the board, he lit a cigarette, crushed it, and went to wash his hands, he lit a cigarette and took his position at the board, he crushed it and went to the john, he took his position at the board, went to wash his hands, took his position at the board, and excitedly began his assignment, my God, fifteen years, fifteen years vanished like a cloud, Jacek executed Nada's simple assignment, we're eighteen again, the September heat beats down on the asphalt roof and outside there's the buzz of a bench saw, underneath the draft of a sewage project the secret sketch of a new opera house for Brno, on the back of a motorcycle to a chalet set in a bend of our "Forest Free-way," the strong scent of felled pines in the noontime heat and the wild whirling of a brook tumbling down "Jost

Falls," on the warm grass tanned, half-naked men and the barefoot Libunka carrying a jug of goat's milk over the warm grass, guitars by the fire, songs reaching up to the dark treetops, Libunka in the grass that warms one far into the night, and in the morning diamonds on the grass sparkling beside the sparkling river, what had happened then and why had what he'd wanted so much not come to pass, was there anything—

"When are you going home?" asked Nada, standing behind him. "For God's sake don't ask me if I want you to stay or I don't want you not to stay, I mean, whether I don't want you to stay or I want you not to stay..."

—and was it only an oppressive fiction, the erosion and the landslides of the last few years, here, all of a sudden, he felt himself again, happy, why should he ever leave here, was it the last day that was the dream or was it the last fifteen years—

I — three

"How do you get long distance here? And what's your phone number?" said Jacek, lifting the receiver off its cradle with his right hand and reading the time off the wrist of his left: 9:14.

"Long distance is ten, my number is four-two-one-eight. But what..."

"Four-two-one-eight," Jacek said into the receiver, "I'm calling Brno three-nine-two-oh-three, urgent, snap to it, pronto!— Thanks, I'll wait."

"I've got a brother in Brno, he's a great guy," he explained to Nada before the call came through. "Brother? Hi! Yep, it's me. Look, let's keep this brief, it's costing me a bundle. Send two telegrams right away, both express— instead of wasting talk, let me dictate—Cottex, Usti. Ethyl acetate still uncertain, stop. Will make unofficial efforts.

Jost. And the other to Lenka at home: Arrive Friday usual train, no later—no, that's not necessary. Arrive Friday usual train. Jacek. What's that? No... Who knows... Maybe we'll be spending more time together and maybe... Seriously, send them off right away and some time we'll celebrate with a few Egyptians... It's a kind of brandy, you yokel. So long."

"You seem awfully concerned about that Lenka you used to know," Nada said softly. "Not that I give a damn about her. But perhaps you didn't realize in your sudden rush that today's only Thursday?"

"I've decided to stay one more day."

"Oh, he's decided. My lord grants me twenty-four hours."

"It's for me, too. One more day."

"OK. So let's start out with a good dinner. I'll let this work go for now, darling Jacek, and—"

"I don't like to see you do that, Nadenka."

"But it's already two o'clock."

"Why couldn't we dine at five, at nine in the morning, or just after midnight?"

"Whew!" Nada exclaimed, she shook her head and went back to her calculations. Not for long, however; Jacek picked her up along with her chair, carried her off, and just dumped her, "Wow!" she cried, "your technique's sure improving!"

At exactly a quarter to five Jacek decided that a quarter to five was the ideal time for dinner, Nada repeated that it would be a bore to go three times in twenty-four hours to the same restaurant, even if it was wonderful and so close to home, in bed in unison they gulped down kippers, honey, and bitter chocolate, and for dessert Nada ate cookies while Jacek had pickled mushrooms, without a word of discussion they both got up at almost the same moment and met by the window, they both dressed quickly and went out into the springtime streets of Decin, walking along the harbor and seeing a boat they boarded it and, for four crowns, sailed all the way to the last stop on the excursion steamer *Moravia*, to Hrensko.

From the harbor jetty, on a concrete ramp, they climbed up to the highway, "I won't check the return time," Jacek said as he passed the timetable for boats and buses.

"The last bus leaves at nine-thirty," Nada informed him.

To the left, below the railing, the Elbe rolled on toward the rum and banana docks of the Hanseatic city of Hamburg and on, now salty, past the dunes and sands of Cuxhaven and under the piles of Alte Liebe out to the sea toward Helgoland and Sylt, all that from his school reader, and to the right, over the highway, twigs and bushes still dark-brown and bare, but snow-strewn with tips, kernels, tendrils, and wicks of bursting green.

At the border station a red-and-white barrier reached across the highway, and Jacek went right up to it. "Don't go over there," Lenka had said once, "Why not?" "They'll want to see our IDs." "Well, haven't we got them?" "But what do you want to see there?" "I just want to..." "Let's go back to the bus!" Jacek shoved his foot as far as he could under the barrier, its tip out into the wide world, of course that other country was actually still some distance away, but even so... "Got a cramp in your leg?" asked Nada.

Alone in the twilight they walked through the canyon of the Kamenice River to the caves, galleries, and tunnels of the fanciful Duke Leopold Valley, in summer an endless procession made its way there, "Resorts are always better out of season," said Nada. "That's just what I expected you to say," Jacek parroted her, and they had a tussle on the little bridge over the rapids.

"I'd like—" said Nada, looking at the menu of the Elbe Chalet.

"Today I'm doing the ordering," said Jacek, and the champagne dinner suited him just fine. "Well, I suppose," Nada remarked, "you haven't spent very much on me."

"But," she warned him ten minutes before nine-thirty, as Jacek came back to the table, "that bus at half-past nine is really our last chance, to call a taxi from Decin would already probably..."

The bus was already waiting on the embankment, Jacek lit a cigarette and smoked with relish, "Put it out!" "No hurry." "But the door's closing—" "I don't feel like putting it out!" Jacek took Nada by the shoulders and, as if uncertain, the bus started off.

"OK, so what now?"

"Leave it to me," he parroted. "Look how the water sparkles..."

"There's ten miles of that sparkle back to Decin."

"No more than eight."

"They might have a vacant room at the Chalet..."

"Resorts are always better out of season."

"But they close at ten."

"So we'll knock."

"They'll sure be glad to see us!"

Shortly after ten, Jacek knocked at the door of the Elbe Chalet, "Good evening," the manager said politely, and he went away without another word. Jacek went straight upstairs, on the stairway he took a key out of his pocket, unlocked the door, and walked through the room to the balcony.

"Hmmm...," said Nada, she sat down in a huge old-fashioned easy chair and when, after a long time, Jacek returned, she said amiably, "So what game are we going to play tonight?"

"We've had nothing but games lately."

"OK," she said, and she took hold of the carved lion heads on the easy chair and locked her legs around its machine-lathed legs. "This old antique is a good deal heavier than my kitchen chair, so you'd better try to remember your simple machines: pulley, lever, screw, inclined plane... I've taken your breath away, huh?"

"I no longer want to ask what you care for most. Not in words, at least."

Nada was silent, she gradually relaxed her comedian's grip on the shedding easy chair as hands slowly slid along her arms and up to her shoulders, "Jacek darling...," she whispered.

"Let's start again from the beginning. Come here."

He reached for her and slowly clasped her hands, she slowly slowly rose toward him from her jester's throne until she was standing beside him, "Jacek—" she said, and her voice broke into sobbing.

The next morning, now almost with expertise, Jacek led the exercise drill, more military in character than Nada's had been, then a cold shower, two quarts of milk, and the commuter bus back to Decin.

"And what if I handed it in on Saturday," said Nada as slap-dash she finished her calculations. "Though last time the boss was hinting..."

"So do you want to hand it in today or don't you?"

"And if it were up to you?"

"I've screwed up a lot, but I've always handed my work in on time."

"So long," said Nada, thrusting her papers into her bag. "I'll come back as soon as I can."

Slowly Jacek walked back and forth through the room and involuntarily he began to pace it off, about 175 sq. ft., the tiny foyer with a WC and an improvised shower in the corner, in the room itself a daybed with a small chest for bed linen, a two-section wardrobe, a table, the drafting table, a bookcase, a little radio, and two kitchen chairs, no more than 5,000 crowns' worth in all, but everything that's needed to live, just what we had then, it seemed so little, but how much of it was left after all the growth, today we've got over 500 sq. ft., pile carpets, a refrigerator, a TV set, the sequence would further dictate a car, then a cottage—all of it well-furnished with cares and more crowded than this poor 175 sq. ft., with Nadezda we could have lived here all along, and we feel like living here with her forever—

Jacek walked back and forth through the room, the morning sun lowered its golden trapezoids from the wall into the room itself, he shook his head and grinned grotesquely, it was a tragicomedy to contemplate one's own life-story, one's *curriculum vitae*, as a gradual growth of the fiction from which the *vita* had evaporated with time and all that was left was the *curriculum* and its transcription, was it a horrible delusion or simply a pile of facts, the sun had reached the floor and Jacek looked out the window toward the harbor, on their ramps cranes were reloading from rail cars to barges and from barges to rail cars, the sinking of the loaded boats to the cargo line and the rising of the unloaded ones above the water's surface, until, completely full or completely empty, they are untied and given permission to sail off, and so on again from the beginning.

"You gave me the right advice," Nada said in the doorway, "Things very nearly went bust. Do you advise that we go to dinner now or later?"

"Later. If we do it this way," said Jacek, kissing her and unbuttoning his shirt, "we can save ourselves a trip back here after dinner."

"After dinner you plan to go— When's the very latest we can eat?" and Jacek and Nada, wildly and tenderly, out loud and in silence, while the sun made its trip across the floor to the opposite wall, cruelly and with laughter, almost to the point of fainting.

"I couldn't make it to the station," Nada whispered, not getting up, "hardly even to the restaurant across the street... You've matured immensely here with me, but you must have had some talent... Buried for years..."

"Thursday, April 2, just after nine," said Jacek, tying his tie at the window, "is when my re-excavation began."

"Come back soon—"

Cross the ends, he could move here, make a loop, and make a fresh start with Nada, pull the other end through the loop, have a second family and a second life, tighten it, or a second fiction, and pull it tight around his neck. That was how it had been with Lenka at the beginning, that's the way things always begin...

"I love you, Nadezda..."

The sun had already climbed the wall and left the room, but it was making its way through other rooms, a single human life and a single fiction are definitely too few... perhaps even two... Nadezda is Speranza, of course, but the Miramar is just a dream, and beyond it the call of the strip leading to the south, the open road of green waves shining toward Africa, into the darkness of other rooms, for thirty-three plus fifteen is only forty-eight—

"It's almost terrifying to look at you when you grin in the mirror like that...," said Nada, but there was no more time, Jacek received one more kiss on the forehead, she crammed some tattered architecture textbooks into his black satchel, and the train pulled out of Decin at precisely 5:29, right on schedule.

On the bank of the Elbe, back upstream along the spring-time river, on the green waves of the warm imitation leather, how curiously those two girls looked us over when we came into the compartment, and with what meaningful affability the one on the left returned our greeting, but how elegantly too we made our entrance, how fluently we put our satchel into the baggage net, trains are full of women and how many more times will we set out, and we won't sleep now either, an electron fired out of orbit has so many chances, so many possibilities—hell, the satchel!

Awkwardly Jacek pulled down his large black traveling satchel with brass fittings and hastily searched through its numerous compartments and pockets to see where Nada had crammed the architecture books, Lenka unpacked his dirty clothes and what would she have said about those textbooks signed Nadezda Houskova, Jacek hid the books among some official papers and up went the satchel fluently as before, why should he be a draftsman in some construction cooperative when he had a degree in chemical engineering and business experience from numerous deals and trips, hurray for trips when we've got a brother who's such a great guy—

With growing excitement Jacek went out into the corridor and leaned against the frame of an open window. "When are you coming home again?" his brother had asked on the telephone, and by "home" he'd meant Brno, "Maybe we'll be spending more time together and maybe—" we were on the verge of saying "permanently," as if with sudden conviction, but I've always insisted to Lenka that we're permanently settled in Usti and that's why Lenka's been planting apple trees, we've got a first-category apartment there, we both have well-paid jobs, of course mine's not so good, but then it's convenient and peaceful, how quickly this sort of faith can spring from nowhere, in a second even, but that could only mean— as if in horror Jacek pressed his hands to his throat, piercing a dam can be just like knocking it down, what else might we learn about ourselves—this time truly in horror Jacek pressed his hands to his throat, a good thing that Usti is only twenty minutes from Decin and the first stop on the express.

I — four

A feeling of vertigo on alighting at our own Usti station, but which station is really ours now—with his large traveling satchel Jacek tottered along the platform in the stream of those getting off, from a fairy-tale pop-up book back to the daily paper and, in his throat, anxiety, new streams getting off newly arrived trains from Most, Uporiny, and Lovosice, all hurrying home to their Lenickas and Lenkas; my darlings, it was only sunstroke, we'll stay home now, as we should, and pull down the blinds, Lenka's a good wife and we have a clever, pretty little girl, but Daddy can't come just yet, my sweet, until his train comes out of its eleven tunnels, that's for Mommy's sake, you see, so she won't cry if people tell her that Daddy came home today on a strange, bad train.

Jacek tottered along the platform and in the gathering dusk he raised his watch to his eyes every so often, the 4:45 to Berlin was late today, God forbid that anything should have happened to it—the platforms emptied quickly, Jacek dragged his satchel from the platform down the steps and up the steps onto the platform, WHERE DO WE COME FROM—WHO ARE WE—WHERE ARE WE GOING, but I live here with my wife and we have a child, a hundred times better than I deserve, my love, I have soiled you... Jacek with his satchel on the steps, going up and going down.

"Express from Prague to Decin, Dresden, and Berlin, arriving on Platform Two—" the loudspeakers sounded, Jacek ran up the steps to Platform Two, the train was already thundering in insignificantly late, and already the crowd was streaming out of its cars, Jacek in its midst, quickly out of the station and home by the shortest route, Jacek in the middle of the current pouring quickly into buses and streetcars, all going by the shortest route, Jacek too, to his Lenicka and Lenka on streetcar No. 5 to Vseborice.

To reach our part of the housing development you ride to the end of the line, today after the next-to-the-last stop there's only one person left, on the rear platform, Jacek had entered the car from the front, it's a man, two daddies coming home from the 4:45 to Berlin, Jacek hurried to the rear platform, but stopped short in the doorway—the man leaning on the brake was Trost.

"Hey, this is a coincidence, isn't it—" Trost bellowed, under his chin a band-aid big as a large coin, "—it's a good thing we caught the Berlin express in Prague, isn't it?"

"It sure is. I've never missed it yet."

"You make the trip often, don't you?"

"Quite often. But you do too, I see."

"Oh, no, not at all. The weather's nice, isn't it?"

"It is now."

At the corner the daddies separated and Jacek hurried past the playground, the carefully swept sidewalk was still damp from having been sprinkled, this week we have clean-up duty in front of the apartment house, and Jacek raced up the stairs, on his door a nameplate ENGINEER JAROMIR JOST, I live here, and even as the door opens Lenicka calls, "Daddy—" and Lenka comes to greet him with a smile.

"Daddy—" our darling cries with her chin on a brass pole of the netting that surrounds her crib, down at once with the netting and his rough chin against her sweet little tummy, Lenicka cries out with pleasure, nothing's so sweet to kiss as our little one, "Daddy gwab me—" cries our pretty little girl, take her in his arms and swing her.

"Daddy don't go way—"

"I'm just going to give Mommy a kiss."

"Daddy come back again—"

"You know I'll come back right away."

"Daddy tell stowies—"

"You know he will!"

Lenka had already taken a bottle of milk out of the refrigerator, she was warming it up, and already she was up to her elbows in our traveling satchel, the official papers she leaves untouched, all she bothers with are the dirty clothes, "Look what I brought you— " "That's wonderful, you're very kind and thanks—but you forgot that white plush again, didn't you—"

"Sure as I breathe, but I won't next time, you can count on it... And Daddy forgot his little darling too—"

"Daddy din't fwoget—"

"You know he didn't, and look what he brought you," show our little one what this strange thing's for, Lenicka went into ecstasy over the water pistol and again the netting came down, trampling her nightshirt underfoot she staggered through the kitchen and covered the walls with water, "Putting that thing in her hand," said Lenka, "means an immediate call to workmen to repaint the apartment," but after all, it's only water, my love.

On kitchen chairs Jacek and Lenka sat across from one another and, in unison, gulped down hot cereal sprinkled with cocoa, "And why did you come back two days late?"

"But Daddy has to tell stowies—" Lenicka called from her crib.

"Once again Chema made up its mind it wouldn't raise the OMZ's balance-sheet allotment over the limit for the second quarter, and KZZCHT wouldn't approve the last quarter's drop in material, whereupon our PZO—"

"Just a minute, I have to go and put the key back in the cellar..." said Lenka, and she was back again soon, "...well, so—"

"Well, so I got home two days late. And what's new with you?"

"The OS inspectors are asking again for periodic reports

on all MS- and TK-data measured against the plan norms,
while USMP insists—"

"Daddy tell stowies—"

"Just a minute, let me go and take care of her— So which
story shall we tell, my darling?"

"The sad pwince!"

"Once upon a time there was a prince and he was very
sad..."

"...because he had to wide the twain so much..."

"...and his little girl at home made yum-yum so little
that Mommy got angry..."

"...thwough many many bwack tunnels..."

"...and since the prince wanted to have a strong, pretty
little girl..."

"...he awways wode that twain and cwied and the pwincess cwied too, because the tunnel had no wight..."

"...light, darling. Light. And so the prince kept riding on
the train and because it was dark he didn't see the princess..."

"...and out of the woods cwop-cwop-cwop came the
auwochs..."

"...aurochs, darling, you're saying auwochs—aurrrochs."

"...and he was all gold, a cow this big with a gweat big
meen..."

"Mane, maaane. A buffalo..."

"...and the auwochs said, pwince, here is youw pwincess and don't cwy, and the pwince went boom! And it
wasn't dawk anymowe in the tunnel and the pwincess
gave the pwince a gweat gweat big kiss wike this—"

"—a great great big one like this. And now beddie-bye,
darling."

"But Daddy don't go way—" and he had to stay with
her till she fell asleep with her thumb in her mouth, he felt
the chafing of the tepid nylon on his wrists and the warming felt of the harness around his entire body.

Clean all his shoes in the foyer and take a hot bath, "You're not going to bed yet, Lenka?"

"How can I, it's Friday!"

"Can I help with anything?"

"Just go to bed, you've had enough with your trip."

"That's true. OK then, beddie-bye now."

Every day the morning theme song of motorcycles tuning up and the rattle of Lenka's alarmclock, Lenka turns it off and goes to get Lenicka dressed, but Lenicka doesn't want to get up, tears, objects falling, and cries.

"Daddy come today?"

"But he came back last night."

"Daddy din't come!"

"But you have the pistol he gave you—you think you just dreamed that, don't you? Hop into your pants!"

"Daddy put on pants!"

"Shh—Daddy's still beddie-bye, we mustn't wake him..."

"...we mustn't wake him...," Lenicka whispered and then screamed, "I want to see Daddy!" and Jacek crawled out of bed, my darlings, and still half asleep he staggered in to help pull on Lenicka's tights and to kiss Lenka, Lenicka sprayed him with her pistol and Lenka was very nervous, he climbed back into bed to get some more sleep, another fifty minutes, and he was asleep before the two of them had left.

The roar of trucks starting up and the stomping on the ceiling always preceded the rattle of Jacek's alarmclock, Jacek raised the clock face toward his eyes, another eighteen minutes, and he turned over onto his other side, think of something pleasant, suddenly he got up, dumbfounded, and walked to the door to the balcony—it wasn't a dream, it had actually occurred—and now he was naked, upstairs they were stomping around, a sprightly army drill, on the other side of the river Speranza was exercising too, only now did the alarmclock ring, he was surprised to find that he could take a fine shower in the tub, after a cold shower the world is at your feet.

The kitchen floor was strewn with all sorts of things, in a mug on the sideboard was instant coffee, already mixed (all you do is add hot water) and three ceramic crackers, why this dieting all the time, and already Jacek was locking the apartment door, but then he unlocked it again, went back to the kitchen, and flushed the coffee down the drain—but in cold water it didn't go down too easily.

"...it really was out of the question. And so I made an effort to arrange it through friends," Jacek slowly told the deputy director of Cottex, he was happy, stuffed with tripe soup, herring, and a stein of beer, and pleasantly surprised by his own suddenly deep and serious tone of voice. "As you no doubt are aware, I studied engineering in Brno and my classmates there represent a significant..."

"Of course I'm aware of that and I'm very glad that, at last...," the deputy said with zeal, "you've finally hit on the proper technique, today unfortunately one can't do without it and..."

"However, there's no ethyl acetate."

"One couldn't expect it, but we would be very grateful if next time... You understand... If you could keep it up..."

"These things are difficult to arrange, of course, and I wouldn't want to press too hard..."

"Of course, I abide by what you're saying, obviously... If you would only keep trying... By the way, I've been reviewing the quarterly bonuses, in your case there must have been an oversight and..."

"That hundred crowns really did bug me. If only—"

"...I've already approved it, you'll get four hundred and ten crowns in all, we were saving the increase for Danek, but now— Besides, I intend to propose to the director that he give you the top pay in your grade."

"Top pay, but that's really terribly— Really, it comes just at the right time. After all these years—"

"The director will certainly okay it if I ask him. Cigarette?"

"Thanks— No, I don't like filters."

"Actually, all I smoke is filters... Well, and so on Wednesday you should go to see KZZCHT..."

"I'd prefer to go on Tuesday."

Jacek leaped through the ridged mud of the courtyard toward the wooden annex to the technical division, whistling the March from *Aïda*, four hundred plus two hundred a month extra, trips to Brno at his own whim, why not stop off somewhere in the forest on the other side of the dam, or even at Pernstejn Castle, we haven't been to Telc yet or Bratislava—

In Jacek's office the chief colorist Petrik Hurt and the technician Vitenka Balvin were waiting—shouts, laughter, and some new anecdotes from Brno, Petrik signed a red issue slip for the 300 grams of Saturday's pure alcohol and Vitenka diluted it expertly: sixty-forty would hit the spot just before dinner, and on Saturday we always get a bit plastered.

When they finally got on Jacek's nerves he kicked them out, it's strange to imagine that Petrik's actually our boss, and Jacek sat down to his typewriter to make his travel report: 3/30-4/1, shit! and a new sheet of paper, 3/30-4/3. I continued my efforts at the main office in Brno..., suddenly he felt again the oppressive sensation of those long corridors in that gray palace, the uneasy backward glances and the whispered reports, "The general director is ready to throw him to the prosecutor... The whole place is to be disbanded immediately... They're hanging that sixteen million around his neck... Hartung broke him sooner than anyone could have expected...," the anxiety and agitation, here one didn't turn one's superiors out the door, Vitenka and I would have fought for a hint of a smile from Petrik, how happy we'd been when they'd had us transferred—

Quickly Jacek finished his report, filed it, and breathed a sigh, he reached for the newspaper and read it through from A to Z, then the arts review, and after lunch a piece of a novel, he opened Armand Lanoux's *When the Ebb Tide Comes* to where the bookmark was:

> *Apple trees rose from the dense grass, wringing their twisted, crippled twigs. The sap wept. Jacques slept with his face buried in the hay. They had fallen from exhaustion... Abel looked at his watch... Three hours passed. They had come from the other village, from the one near the coast, the little valley, the fortified farmhouse, the sleeping bridge, and the yellowish brook. From the south the sound of war roared on, indifferent to them. The sea was no longer in view... With an effort they tried to move their feet. Each boot weighed at least fifty pounds. Jacques took off his boots. When he put them back on, they would hurt him.*

At 1:59 P.M. Jacek banged Lanoux shut, got up, and stretched, this summer would be magnificent, those four hundred and ten crowns for current expenses and those two hundred extra regularly for his secret hoard—again, suddenly, that feeling of horror he'd felt in the corridor of the Decin train, when would he first touch our secret hoard, for what had it been established, and Good God, how awfully soon—2:00, the siren screamed, and he was literally dragged outside by a long-conditioned reflex.

"Suppose we go for a swim."

"Now?!"—Lenka and Grandma were shocked.

"Why not? Better than rooting around in the ashes of this apartment house."

"Wherever did you get that idea? And where would we go?"

"There won't be much hot water today anywhere, we can take the streetcar to the baths. My little darling, want to swimmie?"

"I want swimmie!"

"Well, run along then, Good Heavens," Grandma said, "I can take care of things!" "I have to iron," Lenka said. "But it's nothing for me, I can do it..." "You didn't come to visit for that..." "But I like to..." "How many times have I told you, Mama..."

"I want swimmie!"

"Come along with us, Lenka. Remember how you used to... Come on."

"I'd like to... But I've got to iron."

"Lenunka..."

"So go on then, but be home by five!"

In the glow of floodlights reflecting off the warm green waves, Lenicka shouted for joy and Jacek laughed, twelve minutes till closing, he could still do two laps, but how could he leave the little one alone for even a second, seven minutes left, at least one lap, "I want a wowwypop—" at least five strokes of freestyle, "I want a wowwypop!" just two minutes left, "Daddy'll buy one, but his darling can wait a bit..." "Daddy don't go way—" she squealed, and she grabbed him by the leg, but just then someone came by with an orange rubber ducky and Lenicka was off after it, he had to catch her and she squealed that she didn't want her Daddy, desperately she tried to escape toward the duck, but the blow-up bird had already been thrown into the deep end and a bunch of laughing girls were jumping after it, Jacek picked Lenicka up in his arms and with his body he warmed her already chilled little body, with her fists his daughter struck her Daddy on the face, once again her desire was left unsatisfied, because of one another we don't get what we want, away at once from that golden fairy-tale bird and the sparkling naiads in the green waves around it, we must go to the streetcar, back home to the Residence.

A familiar figure in a green windbreaker with a hood strode nimbly along the broad road—their neighbor Mr.

Mestek was going to the mountains, tapping his carved stick disdainfully on the concrete.

"I'd like to go somewhere where there's lots of grass," said Jacek, glancing out at him from the kitchen window. "My little darling, will you come with Daddy? And you, Lenka?"

"His little darling" definitely wanted to go with Grandma to the movies, Lenka had to make dinner.

"So go alone, at least you won't be in the way."

The development on Sunday morning—featherbeds hung out of the windows exuding the collective dampness left from Saturday's fulfillment of marital duties, last night's satisfied lazily shaking standardized white pails out into trashcans, gnawed bones, molding halves of lemons, dripping garbage wrapped in pieces of newspaper, and the hard heels of loaves of bread, still unwashed children grudgingly dragged shopping nets crammed with clinking empty bottles to the self-service store, while last night's participants with pale veiny legs and droplets of hardened grease in the corners of their eyes, hit by rotating house duty, torpidly pushed along the rice-straw brooms purchased only after repeated, often evening-long meetings of the co-op members, a hundred speakers blared out the same stupid hit, and in the windows a thousand Trosts—Jacek fled onto the bus as out of a tunnel, shaken up amid the shaking throng until, after the fifth stop, he could feel in his legs that the bus was beginning to climb the mountains, so far no one had got out, at the final stop they all got out, Jacek last, with downcast eyes he crossed the highway, stepped into some bushes, crouched, and with his face in his hands waited a while until the last voice had faded into the distance and vanished.

The grass was green again, perhaps it had been so even beneath the snow, on the twigs a billion green micro-explosions—Jacek struck out on one of his guaranteed unfrequented paths, but to be safe he soon deserted it and made his way upward through the underbrush and over the rocks, here you could drink right out of the brook, he tried to walk on all fours, on all fours backwards and somersaults forwards and backwards and sideways, out from under some pine needles he dug up a slightly rotted stick and rapped with it and knocked things down and leaped with the stick across the brook, and with the stick he made a short, deep furrow at a right angle to the brook, then he pushed together a dam of stones, clay, and wood, and when he pulled away a barrier on the bank, the water streamed in the new direction, drove leaves along with it and, aided by the stick, bit powerfully into the soil, tore up pieces of turf, and washed them quickly along—increase the declivity and finish choking off the old channel and the liberated cascades could rush onto the hard, sleeping earth, tear pieces from it, and strike and resound against the very rock of the mountain. Naked, Jacek lay on the warm grass and through the silence the sun penetrated his entire body.

Suddenly it was late, Jacek rose as if he'd been struck on the head, he gathered up the sun-warmed pieces of his clothing, which itched now on his sweaty body, and dazed by the harsh glare he staggered in his heavy, heated boots through the underbrush and over the rocks down to the path and the waiting bus. The Hurts, in their matching homemade folk-style jackets, hardly noticed Jacek, they whispered as they rocked on the plate-metal steps, holding hands in a whitening clasp.

The development on Sunday afternoon—surrounded by young greenery, blocks of buildings with delicate pastel hues, behind the windows vases of pussy willows and lively music, on the clean-swept concrete road a children's carnival, little girls with toy baby carriages and parasols, a gang of little boys on a surrealistic wagon made from an ironing board, their neighbors the Tosnars with their six-tiered pipe organ of girls, daddies with children on their shoulders sitting on sandbox rims.

Grandma, Lenka, and Lenicka were about to leave for the garden plot, but Lenicka wouldn't let them, she'd rather make yum-yum, in perfect unison her Daddy and she put away a huge cutlet apiece, one potato for Daddy and one for Lenicka, "That girl only eats her food when you're around—" and they left for the garden plot, Jacek took the ecstatic Lenicka on his shoulders and carried her across the road to a field, set her up in a tree, and acted like a bear, Lenicka was afraid and ecstatic, her hands around his neck, and wet, great great big kisses.

After unremitting digging, watering, and fertilizing, the tiny square of clay soil had at last sent up its first green shoots. Kneeling, Grandma and Lenka fondled the diminutive beds, Lenicka with them on her knees, in the soil on the bodies of these three generations something eternal and eternally fresh, WHERE DO WE COME FROM, here on each bit of earth a young woman and a half-naked man against the tepid undulation of the reddening horizon. And in the twilight across the broad road in a slow chain of duos and trios with tools on their shoulders, silent, covered with stigmata of clay in the flickering of the fluorescent streetlights. Behind the crowd, sadly dragging along, a solitary figure in a green windbreaker with a hood, his neighbor Mestek was coming back from the mountains, his carved cane tapping out its lonely beat.

Outside their window, in the network of eighty windows of the building across the way, in the open four-sided grottos of gradated shades of gold, young women leaving bathrooms and half-naked men with their cigarettes lit, the unheard trampling back and forth and the springs of tones mixing in the lake of music that rose over the buildings.

"Jacinek, my darling...," Lenka whispered, my wife, we know each other as no one else, a perfect interplay of limbs, love-making simple as milk, a wife with whom I live and with whom I have a child, WHO ARE WE, there is no peace outside existence in an order, never with anyone else but you, my love, I must tell you that—

"Lenunka..."

She was asleep already.

On Tuesday we are going away again. And then again and again.

WHERE ARE WE GOING—and where would we like to go—

Part II — Games — five

Jacek put on his sunglasses before he got off the streetcar, and as he got off he read the time on his wristwatch: 3:28. So the trip from Cottex to the main square
takes 13 minutes.

He walked past the column with its enormous painted
poster of Candy's jazz orchestra, over to the office of the
notice agency: SERVICE TO THE PUBLIC. The notice was
still there.

646 ROOM with balc. in Vanov. Beautiful
view. For rent or for sale.

In the PERSONALS column below, the outcries of a
48-yr.-old bach. farmer and several healthy pensioners a
27-year-old intel. no childr., looking for
intel. husb. up to 35, and a college graduate of the
same age a 25-year-old refined wom. of girl.
appear. offered herself, and she even had her own furn.
apart. For less sensitive tastes there was a 30-year-old
div. woman, native of Usti likes the woods, for
whom Child is no obsticle.

In the crammed columns of POSITIONS AVAILABLE
dozens of appeals blared out for all sorts of people, for
anyone who might be willing to work anywhere, whatever
might come into his head.

Jacek drew in his breath and went through the swinging
door. In front of the counter stood a line of five persons,
all buying tickets for *The Red Gentleman.*

"Six forty-six," Jacek said in a barely audible voice.

Behind the counter a disturbingly beautiful girl typed
out the address on a card and, smiling, asked him for
twenty hellers.

When he reached the bus stop it was 3:44; according to

the timetable, the bus to Vanov leaves every twenty minutes, every :10, :30, and :50 until 11:00 P.M., after that every hour. Since the streetcar arrived at the square at 3:28, it was possible to catch the bus at 3:30, a perfect connection.

The red 3:50 bus arrived at 3:49, it's true, but loading held it up till 3:51. During the ride Jacek took off his dark glasses and memorized the address: J. Krivinka, 71 Dock Street, Vanov. It was 4:07 when he got off the bus, and after two minutes of brisk walking he stood before No. 71, so that—subtracting the time he had spent at the notice agency—it was 34 minutes in all from Cottex.

On the whole, J. Krivinka made a solid impression, right away he laid his cards on the table: he already had six prospective tenants, but he needed money and would sell the separate room on the second floor to whoever would buy a quarter share in the house for 2,760 crowns and thus become a co-owner, the price was so low because the house had been confiscated, all the papers were in perfect order.

On the second floor there was a separate electric meter, running water, a toilet and, besides the bedroom, a small storeroom was available. The room measured some 200 sq. ft., dry, well-maintained, a light switch and two outlets, a washbasin, a varnished floor, two alcoves, glass doors onto the balcony and a large double window with two shutters, as for the furniture we'll come to terms, my daughter will be glad to do your laundry, the grocery store is right down the street, and there's a bar around the corner, it's a five-minute walk to the pool and there's the dock, it has stairs and you can tie up a boat there, in winter you can go skiing just above the garden, we're rarely home, never in summer, it's the real outdoors, you don't need any curtains here, you can heat with coal or with gas, or with oil if you'd rather have oil, it's really nice, it's rare that one finds something so nice and it would really be yours exclusively,

"Just look—" said J. Krivinka, and he went over to the window.

"Thanks so much, but if I could just have a moment here... alone..."

"Stop by on your way down."

With his hand pressed against his lips Jacek waited until the steps on the staircase had ceased, then he spread out his arms as if to embrace all the things needed to live—

Breathless with exhilaration he found the perforated door of a small food cupboard beneath the window, its two shelves were more than enough for a bottle of milk, a quarter-loaf of bread, a can of herring, a couple of eggs, some cheese and a bottle of wine, one pot and one saucepan, the one alcove for his dirty laundry and the other for developing photographs, on the floor there could be a brown shag rug and on the wall a carmine-colored hanging, for the corner a wing chair and a floor lamp, for the wall a bookcase and a small radio, for the opposite one an arrangement of nude photos clipped from magazines and sprayed with shellac, or one of bottle labels, or a globe? No, a guitar and a daybed in the corner, the bed linen in one alcove, the dirty laundry in the storeroom off the corridor, there he could keep his skis and his off-season clothing, a paddle, a tent, and a kettle, a daybed in the corner and on it a black leather cushion, and beside it a little table for a bottle, two glasses and an ashtray, a large mirror, a low ottoman so she wouldn't have to throw things on the floor and so they could see the sky while making love.

With his eyes half closed he silently approached the window, gently opened the door to the balcony, and one step over the threshold: the tops of the trees flowed in a trembling glitter all the way down to the river, through the unbelievable tranquillity and the transparent, gleaming air a barge passed downstream, the open path of sparkling waves to the Decin docks, under Speranza's windows, and on to the docks of Hamburg, the beaches of Cuxhaven, and out to sea—the moist green of the opposite bank stretched up through the tiers of deserted vineyards to the shaggy masses of forests and between gray, stiffened cascades of rock, straight up the sharp curve of the mountain's crest.

The dial of his watch shouted 4:42 and Jacek bit his lower lip hard, gently but hurriedly he closed the balcony door and rushed down the stairs. "I'll bring the money in a week!" he called to Krivinka in the doorway, and he ran to the bus stop and the bus drove rapidly away out of the valley.

Jacek changed at the main square and took the streetcar through the canyon of familiar facades, none of which could be skipped, endlessly to the end of the line at Vseborice, quickly between the solid concrete enclosing strips of long-since-dead grass, trampled day after day, past dozens of ironically identical copies of the four-story apartment house unit model T 03 to his own T 03, No. 511/13, straight up the stairs to the third story, and already from behind the door that bears our name cries of laughter can be heard.

Grandma and Lenka were putting on a puppet show, on the back of a kitchen chair their hands holding the wires, on the seat the action of the fairy tale was reaching a climax, and on a cushion on the floor the spectator, Lenicka, was biting her little fist in excitement.

"Did you bring the money?" Lenka whispered, and then, slowly, with dignity, moving the figure of the water-goblin a little, "...whoo whoo whoo, whoo whoo whoo... I've swum across nine brooks and nine ponds and the princess isn't anywhere, whoo whoo whoo, where is she?"

Gripped by the story, Grandma scarcely nodded, hiding the princess behind the chair leg she lisped, "I'm hiding here, I'm afraaid of the water-goblin—"

"Where is she, whoo whoo whoo, where is she? Lenicka, tell me, where is that wretched little girl hiding?"

"I don't know—" Lenicka lied, choking with excitement, "She isn't here—"

"But she was here just a little while ago—whoo whoo whoo!"

"No she wasn't, watagobwin, oh no—"

"It's water-goblin," Jacek whispered, "and you mustn't tell fibs, my darling—," but no one paid any attention to him, except Lenicka, who cried out, "Daddy go way!" back over her shoulder and then right back with her eyes fixed on the kitchen chair, what was the hurry anyway—

The performance dragged on and on, and Jacek's efforts to enter the action successively as a king, a wicked witch, a bandit, and a giraffe were rejected four times over, "Go way, Daddy—" Lenicka repeated louder and louder until she screamed it, after the performance she and Grandma cut out paper stars, then with Lenka she made necklaces out of bits of folded newspaper, Daddy in disfavor, and she threw the water pistol at his feet, then trampled it, the celluloid cracked and it was all over for the toy from Brno.

On the table and the sideboard a pile of plates and dishes with the uneaten remains of five different courses, "I left you some buns on the tray—" but the cottage cheese in the buns had been picked out by a child's fingers, obviously unwashed, "Well then, find something in the pantry—," but the eggs were for Lenicka, the ham for Grandma for tomorrow, don't cut into the bacon, the cheese is for your snack tomorrow, the sardines are for sandwiches, they didn't deliver the beer.

"And don't turn on the cold water!"

"Do you have to stand right here?"

"Turn off the radio!"

"Out of the way, please."

"Don't smoke here— And not in the bedroom either!"

"You're in the way."

Jacek went out on the balcony among the lines of laundry and lit a cigarette, in the kitchen the entertainment had started right up again, as if some unwanted visitor had just left, we're in the way here—he inhaled deeply as he cautiously paced the narrow concrete floor between boxes, cases, and empty flower pots and gazed at the darkening sky, suddenly an oppressive sense of someone looking— right across the way Trost was spread out in the window.

Trost was pouring out clouds of smoke, behind his elbow on the table a charred baking pan, a bottle of beer on the sill, fists under his chin, and a shamelessly fixed stare—Jacek drew back quickly, stumbled over the laundry tub, and rushed inside, he turned on the light and imme- diately turned it off again, the blind in this room doesn't work, and in a fever he walked up and down in the dark- ness of the room, stuffed his cigarette into the ashtray (its embers could be seen), and what else was left here anyway—

The simplest thing would be to leave without a word— Jacek went out to the foyer, took the key to the cellar off the nail, and went downstairs, the black suitcase would do, he locked the cellar and put the key back on its nail, ten shirts—no, three good shirts and four polyesters, those we can wash ourself, twelve pairs of nylon socks so we only have to wash our socks twice a month, the black leather tie's enough and six pocket handkerchiefs, three pairs of shorts, three towels, wear the gray suit, and then the suede jacket, a pair of dacron slacks, and the black sweater into the suitcase, there's a razor at the office, our toothbrush and comb from the bathroom, two pairs of pyjamas, a dagger, and the secret hoard.

Jacek walked through the foyer, from behind the kitchen door whooping and exultation, silently he closed the door, down the stairs and off across the broad road, the shortcut across the dead grass, and finally the last stop on the street- car line, from over the curve of the mountain range a glow and from the city the streetcar is already coming for us...

...already it was moving into the turnaround, it brought

a worn-out family, Mommy with two shopping bags crammed full, behind her Daddy with a child, the little girl had fallen asleep on Daddy's arm, and now the family was hurrying home— It wouldn't work, we could never make up our mind to do it, not yet, not this way, not today—

Jacek turned his back to the streetcar, from the yellow windows of the restaurant the lament of an accordion and near the door the sad figure of his neighbor Mestek in his green windbreaker with a hood sitting over a melancholy plate of kipper and a glass of stale beer, Jacek downed two double slivovitzes, tripe soup, herring and onions, ten ounces of sausage, and three beers, and quietly returned home.

From behind the kitchen door shrieks and loud laughter, they were putting Lenicka to bed and Jacek went to lie down himself, to sleep, tomorrow Lenka's alarmclock will wake us and we'll go pet Lenicka, and then a second time we'll sleep, and the second time we'll wake up without them.

II — six

The simplest of the other possibilities is to give each other freedom—the famous "improvement" of the Balvins began right at the front door with its double mailbox, double bell, and double visiting cards

DR. MILADA BALVINOVA   VITEZSLAV BALVIN

and in a rigorously binary spirit it covered the entire floor-plan of their conveniently symmetrical apartment: on the left Mija's room, white with a white square yard of foyer, on the right Vitenka's purple room with a purple square yard of foyer. Common ground—the kitchen, the WC, the bathroom, and the center square yard of foyer—was known as "no man's land," and it was azure blue with white and purple enclaves in the two shelves under the mirror, two towel racks, two wings of the food cupboard, and two metal holders for toilet paper.

"I couldn't get along without the gang," said Vitenka as he entered his purple wing, "and Mija couldn't do with it, so why force ourselves on one another—"

On the enormous square dark-red sofa in the middle of the purple room a kneeling girl in a men's nylon shirt was combing the golden locks of a handsome long-haired boy, on a horsehair mattress right on the floor below them slept a girl in a nylon raincoat, and a mirror hanging askew from the ceiling showed a segment of two uninhibited lovers hidden behind a column of four suitcases stacked one on top of another, "Today it's kind of dead," said Vitenka, and he clapped his hands.

The girl in the raincoat sat up, looked at her watch, kissed Vitenka and Jacek quickly and, leaving, held the door open for girl twins in attractive Norwegian sweaters.

"Sweet cherrries have rripened—" sang the twins as they sat down on the horsehair mattress, and before they got to the refrain a slim Congolese with a bluish tint put in an appearance and poured out of his briefcase several bottles of byrrh, the lovers climbed out of their retreat behind the suitcases, and the refrain sounded from all nine throats: "—and how it happennned thennn."

"He had to have a soundproof wall put in for me—" in her white wing Mija pointed out an equally white porous wall, "and I had to promise that I wouldn't encroach on his side even if there was shooting there."

Jacek was given an imitation silver cup containing a milk cocktail, and with the tip of his tongue he fished out the floating strawberries. Mija sat down in a wing chair and, stretching, clutched the two wings of the chair, yawning peacefully. For ten minutes they sat in silence.

Jacek put the cup down on the table, picked up a Swiss illustrated magazine, and looked at pictures of a Soviet Air

Force review at Tushino, we should study German again sometime, "What does *Fahrgestell* mean?"

"There's a dictionary over there. I'd like to sleep."

"Whatever you like, I only wanted to get away for a moment from that caterwauling."

"What's that on your neck—"

Mija got up and sat down on Jacek's lap, ran her fingers over his neck, and then unbuttoned his shirt, she ran her warm palm over his chest and finally untucked his shirt, he embraced her gently and she tapped him on the nose.

"Do you see those white spots? You've got a fungus..."

"I never even noticed..."

"There are dyes that kill that, I can write you a prescription. What color would you like? Red, blue, green..."

"Is it anything serious?"

"No. You've just got a fungus."

"Sometimes I think I'm rotting away. But then again..."

"I'd like to talk to you, but some other time, now I'd rather sleep... Go sit down again, please, button up your shirt and don't be ridiculous... That sort of thing doesn't amuse me."

Mija quietly dropped off to sleep in her chair and her white slipper fell from her foot, through the soundproof wall and the central wall of the apartment the singing of Vitenka's gang, further dampened by the music from Mija's record player, sounded as if at a great distance. "That female has no use for anything—" her husband Vitenka vented his resentment when he divided the apartment into its white and purple wings, "Neither for people, nor children, nor a dog, nor a canary, nor food, not even drink, not even for a goddamn boyfriend—"

"For me the sun is enough, plus two thousand a month net," said Mija, from January to May she drives out in her white two-seater to the southern slopes of the Krusne Mountains and reads and falls asleep in her beach chair or even in the car, at the municipal swimming pool she rents a cabana for the whole year, from June on she drives there straight from her office, pulls a white canvas beach chair out of the cabana, reads in it, and falls asleep in the sun, in November she goes to the Adriatic and in December to Egypt, always the same light, neutral color, the type that never burns—

In the purple room Vitenka had drawn very close to one of the Norwegian sweater twins and had pushed the other one, who seemed willing enough, off onto Jacek, but the gang had made up its mind to head off, "—but someone has to wait here for Milena Cerna!"

"So wait for Milena Cerna," Vitenka told Jacek, "she's a wonder, you must know her from the swimming pool, she's real dark, would you like to see her in the raw? When she rings four times, go into the bathroom and call through the door, "Hi, Milca, take it off!"

Jacek was left alone in the now silent room and involuntarily he began to clean it up: the discarded men's shirt and a black sock into the top suitcase, empty the ashtrays and smooth out the red sofa so you'll like it here with me, lying on his back on the sofa he gazed at himself in the mirror hung askew from the ceiling, waiting for his beloved, come here to me in my room—

Four short rings and Jacek ran to the bathroom, already a key was rattling in the lock, pointlessly Jacek turned on the shower, "Hi, Vitak—" a girl's voice from the other side of the door, "Hi, Milca," Jacek called as he'd been schooled, "take it off!"

Breathlessly, silently, he advanced to the door and opened it a crack, his glance ran to the mirror on the ceiling, in it was Milenka Cerna like Goya's *Maja desnuda* on the red fabric, your beloved waits for you in your room—

Quietly Jacek closed the purple door and walked through the foyer to the white one, now locked, where the sound of soft music could be heard, tomorrow Mija would go to the southern slopes of the mountains and would place herself in the sun, which is needed to live—

With a child you can't divide your apartment that way, of course, and when in the foyer she shouted, "Daddy gwab me—" how many miles of soundproof wall would he need... perhaps the fifteen between Usti and Decin would suffice.

"Tomorrow I'm going to Brno," Jacek said to Lenka, "please put two white shirts in my bag, and no lunch."

"Lie this way... and put your hands behind your head...," Jacek whispered to Nada in the room overlooking the Decin harbor, "I'll go to the door now and quietly steal back...," for a while he stood in the dark foyer, Good Lord, all this should have died out in us long ago—

The next morning Jacek sent Nada off to work, threw back the bedcovers, fetched himself a bottle of milk and some stale rye bread, extraordinary expenditures await us, then he made the bed, swept, and with a cigarette in hand leaned out the window, from under his fingers a bluish ribbon floated up to the clouds, and the cool wet breeze from the harbor, on the docks men leaned on steel cables and one of them all by himself pulled in toward the jetty the prow of a 700-ton barge, the cry of gulls and multi-colored flags on poles.

Sell this two-section chest and buy a three-section one secondhand, it would do for two, buy a folding bed at the bazaar and these two blankets would fit into Nada's chest, a mattress—or just find a canvas army cot, we never slept as well as we did on that, and in the daytime you can stand it up in the foyer—only inexpensive things secondhand from the bazaar, but in the new apartment everything of good quality and new, so a cot then and instead of a three-section chest a lean-to beside the two-section one: two suit-cases on top of one another and a metal coat tree in the corner.

"Wellll—" Nada dragged it out like an expert as she

inspected Jacek's drawing on the board, "you can see the third year of technical school in that and even something of the fourth year—Ouch! you're wrenching my—no, seriously, you could earn a living with that. I've got a surprise for you, but I'll tell you later, because now... I can't... concen—" and so on to the end of our twenty-four hours.

"And now for your surprise," she said, lying on the cushion, he went to the window to tie his tie. "I've got a job for you—and it's right around the corner, it's called Wood-Pak."

"What do they make?"

"All kinds of shipping containers and so forth. They'll take you on at once as a draftsman and in time they'll have an opening for a supervisor, you know, when you haven't had any experience yet... I know a Mr. Dvorak who has designs on Sternfeldova, the manager of our cafeteria, and it'll definitely work out."

Cross the ends, Wood-Pak would hardly be the acme of technology, make a loop, shipping containers are actually crates, pull the other end through the loop, is it really for the birds that he holds a degree in chemistry from Brno, tighten it, a career as box maker arranged by Mr. Dvorak and the cafeteria manager, pull it tight around his neck. Time has become an express train making up its time now that it's running on level ground, should he get off at thirty-three and start all over again as a student...

"You're awfully kind, Nadenka."

The convoy had entered the harbor, the men had run to their stations on the docks, the steel cables from the barges whistled through the air, and now they were being tied to metal posts, and Jacek shivered.

"So bye-bye and good night, darling—" he whispered.

Holding a cigarette he leaned out of the window of the train, hygienic ceramic ware in slat boxes was being rapidly unloaded in a pile right onto the gravel, on the other track a car full of girls on an outing, the boxing material cracked, and the train pulled quietly out, hi there girls, and a couple of them waved, look here, Mr. Jost, what has the railroad done with those boxes, sort it all out again, OK?, and Jacek waved at the girls' car, he sat down on the warm green imitation leather, but it was too hot, in the corridor he leaned out the open window, the April river rushed on, flooding beaches and meadows, this is its high point, ta-ta-ta-dum, that's how time drips from the calibrated bottle with our business card on it, Nadezda is wonderful, I'll come with my suitcase and we'll start a new life, ta-ta-ta-dum, or a new fiction, ta-ta-ta-dum, or keep both and cultivate an isosceles triangle, water it regularly, and shudder at the thought that one of its two sides will break—and which one will that be—but is that all life allots to a man who's thirty-three, where has that sketch of the Brno Opera gotten to, the grass and the sea, when will this train dump us out, is this the overture ta-ta-ta-dum, or is it our NEVERMORE—

II — seven

Jacek was the first to step off the crowded local, he read the time off his wristwatch: the trip here takes 52 minutes.

From a poor, once conceivably blacktop road a good half-mile of magnificent, four-lane divided highway shot out to the right, and a row of fluorescent streetlights towered above plowed fields. From a distance, Interchem looked just like an atomic reactor. The employees' glass-and-concrete bus stop would have been an ornament to any second-class airfield, the laminated-glass entrance an ornament to any first-class one. Projecting ten stories out of the runway-like concrete strip was the silver fairy tale of a freestanding apparatus. Ex-classmate Bachtik was master of it all—two-and-a-half acres worth a hundred million crowns.

The highest level of the hydrogenation tower like the captain's bridge of a carrier, and the job of first lieutenant open. Captain Bachtik had never been in any way distinguished—save that he'd made his decision to leave Cottex at just the right moment.

With a damp hand Jacek grasped the quivering rail, here one could accomplish things, so come on, don't be afraid, we send our leading technicians to be trained first in the Soviet Union and in England, I know both those languages well enough, of course you do, and you can fool around here to your heart's content, I'd introduce a central computer and monitors, that wouldn't be bad at all, in the meantime there are all kinds of people here, but I've already commanded a squad in which half the men were convicts, I remember you could be a stickler for discipline, just give me a free hand and things here will go as at a launching-pad— "Time to come down," said Bachtik, and he began to descend the stairs.

"Just let me fool around here a moment longer..."

A surrealistic domain of silver and from the mountains a moist wind blew, Jacek climbed down the winding metal stairs, once more around the tower and then once more around.

"So what do you think?" said Bachtik down below.

"It's wonderful...," Jacek sighed.

"Better than your two-bit plant at Cottex?"

Jacek sighed deeply.

"I can hold the job for you till the first."

"I'll... I'll give you a ring."

"You're yellow."

Jacek trailed across the runway behind a futuristic, bright-orange, electric-powered truck, toward a glassed-in pavilion which could have taken off without much modification. With a familiar, guilty smile, Pharmacologist

Karel Zacek led Jacek between banks of philodendrons and club chairs.

"Come on," he whispered, "no more of this sitting in the corner."

"Here you'll have the entire floor—" The year before last, Pharmacologist Zacek was master of half a desk and half a Romanian lab assistant, a girl he'd knocked up. Here he has a palm tree, a *Phoenix canariensis,* right by his door.

"On this floor I've got part of the physical chem lab. The rest of it and the organic are downstairs, the inorganic upstairs, and the qualitative in the pavilion."

In front of a row of illusory machines under plastic covers, a row of empty chrome chairs sparkled, and a girl in a surgical smock was crouching in a corner.

"You've even got a real Beckmann thermometer here...," Jacek whispered.

"Two of them and an infrared spectrophotometer," Zacek smiled wanly.

"Can I sit down with this for a moment?" tenderly Jacek pulled off the rustling cover and piously touched the switchboard. "If I were to come here, would you give me this machine?"

"I'd be awfully happy to give you all of this."

"The whole floor?"

"The whole building and the pavilion over there. I'm going to Prague."

"I'll give you a ring on Monday—"

"I'm flying to London on Monday," Zacek smiled guiltily.

"Living quarters are available for singles the day they come in," the manager of the living quarters said as he led Jacek through a vast opaque glass corridor right out of a spy or sci-fi film, "family apartments in nine months." Glass bricks went all the way back to the showers and naked men with wet hair promenaded with towels thrown over their arms like overcoats, behind a white door a

hotel-style room for three and everywhere green upholstery, "I might be able to put you in here—," a gray-haired
roommate was in bed reading a thin volume of James Bond
007 with the help of the thick tomes of a three-volume
dictionary, and under a propped-open window a fellow
was whispering Russian words, "—or upstairs on the
second floor, where the upholstery is blue."

"Engineer Jost? Comrade Bachtik has ordered me to
drive you to Usti—" a well-tanned, dapper young man in
a gray-blue uniform said as he opened the door of a large
silver-gray limousine for Jacek, "—you say your factory's
here between these house lots?" he marveled later when
he couldn't find the entrance to Cottex in the gap between
wooden fences.

In the just beginning drizzle Jacek jumped over puddles
across the ridged mud of the courtyard to the wooden
annex of the technical division, and he sank down into his
wicker chair. Nine-by-twelve feet of creaky boards and a
roughed-up desk of soft wood from the days of the Germans, promoted by the painter's brush to "stained oak,"
on a plant stand a half-century-old Urania typewriter and,
behind a curtain of local manufacture, five bookshelves,
six-by-fifteen feet of files full of letters that had come in
and copies of nonsense that had gone out, a chemical
engineer ten years later—

It was raining hard now and under the overhang of the
roof of the electric plant two men had run for cover, a
seventy-year-old fireman (also a chemical engineer, before
the war the manager of sugar factories: "How much a year
do you make here, Mr. Jost? Twenty thousand? Well, let's
see, I made two hundred and twenty thousand in Louny,
then in Kralupy two hundred and seventy thousand, in
Roudnice only a hundred and ninety thousand, it's true,
but in Lovosice I made four hundred and thirty thousand
plus—") and a fifty-year-old guard (after the war a high
functionary: "I had all those directors called together and

I said to that bunch, goddamn it, gentlemen..."), they crouched together and pressed their backs against the wall, at that moment a heavyset tattooed man rolled a reel of cable three yards high through the gate and pushed it heavily forward, it got stuck in the mud, the fellow roared at the two has-beens under the overhang, the pair rushed out, and all three together rolled the enormous reel out into the cloudburst.

Slowly Jacek lit a cigarette, by degrees he leaned with his entire weight against the right side of the back of the chair, gradually he stiffened the whole side of his body from that point of concentrated pressure down to his knees, and very slowly he moved that whole side left a couple of inches, so that his buttocks rested on the seat in a new position, cool and newly pleasurable, as when in bed one lets his cheek slide down on the pillow.

Vitenka Balvin looked in the door and a short while later Petrik Hurt, the boss, to ask about the big limo Jacek had just pulled up in, but all he had to do was press his fists to his temples twice and look tormented: this pantomime signaled the state known as "Jacek's got neurosis" and the fact that it was necessary to spare him for the rest of the shift.

We too will spare ourselves, Jacek lit another cigarette, stretched the left side of his back and then shifted to the right, twenty-seven more years till our pension and we'll have our whole life saved up, so that then we can mourn it all in one piece—Jacek leapt up from his chair, kicked it, and paced back and forth for the remainder of the shift.

Petrik Hurt jumped off the streetcar at the main square just before the stop and out from behind the column that carried the huge poster advertising Candy's orchestra, Verka Hurtova came running to meet him, Petrik's third wife and his "true love," as Petrik unashamedly claimed, but that third marriage had cost him two furnished apartments for the preceding wives and eleven hundred a month support for their five children, costly enough if one succeeds only the third time, but Petrik didn't complain, "My first wife and I understood one another sometimes, with my second we were both content, but only with Verka did I find out what true happiness is—," and for seven years it had been uninterrupted, he wouldn't have found it if he'd have only switched once...

There was still a lot of spare time, Jacek went to the window of the notice agency, SERVICE TO THE PUBLIC, and read the PERSONALS column, the 25-year-old refined wom. of girl. appear. with own furn. apart. was still available, also the native of Usti likes the woods; Child is no obsticle!, it must require a very special taste to make a spectacle of oneself in the main square.

To kill time, Jacek stopped in at the barber shop, let's wait till Kamilka is free, he picked up the only newspaper on the table, the day before yesterday's *Prace*, and ran through the already familiar news, under different headlines and less of it, we're used to *Rude pravo*—but look, they even publish personals here, nearly two full columns, and it's more tasteful than a spectacle in the main square, it's a real horror how many people there are dying to switch—

"Next, please—"

"The usual?" Kamilka smiled at Jacek.

"No clippers," he nodded.

"You have such thick hair..."

"And yours is as lovely as Egyptian cotton... It must be a pleasure to comb it..."

She giggled and stroked him, perhaps she pressed a bit harder than she need have, but we've known one another for two years now, only so far we never dared try anything, and he kissed her on the elbow.

"That isn't done here," she was pleasantly angry.

"Because I don't get to meet you anywhere else."

"Because you don't go out."

"Because no one ever invites me anywhere..."

"Shall I trim your hairs?"

"I'll do the same to you... and it'll scratch."

She tore the towel away from under his chin and pressed it over his mouth.

"Kamila!—" said the manager into the mirror.

"Check for No. 5!" Kamilka called out, and she began digging in a drawer. "Come here tonight at ten...," she whispered.

"But the last train leaves at half-past nine," Jacek whispered, "and then in the morning..."

Kamilka's neck reddened.

"...at five-thirty...," Jacek lied, grinning meanwhile at the manager in the mirror, "That's why I never go anywhere..."

"Come here tonight at ten," she whispered.

How awfully easy it would be, Jacek inhaled the scent of his cologne and stopped in front of the travel agency window, the smiles of two pretty girls were inviting us to visit the Czech Paradise and a white ship was sailing to Tunisia across the vast green expanse of the Mediterranean, Nadezda was Speranza, should he trust the rest of his life to a chance meeting on a train, the Miramar was already a dream and the open road of green waves shone toward Africa, a superannuated cratemaker's apprentice spending the night in a stretcher for corpses—

As if catapulted, Jacek rushed back to the barber shop and picked up the old newspaper from the table—it would contain the address for notices—and he carried it off in his pocket, the manager called out something, a crowd of people flowed out of a streetcar and dragged Jacek along in the direction of the main post office, quickly past the shop windows of the notice agency, the newspaper sends replies by mail, Petrik Hurt only succeeded the third time around, people said his neighbor Mr. Mestek had gotten as many as thirty offers and had cured his inferiority complex that way, we can have them mailed to the office—

At a speckled counter in the huge hall of the main post office Jacek stood in a sweat over the writing paper and envelope he had purchased, a stamp was already printed on the envelope and Jacek glanced under his elbow into the purloined newspaper, 36-YEAR-OLD divor. with child seeks wife if poss. with own apart., 42-YEAR-OLD divor. eng. seeks young intellect., what nonsense, 58-YEAR-OLD man with artif. leg seeks— and Jacek was already writing:

33-year-old eng., divor., seeks partner

But what sort of partner, they all write something or other, but then this is only an attempt to relieve your mind, after all before making a permanent appointment you have to announce a competition, that way no one can be blamed for anything, they all include a key word, it has to be there, some sort of key word—

Live!

it's short, and at least it won't cost too much.

Jacek threw the letter into the slot, the newspaper into a wastebasket, and then he went out and back to the square, now sufficiently amused.

From the enormous poster a sun-bronzed Candy in a purple tux rolled his eyes at him FOLLOWING OUR SUCCESSFUL GERMAN TOUR, while five fabulously pretty heads gazed up at him ecstatically, you old swindler you, at Cottex years ago Candy had been called Alois Klecanda, a miserable lab-assistant who spent his nights playing in a jazz band and came to the lab only to sleep, if he came at all, at Cottex they put up with a great deal, but for the theft of some tow-cloth and mercury Alois Klecanda got a year in prison and ever since he's been out he's done nothing but play in that band, he makes more in a month than the director of Cottex and his two deputies put together, and in his green sports car he carts around the most beautiful girls in the area.

Jacek stood beneath the clock and observed his own reflection in the black glass, 33-year-old divorced engineer of pleasant appearance—the simplest possibility was divorce.

Lenka and Lenicka were already coming down Revolution Avenue, we can see each other from a distance, but Lenka doesn't run to meet me the way Verka does with Petrik, perhaps she's never run, this is only my first, every fifth Czech is divorced and there are twenty thousand divorces a year, why on earth do we remember the statistics anyway, Lenka's caught sight of us, but she's more interested in that display of knitted goods, but then we might have gone to see it together, the little darling sees her Daddy but runs away, she's more inclined to go for Russian ice cream, Daddy would be more likely to buy her some than Mommy would, of course, but you like Mommy better, "We had a wonderful time—" Lenka says when I come back from Brno, well so did we—

Lenka looks old for her twenty-eight years, soon she'll have as many wrinkles as her mother, she no longer likes to talk in bed, she'd rather sleep, how frightened she was yesterday—watching TV she suddenly jumped up and ran to the bathroom, it happens more and more often, she locks herself in for three-quarters of an hour and then that thief-like crawling into the next bed, as if begging for mercy—please don't—

"Did you bring the money?"

Let's concede that's all that matters to you and the court will determine precisely how much, it will take your side and I'll be glad to send it to you, for three hundred crowns a month a new life, twenty-four hours of freedom for ten crowns, pass by this indifferent wife and child who, in a year, won't even recognize us, and go back along Revolution Avenue in the opposite direction, toward the railroad station and the docks, under the burgeoning chestnut trees, free to take off—

"Daddy swing me like an angel—" Lenicka called, Lenka took her by one arm and Jacek by the other, they raised her up and, swinging her feet, the little girl soared into the sky.

II — eight

The general director leaned back from the oval ebony table and laughed quietly. *Rien ne va plus*—Jacek, his lips in position to pronounce the word "cheese," observed the boss of a hundred and ten thousand employees and an annual turnover of nine billion, here direct attack alone promised any chance of success and already now the little ball was rolling around the roulette wheel, the big boss began to turn red in the face and to wheeze asthmatically, his fingers dark brown with nicotine and too much coffee, it's all too much for you, and a nice big desk would just fit into your anteroom. Let's say "cheese" and look into each other's eyes.

"This isn't badly thought out, I must admit," the general director said at last. "And of course you'd want to be in charge of it all. But there isn't such a position on the chart."

"Let's put it down as a special deputy, Comrade Director. A good gardener needs a ferocious dog."

"The next few months will give us some indication..."

"There's no hurry..."

"But for the time being I haven't promised anything."

"For the time being I haven't asked for anything."

The general director grinned knowingly and shook Jacek's hand just perceptibly harder than was customary, it was boringly simple, one more glance at those three tables, the oval one for conferences, the enormous executive desk, and the long table with its twenty-four leather-upholstered seats of knighthood, of course there were twenty-six factory directors, but you could squeeze in a pair of stools, or three if need be, and out through the padded door into the anteroom, under the palm tree *Trachycarpus excelsa* there's a free corner with good lighting.

"You're to order a car for me—" Jacek said to the secretary, and "To the offices of the Regional Committee—" to the chauffeur. Through the springtime streets of the Brno of his sweet days as a student, since they've held the trade fair here things have been going up and up, "Have you got any children?" he asked the chauffeur and then: "That's fine. Stop here and I'll get out."

Through the long corridors of the gray palace the word had spread that Jacek Jost from Usti had lasted fifty minutes with the general director. Only at dinner upstairs at the Avion was it possible to find all the higher-ups together, and they all came to greet Jacek at his table.

The grotesquely fat Franta Docekal had grown even fatter and was now serving as deputy, his classmate Libor was in charge of exports and was now living, after his third divorce, with a circus acrobat named Manuela, Venca had brought a Mercedes back from Germany and Kikin was stationed in Cairo, they were all on top of things and none of them one bit smarter than we are, maybe less so, but now they're all bigwigs and they look very serious when they fly back from France or Belgium and take off for Argentina or Zanzibar.

"Is Kindl still working in Moscow at COMECON?"

"He's at the embassy now."

"And Valasek... the shrimp who was so frightened all the time, the one who peed in his bed in the army..."

"Oh, he's in Addis Ababa, he sent us his picture taken with the emperor."

On the floor upstairs his classmate, the deputy Verosta, was at the billiard table looking for a weak opponent, Jacek made an effort to scale his game progressively down from fair to poor, "You've got real class," he said, inclining his cue like a knight his lance before his liege-lord, "Oh yes, just so I don't forget it, the general director asked me today what kind of impression you made on people as a student. I covered you with silver and gold..."

"What can that old fart be trying to smell out," said Deputy Verosta, obviously pleased, "it must be on account of the ministry. Many thanks, Jacek, and drop in to see me this evening, here's the address."

"I'd like to, but I'm in a real bind. Our director's raking me over the coals for not coming up with that ethyl acetate."

"How much do you need?"

"A carload?..."

"You've got it, and give me a call the next time you're in Brno."

Another floor up, the great Benedikt Smrcek, the future first member of the Academy from the field of textiles, was playing chess alone.

"You really clouted him, Bena...," Jacek whispered piously, and Benedikt the Great smiled just a bit, "What are you going to ask me for?"

"What does one ask from the head of a research institute?"

"If you're really interested, sign up for a graduate fellowship starting October 1, it wouldn't be a bad idea to have a factory man for a change."

"Bena, do you remember how we once played chess all night in the guardhouse at the Jaromer barracks and we promised one another—"

"I remember that you were black that night, you opened eleven times with a double fianchetto, and you lost twenty-two times," Bena said as he set up the pieces, "that's what I call persistence. The secretary's office will send you the application forms."

His father (66) was just getting ready to go out and play

cards, his mother (61) to see some friends, but they could
stay and talk to Jacek for a while, what was new in Usti,
not a thing, Mom, just as there hasn't been anything for ten
years now, Dad, but here there were lots of new things,
Mom was working in an apiary co-op and Dad was teaching languages to earn money to go to the seashore, then
they'd cut out and make the rounds of the relatives—no,
not to Usti, what would we do there—to Prague and
Carlsbad, in autumn Dad will take foreigners on hunting
trips and live with them in Castle Mikulov, Mom and her
friends will take temporary jobs sorting apples, and at
Christmas time we'll both work for a month at the chocolate factory, "And when are you planning to move back to
Brno?"

"I'm working on it…"

"Why didn't you stay here—" his mother sighed again,
"all your schoolmates…"

"A young man has to go out into the world," said Dad.
"When I was your age, let's see, that would be in thirty-
two…"

"…you were in Morocco."

"That's right, it was great there. Sure, a young man has
to…"

"I've spent ten years now in Usti."

"So many?" Mom was frightened. "That's terrible!"

"I'm working on it. The general director will have something for me, and Bena Smrcek's promised me something
at his institute."

"Of course, you could always come and live with us, but
what would you do with Lenka and Lenicka?"

"I'm working on it."

Jacek's room seemed noticeably larger than the one in
the Usti pre-fab, the window on the magnificent old park,
the wooden saber on the wall, and in the corner the globe
Dad had given him, oh Lord, nothing ever seems to die—

We used to go to school every day along this street,

between the rows of trees below the stadium, as a freshman in high school we hadn't the least doubt that the first
Czechoslovak field marshal would be named Jost ("J.J. the
Great") and he had already planned the reorganization of
the army, up the hill along the wall of the seminary garden,
as a sophomore the brilliant director of a revolutionary
film: the camera looking through the hero's eyes so that his
face wouldn't be visible, but it would show his hands
when he drinks, as they pick up the glass it would come
up in full detail across the entire width of the screen, when
he walks the whole picture would sway rhythmically with
his step, the whole audience would kiss with him and look
down the rangefinder of his gun, along the asphalt of
quietly elegant Masova Street, as a junior the famous spy,
Flying Jacek—the terror of governments, with a wristwatch
that shoots bullets, through the kiosk at the base of the
steps of the University Library, where not even a high-
school senior ventured, until, thrilled, he was a freshman
at the University, the winner of the first Czech Nobel Prize
(that was before Heyrovsky) had come to look for a girl to
serve as his assistant.

Jacek ascended those same steps, in the reading room
beneath fluorescent lamps a fountain murmured, and at
the tables a hundred girls of twenty-five nationalities, near
the Chemistry Department a blonde girl stood with a thick
copy of Gajdos's *Chromatography* in her hand.

"A truly awful book," said Jacek, and he grinned.

"I wouldn't say so," the girl answered icily.

"You're not going to praise me!"

"Why should I praise... you? You're..."

"Dr. Gajdos," Jacek smiled, "and thanks for the tribute."

"Doctor— I'm Libuse Cveklova. And I'm really—"

"When you register for my course, I'll take you out to
dinner."

Majestically Jacek walked out and then skipped down
the stairs, on the door a notice to the effect that Dr.

Benedikt Smrcek, CSc, National Awardwinner, would lecture in the Great Hall—Bena had had persistence and so things had worked out for him. In the streets of the big city, which were just lighting up for the evening, Jacek, the unattached research worker, was looking for his fellows.

And at the White Crocodile, the Bellevue, the Slavie, and the Hotel International they beckoned and waved from tables in the back, with new wives, girlfriends, and mistresses, this is Marcela, Kamila, Jana, Yvette, the girls smiled and shook hands, fresh-looking, sun-tanned, well-cared-for, with pointy breasts, flat stomachs—tennis instead of breast-feeding, sailing instead of pushing baby carriages—dazzling with make-up, perfect, they returned Jacek's prolonged handshakes. Pavel Vrbka had been working freelance for years, writing scenarios about Mendel, proteins, and the Battle of Austerlitz, and at the Black Bear our old Professor Muzikar (58) drinking wine with a marvelous girl from the Brno-at-Night Cabaret.

In the enormous park outside his window strings of lights, laughter, and music from the dance floor, from below the black treetops up to the quivering halo of the city of three hundred thousand, and Jacek fell asleep in his childhood bed, out of the night starlets, sports stars, and upper-class co-eds, today Marcela, Kamila, Jana, Yvette, and we'll stay with them again as we did before.

Jacek woke up before the sun entered the room, he exercised and took an ice-cold shower, at the lunch counter he had a roll and two glasses of warm milk, two crowns forty in all and that can be cut, a graduate fellow in science gets fifteen hundred, and of that three hundred gets sent to Usti, that leaves forty crowns a day, heh heh, four times as much as you had when you were a student, on the way back through Luzanky Park he met a girl with a violin, a music student, you'll never know your whole life long what a timeclock is.

In his room he twirled the globe Dad had given him,

Dad had gone to Morocco at thirty-three and without a tourgroup, by himself, and with his finger Jacek traveled over the blue sea, from Rijeka on the Yugoslav coast down between Charybdis and Scylla, past Malta and Majorca through Gibraltar out to the open sea and to Africa, to the white city of Casablanca... nothing has died in us yet!

Excitedly Jacek waved his wooden saber and piously he hung it up again, from the bookshelf he took down his old *Physical Chemistry* by Brdicka, it would be best to start with that, greedily he began to read, and the forgotten pages came to life again.

And Express No. 7 conscientiously tore along Line No. 1, the main artery from east to west, from Bucharest, Budapest, Bratislava, and Brno to Ceska Trebova, Pardubice, and Prague, in Prague you change for Paris with connections for Le Havre, Calais, Marseille, or to Usti and Decin, our line, on which we've been riding now for ten years, we were leaving home then to go out into the world, but the emptiness of the passing years has maliciously tipped the scales, the world is always at the other end of the line—

"I didn't sleep at all last night," yawned the tousled Nada, rubbing her eyes with her fists, "all night long you kept shouting something in your sleep about Africa, and then you kicked me right here. I'll sleep in the army cot when it comes... What's wrong? No exercises today?"

"I don't feel well, Nadezda."

"Why not?"

"Not well at all. I can't go on this way..."

"Lenka and Lenicka..."

"...and everything. I don't know how to pull myself out of it."

"Get a divorce."

"If that were all there was to it."

"Then go back to them, I told you already on the train that I wouldn't chase you. I really won't."

"So much the worse."

"You still don't know what you want?"

"The trouble is, I do know—precisely."

"And it's—"

"Everything."

"Then you're not so bad off. The opposite would be worse. So let's go, you can lead the exercises."

Imperturbably, the sun glided down the wall and began to cross the floor, Jacek between the walls, the claws of the dock cranes unloaded from rail cars to barges and from barges to rail cars, to be everlastingly on a chain-rope-line-hook would drive one mad, use force to cut through and do it firmly, the barges sink almost to the cargo line, only death is the last possibility, the rising of the barges above the surface, but one does not wish to die so where should he aim, they raise anchor when completely full or completely empty, completely-completely-completely emptied, if both of them were to die at the same time they could sail out, Lenicka and Lenka—and without chains, ropes, or nylon fibers, without straps, lines, or hooks, free to enter the world's splendor—in horror Jacek pressed his hand to his throat, by the window overlooking the harbor, in the windowglass the throttling fingers of my own, this my own right hand are buried almost to the point of vanishing.

II — nine

*I*t's Lenicka's beddie-bye time already, but we've had so little fun, so let's play just a tiny bit more, Jacek took apart the sofa and with its cushions he built her a play house on the carpet, with the coverlet as the roof and a little balcony out of pillows, Lenicka was ecstatic as she crawled through her hut, now she must go beddie-bye, and so quickly quickly once through the obstacle course, Jacek placed two cushions down flat on the floor and a third one perpendicular to them between, the little girl climbed over it, fell and again climbed up, shouted and cheered and had to be put to bed by force, "Daddy gwab me—"

"I'll grab you—where it hurts!"

"Gwab me, Daddy! Gwab—"

And down again with the netting, nothing's so sweet to kiss as our little one, but you really must go beddie-bye, "Daddy won't go way—" Jacek bent over the brass pole, stroked his darling's hair and cheeks, tucked the coverlet under her chin, out of the damp darkness my hand cries out on her little white throat—flee, go away without a word, or get divorced before something horrible happens... you'll never make up your mind to say that first word.

It was raining for the third day in a row, a cold, prolonged rain, and Jacek dozed on the streetcar in the heavy odor of damp clothing, Lenka was carrying a muddy Lenicka along the broad concrete road, Lenicka had fallen down and was crying a great deal, she's awfully heavy and Mommy can scarcely carry her, Jacek took the exhausted wet little girl into his arms and the family staggered home up the steps, Grandma had spent the whole day ironing and on all the chairs shirts were exhaling the warm odor of heated cotton, "I don't feel like doing much today either...," Lenka yawned, "I feel the flu coming on," yawned Jacek, Lenicka had her mouth wide open too, and apologetically Grandma placed her wrinkled fist to her lips, "So let's have a sleep day," Jacek decided, "everyone lie down!" "But not in bed," Lenka added, "I'd never get up again..."

So Daddy and Mommy on the sofa, Grandma in the armchair, but Lenicka screamed that she didn't want to be by herself and so they had to bring in her crib, Lenka fell asleep first and her heavy body warmed his side, Grandma nodded off in the chair, and Lenicka snored lightly in her crib, with sticky eyes Jacek looked over that happily sleeping little flock and then soothing, stupefying sleepiness came to his eyelids.

At two in the morning Jacek suddenly awoke and could not get up, in her sleep Lenka had embraced him and he was a long time freeing himself from her, there was a terrible sensation of hunger in his stomach, quietly he crept into the kitchen but he found nothing edible there, only kohlrabi and cookies, they'd even forgotten to buy bread, a ravenous Jacek greedily guzzled cold chlorinated water and he quivered with disgust, now we won't get back to sleep again, a pain seemed to be developing in his throat, we used to have some Swiss chocolate in the bookcase, but someone's eaten it, the triple snoring in the living room and the sleepy but angry Jacek shuffled through the nighttime apartment coughing experimentally, it could be the flu, in the refrigerator he found some frozen yogurt and vengefully swallowed it in the largest pieces he could get down, then water "on the rocks," an inflammation of the lungs, fine to neglect it, with a pack of cigarettes and a chair he went out on the balcony and sat down, a blanket thrown lightly over his shoulders and so till morning...

Although his temperature was only 99° the whole apartment was turned upside down, a struggling Jacek was quickly stripped, on the kitchen range Grandma's teas and decoctions were boiling, "Daddy is ticky and you must be quiet," Lenka whispered to Lenicka, to be "ticky" was one of our favorite childhood games, the pleasure of being manipulated—fingered, measured, picked up, carried from place to place, put to bed, covered up all the way to the eyes, and left to follow all the bustle and excitement, already Mommy was bringing a pint of cranberry jam, there weren't any seeds and you didn't have to cut it or even chew it very much, just the first bittersweet taste, and already Lenka was bringing a good two pounds of cranberry jam, and spoon in hand she sat on the edge of the bed.

"You faker," Lenka threatened him with her finger when for two days now Jacek's temperature had failed to go above 97.9°, "you're just pretending, right?"

"But I kept saying there was nothing wrong with me..."

"It's OK, as long as you get to spend some time at home..."

"You shouldn't have gone to so much trouble..."

"That's all right, I'm glad to do what I can..."

My wife has the sincerest blue eyes in the world, and Jacek quickly drew her to him.

"Lenunka..."

"Wait a moment, I'll just close the door—"

Like milk, my love, there is no peace except existence within an order, "Jacinek...," my wife whispers, and she presses her delirious lips against the ridge of my stroking hand: "Jacinek... I'd like one more little one..." On her white throat my black hand roared, and a bitter, salty hunger.

"This is the first time I've been here for two years," Pepik Tosnar said absentmindedly as he sat down at Jacek's table, he was the creator of the six-tiered pipe organ, daddy of six girls, and their neighbor from the apartment house, "I'll start with two beers, bartender!"

"You've only been to a bar once in the last two years?"

"No-o, I'd be telling a fib, last Easter I went to The Five Arches."

"Then you're my guest, let's make it worthwhile—" impressed, Jacek looked at this balding man who spent most of his time in the playground below their window and who earned extra money fixing blinds delivered in a state beyond repair, "—two more, let there be six in all, like your daughters, and I'll get the check!" A good man, but beyond daughters and blinds he didn't know too much.

Not taking no for an answer he dragged Jacek to his own place for "slivovitz twice distilled and three times passed through charcoal," well, let's have a look at that apartment underneath which we've been living for two years, where there's so much trampling every morning—right in the doorway an acrid mixture of odors hits the nose like a blow from frozen reins, the same apartment as ours but what have they done with it, six little beds like coffins in stacks, on the floor a foot-deep pop-art layer of a thousand unnameable things dragged in by the children, the wild romping of six filthy little devils, "I've made them all with clefts down below, nothing but rejects so far," roared the circus manager to outshout the wild beasts climbing all over him the way the chimpanzees at the zoo climb their tree, and into mustard glasses he poured out more lethal doses of wood alcohol incompletely distilled, which this innocent fool had evidently spiced with brown coal rather than filtering it through absorbent charcoal, "But the seventh time's in the bag, it'll be a boy," roared his cannonball of a wife while the slobbering monkeys clambered over Jacek's limbs as over tropical vines.

If Lenka were to have triplets, there'd be seven of us, including Grandma—the frightful alcohol flamed up inside Jacek and Lenicka rapped her head against the bathtub, terrible screams, if she rapped it harder she wouldn't scream anymore and from your slippery hands a child could easily slip and fall, "What are you up to in the bathroom—," Lenka with gas, "We're almost done...," take them both up to Maria's Rock and push them out between the wires, the little one tore away from me and my wife leaped after her, "Hey you two, march to dinner—," from her ten containers of sleeping pills somehow procure the right substance and then throw the ten empty containers on her night table, wear gloves, perhaps she'd find out about my girlfriend N. Houskova and solve it all that way: Lenicka to Grandma's with two hundred a month, everything immensely simple all of a sudden, exchange the apartment for a room or a one-bedroom co-op, also first-category, and take as much as ten thousand under the table, sell the furniture, rugs, curtains, and then with his savings he could manage a Hillman Minx, "—we're working on it!"

Jacek stuffed himself to the point of numbness, pass the roast, with his fingers he tore crisp meat off the bones and standing over the refrigerator he drank his fill straight from the bottle—an imaginary line to the window right across the way, Trost with a piece of meat in one hand and a bottle of beer in the other, that unbearable alter ego, and Jacek ran off to the bedroom, Grandma and Lenka had already tuned the TV to their favorite Dietl soap opera, you bet Trost and his Mrs. were also watching Dietl.

On Sunday morning Jacek and Lenka took Lenicka into their bed, the little darling crawled along Daddy's leg and up to get a great great great big kiss and then a second one, still sweeter, and with his knee under the coverlet he once again played polar bear, Lenicka was frightened and ecstatic, "Daddy don't go way—"

On a bus up into the hills Jacek fled under the windows of the Tosnars and the Trosts as from a prison cell, at the summit, on the vibrating metal floor, two pairs of lovers— the two Hurts and Vitenka Balvin with his guitar and Milena Cerna, off on the most secret of the secret paths to the very top, at the base of Mt. Kneziste the white spot of Mija's two-seater and the smaller white spot of Mija in her beach chair, he turned and fled through the waves of gleaming emerald grass with a million gold dandelions like medals on green velvet waiting to be awarded, now only to kill on a Maytime meadow with so many women and horses, Lenkas for the world or the world for Lenkas, now only killing was left—

After a Sunday cutlet with potato salad and a slice of crumbling cheesecake we, the Josts, and Grandma go to the zoo, and Lenicka in ecstasy in front of the monkey cage. "Come, darling, Daddy will hold you up—"

At the office his fists were now constantly pressed to his temples and his face looked tormented, "Jacek's got neurosis," he was depressed for the fifth day in a row, *alles ist schon egal*, "It's Jacek again, Mija, write me a prescription for three containers of those pills—I said three!" "And today will be another sleeping day! What's that—OK then, I'll do it myself."

On Sunday morning he and Lenka took Lenicka into their bed and before dinner out to the high Maytime meadows, the gleaming grass gleaming straight up to the gleaming sky calls like the shore to the sea, we will swim out, something will happen, SOMETHING WILL COME, the humble expect to be exalted and the masters are afraid of loss, all count on change and so it must come, SOMETHING WILL HAPPEN, faith is needed and an amused interest in how we'll be violated this time, SOMEONE WILL COME AND SHOW US WHERE TO GO, all that's left for us is to prepare for that coming, IT WILL BE RESOLVED AND IN GRATITUDE WE WILL SUBMIT, already the bolts of the catapult are being tightened and the flight path adjusted, LET'S TAKE OFF SOON—we pray and we prepare.

Part III — Preparations — ten

A flat green ceramic ashtray, two plain wineglasses
made of leaded glass, a pot, a saucepan, and a guitar
pick, only three hundred from the secret hoard and we're
all set—carefully, on his stomach, the way a woman might
carry her child, Jacek carried his black traveling satchel
onto the bus to Telnice, "Let's have that, Mr. Jost, I can
hold it on my lap—" "Good day, Mrs. Klusakova, that's
very kind, but I'll manage—" "Just hand it over!"

The bus left the square at 3:55 sharp, Mrs. Klusakova is
our new neighbor, her husband works for the police and
she wants to sell us strawberries, he must not make very
much, it's useful to seek out support from the local authorities and strawberries too in the bargain, you can eat them
just as they are, with sugar or with cream, you have to try
them with condensed milk, "You're so very kind, really—,"
the bus drove through the canyon of familiar facades
infinitely faster than the streetcar on its way to the last stop
at Vseborice, outside the window the model T 03 cinder-
block buildings flashed by and then, as if demolished, they
disappeared to the rear, right after them the garden colony
unrolled, made up it seemed more of wire mesh than of
commonplace young radishes and carrots sown from packets for a crown apiece, and we're on our way—

Between rows of old chestnuts covered with pontifical
candle-blossoms, through unending fields of spring grain,
a sharp turn around the chemical plant, and the enormous
shallow crater of the strip mine with ramparts of trans-
ported bare earth, towards the monument with the green
bronze lion and along a granite road straight into the
mountains, through waves of meadows, tiny houses buried
in the tops of trees, and now that linden tree with the sign,

and we're home, "So don't forget, Mr. Jost, they'll be ripe in a month and I'll let you have them for eight crowns a box."

Into the transparent air, intensity fifty thousand candle-power, and a blindingly lit dirt path leading upwards, down the slope a flock of butter-fat goslings rocked to and fro, and by the trunk of a pink apple tree a snow-blue kid goat, as if posing for an Agfacolor, but the kid had three dimensions and could be petted in the bargain, "Good afternoon, Mr. Svitacek, I'm just..." "But we play with him too, he likes it best when you scratch him on the horns...," Mr. Svitacek delivered the mail in Ritin and his wife was chairwoman of the local town committee, he'd brought her the box of detergent that had stood around too long, a token tribute to their power, so that they would leave him in peace, "Here's some of that American laundry detergent for your wife, you pour it into a little hot water and then shake it up till the tub is full of foam, then pour all the water in at once..." "But how can we thank you, Mr. Jost, really we can't take it for nothing..." "But I've had a good time playing with your kid." "Then we're very grateful to you... and you must stop by sometime..."

Our main street here is a curved pasture with a little stream and marsh-marigolds, ours is the last yellow house, Mrs. Heymerova would come back from her daughter's in the fall, Jacek unlocked the door with a key that seemed made for a church and then impatiently up the wooden stairs to his "retreat."

The room measured a little over 200 sq. ft., on the brass bed an orange blanket made of merino wool, a dark oaken wardrobe big as a closet, and four heavy chairs around an oval table, on its cover a scene of stags rutting and more deer hanging on the wall above the bed, made from the same antique woven material, an unbelievable sofa in the shape of a sitting bathtub, and outside the window a strip of shiny green grass all the way out to the horizon—all for fifty crowns a month.

Cautiously Jacek unpacked his satchel, an ashtray between the horns of the rutting stag, two glasses onto the shelf in the cupboard next to the bottle of Beaujolais, the pot and saucepan onto the shelf by the cooking stove, and the guitar pick behind the strings of the instrument, all the wrapping paper into the fireplace, in a sudden inspiration he brought an armful of fir brush in from the courtyard, lit a match, and a fire roared in the fireplace, the crackle of dried wood and the sweet, pure scent of a real fire, what was time—

"You've practically moved into that 'retreat' of yours...," Lenka mumbled, but she had no time for conversation, for outside there was laundry to take down, and Lenicka decisively preferred to go with her, it seemed that three times a week with Daddy was enough, "And do you really have to study so much for your work?" Grandma asked again, "Technology is moving forward with seven-league boots—" Jacek said firmly, "and what I learned ten years ago—" "I know, they were saying the same thing on TV the other day..." and she followed the two Lenkas out to get the wash.

It had gone easier than he had at first supposed, everyone was out so let's start getting ready, Jacek strolled through the apartment as if he were taking inventory, or more like a future heir through the apartment of someone who has not yet passed away, leave all the pictures here, we'll swipe a thermometer from Cottex, take the desk lamp to the retreat with him, leave the glazed plastic red hippopotamus at home, don't take any junk, as with cattle out on the range so on all his things Jacek saw one of two brands: TAKE or LEAVE—the polyester shirts, the good shirts, the black leather tie, the suede sports jacket, the black sweater, the dagger, all glowed in the dusk of the vacated apartment like a neon sign TAKE, the undershirts, the worn-out shorts, the knitted vests, ten Christmas ties from Grandma, all the glass and porcelain, the slippers worn till they shone, and the gardening jacket labeled LEAVE, a bottle of Yugoslav Badel brandy TAKE, the ficus LEAVE, in the kitchen there are perhaps hundreds of things which we learn about only in a closing inventory, for what in God's name are these funnels, mashers, glass spoons, sieves, jugs, saucers, and slicers, the technological furnishings of industry that have gradually pushed us out onto a corner of the balcony, allotting us just a slot for depositing paychecks, a slot without a bottom.

The three women (how many of them did we actually freely choose?) were returning from collecting the wash, more excited by what was going on in the yard than they'd been on that excursion to the Giant Mountains, and almost surprised that we were still home—surprise on both sides would have been appropriate—and without delay two of them recommenced that bubbling, hissing, baking, and boiling, that costly sixteen-hour chemistry on conveyor belts out of which there emerges for us, most of the time, a warmed-over sausage or cold toast and watery tea.

"Why do you always wear those old socks when you've never worn the red ones?"

"Why do you have to wear those black suede shoes in this heat?"

"Why don't you ever wear your suede jacket?"

The old socks and the suede shoes are things on their way to wearing out, thus LEAVE, but save the red socks, thus TAKE, and the suede jacket is a component of the Suitcase, worked out a hundred times in the finest detail and packed as perfectly as the luggage of a cosmonaut.

"Daddy gwab me—" Lenicka says for the first time today and in ninety seconds "Want down—" and right back to Grandma's skirts, counting Lenka's question, what is confectioner's yeast, together with the appropriate answer, plus bringing potatoes up from the cellar, we were needed today for only six minutes in all, of that really needed for only a hundred seconds. To the sound of triple snores Jacek selected a suitable knife from among six candidates in the now silent kitchen, the one selected was thoroughly put to the test by cutting into the sideboard: the knife TAKE, the sideboard LEAVE.

From Cottex he could now make it comfortably without haste, after 2:00, to the self-service store to buy a quarter-loaf of bread, a bottle of milk, and a chunk of Swiss cheese, the bus to Telnice leaves at 2:28 and stops around the corner, "Good day, Mrs. Klusakova!" "How are you, Mr. Svitacek!" and at three we're already at home in the retreat. Jacek put the provisions away on the shelf and from his empty satchel into the waiting dark oaken wardrobe only one hanger for his cosmonaut's suede jacket, take off his wristwatch and lock it up in the wardrobe.

With the orange blanket slowly to the grassy strip at the edge of the forest, from the sparkling green clouds of the treetops the dark flashes of treetrunks down to the high grass, lying there seeing only a half-circle of grass against an ocean of sky. And then hour after hour by the window, until the grass turns gray and then black, from the ridges the night breeze of eternity and freedom, when did we last have time for the stars, I'm coming to see you, I'm here, your new neighbor, hello, Cassiopeia, how are you, Big Dipper—

III — eleven

A large yellow envelope, METERED MAIL, a good half pound, another book no doubt, Jacek tore open the paper and from the large yellow envelope a stream of dozens of variously colored smaller ones splattered onto his desk, on all of them written, in different hands and in different places, the same thing:

Key word: .Live!. 63064-v

Fifty of them perhaps and another fifty remained inside, in terror Jacek crammed the flood into his desk drawer, banged it shut, and locked it, horror—

From the desk to the window and to the curtain from the plant stand, at least one, Jacek unlocked the drawer and in the concealing frame of his chest and both his arms he tore open a small blue envelope:

Dear Sir!

I read your advertisement in the newspaper Prace, and because I have the same interests as you, I took the liberty of writing you.

I am 17 and I work as a salesgirl in a food store. Should you be interested in making my acquaintance, write to this address:

Milena Klimtova
Rorysova 28b
Litvinov.

Seventeen, aren't you ashamed, and Jacek again banged the drawer shut, then opened it again and greedily read on:

Dear Friend,

because I too seek an acquaintance and a new life, I am taking the liberty of intro-ducing myself to you.

My name is Kvetoslava Mozna. I am a

teacher in grades 6 to 9. I have dark
chestnut hair. I am 5 ft. 5 with a good
figure and nice features. I will soon be
27. I have varied interests, a serious
character, and a sensitive temperament.

> Address: Kvet. Mozna
> Teacher, Secondary Public
> School, Pikhartova St.
> Carlsbad
> Best wishes, Kv. Mozna

Dear Sir,
 I am taking the liberty of replying to
your ad.
 I am 31 divorced the innocent party medium-
thin figure all sorts of interests.
 I have a daughter five years old pretty
and clever.
 I live in Ceska Trebova where I have a
furnished apartment in my own house and
besides that my own car.
 I am answering your ad because I want to
find a good father for my child and a good
husband for myself whose strong and not to
tall—Im 4 ft. 8 1/2.
 I am answering your ad for a friend, whom
I am very fond of and who doesn't know
anything about it.
 She is 27, an office worker, a pretty and
intelligent girl She has a little boy by
him She has a late model car. She does
badly, because she avoids all action ever
since that bad thing happened to her. That's
why I'd like to help her. If her good
points suit you
 I have a mild, sensitive nature. I am 5
ft. 5, I have light brown hair, blue eyes
and a sincere heart Surely you are full of
ideals and you believe that at least some

of them will find fulfillment. I believe
that too and if it isn't too much trouble
for you, please write to me at this address
   I don't know what your further require-
ments might be. My hobbies are culture and
nature. I've been in a number of countries
on agency tours, and I take pictures
sometimes
   If you haven't found your partner yet,
write to this address
   you too are divorced, I believe, as a
matter of fact, that a divorced man has a
better basis for understanding and friendship and then marriage and also that he can
steer clear of unpleasant experiences from
the former marriage you won't be sorry and
you won't be disappointed When the hand of
Fate has cheated us so
   Dear Sir! I am a civil servant, 28, and
I am looking for a man who doesn't acquire
anything too easily or without effort and
who is familiar with losses and difficulties.
Eliska Rejckova, Cheb, Obrancu miru 1182.
   I haven't the least idea how to answer an
ad and so I haven't any idea how to go
about this, but I am very interested. I am
an architect (4 yrs. professional school),
twenty-three years old, a slender blonde
they call me Dada.
   By chance I was attracted to your ad today
of course I really would like to meet you I
have an active interest in literature and
culture a charming little boy culture and
nature 25 years old I have a daughter who
doesn't know anything 5 ft. 8 for the
purpose of negotiating conditions with a
daughter for each one to pour strength into
the other Dear Unknown still the highest
form of love the slogan we share is LIVE!

```
single lively 5 ft. 5 slender figure When a
dear one dies culture and nature 29 years
old be everything for one's husband 26 yrs.
5 ft. 6  29 yrs. 5 ft. 3  5 ft. 5  so he
would love me dark chestnut 22 yrs. fine
figure 24 yrs. 5 ft. 5  We live in a forest
ranger's lodge 26 yrs. really pretty 5 ft.
6  nature  blonde 23 yrs. true love 26 yrs.
5 ft. 4  slender figure 33 years 22 yrs. 21
27 27 23
```

"I'll be late today," Jacek telephoned Lenka, "No, I'm not going to the retreat, a mountain of work's piled up here all of a sudden…"

A total of 114 female readers of *Prace*, from 17 to 38 years of age, were willing to begin, practically right away, a new life with a 33-year-old divorced engineer. After throwing out the ballast, there remained 22 potentially interesting cases, 10 as a reserve, and the rest to be disposed of along with all the envelopes.

On a metal shovel Jacek fed letter after letter into the fire, and he carried off the black heaps of ash to flush away, with strong coffee and a cigarette he sat down to his old Urania, prepared 22 requests for further specifications, as detailed as possible please, and dropped 22 letters into the mailbox.

Within a week a second large yellow envelope with 19 additional offers, one of them for the interesting and two more for the reserve—and 22 replies, 16 of them within two days' time, i.e., immediately:

```
When from a distance I saw your blue
envelope, I have a mailbox with holes in it
and no letters ever come for me
   terribly happy, of course don't make
anything of it, but I'm awfully happy that
you answered. Maybe you can understand how a
person feels when he's terribly happy, and
that's me today. I really mean it honest.
```

please forgive my answering so late. But
it wasn't my fault. The letter came to my
home and from the typed envelope Mother
thought
     I am an entirely normal girl, maybe a
little above average. Of course, that's just
my say-so. Many people at school say I'm
pretty
     I really don't know where to begin. You
ask me to tell you everything that can be
told in a letter, so I will try as hard as
I can to
     well, as for my head (I mean the hair),
that's worse. I wear it red. So much for
the head.
     I graduated from college in Brno, a copy
of my diploma may not be necessary. It
would be nice if by chance you were a
chemist too, but of course be assured
     I'm a blonde, not so pretty, perhaps
rather striking, from time to time people
turn around and stare at me, but I hope
it's not because I look like a freak.
Modern dancing can really arouse me
     I'm happy when lilacs are in bloom,
especially white ones, and I'm terribly
fond of jasmine. You know, at the back of
our garden
     I spend my free days at home, we have a
large house. For me it's bridge, which under
all circumstances
     I love the sun, we could go sunbathing
together
     especially in German and I can't resist--
suddenly you seem so close to me—
     I like the wind, the rain, Armenian
cognac, I don't like rice, noodles, or long
intermissions
     for five years now in the chemistry of

fats and I tell you it's an extremely
interesting field. I don't know what you do,
but the chemistry of fats
  and so I began to study Italian. It would
be wonderful if you could go to Florence
with me in September. All formalities
including liras would be taken care of by
my brother, who has an important position
  I too was disillusioned, but believe me,
life is wonderful. Sometimes strange, but
always wonderful. Imagine that all talent,
experience, longing and dreams are possible,
that it is truly possible to live. I will
be waiting.

Jacek wrote 19 answers, this time with a carbon for the files. "This is Jacek again. No, Mija, not for sleeping, rather the opposite—to keep me from sleeping... Five containers or so. Oh yes, and what you said that time, that I was getting gray, that fungus on my skin, well— You said that you could give me a prescription for a dye... Yes? Well then, make it red!"

Naked, Jacek stood in front of the bathroom mirror and rubbed a solution of Tinct. Castellani onto his skin, you only needed a little and even that would stain his clothing, but then these pajamas are LEAVE, the healed and attractive skin TAKE, and people would look when we go sunbathing together—straight from the bottle he poured the red ink onto his body and rubbed it into his skin, Lenicka ran away in terror at the sight of her Daddy bleeding horribly, Grandma crossed herself, and Jacek laughed softly as he lay down in bed beside a dumbfounded Lenka, not even an executioner could have produced such an effect.

III — twelve

*H*e left his new iridescent raincoat unbuttoned so that the suede of his jacket could be seen and the narrow strip of his black leather tie could stand out against the dazzling white of his nylon shirt, Jacek clicked his tongue in the mirror, walked slowly down the stairs to Platform Two at Usti Main Station, and at 6:20 sharp set out on express train R 12 to Prague.

Sitting by the window and facing forward, Jacek glanced at the headlines and then tossed the paper into the net above his head, the chocolate-colored Elbe sparkled out of the milky vapor hanging above the green fur of the opposite bank, in Lovosice at 6:41 according to the timetable, by Vranany an hour of refreshing second sleep, in Vranany Jacek woke up gently, now quite himself, a Carmen cigarette and from his black traveling satchel an azure blue spiral notebook.

The first two engagements were in Prague, sheets I and II.

    I. Engineer Jarka Vesela (27), chief analyst at Foodcorp
       Grad. of Chem. Dept., Brno
       Passion: chem. of fats
       Erot: uncryst.
       Other: tennis before work, camping
       Charact: enthusiastic about chem. of fats
       8:02 on arrival of R 12 CAUTION: II at 8:30 at the Palace Hotel, 2nd fl.

    II. Engineer Anna Bromova (37), dep. dir. VUGMT
       Grad. of the College of Eng. of the VST, Prague
       Likes wind, rain, Armenian cognac (remember when ordering!), dislikes rice, noodles, and long intermissions.
       Erot: ironic. Divor.
       Other: Russ., Eng., Ger. Terribly erudite

> *Charact: high intellect, high style!*
> *8:30 Palace, 2nd fl. CAUTION: train leaves Main Sta. at*
>   *9:11 R 30*

R 12 drew into Prague Central one minute after 8:01, nervous Jacek got out last and was the last to leave the platform, at the exit gate a rather short powerfully built blonde with a white box (the obligatory identification sign for all of them) held timidly under her arm, Jarka Vesela—the fats chemist—erot. uncryst.—doesn't like rice, noodles—no, that's II, this is I, Jarka Vesela—the fats chemist—what else, quick—8:30 at the Palace—

"It looks like you're waiting for me—"

"Yes, that is... Hello, I'm Jarka Vesela..."

Calmed by the nervous way she played with the white box, Jacek offered her his arm, they threw the box into a trashcan and smiled at one another.

"You see, and I thought it was done by heat—" Jacek said at the soiled table in the station cafeteria.

"Oh, no, that would burn it! I tried countercurrent extraction, but the middle layer contained enough biological crap to puke, seriously I felt like throwing up, even though I don't mind chewing frozen spinal cord and I love a bite of raw pork gall bladder now and then."

"So you went to school in Brno too...," said Jacek, pushing away the untouched bouillon with inconspicuous speed, and quickly gulping down air.

"Yes, and I have pleasant memories of the slaughterhouse there. Once they brought in three animals dead of hoof-and-mouth disease, and my colleague Kousal and I first cut out the guts—"

"It's a terrible shame I've got to run," said Jacek, sweating and unable to down even a spoonful of the bilberry compote, "but I really have to..."

"I'm awfully glad I got to know you. Next time I'll take

you to the lab, now I'm busy with bones from the salvage collection, and if there weren't so many flies on them—"

"I'm on my way to Poland for four months, after that I'll definitely write you!"

"Just wait, I'll make a fats chemist out of you yet!"

"...except for the fact that I'm a little old for you," said Engineer Anna Bromova (37, dep. dir. of VU) in the 2nd fl. café of the Palace Hotel, playing with a white pack of Kent Micronite Filters (a crown per cigarette, remember when ordering!), "but I've already scored my first point."

"I can assure you...," Jacek said over a bottle of mineral water, and it wasn't easy.

"You could have turned around in the door and disappeared. You're reassuring, I like that..."

"...and you like the wind and the rain and—I'm awfully fond of taking walks in the rain."

"Rudolf, two Armenian cognacs. If you'll permit me—"

"I was just about to say the same thing."

"Only five minutes left. I've been thinking it over, but I haven't thought of any job for you in Prague."

"But I wouldn't think of bothering..."

"Not a thing. No prospect even."

"Please don't think it depends on..."

"In any case you couldn't live with me. I can't do anything for you. Shall we go? Rudolf, I'll pay for the gentleman as well."

"Waiter, we're going! —Two more double Armenian cognacs and I'll pay for everything on one check, for the lady's Kents as well!"

"Those I brought with me from home..."

"That doesn't matter, you can divvy up with Rudolf. I'm glad to pay for your taxi in the bargain, and for the postage on your letters. The stationery looked very official, in any case."

"So did yours— That'll do, Jacek. If you're pretending, you're doing a marvelous job of it— No, you have two

more minutes, don't be ridiculous... that was only to filter
out.... Do you really think you could bear having me
beside you—with your eyes open?"

"Yes, but first I'd have to stuff a towel in your mouth."

"I'm glad you didn't turn around in the doorway and
disappear...," she whispered to Jacek when he got out of
her black official limousine at the Main Station, ugly but
very interesting, tanned and skinny, her eyes sparkled and
her slender fingers were warm. Jacek kissed them and left
Prague on express R 30 precisely according to the timetable.

> III. *Hanicka Kohoutkova (22), elem. teacher*
> *Teachers Inst. with honors*
> *Passion: children and animals*
> *Erot: undevel.*
> *Other: lilacs, esp. white, jasmine*
> *Charact: a kid, naïve, sinc.*
> *10:34 on arrival of R 30. 192 minutes. Depart 1:46 R 28*

A large white box with a pale blue ribbon, held like a
baby, on the platform of the Pardubice station—it belonged
to a tall (5 ft. 7) girl with light chestnut hair.

"It looks like you're waiting for me—"

"Yes."

"I recognized you by the box."

"Yes."

"Should we go for a little walk?"

"Yes."

From the station to the tiny park in front of the chemistry school and then to the main street, "Wouldn't it be
better to turn off somewhere?" said Jacek, "Why?" she
retorted, and down the main street to the square with the
Green Gate, fortunately Pardubice soon comes to an end
and from the square there are stairs leading to a large park,
on the bench between the two lovers the barrier of the
black satchel and the white box with the ribbon.

"We should have a little talk, Hanicka."

"Yes, Jacek."

White clusters of lilac burst forth from the tops of bushes, Jacek walked across the lawn and with repeated jumps gathered some flowers, Hanicka ran after him, clapped her hands, suddenly took off her shoes, and hop hop we've got a beautiful bouquet, flushed Hanicka laughed and Jacek tried to kiss her, "What are you up to?" and she patiently offered him her tender forehead.

"You taste like condensed milk..."

"Hey, I like that, and the best thing is eating it with strawberries!"

"And what else do you like?"

"Are we going to be so familiar right off?"

"Yes."

"First of all I like children. That's why I teach. Children are terribly sweet. I like them very much... And then white lilacs and jasmine... I like all white flowers very much, especially white lilacs and also—"

"And animals?"

"I like animals very much. At home we have lots of animals. We have chickens, rabbits, ducks—"

"And your Mother?"

"I like Mom and Dad best of all."

"Could you like me too?"

"That's why we're meeting—"

A Maytime fairy tale on the succulent meadows of Pardubice, where everything asks for caressing and where there is only a single mountain far and wide, Kuneticka, a green angelfood cake on a warm green plate.

On the train now, Jacek placed the white box with the ribbon in the baggage net above his seat, Hanicka herself had baked him the poppyseed coffee cake inside, she smiled at him from below the window, "I'm so happy that I have my own boyfriend now—" and R 28 left at 1:46.

IV. Lida Adalska (25), forest ranger's widow
Schooling: scarcely
Erot: sincere
Other: lives in a forest rang. lodge
Charact: ?
2:48 in the car, 14 mins. DO NOT GET OFF! Depart 3:02

On the platform at Ceska Trebova a woman with a white box, Jacek leaned out and waved, the woman came to the window—just 14 mins!—with a placid smile.

"I'm Jost."

"I'm Adalska."

"Unfortunately, I can't get out, because I have to—"

"That doesn't matter. I just wanted to see you."

"I'm terribly sorry, but in a couple of minutes—"

"That's enough. Don't say anything more, please."

She looked up at the window and smiled, a beautiful woman at life's summit, all around her the flow of those transferring for Ostrava, Krnov, and Zilina, they bumped into her but with dignity she held her place all fourteen of those minutes, one after another, as if embedded in the stone of the platform, and finally now the whistle, "Mrs. Adalska, next time I'll come for longer..."

"It really was kind of you. This is from me—" and she handed Jacek her white box, already the train was getting under way, "—it's what I always gave my husband when he went away."

"Lida, I... I thank you and definitely—"

"It's me who should thank you."

R 28 continued on its way east through meadows and woods, in Lida's box there was bread, meat, salt, and a large dry apple in a dazzlingly white napkin, Jacek bit his lips, what else in God's name do you want, and with horror he opened his blue spiral notebook.

V. Tanicka Rambouskova (20), bookkeeper at a flax mill.
Business school graduate
Passion: Tanicka Rambouskova
Erot: novels for girls
Other: terr. chaos
Charact: an incred. ambit. brat
3:23 on arrival of R 28. 115 mins. Depart 5:18 R 8

"...and we'll leave this place for good. Some time in Prague and then out into the world—" Tanicka danced far ahead of Jacek and only from time to time glanced back at him, in addition to his satchel, he had to carry her enormous empty white box, most likely visible to jets seven miles up, "I know men too well already—" she asserted at one corner of the station building, "—never has one of them had me and none of them ever will—" at the other.

"That of course makes any further correspondence dubious," said Jacek.

"No, just the opposite, you'll fall in love with me and I'll flirt with you and that will attract you most!"

"How old are you really, Tanicka? Show me your ID card."

"And suppose I'm only eighteen? What does it matter—"

"In the letter you said twenty."

"A little white lie, so as not to discourage you from the beginning. Next time I'd like to meet in Prague or at least in Ceska Trebova. What kind of car do you have?"

"A white eighteen-cylinder Cadillac with a trailer."

"Why did you come by train then?"

"My left carburetor exploded and I had to wait for a repairman from Washington. They won't give him a passport..."

"I wish I had my own passport..."

"The foreign minister himself would provide one for my wife."

"Why did you get divorced— oh, that's a stupid question! You felt hemmed in, you longed for freedom, air, the sea, distant lands... and women. Your wife became indifferent soon after marriage, only for the sake of the child you kept up the appearance of a happy marriage, until one day a woman crossed your path like a ray of light in the darkness, and the garden of singing roses opened for the mournful knight... Come, let's sit at the station, I like the tracks and the smoke... We'll have a fine love affair."

Tanicka's white box didn't fit into the net above his seat, Jacek carefully placed it on the seat beside him and for the last time he leaned out of the window.

"You see—" whispered Tanicka below him on the platform, "no, you don't see in the slightest how beautiful life is, how terribly beautiful—" and R 8 pulled out of Svitavy at 5:20, two minutes late according to the timetable.

> VI. *Dr. Mojmira Stratilova (29), translator*
> *Studied at the Fac. of Phil., a year in Paris*
> *Long sents. w/o commas or content*
> *Pure flame of soul w/o body, pure abstraction*
> *Charact: delicate, subt., ether., immater. angel*
> *6:35 according to the sta. clock*

By 6:50 according to the sta. clock six women had come and gone, one after another on someone's arm, at 6:52 a seventh rushed up, grotesquely tousled, straight toward Jacek who, leaning against the wall in a semi-recumbent position, already half-asleep, was now as ransacked and empty as the white boxes traveling by express to the east, "You're the one, yes—Jacek? All happiness, hi! Listen, weren't you supposed to have a rolled-up magazine in your right hand? What's that—me and a white box? Ha-ha, that's a good one! I'm frightfully hungry and if you haven't got any money let's go dine at a stupid couple's I know, you don't have to pay any attention to them... You've got money? Do you feel like investing in me?" Distracted, Jacek only nodded apathetically.

Two vodkas, two eggs with horseradish, two Rumford soups, two Moravian skewers flambée, two bottles of red Moravian wine, "What else?"

Two portions of kidneys en papillote, two portions of carp à la Moulin, and two bottles of white Tramin, "What else?"

Two orders of fried Swiss cheese and, worn out, Jacek gave in, it'd been a long day and tomorrow we want to get up at half-past five, two double cognacs "Armenian, and salvage me two portions of bones besides—" Jacek ordered for Mojmira, and he asked the headwaiter to find him a place to room and board in Prague, preferably in the forest ranger's lodge, then all of a sudden a car of some sort and on the back seat he clapped shut like a pocket knife.

A terrifying clatter like a tank in a scrapyard, a monstrously beautiful alarmclock from the days of the Austrian Empire set for half-past five, on the floor slept a woman in a sweatsuit, Jacek stepped over her, the walls lined with books high as his chest, above them on all four walls a connected strip of reproductions of the Impressionists *(here reality has been tranformed into spots of color)* without frames, even the white margins had been cut away and all the pictures exulted together, above on the molding a display of empty bottles, So long, angel, and thanks a bonch! Jacek typed on the paper sticking out of the typewriter, below some French poetry, and he ran downstairs, the gate was locked, he burst into the courtyard, hop onto the garbage can and skip over the fence, the scent of fresh asphalt and with it lilacs in full bloom, from the shrubbery four legs projected, and Jacek skipped across the lawns, suddenly a familiar giant plane tree and behind it a small pink palace, at seventeen, behind that bench, he'd been initiated by Mrs. Sbiralova from Medlanky, the second circle of the spiral was beginning to unwind—

On express train R 21 he could sleep his rosy fill from 6:38 to 10:53, there was no need for sudden stops, in

Prague baked lamb with spinach and a good local beer, at 1:59 R 55 leaves, up along the current of the springtime river, but why home so soon, what else have we got on the menu:

> VII. *Tina Vlachova (27), occupation?*
>   *Address evident. false*
>   *Letters very brief, techn. matter-of-fact*
>   *Erot: snapshot in bathing suit, like a Modigl.*
>   *Charact: ? WATCH OUT!*
>   *Bus: CSAD from Usti at 4:00, stops Bohosudov Fun. 4:31*
>   *63 mins. Dep. 5:34, arr. Usti 6:05, as from Berl. expr. R 151*

Near the Bohosudov Funicular, at a corner, a golden-orange Tina de Modigliani was unaffectedly smoking, "Looks like you're waiting for me—" no white box, a type you can't help but speak to and in half an hour you're talking to as if you'd known her for years, "...and then they made Prague off-limits for me. But it's OK here as a waitress. I can make out anywhere."

"I thought you were giving me a fake address..."

"I've been here for three months—" and she gestured with her chin toward the vista beyond the funicular, in the pervasive fragrance the numbered metal pylons ran up through the forest to the peak of Supi Mountain, five hundred years ago, it was said, Archbishop Jan came here to sin, then meadows and further on above the precipice of Mt. Kneziste, at its summit the Mosquito Tower chalet, and at the tip of the tower Tina's room.

"Take me up there sometime... soon..."

"So come back."

"I've traveled five hundred miles to find you... And from my retreat it's only an hour's walk through the woods."

The bus back was already pulling into the turnaround, "Come whenever you want to—" Tina de Modigliani whispered, "but you must always call first!"

Depart 5:34, arr. Usti 6:05 as from the Berl. expr. R 151, streetcar No. 5 to Vseborice, even as the door opened Lenicka's voice, "Daddy—" and Lenka was coming to welcome him with a smile, "You forgot the white plush again, didn't you—"

III — thirteen

D addy don't go way—" so stay with her until she goes to sleep, in a couple of years she'll be coming home only to eat and sleep, Daddy the cashier and hotelier, in any case he'd be good for little else by then and this eager child of the electronic age would only be bored by an aging man who had never achieved anything and who himself had never lived, I can only advise you, daughter, not to take after your father—the art of leaving in time—but since they've tied us here, the wrists bloodied by sharp nylon cords and the arms weakening with vain twisting, dragged in harness to one's retirement and then one's death, a man who once was able to live but who didn't come up with the courage needed to live, who started to die at the age of thirty-three on a cross of his own construction.

Polish all the shoes in the foyer and take a hot bath, "You're not coming to bed yet, Lenka?"

"How can I, it's Thursday!"

"Can I help with anything?"

"Just go to bed, you've had enough with your trip."

Go to bed after your trip and get some sleep before another one, the rest of the night is spent ironing, sewing, or bathing, during the day we don't see each other and if we do it's only for a new verification of the fact that we get in each other's way, what's left of you, my love—

"Daddy come home today?"

"But he came home last night... So hop into your pants!"

"Daddy put on pants!"

"Shhh—Daddy's still beddie-bye and we mustn't..."

"I want to see Daddy!"

And Jacek crawled out of bed, my darlings, and pulled on Lenicka's tights, she played, she was affectionate, flirtatious, she showed her belly-button and again so many many great big kisses, nothing's so sweet to kiss as my little one, "Daddy take me to school!" "Daddy has to go beddie-bye some more!" fifty minutes more and then wake up again to the horror of desertion—

On the bright June morning Mommy and Daddy cross the lawn and the little girl flies up between them swinging on their hands, Lenka's happy laugh and her hair in the wind, "We still know how to run, Jacek—" up to the bronze gate of the institution for discarding children.

"When you're wittle, Daddy, and I'm all gwowed up, I won't send you to school."

"And where will you put me during the day, my darling?"

"I'll take you by the hand and take you to the pond and the movies and the swings—"

"So give me your hand and we'll go—" "But Jacek, how about your work?—," a few work days have already gone for experiments, so today we'll try a negative one, the little one and Daddy both had to be shown that it would bore them very quickly, Jacek took Lenicka by the hand and systematically led her through the child's vision, first to the pond to pick posies and bathe her tootsies, a pond in June is not so bad, actually—well, she's not bored so far, but what next, at ten to the movies to see a silly film in which a little boy and a little girl engage in a moralistic discussion on how to rehabilitate their drunken Daddy, but Lenicka's spoken subtitles transformed it into a larger-than-life story, half grotesque and half myth, the experiment went aground but, touched, Jacek swung his little girl in the swing for his sixth crown's worth, "Fwy wif me, Daddy, into the sky—"

In front of the gate of Lenka's factory a young man
waiting with a motorcycle, when was the last time we
stood like this, so impatient, of the crowd of exiting women
Lenka is still the prettiest, happily the little family makes
its way homeward.

Water our strawberry vines, why buy berries from the
policeman's wife in Ritin, all three of us sit down on the
grass in the sun and from both sides we smell the scent of
a loved one, on our own land, WHERE DO WE COME
FROM, our daughter gets her beauty sleep and on the other
side of the wall we come together, our longing contained
within an order, WHO ARE WE, my wife and I—half-
naked, Jacek leaned out the window with a cigarette in his
mouth and inhaled deeply, directly opposite was Trost,
leaning equally far out his window and equally half-naked,
he inhaled deeply too, and behind him the same dull glow
of the lamp placed in the same spot as ours, over our beds.

"So yesterday I sank a German steamer," during Saturday's sixty-forty Vitenka ecstatically described an international collision of riverboats on the frontier at Hrensko, we
were lying in the garden in back of the house, WHERE WILL
WE LAND, the afternoon before, Mija had flown off to
Tunis.

Mr. Stefacek came out of the tow-cloth storeroom with
a new toy for men, a sort of tiny TV set, and when you
turned the switch you saw color photos of film Venuses,
"My Verka's better—" Petrik Hurt said with conviction, all
that sated happiness in his voice had the sound of
conviction.

On the ridged mud of the courtyard a large black limousine with a Brno license plate swayed magnificently, and
out of its door, held majestically open for him, floated the
general director's deputy himself, Franta Docekal (the
director of Cottex suddenly grew smaller and his two
deputies shriveled up completely), in the front part of the
director's office the stout marshal of the courtyard was

fanning himself with a handkerchief from those two precious sets we'd been having engraved for months, like
gems, one for the Czechoslovak exhibit at the Montreal
World Exposition, the other for the Shah of Iran.

Jacek was praised by His Majesty and rose, he grinned
mockingly, don't bother, one possible way to start a career
is to clear out, as you know so well yourself—an undistin-
guished planning expert, Franta Docekal had fallen ill here
some years ago with an inflammation of the lungs, "Usti
Syndrome," and the doctors had recommended a healthier
climate, the Brno one for instance, here in unhealthy Usti
Franta left behind a miserable apartment with a hateful
wife and a lame malicious brat, there he married a pretty
doctor with her own house and went rapidly to the top, a
dizzying career built on an inflammation of the lungs, why
not inhale some hydrochloric acid—

On the column in the main square a new color poster,
Candy in a white tux BACK FROM HIS TRIUMPHANT
YUGOSLAV TOUR, he had it thanks to some stolen mercury and tow-cloth, if it hadn't been for their mishaps
today we'd still have lab assistant Klecanda and planning
expert Docekal and Vitenka, with his inferiority complex,
came to life only when Mija stabbed him with scissors in
a fight and thus provided grounds for the start of the
highly successful Balvin Improvement, only through the
alcoholism of his first wife and the infidelity of his second,
through two misfortunes, had Petrik Hurt found happiness
with his Verka, from the depths of failure one bounces
back—

The flagellant Saturday ritual of cleaning up was going
full blast, Lenka with five things at once and already gray
with exhaustion, "If only you wouldn't keep getting in the
way—"

A 28-year-old pretty intell. off. worker with an interest
in culture and nature and with own 1st-cat. apart., forget
that pudding, which we won't eat anyway, come and stab

me instead with the scissors, it'll give both of us infinite relief, don't buy me new shirts I don't feel like wearing but buy yourself a case of that cheap Georgian cognac you like so much and invite over all your friends it wouldn't occur to you to invite without some reason, give me a pretext, bring someone you'd like to have home for the night, neglect me, get drunk, deck me out with horns, beat me, lose your mind, desert me or kick me out, and if you still love me then out of love be the cause of what I must commit, I WANT IT TO BE AGAINST MY WILL, the inability to make an end, to change, to begin, and the desperate desire for an end, a change, a beginning, we do everything for change except change itself and only out of failure can we rise to the top, SOMEONE HURL A BOMB, we thirst for the sweetness of the whip of necessity, at least throw a firecracker, then let me begin to throttle you, I HAVE PUT EVERYTHING IN A STATE OF READINESS, I ONLY AWAIT THE SIGNAL, on the catapult the last bolts are getting their final twists and the flight path is being synchronized, I am taking my seat in the flight chair, WHICH CAPTAIN FAILURE WILL NOW FIRE OFF—send him a car and driver.

THE SECOND HALF OF THE GAME

*All roads lead to paradise if we follow
them long enough.* —Henry Miller

Part IV — Beginnings — fourteen

*T*he driver braked hard and turned to the left, the
springs of the limousine undulated, through an open
bronze gate they drove into the château park, Jacek let go
of Anna Bromova's warm fingers and gravel drummed
against the bottom of the car.

Outside their windows stretched a row of gray statues
of saints and on the court behind it a rather tan young man
dressed only in white shorts was playing tennis with a
charming black girl, "Now the backhand, look—" he called
to her, laughing, and the ball flew past the golden arrows
projecting from St. Sebastian's body.

Behind twelve-foot glass doors a red runner went up
marble stairs to the second floor and on a white tablecloth
a forest of bottles, "Have some Campari," Anna advised
Jacek in a whisper, "and some of that red caviar before
they gobble it up—," and on the way to the table Jacek was
introduced to twenty-three big shots, any of whose visits
to Cottex would have forced them to interrupt production
and press whole work shifts into clean-up and decorating
activities.

The young tennis player came to lunch promptly at one
in a consummate suit of dark-gray natural silk, he shook
his head no to an aperitif and gave Jacek a friendly smile:
"Physicist?"

"Chemist," Jacek said with a friendly smile.

"Isotopes?"

"Cotton."

"Please excuse me," said the young man (as if Jacek were suddenly dead as far as he was concerned), and while a waitress served sirloin steak (real sirloin in real cream) and poured out some white Melnik wine, the young man silently, carefully, and rapidly ate his bouillon with raw egg, cold smoked mackerel with three carrots, and a pint of warm milk ("He's on a high-protein diet—" Anna whispered as she heaped on Jacek's plate a second helping of dumplings Esterhazy with bits of bacon, boiled in a napkin, sprinkled with sautéed breadcrumbs and chopped parsley, and drowned in butter), he looked at his watch and left at once ("Now he'll sleep for ninety minutes—he wants to keep up full efficiency for another fifty years..." "But who is he?" "An atomic physicist. A leading one." "No, no more dumplings, please.").

Jacek followed Anna down a path between hazel bushes and toward a vine-covered wall, Anna leaned her back against it and drew him to her, "I love you because you don't close your eyes when you kiss...," and she stepped onto a rock in order to be closer to his level. From behind a giant treetrunk in the middle of almost a half-mile of lawn a black-and-red figure emerged, skipping strangely and jerking its arms and head it aimed straight toward the lovers, suddenly it performed a series of somersaults and again that crazy rhythm, "Anci—" Jacek whispered uneasily, "there's something coming this way..." "But that's only Jozef... the atomic physicist."

The atomic physicist Jozef, in a black sweatsuit with red pleats, danced the *letkis* across the lawn snapping his fingers, when he reached the wall he looked at his watch and trotted back, disappearing into the hazel bushes.

"Clown!" Jacek gave vent to his feelings.

"Not really. He pulled off a couple of terrific thermo-nuclear stunts."

"But they only do that in Russia and America..."

"He just flew back from America and now he's going to spend half a year in Dubno, outside Moscow."

"Is he really that good?"

"He is."

"Good God, how old can that kid be?"

"Thirty-three."

"Ouch... That's the age when you've got to do something. Or else die."

In the sitting and the assembly rooms of Academy House the furniture looked like something out of a museum, Anna explained to Jacek what Empire, Baroque, and Rococo were, "...but that's all rubbish compared with a Florentine chest in the little Yellow Salon, come—" The "little" Yellow Salon was big enough for a proper bleaching-room with a kettle for pressure boiling the skeins, along the back wall were two billiard tables, one the usual barroom size and a giant one for experts, between them, against a background of gold brocade, Jozef in a striped T-shirt and blue jeans making caroms at both tables in turn (Anna was trying to drag Jacek off to one of the windows), on the ordinary one with powerful blows of the cue the quick movement of individual balls all over the table, on the big one with fine pecks pushing all three balls close together along the cushion, which he was using to advantage, so they play in country inns and so in championship matches, a carom every time, Jozef never even waited for them, he shot a ball on one table and then started toward the other, behind his back a carom every time, "Look at this workmanship—" Anna said, now kneeling, and piously she touched the medieval bands and bolts.

"Excuse me," said Jozef as he bent over the small table, "but do you know if there's a cellulose yet with carbon 14?"

"I believe... they're working on it somewhere..."

The crack of balls on the small table and a carom, "Please excuse me, in five minutes I'll score three hundred and give up both tables." A fine peck on the big one, behind Jozef's back the balls caromed and assumed position for another one.

"But you aren't even looking at it—" said Anna, and she stood up.

"Yes, it's very beautiful—" said Jacek, crawling around the chest on his knees.

Along the row of saints wrought-iron lamps lit up and Anna led Jacek further, behind the slender junipers a sheet of water sparkled like the one behind the cypresses, "It's like an evening at the seashore...," he whispered, "Let's go to the seashore together...," she whispered. On the facade of the château dark windows yawned, in the game room only the TV flickering, in the dining room the light of the chandeliers, and on the top floor a desk lamp by a window. "Of course," said Anna, "that's his room. I wish I could start life again at thirty-three—"

Jacek stroked the head on his shoulder and suddenly felt a fine pricking, he touched Anna's hairpin, passed his fingers over it, and then pulled it out, "Give it to me, Anci—I'll keep it in my wallet..." "And give me in exchange...," and Jacek gave, took, took and gave in that gift of a château park.

Later, on the 4:45 to Berlin, he carefully stuck Anna's hairpin into the dirty clothes in his satchel so that Lenka would find it, and in silence he looked at the river along the track, rising beyond Lovosice are the wavy hills of Stredohori, Varhost, then Ostry, then the thermal swimming pool, then the locks and the Strekov Castle, the Germans call it Schreckenstein, but the Czech name doesn't imply any sort of horror, the final time it will all go by in reverse order—

"It's thoughtful of you to bring me back my hairpin,"

Lenka said over the open black satchel, "you can't get them in the stores now and Lenicka needs more and more. But you forgot the white plush again..."

"Tomorrow I'm going to Brno, please pack two shirts in the satchel, and no lunch."

R 30 was given permission to leave Prague Main Station only eleven minutes late, but on the plains beyond Kolin it made a fine showing and arrived in Pardubice at exactly 10:34, by the railing in the sun Hanicka Kohoutkova was smiling, she wiped her right palm on her skirt and stepped out to meet him, 192 mins. free.

"Were you good all week?"

"I was, on my honor."

"You didn't upset your father?"

"Yes. On Tuesday instead of doing my German I was staring out the window, and when he tested me I didn't know the second person plural."

"What is the second person plural?"

"*Ihr habet* or *habt, ihr seid, ihr lernet* or *lernt.*"

"Good. And why were you staring out the window on Tuesday?"

"I was looking forward to your visit."

On the other side of the lazy Elbe a vaporous blue glow quivered above the yellowing wheat, and along the country road the red of the poppies cried out, Hanicka stuck one in her mouth, stood with arms akimbo, pulled her belly in, and "Now don't I look like Bizet's Carmen?"

"Not in the least, you lamb. These cornflowers are more your style..."

"That's a bit insulting. I'd like to be like Carmen and dance wildly on tables in some cheap bar, just like her."

"I'd be afraid for you and jealous of the barflies."

"Don't be afraid, anyway I wouldn't be happy. I'm only saying that. I like the *mazurka* best. It must have been wonderful to be a Polish noblewoman!"

"Is that what you tell the children in school?"

"I should say not, that would really do me in! There was a great oppression in those days and the collective farmer had to pull wooden plows with his family."

"Good."

"While the great landowners and later the city manufacturers went from feast to feast. I'd like to have been named Jadwiga."

"And I Tadeusz."

"Hey, that would be just like Mr. Kutil from Rosice! No, wait, I thought up a name for you long ago—Jastrun."

"What do you mean long ago?"

"When I was still a girl, before I got to know you...," and she ran off into the grass, Jacek after her, they chased each other and frolicked until they were out of breath, then they sat down on the warm grass, Hanicka picked flowers and braided two garlands, she put the larger one on Jacek's head and, thus crowned, Jacek glanced at the timetable, Mojmira can't make it today and it's too hot to travel, it isn't so important anyway and a no-show would be a blessing, so he squandered 242 minutes with Hanicka and left at 2:46 on the R 7 for Prague.

No, it isn't so important anyway and a disaster would be a salvation, Jacek was coming back on his usual express from Brno to Usti without actually having been to Brno at all, but at Cottex they'd swallow anything now, their confidence in Jacek was limitless, the director and his deputies had called the factory guard to deal with that crazy shipping clerk come to announce that there was a whole carload of ethyl acetate waiting on our siding, they were convinced that the shipping clerk was soaked to the gills again, but there was the car and two more were confirmed for arrival from Brno, Cottex couldn't use up that lake of ethyl acetate in five years and it couldn't be stored, so it would be traded to Chemopharma for roofing, oxygen, and three hundred porcelain cups for the plant cafeteria, instead of inevitable shortage a gratuitous prosperity, careworn Jacek gazed out of the train at the Elbe, today we're coming home from our trip a day early but next time a day late, Lenka's no longer surprised at anything, so I have to reach for a higher caliber, you compel me to do it, my love—

> *Darling: This evening it's raining, I'd like to crawl in beside you and watch the rain with you.*

one from Anna or from Tina

> *Expect you definitely 11:00 P.M. Something's come up. Arrange it at home so you can stay till morning*

or best of all both, in the Lovosice station Jacek decided on the 4:45 to Berlin and he stuck both letters in with the dirty clothes in his satchel so that Lenka could not avoid finding them, the world is calling for us and at home it's always the same old thing, how many years do we want to consume going out to meet that call, how long will that call persist without an answer—

"About the sad pwince!" Lenicka wanted a fairy tale, Jacek stood nervously over her bed, why is it that today Lenka hasn't opened his satchel yet—

"...and he was vewy sad, because he awways had to wide the twain..."

"...train, trrrain..."

"...and in the tunnel they wasn't no wight and out of the woods cwop-cwop-cwop came the auwochs..."

"...aurochs, little one, you say auwochs, aurrrochs..."

"...a gweat gweat big cow and he said, pwince, here is your pwincess and don't cwy, and pwince went boom! And now they was wight in the tunnel and the pwincess gave the pwince a gweat big kiss wike..."

"...great great big like this. And now beddie-bye, darling."

"Daddy don't go way—"

"What's this you've got here...," Lenka said from outside. "Some sort of letters..."

Jacek waited in the dusk of Lenicka's room, her little fist in his hand, and held his breath, the pwince went boom! And now they was wight in the tunnel—

"Why these are great—whose are they?" Lenka said from the other room.

"Ohh—they're someone's, a pal's."

"I can see they're not yours."

"What's that?" said Jacek to the lighted glass panel of the door.

"You'd hardly have stuck them in here so stupidly. *Watch the rain with you,* but when it's raining, Jacek, you just start to yawn, you pull down the blind and go to sleep right where you are—"

"Huh— and what do you make of the other one?"

"There's another one here?— How many women does your pal keep up a correspondence with?"

"Let's see... with seven."

"And it amuses him?"

"Tremendously!"

"Today I'm celebrating," Mojmira called as she stood at the counter of the Brno Main Station cafeteria, from a cellophane bag she poured the remainder of the potato chips into her mouth, finished her beer, and as if it were a handkerchief stuck the crumpled cellophane bag into Jacek's jacket pocket, "after less than seven months they sent me my check! Let's go."

At the Petrov lunch counter they ate two grilled Moravian sausages with their fingers and Jacek clasped his black satchel between his legs, "Today I'm celebrating, they sent me my check!" Mojmira cried across two counters to a young fellow in white-rimmed sunglasses, "Buy me a beer?" the young fellow called, "Make it three," and he got the five crowns change for carfare.

By the time they reached the milk bar on Freedom Square they'd added a freckly archeology student from the

Low Tatra Mountains, and Mojmira paid for four strawberry cocktails, "I got it for my translation!" she cried,
crossing the square toward a motorcyclist in leather pants
and suspenders, the driver stepped on the gas, drove
around the square, and held the door open for them at The
Four Ruffians, during the goulash soup a bearded radio
technician joined them and all six of them went on to The
Noblewomen, at a long table fourteen people were sitting
and talking quietly, in their midst, like a priest, the poet
Oldrich Mikulasek was stroking the edge of his wineglass,
"We just heard you're celebrating," a pretty blonde on his
right told Mojmira, "I got it for that Spanish story,"
Mojmira confirmed happily, and she ordered two bottles
of Mikulov Sauvignon, the procession of some eleven
people now went to the seafood restaurant on Jakub
Square, at their head the motorcyclist in leather pants and
bringing up the rear Jacek with Mojmira and the large
black satchel, at a necktie store they were joined by a long-
haired unisex creature, "The fellows at the Slavie Café said
you got paid for that 'Executioner's Afternoon'—"
"Here—" said Mojmira, thrusting a crumpled three-crown
note into his (her) proffered hand, and (s)he joined the
group, from St. Jakub's on a gray-haired woman limped
along on crutches, "I got paid today—" Mojmira called
after her. "I heard," the old woman rejoiced, "For that
Alvarez translation!" and she hobbled after them, in the
Typos Arcade a fellow in a black waterproof hat was
pissing into a grate, "Vitek," Mojmira called after him,
"today—" "I heard," he muttered, and he joined the gang,
by the portal of the Viceregent's Palace Pavel Vrbka stood
with an Admira movie camera around his neck, "Mojmira
got paid today—" Jacek called after him, "I can see," said
Pavel Vrbka, already in formation, and at the M Club there
were almost thirty of us.

"Ten days I worked on it like a mule till late at night,"
Mojmira cried, kicking a trashcan down the stairs into the

Vegetable Market. "I played with it as I would with poetry
and I made a hundred and eighty crowns, I've found a job
in a dairy, I'll handle butter with a sterilized coal shovel,
fifty-five crowns a day, I have to supply my own rolls..."

"We hear you're looking for a job in Brno," wheezed the
man in the waterproof hat as he trotted beside Jacek along
the rounded cobblestones and down the hill after Mojmira.
"I would like something—" Jacek wheezed back, fending
off the jolting satchel with his knee, "We could take you
onto the editorial staff of the *Technical News*—" "But I—"
"We know all that, I've already sent up the proposal—"
each of them caught up the trashcan at his side, swung it,
and threw it over the edge of the fountain, it wasn't on so
Jacek stepped into it and climbed up the possibly Baroque
stonework, the Vegetable Market turned upside down, the
lights above and the dark below, "I greet you, Brno—"
Jacek cried, and to the shouting of fifty throats he stretched
out his arms like the pope for *Urbi et orbi*.

A flowering linden gazed into the window and around
the wall the continuous strip of Impressionists, on a collar-
bone a hairy leg in a red sock, half-past six in the morning,
Jacek extracted his black satchel from beneath the golden-
haired admirer of the Great Poet Oldrich and kissed her
half-open mouth, Mojmira evidently hadn't made it home
yet, into the courtyard onto the trashcan and skip over the
fence, along the asphalt, and across the park opposite his
house, the old folks were still asleep, in his bookcase Dad
kept hidden behind *The Count of Monte Cristo Ten Years
Later* a bag of chocolate-covered raisins, Jacek gulped it
down and collapsed on his boyhood bed.

A huge tree with reddish leaves gazed into the window,
by the window a globe and on the wall the wooden saber,
11:16, and at 11:30 in white shorts on the Luzanky courts,
an hour of practice hitting the ball against the wall, now
the backhand and then into the shower, at one sharp Jacek,

wearing his father's gray English suit, entered the University cafeteria, a well-built girl in rimless glasses made room for him beside her, Jacek silently, carefully, and quickly ate his beef broth with Russian egg, his kipper with three pickled onions, and a pint of warm milk, nothing but protein.

The large park was almost empty at the time, and it was quiet beneath the tops of the century-old trees, one after another they revealed themselves, and simply by walking past you could see a continuous live cyclorama *Trees in the Grass*, and Jacek took a turn through it across the lawn, ta-ta-tatatata, why not snap your fingers, ta-ta-tatatata and, dancing through the treetrunks as far as the playground, he looked at his watch and out of the park at a trot.

At Under the Lookout three old fellows were nodding over their stale beer, evidently they didn't want to go home from work so early, and the bargirl was lazily sucking her wine spritzer from a wineglass, Jacek held his cue and concentrated on the green cloth of a battered and cigarette-burned billiard table, a cushion shot for this one—no, go back to the starting position and again—no, try again, nothing, again and again nothing, at last, chalk up the cue and keep it up, twenty-three caroms is our longest series and now our exhibition game, with fine pecks keep three balls going close to the cushion, a carom is easy enough but the trick is to get the balls back into position again, that's not it, once more— "Mister," someone said from behind Jacek's back, "let's play to a hundred and fifty for coffee and rum, I'll spot you thirty-five—" "Excuse me, please," Jacek said without even turning around, "in five minutes I'll finish and give up both tables—," in five minutes he put the cue away, at home he lay on his bed and slept for ninety minutes.

Penetrating into his room from a great distance were radio music, the rumble of motors, and the whiz of pneumatic drills on pavement, then from many sets the same

TV program acoustically reinforced itself, the day was long in coming to an end and, as if uncertain, the city put off its decision to go to sleep, what was the day good for, an invigorating breeze of silence lifted the room from its chance surroundings, over the roofs of the houses and up above the night itself into the space beyond earth's orbit, where it's always light, the desk lamp's halo awakens the old wood to a warm breathing and in an open red binder a white sheet of paper flares up, cigarettes and matches on the left, an ashtray on the right, an eraser and a pencil sharpener in front, Jacek sharpened a pencil and studied how to reckon with the elements all things are made from, physical chemistry is the backbone of the two principal sciences and a serpentine going upward, marked by constantly higher mathematics, heat content H, free energy G, entropy S is the measure of the chaos of order, with organization it approaches 0, freed from interference it rises to the number 1 of absolute chaos, where are we on this continuum (0-1) and where are we going through sheer inertia—

Jacek walked quickly down the long corridor of the gray palace to the general director's office and marched in through his door, "Did you get my proposal dated the fifth of July?"

"Sit down, please...," the chief said with an affable smile.

"No. What did you think of it?"

"Let's have some coffee, at least..."

"No. What do you plan to do with me?"

"You're a sly one, aren't you!"

"Sly?..."

"You must be the first person in the world to propose the abolition of his own job—hahaha!"

"But I really don't want it anymore."

"So why not hand in your resignation? Hahaha!"

"I've been there for ten years and understand, it isn't easy... People I like..."

"Don't make me cry—hahahaha! Sit down and let's have that coffee!"

"No. I'm asking you to abolish my job—"

"Hahaha—"

"—or I'll start making trouble for you!"

"Hahaha, you needn't do that anymore, you've already snared another two hundred crowns that way and praise from the general director for initiative, and they've put you on the Management Reorganization Committee, we'll be sitting there playing tricks together—"

"Ow," said Jacek, and he sank down in his chair, instead of the abyss another lift, "so shoot that coffee over to me, Anton boy, let me get a grip on myself."

Jacek swayed along the long corridors of the gray palace, another couple of stunts like that and I'll be boss of the whole building, on the stairs a girl in a white apron ahead of him, on a tray she carried six bottles of domestic Gold King whiskey wrapped in cellophane and ribbons, "Come, kitten, let's drink it together in the boiler room." "What's left of it—" she giggled, and Jacek set out after her, she stopped in front of a pair of tall white doors and looked helpless, "Where are you taking that?" "To some West Germans—will you open the door for me?"

Jacek grabbed the handle, but the door was locked, he knocked with his fist, nothing, and then a bit of kicking, both doors flew open and a petty official with a black tie and a stripe on his sleeve, evidently entrusted with watching the door, looked fearfully out, "Engineer Werther hasn't gone yet?" Jacek shouted close to his face and walked in, the speech was evidently over and, at the head of the crowd, Franta Docekal was walking toward a table covered with a white cloth, his hand met Jacek's over the Hungarian salami, people always go for the most expensive things first, for the last ones all that was left were some disgusting looking meatballs, Jacek clinked glasses with an athletic-looking blonde in white silk with diamonds on her neck, ears, breasts, and belt, why drink with the waitress in the boiler room, the party lined up to have its picture taken, "The lady in the center—" the photographer commanded, the blonde wanted a profile and, with a smile, Jacek looked over her shoulder at Franta Docekal, who had just eaten the last meatball, wiped his fingers on the napkin, and placed in his now healthy wind-pipe a log-like, gold-banded cigar.

"But there's no place to go here," said Tanicka Rambouskova on the bench of the Svitavy station, prop-ping her feet against Jacek's traveling satchel and looking at the tracks, "there's nothing here, it's only for people who don't want anything anymore, only to stuff themselves and sleep—should I hand in my resignation?"

"What would Mom and Dad say about that?"

"We haven't lived together for a long time... It was a great romantic love affair, they addressed one another very formally, every day he kissed her hand and brought her flowers and when he left her a note in the kitchen to say, for instance, that he'd gone out to feed the rabbits, he addressed it to My Beloved..."

"But then why—"

"One day it all collapsed and we had to throw him out."

"But that's awful, really terrible, what must have happened to—"

"He was a thief and a degenerate."

"Really? Explain it to me in detail, I'm immensely—"

"He stole candy from the store, pickles, rum, powdered coconut, and gave it to the boys in the dorm. When should I hand in that resignation?"

"It'll happen this year, I know it—" she whispered up to Jacek at the window of the express, she was magnificently resolved to pick up and leave without a suitcase on that very train, it was already starting and Tanicka began to run beside it, "—I feel it already in my feet, something like a tingling—" and Jacek stroked her on her dark head, Tanicka couldn't reach him, she stroked the train, it was already leaving and Tanicka was left behind, she grew suddenly smaller and with her hand above her head like a soldier's salute she disappeared around the bend, Jacek was still returning her salute and now the express carried him off to the west, ta-ta-ta-dum, on green cushions through green meadows and forests, ta-ta-ta-dum, as on the green waves of the Mediterranean from stairs to stairs, the Belvedere, the Jeannette, the Palma, the Stefanie, the Kvarner, and on each tiny beach another naiad waits, Speranza has been realized and the Miramar is no longer just a dream, ta-ta-ta-dum is a hymn of freedom, only two more cliffs and in the sun beyond them the open strip gleaming toward Africa—

"You forgot the white plush again, didn't you..."

They'll call him a thief and a degenerate, still it's better than inhaling hydrochloric acid, at lunchtime Jacek entered the tow-cloth storeroom, not a soul anywhere, and he pulled down from the shelf a parcel of tow-cloth, more than a sixth of a mile of it, material for white and purple tuxedos for the barons of jazz, and he dropped by the chemical storeroom, "You've got a visitor at the gate—" he told the old woman, who was hooking a curtain, "Could that be my old man I wonder—" she said, and she ran off. Jacek took a bottle of mercury under each arm and dripped a bit from one of them—that was how Alois Klecanda had got caught that time and how he'd become Candy, the silver drops ran their crazy course over the concrete, both of us await our triumphant return tour—

In his office Jacek propped the roll of tow-cloth against the shelf with the files, the bottles of mercury on the edge of the lower shelf with the curtain only half concealing them, and he sat down at his antiquated Urania:

Dear Mrs. Jostova:

You don't know me, but I know you very well. We have windows across the way from you and it's terrible to watch what your husband's been up to, the degenerate, when he's in the bedroom by himself and you, poor woman, are working in the kitchen till late at night. I can't even tell it in a letter. Dad said if I didn't write to you, he would inform the Security Police. There are children here, after all!

Your outraged neighbor across the way

On the envelope: *Mrs. Jostova* and seal it and when Mr. Stefacek comes back from lunch to his burgled tow-cloth storeroom, he'll lend us some photos of nudes.

The letter into our mailbox in the lobby, the pictures into the pocket of my bathrobe, the belt from Lenka's sewing machine, fasten it with wire to the handle of the can opener, and a whip under the pillow.

"It's from that Dvorakova hag," Lenka laughed as she read the letter, "she's mad because Thursday at the cafeteria I grabbed the last milk out from under her nose," and the letter became a paper steamboat for Lenicka and from the bedroom revels and shouting, Grandma was lying on her back, Lenicka sitting astride her and waving the whip, her "fishing wod," the "fish" is Grandma, the poor old woman tried conscientiously to bite the line and so lost her last incisor, "Now you, Daddy—" "With a stomach like that I wouldn't dare have my picture taken," Lenka grinned and tossed aside Mr. Stefacek's photos, "That's Mommy—" Lenicka rejoiced over them and shuffled them like cards, "Here's Mommy and here's another one—" "Let's go eat," Lenka decided, through the closed kitchen ventilator one could see in spite of the curtain the eighty windows of the apartment house across the way, the perpendicular strips of shining kitchen windows, the whole development is eating dinner now and above the apartment house only a crack of sky turning pale, stabbed by antennas, crying from the cage of those antennas—

Outside the open window a magnificently undivided blue hemisphere, the surging crests of the Krusne Mountains and a view as far as Germany, in the bar of the Mosquito Tower music from a tape recorder and weaving among the occupied tables the golden-orange Tina de Modigliani, tourists from four countries watch her go by, she's something to stare at, but you stare in vain, she's mine, in the aisles Tina raised her tray over her head, leaned over, thrust forth her chest and laughed, and no one looked at the beautiful view from the window (the chalet's take was up forty percent from the preceding year).

A bell sounded for the last funicular down, Tina pursed her lips, Jacek nodded imperceptibly, finished his unbilled Cinzano bitter, and chewing on a slice of lemon walked slowly out onto the terrace, the sun bled on the mountain chain and in the valley the reddened meadows flamed, beyond them a strip of fields and then a gray imitation mountain where a huge mine was murdering the soil, and beyond the spreading gray corpse of the strewn waste rose the gray-brown crepe of smog beneath which the city of Usti was suffocating, and Jacek turned around, the last tourists were hurrying to catch the funicular, the terrace was empty, buses and cars were going down the serpentine to the valley, and on the gravel parking lot only the couple's Renault, the family's Wartburg, and that Opel Admiral.

Jacek slowly lit a Kent and gaped at the increasingly washed-out sky, Tina's window in the tower was open, when he lit another one the family rushed out the door and into the Wartburg and started down the mountain, the couple with the Renault was evidently going to stay the night, Jacek leaned on the railing and smoked slowly, Tina's window was still open and night was coming up from the valley, Jacek approached the glass doors to the bar, the couple were kissing in the corner and the Opel Admiral in the cafeteria was whispering with Tina.

The blue woods began to turn gray, in the valley the first lights and the first stars in the sky, Jacek glanced at Tina's window and relished a pleasant feeling of tension, his fingers played with another Kent but he didn't light it, it was as if the silence grew stronger and with a bang the window in the tower suddenly slammed shut.

Jacek broke the cigarette and tossed it away on the run, through the side entrance and up the winding stairs, one more landing and he rushed through the peeling door, "Was machst du hier, du Saukerl—" he hissed, Tina grabbed her head and took refuge behind the wardrobe, the Opel Admiral began to protest, Jacek pulled out a camera, Tina screamed, and the fellow dressed quickly, shook his fist at them, and rushed out, the start of his engine, the lovers' Renault was left alone in the parking lot, and the lights of the Opel Admiral traced a zigzag down the serpentine.

"Superb," said Tina, she detached a ten-mark note for Jacek and went downstairs to give the couple their check, out of the green box on the wicker chair Jacek took a cigarette (Yenidze No. 6 Mild Virginia) and a silver lighter (Hasenlaufer und Sohn), Jacek's new lighter worked marvelously, from deep inside Jacek exhaled the blue smoke out into the night air and waited for Tina.

His whole paycheck transferred to the secret hoard, Jacek walked nervously through the empty apartment and waited for Lenka, nothing at all was happening, LEAVE and TAKE, the various objects unanimously mocked him in the darkness of the drawn blinds, dust was gathering on the cosmonaut's luggage so that he could write on it with his finger BECAUSE OF DAMAGE TO FIRING APPARATUS FLIGHT WILL NOT TAKE PLACE—

"Did you bring the money?" the launching pad asks.

"No—" the apparatus begins its countdown.

"How's that?"

"You know, I had a few drinks in Brno with some friends... I had to send them some money."

"Nine hundred crowns' worth?"

"Twelve. I'll send three hundred more next payday."

"As you like," Lenka shrugged her shoulders. "I'll take it out of the savings account and you'll have to put off buying that dark suit another year. Are you coming along to the garden?"

"No!" and again Jacek roamed through the empty apartment, the rocket was to be held on the launching pad a while yet, the dark suit would have been of use for the first time in his life, again the Lenkas' fortress had repelled the attack, but the besieged can be starved out, like a tornado Jacek burst into the pantry and went through it shelf by shelf, try bacon with cheese and put condensed milk on the sardines, chocolate'll do the trick, but it didn't, and white as a sheet Jacek opened the door for the Lenkas, "You must have been hungry—" Lenka made a wry face, "well, Lenicka, Daddy ate up our supper—" "He just stuffed himself a bit, like a man—" Grandma called, "wouldn't you like some garlic soup now?" Lenicka rejoiced that she didn't have to have any din-din, while Lenka and Grandma deliberated whether to cook macaroni, lentils, potato pancakes, canned goulash, toast, braised beef, bilberry dumplings, or dried peas with bacon bits and onion.

"Tomorrow I'm going to Brno," Jacek whispered, "please put two white shirts in the satchel, and no lunch..."

Jacek strode along quickly behind Dr. Janzurova's copper headdress, over the magnificently maintained parquet floor from hall to hall of the Government Information Bureau, Anna's gift to him, enormous ceramic vases under the windows and through the panes a forest of tropical foliage, the walls were covered up to the ceilings with books bound in black and the ladders to reach them were made of stained wood and ringed in brass, at polished, statesmanlike tables people leafed through illustrated magazines and drank coffee from glass cups, the telephone rang in the hall and no one bothered with it, "Nobody breaks his back here, does he—" said Jacek. "It's quieter at the beginning of the month," Dr. Janzurova smiled charmingly, "now we'll take the elevator down to the ninth floor, where we keep the encyclopedias, dictionaries, and manuals, on the eighth there's only a card-punch machine, the photo lab, and the bindery—" "That's enough for now," said Jacek, "I'm sure I'll like it here..." "Comrade Deputy Bromova gave us the best report imaginable concerning you and we're all looking forward to having you here..." "You too?" "Me... especially, I left that for last, but if you should need anything from the start I'd be most happy to help you..." "I could see at first glance that you were friendly..." "Thank you, I felt the same way and I'm really looking forward...," "My God, they have forced air, real leather everywhere, chrome knobs, even an aquarium," "And here's your desk—" a desk like a steamboat, on the first, glassed-in deck a regular library, on the upper deck two telephones, a metal vase for a smokestack, and as a mast towering above it all a magnificent *Palma areca.*

The chauffeur opened the door of the stretch limousine for Jacek. "What do you think," said Anna, sitting down on the back seat. "Fan-tas-tic—" sighed Jacek, and he sank back into the cushions.

Jacek leaped out of his wicker chair and with a look of disbelief took in those nine-by-twelve feet of creaky boards, the roughed-up desk from the days of the Germans, the plant stand with its half-century-old Urania, and the five pine shelves behind a curtain of local manufacture... where was the mercury and the material that would put him in tuxes—

"I stashed it all away when that inspection party was here from Brno," said Vitenka Balvin, "you should be a bit more..." "Till next payday—" said Petrik Hurt, despite his eleven hundred in alimony, he pushed a fifty-crown note into Jacek's hand. "Get lost—"

In the empty office Jacek breathed in deeply and dialed the main office of Cottex, "Security Police, give me the director... Comrade Director? District Office of Public Security, Sergey Sniper speaking. Do you have a certain Jaromir Jost working there?... That must be him. Have you noticed anything suspicious about him lately?— no, I can't tell you on the phone, we only want you to inform us immediately about everything involving this matter, goodbye."

Within five minutes the director came to see Jacek with a newspaper in his hand. "Have you seen the latest issue of *Textile World*? Just look here, at the top..."

> In the photo, from left to right, Cmrde. General Director
> Josef Novacek, the central secretary of UNICAG Prof.
> Erika Ursula Marie von Wittig-Hohenmauern, Eng.
> Jaromir Jost, and the general director of CHIAG and
> president of WIPAG Dr. of Phil. and Dr. of Sci.
> Siegfried Postolka, all engaged in hearty conversation.

In the photo were the two general directors and the blonde in the center, all looking in the direction of a smiling Jacek, "I shouldn't tell you this," the director whispered, "but just a little while ago the security police were asking about you, so be careful... we'll all stand up for you, but watch out... You know how in Brno they're always trying to discredit us, we need you badly...," and the old man put his hand on Jacek's shoulder.

On the porcelain tray five checks and three asterisks had arrived, Jacek gulped down his third rye and turned resolutely to the fifth beer, by the door neighbor Mestek pining in his green windbreaker with a hood, still drinking his first beer, and at each of Jacek's successive drinks he shook his head, inside Jacek a cold, damp sense of revulsion suddenly rose up but he drank on heroically, it was necessary to drink up all twenty-five of those crowns stolen from Lenka's rent envelope, in the twilight of the Vseborice tavern the gloomy drinkers looked up from their glasses each time the door opened, a boy came in with a jug for two quarts of beer and two packs of Partisans, as he left he took a deep drink from the jug, and again we look into the fragments of that little round mirror between the floating wisps of stale foam, just stir it and it'll bubble up, the bubbles will float up to the surface, and that cruel mirror will disappear beneath the thin foam for a while, the door creaks and we all look up again quickly, the next guy comes in for beer and enjoys the thick foam, but just wait a while, and silence in the bar waiting for the next arrival even though the preceding ones have been so disappointing, mix it all up by stirring and when the door creaks we'll all look up—

The development blocks were all playing musical chairs and on the walk in front of his apartment house Jacek began to sing, how many more stairs there are now than before, and he scratched at the door like a dog, inside too there was scratching, and when the door opened Lenicka was down on all fours on the carpet, Jacek got down on all fours, too, and barked, "Woof-woof—" Lenicka answered in ecstasy, and the two puppies ran into the kitchen, "I'm drunk as a monkey—" Jacek announced triumphantly, "You took twenty-five crowns from my rent money," Lenka accused him, "But how can you leave your husband without a single crown?!—" Grandma spoke sternly to her as she poured Jacek a glass of herb liquor to stop his burping, and when the barking puppies had crawled under the bed, Grandma stuck fifty crowns of her money into

Jacek's pocket, "So you don't have to borrow anymore—" Lenka said, and she reached under the bed and stuck a hundred into Jacek's pocket, "Get dwunk again soon, Daddy—" Lenicka whispered in her crib behind the netting, "and pway puppy again..."

The official limousine of the director of VUGMT stopped at the Ministry of Heavy Industry, Jacek followed Anna through the vestibule and the passageway to the courtyard, between stacks of old papers out of the building and onto a bus, out of the excavated earth towered ten-story apartment blocks with curtains, twelve-story ones with whitewash crosses on the windows, and fourteen-story ones still only crudely assembled from sections, Anna's high heels disappeared into the masons' rubble of the boxed-in staircase, and here on the sixth floor we're home, I'd like to have this room with the view of Prague, "This room with the view of Prague is yours," said Anna, "and the first time it rains we'll sit and look at it together..." "And at night Prague will shine in here on the ceiling..." "You know, all my life I've wanted this city so much..." "Take this room, I'd be glad for you to..." "No, I'll come here to see you..."

Outside the frameless window, the hills of the capital spread out at their feet, the head of the Government Information Bureau with his second wife in their Prague apartment— "Come here, let me show you where we'll put the dinette," said Anna, happily leading Jacek by the hand, "... and wouldn't you like a wall-hanging with a large abstract design? I like to cook in general, but not every day... although here it will be something entirely different, I don't know how much I'd give just to peel potatoes and listen to you singing in the bathtub—I still can't believe it..." "Nonsense, I only have a couple of trifles to take care of—"

"—first you must break off with that Cottex, the pay

there is shameful. At first I thought we could rent a lodge in the mountains, but I've found something better," Tina raved, sitting on the bedspread with her knees tucked under her chin and her dark hair, let down, quivering on her calves, "a gas station, you know... Instead of starting at zero you start at five, at night ten, but you get ten crowns for just one gallon, maybe five hundred a day and in three years half a million..."

"Great," Jacek whispered, "but first I have to break away and you've got to help me... Throw something over yourself and let's go down to where there's a telephone..."

Tina led Jacek by the hand down through the sleeping chalet, from behind a thin door the snoring of a couple from Krakow resounded along the corridor as if they were choking to death, and that West German sedan from Hanover was snoozing pronouncedly after spending eighteen crowns on his wife and then a hundred marks on Tina, with the key to the bathroom Tina had no trouble opening the office door.

"So what will it be?"

"I'll dial the number and as soon as you hear a woman's voice, say right off, 'Jacinek...,' and then maybe how wonderful it was yesterday and how next time I should stay all night..."

"OK, but I'd never call you Jacinek..."

"That's just the point, that's what she calls me at the moment of climax," and trembling Jacek dialed his apartment, "You're a real snake," Tina sighed, "well, at night it'll come in handy at the station—Jacinek...," she whispered passionately, theatrically, into the receiver, "Oh, Jacinek, it was so wonderful yesterday and next time I know you'll stay all night... Jacinek, do you hear me... Jacinek...," and she banged the receiver onto the hook, "She's bawling or something... I can handle a lot, but I don't have the stomach for this..."

"Lenka's crying..."

"But so strangely, as if she were choking or…"

Jacek rushed through the nighttime meadows down to the black forest, on the black sky the brutal stars burned white, the millionfold Milky Way like the road to hell, he rushed over the silvery grass and the heavy traveling satchel struck his legs, thorns like fetters of barbed wire and persistent twigs struck his arms and face, into the evil, tense, lurking forest of the enemy, where from dark damp beds moss-covered boulders roll out their worm-ridden bellies, concealed in daytime, and the dry crackle of dead twigs like shots that missed, how hard on the soles that road from the forest can be and through grain up to his chest along the field roads, through the sleeping village where all the dogs go crazy on their chains, and along the concrete of the coal-conveyor under those phantasmagoric mountains of uprooted earth and thus murdered soil from which now only strange sparse pale weeds can grow, and around the moon-like craters and dunes from which nothing will ever grow again, through the labyrinth of undermined cave-ins, how ghastly far off home is, the lights of the development have long since gone out and like steamboats the apartment houses are lying in their winter anchorage, the silent pavement between the buildings is still warm with the tramp of children's shoes and once again the stairs to our apartment have multiplied, "Lenka, I have to tell—"

"Please don't say anything…," she whispered, sobbing softly, and passionately he kissed her hands, "… and get up, please get up… my Jacinek."

On the banks of the Elbe, on Sunday before noon, three thousand people, there would be more room in back by the wire fence under the poplars, Lenka spreads the checkered blanket out on the grass and Lenicka is already bare, "Cawwy me piggyback, Daddy—," Jacek crawled on all fours and on his back Lenicka exulted, her little legs clasped his ribs and on his shoulders that tender little body, they tumbled onto the ground, "Mommy, look, I'm wessling wif Daddy—" and Daddy and his daughter were like lovers in the grass.

Daddy stood in line for a boat, he seated the two Lenkas and pulled on the oars, the heavy rowboat flew with the current, a tanned brunette flashed by in a red canoe and behind her four girls were laughing in a white motorboat, Jacek pulled on the oars and the rowboat made its way heavily through the wake, Lenicka had fallen asleep lying in the prow and Lenka was carefully surveying the banks, the oars creaked in their metal locks and from his soaked brows salty sweat trickled into his mouth, "Look, pears already—" Lenka whispered excitedly, and Jacek turned the boat toward some stairs on the bank.

Up the hill to the railway embankment, through the dark, narrow underpass to a forgotten paradise of silence and warm, free grass, Lenka and Lenicka jumped to reach the hard, green pears and Jacek set out to find some hazelnuts for his little girl, he entered the hazel jungle and the springy, sap-filled twigs pressed stiffly against his body, beyond the bushes a small glade with a hut six-by-six feet and in front of it a dark, heavy woman was sunbathing, she sat up slowly and looked Jacek straight in the eye, "I only wanted to pick a few nuts...," he whispered uncertainly, and she got up and gestured—her finger in the hole—toward the door to the hut, Jacek followed her through the high grass and entered with his head bent, the ground inside was spread with sacks except in one corner where there were pots, saucepans, cigarettes, linen with black lace, cold cream, and lipstick in a straw hat along with baby oil and a yellow sandal turned upside down, the woman fished out a bar of cheap chocolate with peanuts and broke Jacek off a piece like a slice of bread, "I meant hazelnuts, from the tree...," he stammered, he tripped over a red parasol and sank on his knees into the sacks in front of her, "Daddy—" they heard from outside, "Daddy, wherre arre you—" "I'm coming—" he shouted, and he tore his hand free from the woman's, crossed the lawn, and leaped into the hazel thicket without any idea where he was going, until whipped and scourged he found the Lenkas among the pear trees, they took him each by a hand and together they ran down to the boat, Jacek leaped to the oars and pulled at them with all his might, the heavy rowboat turned its snout against the current and Jacek labored conscientiously, the grating of wood against metal and streams of sweat uniting in a hot salty veil over his face like a burst of tears, the old crate crawled against the current and playfully the current pushed its prow now to the right, now to the left, around the bend came a steam-boat, aroused waves rocked the rowboat like wind on the sea and the now wet daddy hauled his family back to their dinner.

Lenka carried two large bags for her hungry family under the poplars, "And now let's give our faces a good feed—" she laughed, and Lenicka helped her unpack a thermos, bottles, packages, sacks, and a perforated tin box.

In the afternoon heat, yachts sailed out from the jetty on the other side of the wire fence, their keels, polished like jewels, whizzed over the surface and, nearly naked, their tanned crews of both sexes hung over the sides and from the rigging, handsome and free as the gulls above their masts, the whole river to the south was full of white sails—

"Hello," Lenka was smiling in some direction, from the boat-rental stand Trost was coming with his family, his wife was unpacking from two bags a perforated tin box, sacks, packages, bottles, and a thermos, Trost played with little Trost on the same checkered blanket that we have, "Daddy cawwy me piggyback—" Lenicka cried, she climbed up on Jacek's back and kicked with her heels painfully into his groin, Jacek the Horse snorted on his knees in the warm grass near the wire fence and across the

way Trost the Horse was snorting with his screeching
jockey on his back urging him on.

One mountain slope on the left, another on the right,
above the point of intersection the crest of a third, dark
green needles of two shades: muted and bright, light green
foliage of a thousand shades: muted, bright, reflecting,
translucent, absorbent, half-, quarter-to-1/2, packed into a
complete progression of gradients from 0-360° times the
third dimension, all in motion on a conjectured poly-
structure of spatial branching drawings and a proportion-
ally motionless static eruption of inelastic explosions in a
Niagara of light—
"This is our forest," Lida Adalska smiled, "come—"
Inside, twilight and bright spots strikingly focused now
on the roots and now on the crowns, here in a plain of dead
needles sad telephone-pole spruces aren't making it, here
the floor of the woods is like a bombarded city square,
behind the trunks of the larch trees rise the ruins of forgotten castles and below you the tips of young spruces growing up out of the ravine, gray stumps, lustful as Turks, roll
their huge deformed members into the tender bilberries
and from the spruces' armor trickle stalactites made of rock
candy, the spider's diamond lace closes off the dragon's
cave, an art gallery of wood sculpture and the path to it
spread with pinecones off a grandfather's clock, a forest of
fairy tales and happenings—
"... I used to come and meet him here," Lida whispered,
"and the children ran here with me. He was so fond of
us..."
"... and then there was the time he brought us a fawn
on his back," Lida laughed, "Arnostek polished its hooves
with boot polish and Janicka made him little silver antlers
from the paint we'd used on our stove..."
"... and once when the snow was up to your waist, I put
a kerosene lamp in the window and the children kept

waking up all night long to see whether their Daddy had gotten home…"

"… 'grrr-grrr,' he growled from his hiding place in the hayloft, and Janicka looked out the window and said, 'Go way, bear, Daddy's coming and he might be fwightened of you—'"

"… he lies under that young fir tree, like you he was thirty-three when he died…"

Up to their calves in flowering grass, they walked down the mountain together to the ranger's lodge, and a boy and a girl ran out of the white house, they were afraid of the stranger with the black satchel, Lida stooped down in front of them and there were three faces peeping out from under her brown hair, Jacek tossed his satchel into the grass and stooped down with them, he made a rabbit face, he made Janicka laugh, we've got a way with kids, he barked at her and she barked timidly back, he didn't have to ask her twice to climb on his back, and Arnostek looked on jealously as he observed how his little sister was playing with her new uncle, "Now me, Uncle—"   "But you're a boy, we should box a bit together—," but Arnostek didn't know what that was, "My husband didn't do that with him…," Lida laughed while Jacek explained to her son what's a jab and what's a hook, inside five minutes Arnostek was a passionate boxer and now it was Janicka's turn to be jealous, Jacek picked them both up, "One more time—" Janicka called. "You're as strong as Daddy, Uncle—" Arnostek whispered.

Daddy's workroom was to be Jacek's temporary bedroom, outside the window a mass of spruces pierced the sky like Asiatic towers, and from a wide frame of dark wood with a black ribbon over the glass the forest ranger, the late Mr. Adalsky, looked down, a thirty-three-year-old with an oval face, eyes and hair apparently brown, no special markings, no feature betraying any special quality, an easily exchangeable anybody in the best years of his life and dead at thirty-three, you came to an end right at the time I'm getting started—

The strong scent of felled pines in the afternoon heat, the wild swirl of the brook, and in the warm grass a half-naked man was eating, like that time eighteen years ago, my God, nothing ever dies, the summer heat beat on the asphalt roof of Forest Building No. 06, the buzz of a circular saw outside, Jacek played with the jointed weight of the drafting board, tried out the T square, and attempted a couple of drafting techniques, "We'd be very happy and don't worry, I'll break you in myself. I like you—" said a magnificent man with white hair above a deeply furrowed, copper-colored face and the chest of a Laocoon in an unbuttoned Canadian shirt. "Well?" Lida asked out on the highway, "I've been accepted—" Jacek sighed happily.

Ta-ta-ta-dum, the express tore along through fields and woods, thundered at crossings, and rumbled through village stations overgrown with weeds, after the change of engines it quickly made up for the delay and at Kolin it was already two minutes ahead of schedule, I won't be the one to push our train on to its destination, my love, you take charge of the string of cars, the changing of engines: you be the one to push me off on my way—

"Just one more, this one will really be the last—" Jacek insisted on pouring Lenka another glass of Georgian cognac, "What's gotten into you—" her tongue now tripped confusedly, "you put it into the desserts, into the stewed fruit, the tea, I even tasted it in my mouthwash..." "It only seemed that way, you're acquiring the taste..." "But I don't want to acquire any taste, I'm afraid I'll get drunk..." "But how can you from just this little bit, come on, let's clink glasses—," they clinked glasses and Lenka emptied another goblet, she got up with difficulty and staggered off, under her thinning hair the sinking shoulders of a suddenly old woman and on the other side of the wall the revolting sound of splashing, then her sour breath,

"Oh, Jacek, I feel so sick—" and she laid her head in his lap, "Mommy," Lenicka called from her crib, "come and give me a kiss... Mommy—" "I can't come now, darling, tomorrow—" "Mommy, pwease come now—" "I can't—" Lenka moaned and collapsed on the floor, her head shook as if at her final gasp, "Mommy, I'm down on my knees, pwease come, pwitty pwease—" the neighbors' brooms were beating on the floors and ceilings as on a tin barrel and like a rat inside it Jacek ran back and forth in the dark, he was afraid to turn on the lights, the Lenkas moaned on the other side of all the walls and, near madness, Jacek howled under his pillow.

"... and greet him nicely and tell Comrade Dr. Mach that Mama and Papa send him their best," Hanicka Kohoutkova repeated her instructions in front of the pale-blue entrance to Kolora, a firm in Pardubice, "in the event of a successful outcome, Mama will fatten up a goose for him, but better not say that, Comrade Doctor's very strict. And don't forget to greet him with 'Honor to Work.' I want so much for you to pass the exam—come around the corner and I'll bless you on the forehead..."

With a glass rod pull the skein out of the boiling dark-red bath, with another rod stretch it out and by twisting it in the opposite direction wring the specimen out to a pink color, untwist it, submerge it, and with both rods put it through the color bath evenly, as when you turn a hoop with a stick, that's the way we learned to do it at school, to get the color even— "It takes a bit of practice, but it'll come: a colorist has to be born," Dr. Mach laughed, "so how about starting on the first of October?"

In a small, cheerful lab with windows looking right out onto fields ("We tore down that terra-cotta smokestack across the way, so it wouldn't throw a red reflection into the lab—"), bright skeins were hung everywhere and the dyed pieces looked like garlands and streamers, there are only four shades of black, no one knows how many whites there are, and no one has ever counted the browns, the keyboard of colored tones is over half a mile long, life as a colorist is a life of visual music, come here mornings, compose a Spanish moss or a bishop's cyclamen in silk and we'll put sixty crowns a day toward your account, on the wooden racks saturnine brown, bittersweet, Victorian blue, passion auburn, salmon pink, and cardinal red had dried, and on the pole below Jacek's first harmonious chord after fifteen years, the color of flesh from that dark-red bath— "Starting on the first of October!"

By the entrance Hanicka was fidgeting and biting her nails in agitation, "Jacek—" she cried out, and she ran toward him, "well—did they take you?" "They took me!" "Was it hard?" "I absolutely pulverized it." "Oh Jacek, I suffered as much as when I took my high school exams. Mama will start right away fattening that goose for Comrade Dr. Mach, and for you too we have a reward—"

A warm breeze blew over the solitary tract of beardless wheat from horizon to horizon under the hot clear sky and wave after wave rushed across that endless sea of grain, without an effort the path through the fields became a quiet street of well-swept clay and neat green fences with red knobs on top of the poles, behind each fence a little garden with a circle of flowers in the middle and a wooden bench and from each green gate, surrounded by roses, stairs up to a pretty little house, ours is that pink one with wild rose bushes along the stairs, on a concrete platform under the apple tree on a bench Mr. Kohoutek, my father, in a clean white shirt, his skin like a young woman's, not even a single gray hair and a dry, firm palm, and out of the house comes my mother, Mrs. Kohoutkova, in a clean white apron, a thousand lively wrinkles from so much smiling and a hand soft and warm, in the parlor on a clean white tablecloth four deep dishes on four shallow ones and four settings of heavy, antique silver.

A nice little house, a nice new job, a nice little garden, Jacek looked and Hanicka was beautiful, she was full of joy and the eyes of all four were damp, touched, Jacek fought for the huge glass jug so that he could go for beer, but he wrested it from them only to find a ten-crown note on the bottom (*"We're* entertaining *you*—"), a quiet, pretty tavern with a sparkling brass spigot, in front under a linden tree sat tanned, sturdy men in white shirts on red garden chairs on yellow sand under the green linden tree, all the tones unbroken and rejoicing together, from all the windows came the clean smell of roasting and frying, walnut cake and strawberries with cream.

When dinner was over it was already six in the evening, Papa went out to drink beer and Mama disappeared into the kitchen, Hanicka had wiped her mouth thoroughly with a stiff napkin, but even so her conscientious kisses tasted of strawberries and cream. Today she had to sleep downstairs between Papa and Mama, but she could go out for a while on the bench in front of the house, on all the benches in front of the houses there were couples in the twilight, "I want to have three children," she whispered, "two at least. The first one will be called Jastrun or Jadwiga. It's practical too, they'll have the same monogram as you do, that is, as we will. I've already started to embroider two red J's."

"So go ahead and kiss each other, you're as good as engaged now—" Mama smiled, one more warm silver goodnight spoonful of strawberries and cream and up the wooden stairs behind Mama, she showed him where the toilet was and also stuck a porcelain pot striped with flowers under his bed, the black traveling satchel rested like a purring cat on the little round armchair, a white basin and a white pitcher as in a summer cottage, the warm stars squeezed their way through the little window in the slanting wall, and out of the perfect silence rose the breathing of the dark earthenware oven of the endless Elbe plain.

The morning was shining vigorously as Jacek ran down the stairs of the pink house, down the sleeping clay avenue to the train, he stayed out in the corridor by the window and again ta-ta-ta-dum, the express pulled out with an insignificant delay from the gray platform deserts of the new Pardubice station and it rumbled westward through meadows and fields, ta-ta-ta-dum, past green tablecloths and endless fields wave after wave to the stairs leading to the platform gardens with benches around the houses with their loving bright facades, it's the hymn of freedom, this ta-ta-ta-dum, or is it only the theme song of parting—

"Did you bring the white plush?"

On the ridged mud in front of Cottex a scaffold was being raised and with latex paint an ancient mason was potemkinizing the facade of the electric plant, but the wall had nothing but contempt for this vain endeavor, the paint rotted, peeled, and fell off, and beneath it the inexorably naked bricks of the old barn which should have collapsed long ago, like the gaping teeth of a corpse overgrown with grass and still unburied—

At the ring of the phone Jacek started, perhaps this was it— "Petrik?..." said Verka Hurtova, "Darling Verka...," Jacek mumbled like Petrik Hurt. "I'm looking at the wall clock and the time doesn't move, I wish I were at the square watching you jump off the streetcar. Petrik?..." "Darling Verka..." "I thought that crazy Jacek was with you, Petrik, I can't wait for the afternoon anymore, you'll buy me ice cream first, won't you darling, and we'll lick it together, one lick for you and one for me, why must we leave each other in the morning and spend so much of the day apart..."

Petrik Hurt rushed into the office and Jacek handed him the receiver in full stream, for another half hour they chirped and then Petrik was wiping the sweat from his brow, "Excuse me," said Jacek, "but what are you doing this afternoon?" "We're going to the swings!" "And then?" "Why home—" "I accidentally overheard and got the impression that you're doing something special today..." "With us, you see, every day is special. Verka is... but you wouldn't understand. Verka, you see..." "It sounded like a poem." "Verka writes poems." "About what, for heaven's sake?" "Why, about the two of us—"

Jacek dialed the director's office, "It's Jacek Jost; greetings, Jozef," he spoke quickly into the speaker as Verka had done earlier, "I can't wait any longer to break with this Cottex, I look at the wall-clock and the time doesn't move, I wish I were at the square in front of our institute in Prague, I can't wait to start working there, meanwhile you should supply me with a new typewriter for the lab, in ten years of service here all I've got is this old Urania from the time of Franz Josef—" Bang! and the director hung up.

When they met, the director pretended that nothing had happened, he only upped his affability, the old man has refused to collaborate so we'll force it out of him, Jacek rushed to Cottex with Tina's camera, at 12:00 sharp he conspicuously stepped straight from the courtyard onto the fire ladder and up onto the roof of the electric plant and in full view of the director's windows he whipped off two rolls of industrial espionage, twenty-four shots so perfect they could go directly to the desk of the director of the CIA—"What f-stop are you using, Mr. Jost?" the hulking guard with the heavy revolver in his belt took an interest, "You haven't seen anything—" in a theatrically threatening half-voice Jacek tried to provoke some action against himself and out of despair he even hinted he might take flight, "Today I'd step down as far as f22," the warrior yawned instead of shooting and climbed into his glassed-in cage, it was maddening—

"Oooooo—" went Jacek to Lenka in the doorway when

she came to open the door for him, and right after that he kissed her, as usual, "But I said hi to you—" Lenka said in surprise, "But I gave you a kiss—" "But why did you bellow so?" "I bellowed?—" "You did, right when I opened the door—" "I didn't bellow, are you mad?—" "But I heard you with my own ears, you went ooooo—" "I'm really scared, Lenka, what's wrong with you?"

Lenka was doing laundry in the bathroom, Jacek snuck into the kitchen, turned on the mixer, and snuck out to the bedroom, Lenka went to the kitchen and the mixer was silent again, she went back to her laundry, Jacek snuck into the kitchen, turned on the mixer, and disappeared, Lenka went to turn off the mixer and went back to the laundry, Jacek turned on the mixer and hid behind the bathroom door, Lenka went to the kitchen, in the bathroom like lightning Jacek turned on the wringer and the washer and rushed into the kitchen, "Have you been turning this on?" she asked in confusion over the screeching machine, "Why would I do a thing like that?" "Well, for no reason at all—," the mixer was silent but in the bathroom the roar of the two motors and Lenka stiffened, "What's that—" "You've left on the washer, dear." "But I'm done with the laundry—," together we ran to the bathroom and were horrified at the two motors running, "What's wrong with you, dear?"

And at night lay all the knives out on the sideboard with the handles together and the points facing outwards, a fan of blades pointed toward anyone who comes near them, in the morning when Lenka gets up not a word from her, only Lenicka's voice from behind the wall, "Mommy, why don't you talk to me today, even when I make you angry—"

Tanicka's room was noodle-shaped, about 140 sq. ft., only an iron bed, a wardrobe, a stove which would never warm anyone, outside the window facing the Svitavy station plain little parcels wrapped in oiled paper and on the wall a prewar tin poster advertising the Papez Company with the legspread of the Eiffel Tower against a yellow Parisian sky, "I'm dying here—" in a theatrical posture Tanicka stretched out her skinny arms clad in a none too clean blouse, "Of impatience," said Jacek, "Absolutely!" she cried, collapsing on the bed to show just how absolutely, but she couldn't endure lying quietly more than two seconds at a time, so already she was churning her legs in the air like a cyclist and bursting into laughter, magnificently unaware what dying was.

"Would you like some bread spread with lard?" she said from the bed. "I've started to write a novel."

"I'll take a slice. Of course it's about the two of us."

"The knife's on the wardrobe. You come in in Chapter Two."

"How many chapters do I last? Do you have any salt?"

"No. I'd like to have lots of lovers..."

"I'm not enough for you? So advertise."

"What woman wouldn't want to have lots of lovers? The novel will have a hundred chapters."

"Seriously, at our place there's a couple by the name of Hurt and the wife writes poems... about the two of them. Really, I wouldn't believe that in the world..."

"There really isn't any novel, I made that up, maybe I will write one, but I've already got more than thirty poems about us. For instance:

> *I don't care*
> *for crumbs*
> *fallen from the table*
> *I want to be a feast*
> *for you the unsated*
> *I am virgin soil*

"What do you say to that? Would it do for a blues song by Vasicek Neckar?"

"You write poems about the two of us...," Jacek whispered with enchantment.

"Did you bring the money?" Lenka said, and she went to the bathroom to do the laundry, Jacek snuck into the kitchen and turned on the mixer.

And before the pale Lenka could go downstairs to hang out the wash, Jacek had gone for cigarettes then slipped back into the empty apartment, turned on the washer, the wringer, the mixer, the radio, and the TV, a fan made of knives on the sideboard and away quick, with his cigarettes he went down to the drying room and helped Lenka hang out Lenicka's shirts and tights, who will do your wash, little one, when they take Mommy away—

One step behind Lenka up to our place, in the hallway the roar from our apartment, "Someone must be in there—" she whispered, "But who could—" "Don't go in there, wait—" she leaped to the door opposite hers, bearing the nameplate JAROMIR MESTEK, and leaned with all her weight against the bell.

In his green windbreaker with a hood and carrying his carved cane, Mestek came right out, although evidently prepared for an excursion he quite willingly let himself be led into our apartment, "It's happened again," Lenka whispered to him, "just like last time..."

Mr. Mestek seems to know his way around our apartment well enough, he looked it over expertly and turned off all the roaring electric appliances, then went back to the hallway to check the fuse and returned right away, "It's nothing," he smiled, "just the current acting up." "But look here—" Lenka whispered with horror, pointing to the knife fan on the sideboard, "just like last time..."

"But it's nothing," Mestek smiled comfortingly, "it's just Lenicka playing, or Grandma being absentminded..."

"But they're both at the movies and when they left it wasn't happening—" Lenka whispered in a terrified voice. "Exactly like last time—"

"You've been terribly overwrought lately," Jacek interrupted her, "and evidently so preoccupied you..."

"But then it wouldn't be—" and Lenka tried to swallow, "quite normal..."

"But what are you thinking of," Mestek interrupted her, "why should you imagine such negative things..."

"Someone must have been in the apartment..." Lenka whispered.

"Well, since it disturbs you so," said Mestek, "it's nothing, of course, but for the sake of your peace of mind—" and he took a clean dishcloth out of a drawer—he really knows his way around here—and he deftly wrapped all the knives in it without touching a single one, "—I'll take this to the police, the fingerprints will explain everything—"

"Give that here!" Jacek exclaimed, and in a cold sweat he grabbed the bundle out of Mestek's hand, "I'll take it there myself."

"And so the movie's over," Mestek smiled good-heartedly, "or did the ghost do something else? Who put that balloon up there on the sideboard?"

"But you put it there...," Lenka was smiling now and blushing, "so Lenicka could see it from all directions..."

"Maybe I did that thing with the knives too," said Mestek, "you know, I do occasionally have blanks..."

"But what are you thinking of," Lenka interrupted him, "why should you imagine such negative things..." and she was laughing now, in a little while Lenicka and her grandmother came back from the movies and straight up to Mestek, "Uncle gwab me—" Lenicka insisted, and Mestek held her a while and then seated her up on the cupboard, Lenicka was afraid and ecstastic, "Uncle don't go way," he wouldn't go yet, Mommy has to pour him some cognac to thank him for his help and Grandma brings him a plate of brittle cookies, Lenka and Mestek clink glasses and right away she's poured another one, for herself as well, conversation and laughter from the room, the two of them sitting on the sofa and the husband outside the door, great, what woman wouldn't want to have lots of lovers, great, but not like this, so pointlessly guiltless — In the middle of the table a pink rum cake for Lenka's birthday with a twenty-eight made of Dutch cocoa icing, around it are neighbor Mestek (the timid suitor), Vitenka Balvin (the experienced seducer), Mija Balvinova (as a bad example), and we two Josts (fissionable material), Jacek (the procurer), who has unpacked from his black traveling satchel onto the white tablecloth one bottle of Georgian cognac after another, until there were ten of them in all (66 crowns a bottle—, his last special bonus was 900, so 240 left over for the secret hoard, the special bonuses from Cottex had become a sure thing now), "But they're only pints—" Jacek called as he poured out the second, Lenka was chatting with Mestek about baby powder and Mija was doing her best to no avail, "It's kind of dead here...," Jacek whispered to Vitenka, the expert on relaxed parties.

"Table and chairs out of the way—" Vitenka ordered and clapped his hands, "take apart the sofa, the mattress goes on the floor and from now on everyone onto the floor—" Lenka was for it and with the third bottle the party moved down to the floor, Jacek put his head on Mija's breasts, but across the way Lenka and Mestek had just gotten onto the cementing of linoleum, "Vitenka—" Jacek addressed the master of the revels.

"The light really gets in your eyes," Vitenka said loudly and clapped his hands, "haven't you got a candle—," Jacek brought one at once and conscientiously loosened all the bulbs in their sockets, he sat down next to Mija and kissed her hair, Mija put her arm around his shoulders, she was cooperating marvelously, and Jacek strained his ears, "... on a hill the mornings are always the finest," Mestek prattled on, "Yes, the air is clearer then," Lenka babbled. "Vitenka—" Jacek almost burst into tears.

"Everyone drink up his drink and the men change ladies clockwise—" Vitenka ordered and clapped his hands, "hop-a-hoppity-hop," movement and laughter, Vitenka sat down by Lenka and took things expertly in hand, in a while they were lying beside one another and out of the darkness Lenka's quiet laugh could be heard, Mija lay on her back and drew Jacek toward her, she was really out-doing herself and Vitenka too was exerting himself, at first they hadn't even wanted to come and now they were almost conquerors, the vessel was taking wind into her sails, Jacek emptied the third bottle from the burning slopes of Georgia and opened a fourth.

"I'll go make coffee," said Lenka, and she got up, "I'll go with Lenka and we'll come back soon, in no more than half an hour—" Vitenka said loudly, and he jumped up, "If you don't find Jacek and me when you come back, we'll be behind this door and please don't disturb us!" Mija called to him, and already she was pulling Jacek in that direction, one couple in the kitchen and the other in the bedroom, poor Mestek was the odd man out.

"Let go—" Mija hissed from the other side of the door, and firmly she pushed Jacek away, "But Mija..." "Just sit down, I've had enough of this low comedy routine, we haven't got an audience anymore—," they sat on the bed in the darkness, a whole yard apart, minute after minute, Mija bent over until her forehead touched her knees and she wept quietly, "Mija, what's happened—," a quiet sob, "Mijenka, please—" Mija's broken into tears, but don't make noise, please, there's no acoustic insulation here like you have in your white room at home.

Both couples came back to the living room in silence, Mestek, sadly sipping his drink, was shaking his head in disapproval, "Vitenka...," Jacek whispered in despair, "do you know anything else to do?"

"Why are you so anxious to turn your place into a whorehouse?"

"I like the way you keep yours."

"If I had a wife like Lenka..."

"Come on then— And pour yourself some more—" and Jacek got up, clapped his hands, and ran around the room pouring diligently, he drank with each of them in turn and with all of them together, he was as pathetically assiduous as the owner of a tavern on the eve of bankruptcy, Lenka quickly cheered up again, she stroked the limp Vitenka as if he were Lenicka refusing to eat, and Vitenka revived and snapped at her stroking hand, Mija kicked her legs in the air and her shoes flew off into the darkness, Jacek rubbed his hands, he lit their cigarettes, freshened their drinks, asked what they wanted, drank with all of them, and smacked his guests on the back, he bent down to them and laughed officiously, keep the action up the way a hoop is kept going with a stick, up the stairs to the platform near the little pink house for strawberries and cream, "But certainly, Mr. Mestek, make yourself at home here—" and Mestek unfastened his shoelaces, kneel down and officiously remove those stinking shoes, for the Government Information Bureau and an apartment with another wife with a window overlooking the metropolis, "I've had one too many—" Vitenka sighed, intoxicated, lead him off to the bathroom, take especially good care of him, refresh his breath with our own toothbrush, and wash him with our own washcloth—the Balvins' great improvement was somehow collapsing—if only his respect could be that of a rival, I want to be a feast for you the unsated under a yellow Parisian sky, meanwhile Mestek's gone down, lead him off to the bathroom, a cold shower, give his back and belly a nice stimulating rub with the fine sponge reserved for Lenicka's face, I have a girlfriend by Modigliani, but all of a sudden they're tired out and want to go home, what's so wonderful there, don't run out on me yet, green waves from stairs to stairs and on each terrace another naiad waits, they're all in the doorway all of a sudden, they tie up my boat and lock my plane in a hangar, they're running down the stairs, they've stolen my sea and my air and in the sudden silence after the closing of the door Lenka is coming toward me with a smile.

"That was a wonderful evening, I want to thank you very much for thinking of it," she whispered, and with her hair disheveled she looked inordinately pretty, "I had a nice talk with Mr. Mestek and Vitenka really courted me in the kitchen—," she giggled and her eyes gleamed, that's her hand stroking me again and petting me, her sensuality is aroused but, as if to spite me, in the wrong direction, but how newly beautiful Lenka looks today, newly aroused, "Jacinek, my darling—" she whispers the magic greeting and her arms are firmly around his body, "Lenunka—," like milk and like that cognac, how sweetly it had failed this time, it'd never been like this before, "It's never been like this before," Lenka whispered, and she went to open the curtains, the aviation-blue sky was already bright and Jacek ran to catch his R 12 with cars direct to Brno, "... and don't forget the white plush..."

Like an airplane hangar, over each metal entrance laminated glass like an outstretched wing, excitedly Jacek climbed the stairs of his classmate Bena Smrcek's institute in Brno, a hodgepodge of concrete, glass, and steel, up and down around him young men in white labcoats, the uniform here, physical chemistry is on the fifth floor, "I've just come to look since I'm one of the applicants for the fellowship..." "Our new fellow will have this desk—," in streams of light a white-and-pale-blue laboratory desk with silver taps for water, gas, vacuum, and coolant, silver burners and, under a cover, a row of electrical outlets, inside, on black shelves, the gleam of laboratory glass, that almost forgotten glass with which one might still make a hole opening onto the world, at the next desk a hirsute young man looking fixedly into a golden brew as if it were a spinning roulette wheel, and by the large window in the corner a cheerful scholarly debate, presenting for your approval our new fellow, I'm not dead yet, Jacek walked out of the lab and back down as slowly as possible so that he could imprint as much as possible of that blue-and-white room where intellect still lives and where there's still adventure, of that room prepared and waiting in this airport of a building.

Outside the window in the mud-ridged Cottex courtyard the ancient mason was asleep under his crooked scaffold with his mouth wide open, and on the speckled desk from the days of the Germans work that had piled up for two days: a directive from the general director's office, sent again in error.

Jacek sat down at his Urania and, mentally counting up how much was available from the secret hoard, replied mechanically that we will proceed without delay, paragraph, As we have informed you many times before, we cannot proceed in the foreseeable future, five spaces and in the center the greeting, Peace on Earth, just then the telephone rang, this was it—some Carmen Pospisilova was calling angrily to ask where her daughter was, she hadn't been home for two days and her name was Carmen too.

Jacek banged down the phone, pulled out of his drawer the twenty-four spy shots of Cottex enlarged to map size, for two days he'd fiddled with them in the factory darkroom, he put them in a fiery red folder with the letter to the general director's office, added a ten-mark note from Tina, and tossed it all on the director's desk, a time bomb ready to go off—he went back to his office, lit a stolen Winston cigarette, and waited happily for his stage-call.

At last a stomping outside the door, there were more than one of them—the dyer Patocka come with a suggestion for improvement: fire the color-room foreman and we'll save twenty thousand a year, his explanations weren't convincing, the dyer stood on his rights and so

Jacek had to write it up in duplicate, record it in the log, write a confirmation, and thank the man for his initiative.

The phone rang, I'm coming and I'll take all the responsibility—Lenka was calling to say that Grandma had gone off to Brvany for unknown reasons and Lenicka had run through a closed door, buy some glass, twenty-seven by forty-four-and-a-half inches, beige enamel paint, crepe paper, and especially the white plush, the telephone rang and informed him that the boys had pulled out lab assistant Palanova's chair as a prank and that she'd suffered a light concussion, the telephone rang and officially informed him that tomorrow Dr. Bruno Deleschall would arrive from the Basel firm of Ciba, he had nowhere to stay and tactfully take away his camera right at the entrance, so that's how you want to frame me, OK, I accept your game and out of all the stalemates up till now I'll somehow manage a checkmate—

Heavy steps outside the door, there are at least two of them coming—three arrived, first the director with the fiery red folder and, now liberated, Jacek stood up, I'm ready—the director placed the folder on his desk, "The letter to Brno is marvelous—" he said and then whispered, "Those shots of our grounds are handsome, but for the sake of security I locked them in the vault—," behind him an aged secretary and the firm's legal expert made sour faces as they carried off the fifty-year-old Urania and left in its place on the plant stand a brand new blue-gray Zeta, the director winked archly, the doors banged shut, and Jacek was left alone with his new typewriter, for another fifty years there would be peace between Cottex and his department, blue-gray is the color of aviation, CAPTAIN, I DON'T UNDERSTAND YOUR CODE—

Outside the window a mass of spruces pierced the blue blue sky like Asiatic towers and behind the glass with the black ribbon the portrait of the dead thirty-three-year-old

Adalsky, how delightful sheets bleached in the sun feel against the body, how young it is to be only thirty-three—

Jacek dashed through the blossoming meadow from the forest ranger's to the mountain, through the woods, and by bus to the station, on the platform deserts loudspeakers summoned passengers to board trains for the west and the east, Jacek with his black satchel going up and down the stairs, the greatest torment is not to be able to decide, but if deciding fetters one so isn't that torment one's last remaining liberty, depart by the first train that stops here to pick us up, Jacek laughed into the faces of the hurrying throngs and snapped his fingers, so quick, quick, children, off to school, the bell's rung and the teacher's already raging on the podium, she'll put a black mark in her record book, Jacek set his satchel down at his feet and raised his finger like a preacher, they had to go round him and Jacek guffawed in their faces, life is such a wonderful game of chance and so terribly one and the same for all time, every-thing that passes you by, you who never venture anything, and where do you get your firm belief that you couldn't live MAGNIFICENTLY SOMEWHERE ELSE than where you live according to a concatenation of chances, you maggots and roundworms, MY FAITH IS IN FLIGHT, ta-ta-ta-dum, on the green cushions into the green waves of the sea which never ends, ta-ta-ta-dum, I TEAR UP MY SEAT TICKET and sit wherever I like, ta-ta-ta-dum, what, we're in Usti? Train, ride on—the train stopped.

And the crowd had already surged from the cars, all by the shortest routes to their Lenickas and Lenkas, ride on, train, I beg you, my Poseidon, from your compartment I pray to you, ride on, I must go to the end of the line, Speranza is there waiting for me on the first terrace beyond the Residence, where we used to go swimming, we'll sit on chairs facing one another and call on you, ch-ch-ch-ch—I wasn't asleep then, ch-ch-ch-ch—I can't fall asleep any-more, ch-ch-ch-ch—I don't just want to sleep until I die,

I've already torn up my seat ticket, ride on, train, ride on,
ch-ch-ch-ch—

IV — fifteen

The stream of passengers leaving the Decin station poured quickly onto buses and streetcars, we've only got a short walk from the station, Jacek hurried down the street past our third-category, on the staircase that stinks of sauerkraut he pulled out of his pocket a metal ring with a mass of keys, the Decin key is the gold one and this tiny beach is the Naiad's, in the foyer he kicked off his shoes and slipped into waiting leather slippers, Nada was reading Páral's novel *The Trade Fair of Wishes Come True*, and already she was tossing it aside, "Jacek, you've come—"

"I'm here now, my love—"

"Wouldn't you like something to eat? I have a big can of herring in oil—"

"Later, now all I want is to look at you and listen to you talk. Sit here on this chair and I'll bring the other one from the foyer... ch-ch-ch-ch—I love you so ch-ch—repeat after me: ch-ch-ch-ch—" The overturned chairs laughed with their legs in the air while the lovers lay on mattresses as if on waves.

A cigarette by the window, the barges on the Elbe sailed out from the docks and formed into a convoy, the afternoon sun with its golden trapezoids moved through the room and the room was full of light, "Jacek," Nada whispered from behind him, "I've already signed up for the new co-op they're building, in your name... In three years we'll have our own apartment, two rooms, a bathroom with hot water, central heating, a telephone..."

Jacek jumped out of the bus and hurried across the excavated plain up the hill past the ten-story buildings with curtains and now with antennas as well, the twelve-story buildings have curtains already, and in our fourteen-story the windows are in with whitewash crosses on the glass, on the spattered staircase he pulled out the metal ring with its mass of keys, the Prague key is this silver one with the notch and this lofty beach is the Palma's, Anna was kneeling on an old coat, varnishing the wood floors with a brush, and already she was tossing it aside, "Jacek, darling—"

"I'm here now, my love—"

"Wouldn't you like to take a bath? They're trying out the hot water system today—"

"Later, first let me help you. What should I do?"

"First change your shoes, darling. The blue ones in the foyer are for you..."

"Anci, you know, it would be great if we had a phone here—"

"I've already applied for one... in your name."

On air mattresses Jacek and Anna lay side by side on the floor and their shoulders touched, "As if we were floating on the sea...," said Jacek, "Farther and farther away from the shore...," said Anna, and they lay on compressed air as if on waves.

A cigarette by the window, out of the night the metropolis shone from its invisible hills, the lights blended with the noises of the enormous development and in thus permeated waves they shrilly broke on our ceiling like the tide, "Jacek," Anna whispered from behind him, "I'd like to have a cottage somewhere in the country, you know, where it's dark at night and quiet and where even the open air goes to sleep..."

On the path through the fields Jacek hurried across an endless expanse stretching from horizon to horizon, huge red farm machines drove into the yellow sea and sacks of harvested grain lined their incursions, on the steps between the wild rose bushes Jacek pulled out the ring of harvested keys, the Pardubice key is this homemade one, already Hanicka is running full tilt onto the platform with the circle of flowers, "Jacek, this is so wonderful—"

"I'm here now, my love—"

"Wouldn't you like to go see the rabbits?"

"Later, first I'll go say hello to your parents."

In the corridor Jacek tossed off his shoes and put on a checkered slipper with a tassle, "Don't take off your shoes—" Mrs. Kohoutkova said, "we've been holding supper for you, you can go straight to the tavern for some beer—," the clean scent of roast meat and the glass jug with the ten-crown note on the bottom.

On all the benches in front of all the houses couples in the twilight, "The goose for Comrade Dr. Mach will be remarkable," said Hanicka, "Mama thinks fifteen pounds is big enough. I've been arguing that it ought to weigh at least eighteen pounds... Why don't you say anything?"

"I'm listening to the magnificent quiet here..."

"I'll be quiet too. It *is* magnificent..."

A cigarette and blow the smoke into the prism of light coming from the window, the couples got up from their benches and entered their houses, downstairs the lights went out, in a short time they went on upstairs, and then one light after another went out into the majestic quiet. "Jacek," Hanicka whispered, "we must wait a while yet, but I'm so looking forward to having children... First a boy, he'll look like you and go out into the world, and then a girl, she'll stay home with me..."

Through the blossoming grass Jacek sped down the mountain to the forest ranger's and involuntarily reached for his key ring, but here they don't lock their doors, with a cry of joy Arnostek slid down a ladder and from the woodshed Janicka came running, in the yard Lida was feeding the hens from a wicker basket, and already she was tossing it aside, "Jacek, you've come—"

"I'm here now, my love—"

"Wouldn't you like to go for a walk?"

"Later, first I'll quiz Arnostek on his new vocabulary."

In the foyer Jacek took off his shoes and put his feet into the enormous leather slippers of the late Adalsky, "Uncle gwab me—" Janicka begged, so hold her in his arms a while and then set her up on the cupboard the way neighbor Mestek does, Janicka was afraid and ecstatic, "Uncle don't go way—," he wouldn't go, but now Arnostek must recite the thirty new words he's learned, the boy must get ready to go out into the world.

In early evening behind Lida along the path to the woods, then turn off the path and straight up through the glades to the grassy dunes, "My husband used to call this our Nude Beach...," said Lida, "It must be nice to sunbathe here...," said Jacek, "It is, people come here from Prague and some of them don't bother wearing suits..."

A cigarette on a stump in front of the forest ranger's, in the lighted window two children's silhouettes and their little faces pressed to the glass, "You're a good man, Jacek," Lida whispered, "but here life isn't easy, there's a lot of work to do, the house, the farming, the children... It would be fine to begin again from nothing, to be young again from the very beginning..."

Jacek stepped out of the express and hurried across the tracks of the Svitavy station, it's right across the street, on the warm dark staircase grope and find in the mass of keys the one for this place, big as a church key, under the tin picture of the Eiffel Tower the little Jeannette beach, Tanicka was mending a stocking, and already she was tossing it aside, "Jacek, you devil—"

"I'm here now, my love—"

"Wouldn't you like to hear what I've written?"

"Later, first I'd like to change my shoes..."

Jacek took off his shoes and looked around in vain for something to put on, all Tanicka had were three pairs of shoes under the bed and otherwise nothing, "I go barefoot at home, but I've heard that in Prague they've got real Chinese sandals for sale..."

"Wouldn't it be better to buy a table and chairs first?"

"They're dull, unnecessary things—" Tanicka threw all the bedding off her bed and under the yellow tin Parisian sky they rocked on the cross-wires as on a canoe, Tanicka read eighteen new poems aloud and then suddenly fell asleep. Scarcely had Jacek begun to read the newspaper than a skinny arm slipped before his eyes a chewed-up piece of paper containing the nineteenth:

> *With my longest nail*
> *on my master's back*
> *I'll engrave*
> *childish obscenities.*
> *Surely*
> *it will get through to him then*
> *that*
> *this is no time*
> *to read the paper!*

A cigarette by the window looking out onto the sad Svitavy station, through the bubbly windowpane plain little parcels wrapped in oiled paper, "Jacek," Tanicka whispered, "I'll die here longing for the big city, where the store windows shine and the streetcars clang..."

Jacek stepped out of the express and hurried with the crowd through the din of the Brno station to the cafeteria, over a stale beer Mojmira was reading *The Trade Fair of Wishes Come True* and suddenly she lit up, "Jacek, welcome, all happiness—"

"I'm here now, my love—"

"Wouldn't you like to go to the publisher's, I have to take you there sometime to explain to them that you're not ready to come right now..."

"Later, first let's stuff ourselves. I'm so huuungry—"

The magnificence of the city of Brno begins right outside the station, streetcar after streetcar in three rows, directly across the square the airline office with its heavy chrome swinging doors, and on both sides a gleaming, unending strip of shop windows and glass doors.

Through glass doors, swinging doors, and turnstiles, down from refrigerated glass shelves, out of bowls and out from behind curtains, onto spattered counters, onto wood, and onto ever new damask tablecloths and paper trays, plates made of plastic and of gilded porcelain, crackling sausages, crunchy french fries, and meat from the spit, and into steins, paper cups, crystal goblets everything that can conceivably flow, at first icy and then warmer and warmer, "You're the last man left who knows how to eat—" Mojmira said, "You're the first woman I've enjoyed food so much with—" said Jacek, and gargantuan kisses in front of the dried-up cloakroom attendant at the Hotel Continental.

A cigarette inside the glass doors, along the garden wall down under the tops of the old trees the street leads to our house, the street is pasted up with a thousand posters on which long ago we used to dream of seeing our name in huge letters, "I'm ashamed now I made such a hog of myself," Mojmira whispered, "but I've been hungry all my life, before the war, during the war, since the war, and I'm still hungry now, it's wonderful not to have any money, but sometimes a sense of horror comes over me..."

Jacek jumped from the funicular seat and hurried up the hill to the Mosquito Tower, on the spiral stairs he took out the key ring, from the round windows now the crests of the Krusne Mountains, now the peaks of the Czech Central Range, and now the view into Germany, this thin skeleton key belongs to the Belvedere beach, Tina lying on the bed smoking a cigarette, and already she was tossing it aside, "Jacek—"

"I'm here now, my love—"

"Wouldn't you like to go down to the bar? We just got our quota of Dubonnet—"

"Later, now I'd like to be with you. Do you have anything for me?"

Tina gave Jacek some paper money fastened with a hairpin, each bill from a different country, the prettiest of all, like a postage stamp, a colorful franc note, "But now you have to go down to the bar, Jacek. Right away."

Without a word Jacek changed into heavy half-boots with tire-tread soles, in these he could go up and down the stairs like a ghost, they could serve for attack or defense, "You won't need them today," said Tina firmly, "wait till I come down. Scoot!"

On the way downstairs Jacek passed a huge fellow with a thick cigar in his bared, vulgar teeth, in the bar Jacek drank Dubonnet and in hot breakers again and again he beheld Tina's tormenting gold-and-orange skin, he breathed in deeply like a drowning man that hitherto unknown smarting sensation, and again hot wave after wave.

A cigarette by the window, Tina's hair let down and quivering like an animal's, he poured another two glassfuls and looked out in silence, "Jacek," Tina whispered from behind him, "I'd like some milk now, sweet white warm milk..."

The funicular down to Bohosudov, the bus at 5:34 and in Usti at 6:05 as if from the 4:45 to Berlin, streetcar No. 5 to Vseborice, Jacek hurried along the road past the playground, on the well-scrubbed staircase he pulled out his mass of keys, opened the Residence with the one with the letters FAB and the dog's head, Lenka was wiping the foyer with a rag, and already she was tossing it aside, "Jacek, you came back today, already—"

"I'm here now, my love—"

"Wouldn't you like some strawberries, they're fresh from our garden..."

"Later, first I'd like something to drink. You didn't

forget the milk... No hot cereal, just warm up the milk for me and put in five cubes of sugar..."

"You forgot the white plush again, didn't you—"

"Yes, I did, darling, but I'll bring it, really I will—" said Jacek, putting on his old slippers worn smooth to a shine.

"Daddy—" our little darling calls, her chin on the brass pole, down with the netting at once and his rough chin on her sweet little tummy, Lenicka cried out with pleasure, nothing's so sweet to kiss as our little one, "Daddy gwab me—" cries our pretty little girl, and so swing her back and forth and set her up on top of the cupboard, Lenicka is afraid and ecstatic, but now she must go beddie-bye, "Daddy don't go way—" and stay by her bedside until she goes to sleep with her thumb in her mouth.

A cigarette by the window, outside children being called home to bed and now the stars like urchins on a fence slide on their rumps down the antennas into cribs with netting, just across the way Trost with a cigarette by the window... that fellow's gawking right this way, from that window he's goggling right at my face—

By bus at 3:55 from the main square through the canyon of facades none of which can be skipped, down the row of old chestnuts, around the sharp curve past the gas works, and through the mountains of dead soil torn up from the earth to the monument with the lion eaten up by verdigris, now the linden tree with the sign and along the clay road up to the retreat, the yellow house isn't ours, it belongs to Mrs. Heymerova, who'll come back again very soon, on the oval table and on the wall stags bellowing in rut, they don't bellow but they're embroidered with open jaws, and out the window of the retreat the undulation of gleaming emerald grass rearing up to the gleaming sky like the coast to the sea, we've already set sail, but we forgot to pull up the anchor, the boat has only a lookout deck and the train keeps hauling us around and around and back to the launching-pad at home, try it once on foot or perhaps on a horse, MY KINGDOM FOR A HORSE that will carry us away from the plain of too many victories and hurl us into the bloodspill of salvation because it is the bloodspill of a single defeat, MY KINGDOM FOR A KICK-OFF so that instead of going a little way with a satchel of dirty clothes we can take off once and for all with the cosmonaut's luggage, I already know the timetable by heart, CAPTAIN, I REQUEST THE SIGNAL TO TAKE OFF— This is the last time I'll ask.

Part V — Autosynthesis — sixteen

L ate, as usual, express No. 7 from Bucharest, Budapest, and Bratislava was just pulling into Platform One at Brno Main Station. In the midst of the usual confused rush of travelers Jacek took in the always unexpected sequence of numbers on the reserved cars until, sufficiently amused, he finally caught sight of his own car, No. 53, hooked up between Nos. 28 and 32.

In compartment F by the window on seat No. 67 a fat old man looked up, we have No. 68 across from him, Jacek put his traveling satchel up into the net, hung his beige iridescent raincoat beneath it, and when he'd sat down another passenger entered the compartment with a seat ticket in hand, he had the odd number 69, next to the fat man, he put his suitcase up into the net and he hung beneath it his blue-gray raincoat of the same material and cut as Jacek's.

"Excuse me, gentlemen," said the fat man by the window, "do either of you play chess by any chance?"

"I do," said Jacek.

"I wouldn't mind a game," the third passenger said simultaneously, he and Jacek looked at each other, laughed, and the train pulled quietly out.

"So you two come to an agreement which of you I'm to demolish," the fat man roared joyously, "meanwhile I'll set up the pieces—" and he was already sticking them into his portable chess board.

"You play, since you're sitting there," the third passenger said to Jacek, "I'll kibitz. To myself."

"You can do it out loud," Jacek smiled as he opened P-Q4.

The fat man opened up on the same column, P-Q4, mechanically Jacek moved P-KB4, the fat man again the mirror image, P-KB4, another couple of moves and similar countermoves and we've achieved that double interlocking barrier known as a stonewall.

The train rushed on through meadows and forests, a girl waiting behind a lowered barrier flashed by, she was wearing a red polka-dot dress, and on the little table by the window two players sweating over their total blockade, nothing could come of it, both were waiting for their opponent to make a mistake and that's a terrible bore, "I've got to step out a minute...," Jacek grumbled a good quarter hour before reaching the Svitavy station, and he stood all that time by a window in the corridor.

Tanicka Rambouskova had been waiting at the far end of the Svitavy station and she ran up to Jacek's window, we stop here for just a minute, "Don't think I came here just to see you—" she lied, out of breath from her gallop.

"I wouldn't have imagined it even in my sleep—do you sell lemonade here?"

"You're a disgusting cynic and I don't want to see you ever again, ever—understand!"

"I'll jump off the train!"

"That would be wonderful... I'd lay your bloody head in my lap... Jacek, please, get out—"

"It isn't that simple..."

The train pulled quietly out and Jacek waved to Tanicka until she disappeared around the bend, why didn't we get out, he sighed and went back to his compartment, on the table that nightmarish unfinished game and both passengers preoccupied, making faces over it, "You said you'd like to play," Jacek told the third passenger, "so if you're still inclined—"

"If it's OK with you—" said the third passenger, and he eagerly moved over into Jacek's seat No. 68 opposite the indefatigable chess player, while Jacek moved into the thus emptied No. 69 and with relief he now observed how his substitute was tormenting himself, he tormented himself another hour, as far as Chocen, where the two of them, quite exhausted, settled for a draw rather than an endless repetition of the same moves.

The third passenger fished a timetable out of his suitcase and compared it with his watch, "Twenty minutes late, right—" said Jacek. "Yep," the passenger agreed, "I wonder if we'll catch the 4:45 to Berlin—" "You can rely on it—" Jacek assured him, "are you going to Usti by any chance?" "Yes, and you?" "Me too. For a long time?" "Possibly for good. You know the place?" "For ten years now almost too well. What would you like to know?" "Do you know anything about the chemical plant?" "Everything. I work next door at Cottex. You're a chemist?" "Yes. If you'll permit me—" and the passenger pulled a card out of his wallet and handed it to Jacek,

ENGINEER NORBERT HRADNIK

Jacek read the card, got up, and almost embraced him. "We're in the same profession then, I'm very happy..." "It really is a lucky coincidence..." "Most happy to do anything for you..." "You're really very kind...." "With the greatest pleasure..." expressing their affability they rushed to the dining car and shared a large dinner, Hradnik was running away from his wife and two children, from an awful job in Brno to Usti, we from Usti to Brno, two more beers, "I'm Jacek—" "I'm Nora—" and two carafes of wine, "I'll find you jobs, Nora, as many as you want—" "I'm more worried about a place to stay, Jacek, they'll stick me in some dorm—" "Tonight you can stay at our place—" "At home, Jacek, I had to cook hot meals twice a day—" "Nora, I've got fantastic chicks in Svitavy and Brno—" "Two cognacs!" Nora ordered, "Georgian!" Jacek added, and just before Prague they stumbled back to their compartment, in the dark of the tunnel they fell laughing into their exchanged seats and here was Prague Main Station already, both got up and put on their raincoats, "But Jacek, you've got on mine—" Nora guffawed in Jacek's beige iridescent, "And you've got on mine, Nora—" Jacek giggled in Nora's aviation blue-gray, they fit and suit us, CAPTAIN, NOW I UNDERSTAND YOUR CODE—

"Why you're like twins," the fat man grinned from his window, "Let's exchange them," Jacek cried out, "I'm awfully fond of this aviation color—" "Sold!" Nora cried out, "we've both got a new coat for free—"

"Darling—" Anna Bromova called from the exit of Prague Main Station, and she ran up to Nora, only a step away from him did she realize her error, "Jacek...," she whispered in terrible embarrassment, Jacek laughed and put his arm around her slender shoulders, "Jacek, stay in Prague today...," she said on their swift trip through the little park, "...you know no one's expecting you in Usti..." "Today I've got something very important to arrange," Jacek muttered like a conspirator, "for both of us...," and at least Anna was able to see him off at Prague Central Station, Jacek and Nora easily caught the 4:45 to Berlin and Jacek had time to come out to the window in the corridor, Anna stood for a long time by the car, she kissed her palm, blew the kiss up to him, and the train pulled quietly out over bridges high above the streets of Prague, it passed through the green shadows of Stromovka Park and then beneath a hillside of millionaires' mansions and the Byzantine skyscraper of the Hotel International.

"With your right foot!—" Jacek called out at the Usti station, and Nora had to step out right foot first for good luck, streetcar No. 5 to Vseborice, the last stop, the two men hurried past the playground, the steps up to our place have multiplied considerably again, "You go first—" Jacek pushed Nora, reshod in his old slippers and carrying Jacek's black satchel, into the dark foyer, Lenka came out to meet them with a smile, "Who are you bringing home, Jacek?" she said to Nora, she took the traveling satchel from him and went back into the kitchen, Jacek stepped ahead of Nora and entered behind Lenka, "Mr. Norbert Hradnik."

Nora kissed Lenka's hand and she took it unexpectedly well, heaven knows when the last time was that anyone had greeted her that way, Nora moved through the kitchen with agility and prepared a marvelous omelet, but then he's had the training provided by five years of married life, Lenka clapped her hands in admiration, Nora took Lenicka by the legs and taught her to do backward somersaults, you can see the routine of a father of two children left behind in Brno, after supper he talked about the Margrave Jost and Lenka showed a surprising familiarity with Moravian history, she must have read up on it sometime, the substitute had taken and they put him to bed in the living room with two pillows under his head, depleting Jacek's customary stack.

From Cottex home as slowly as possible through the town, at the Hranicar movie house they're playing *No One Will Laugh* for the third week in a row so let's go to the movies for a change, herring and onions at the Svet Cafeteria and a small carafe of white Burgundy at the Zdar, everywhere he goes a bachelor lives it up, even when he's alone, paradise must be solitude with the possibility of choice, Jacek stopped in at the barbershop and spent a pleasant time in Kamilka's soothing hands, "Why didn't you come that day at ten...," she whispered when he kissed her on the elbow, "That day I couldn't, but today's no problem..." "Today my Dad's here from Mimon, but come tomorrow—," Jacek inhaled his cologne and gazed contentedly at the travel agency display next to the notice agency, two pretty girls invite us to visit the Czech Paradise and on a green sea a white boat sails along, on the column a new poster with Candy in a red tux, LAST APPEARANCE BEFORE OUR GRAND TOUR—

Toward evening Jacek came home, in no way missed, in Jacek's T-shirt with Lenka's apron tied around his waist

Nora was preparing Hungarian fish soup and Mexican goulash, Lenka was merrily grating the cheese, and together they went to bathe Lenicka, "I thought that kind of husband had long since died out...," Lenka laughed, "That's nothing," Nora laughed, "I used to do the ironing, and one winter I even did embroidery with my wife..."

After supper both of them took a cup of rosehip tea with jam into the living room and talked about Stravinsky and Kandinsky, what sort of men they were, Jacek went out onto the balcony with a chair and a glass of cognac and facing the strip of dark blue sky he smoked cigarette after cigarette, the couple on the sofa and the husband outside, it would be only an occasional release from the barracks to visit the town's dance hall, and after all Lenka doesn't want to commit a sin, so just bring a new husband into the apartment and thus preserve the numerical status quo, soldier for soldier, CAPTAIN, THANKS FOR THE SIGNAL, when the bottom of a gasoline storage tank cracks it's best to call the firefighters, all that has to be done is to let water in, and then out of the hole in the bottom only water will flow, it's heavier, and the gasoline will remain undisturbed in the cracked storage tank until you pump it into a new tank—since Lenka and Nora had forgotten about Jacek, they were almost frightened when he suddenly came in from the balcony, "Don't bother getting up—" said Jacek, "tomorrow I'm going to Brno, please put two white shirts in my satchel, and no lunch..."

"Don't forget the white plush..."

Outside the window above the houses a shining blue hangar, Jacek tiptoed through the apartment, away from the sleeping Lenka past the sleeping Nora into the foyer, take the traveling satchel and the blue-gray raincoat, CAPTAIN, THANKS FOR THE UNIFORM—

A great four-day cruise on the green cushions of the black steamship from beach to beach along the entire coast, Jacek stepped out of the sea and up the steps with his black satchel like a trident in his hand, like Neptune himself, greeted and welcomed by naiad after naiad, fed, indulged, fondled, loved, and respected, the Belvedere, the Jeannette, the Palma, the Stefanie, the Kvarner, the Naiad, the Speranza, and in exchange for just the one beach at the Residence he got the Miramar as a point of departure for Africa—

"What's happened here?" Jacek was frightened, Lenka locked in the kitchen and Nora throwing into his suitcase the things he'd laid out on a chair, "Nothing, to be precise."

"You want to leave? Why?" Jacek whispered, crushed.

"Didn't you know that tomorrow Grandma's coming back from the hot springs?"

"But that can be taken care of... Would you rather live in the chem plant dorm, in a room for four with bunk-beds?"

"I've been living in one for three days now and there are nine of us in a room."

"Did Lenka do anything..."

"Lenka didn't do anything. When you described her to me on the train you said that she's intelligent, decent, a good cook..."

"And isn't all of that true?"

"It is, anyone can tell that in half an hour himself. But you forgot to tell me the main thing about her."

"What main thing?"

With a sigh Nora picked up the suitcase and shook it, it was almost empty, he carried it into the foyer, tore his blue-gray raincoat off the coat tree, and threw it over his shoulders, CAPTAIN, WHY DOES HE GET TO MAKE THE FLIGHT INSTEAD OF ME, "Couldn't you possibly change your mind...," Jacek groaned, "if I were to ask you—"

"I'd come to fear you," N. Hradnik said. "Farewell, Mrs. Jostova, and thanks for everything—" he called to the glass panel of the locked door, and he left in silence.

"Nora was fine at first," Lenka said, holding Lenicka in her arms, "but when you went away he tried to take advantage of the situation, I had to go for Jarda Mestek at once…"

"Jarda?"

"… and in the meantime Mr. Hradnik had vanished. Today he only came back for the things he'd left behind in his haste. Jacek, when are you going to bring me that white plush—"

"Next time, definitely."

Post another man at once in the deserter's place, "And so I'm extremely grateful to you, Mr. Mestek," Jacek said in his neighbor's bachelor apartment, "you've done so much for us already…"

"But it's nothing, I was glad to…" Mr. Mestek smiled. Jarda.

"And why shouldn't we call each other by our nick-names, after all, when we're almost like members of the same family. Mine is Jacek—"

"Mine is Jarda—

"I know. Lenka uses it more and more lately: Jarda says this, Jarda thinks that, Jarda would never—she likes you, you know…"

"I'm not so sure myself…"

"But she does. Just now she was saying how surprised she was that you're alone all the time. Such an intelligent, decent man—those were her words—and then such a good-looking one, very good-looking, in fact… Why once in the middle of the night she whispered your name in her sleep…"

"Oh, that's hard to believe!"

"She did, but I'm not jealous, on the contrary—"

"You'd have no reason to be."

"But you see I'm very glad to know that Lenka has someone to depend on when I'm not around, someone who… who…"

"You don't know her very well, Jacek. Not very well at all."

Jacek got up, took in at a glance the saucepans with old, hardened grease, the bundle of filigree carved canes, the piles of crossword puzzles, the socks drying on the string hung from the windowlatch to the latch on the door, all that bachelor squalor, he sighed and stole away.

Darling, come, please please please, wrote Anna, WAITING LIKE LAST TIME, Tina wired, and from Tanicka an exclamation:

> *Sweet drop of honey*
> *Trickle into the comb!*

Jacek paced his office at Cottex like a beast in a cage, CAPTAIN, I REQUEST INSTRUCTIONS, your parachutist has deserted and the next man from the local reserves is unsuited for the task, how can I attack without troops—

On his desk Tanicka's poem, the telegram, and the envelope from Prague, did we dream it or did a ray of sunlight really fall on the blue-gray metal, the Zeta flashed a gleam and Jacek stopped short in the middle of the room, CAPTAIN, SIGNAL RECEIVED, carry out a paratroop recruitment drive, the escalation will culminate in a mass parachute drop, and already Jacek was pressing the corresponding keys of the newly assigned Zeta:

```
28-YEAR-OLD wom. off. work., divor. with
3-year-old charm. daught. and own furn. 1st-
cat. apart. seeks partner, key word: "LIVE!"
```

and then on the envelope the address of the Personals section of *Prace*, Jacek tenderly caressed the aviation-blue machine, *zeta* is the last letter of the alphabet, and he stopped to reflect: flight wouldn't be as easy as an ocean voyage, the failures up to now dictate a revision of the old maps, one must get to know the squadron assigned and, most important, become familiar with the terrain to be conquered, to learn where the stores of oil are, where the communications, the junctions, and the dams, where the artillery units and where the staff, perhaps our conjectures concerning the territory are incorrect—

V — seventeen

A large yellow envelope, METERED MAIL, was already there, not much more than a pound, Jacek tore open the paper and from the large yellow envelope a stream of dozens of variously colored smaller ones splattered onto his desk, on all them in different hands and in different places the same thing:

Live! 64063–v

Jacek piled up the letters and then he counted them, only 62, that's because of Lenicka, he took his letter opener out of the drawer and began to open the paratroopers' applications:

Dear Lady!
  I read your ad in Prace and I'm in just as bad a fix as you, my girl is six, only we don't have a 1st-cat. apartment and that is certainly a basis and condition for
  Dismissed, next—

Madame:
  Your advertisement today strongly attracted my interest. Although I'm 44 and I limp a little on my right leg

Dear Comrade!
  I'm also an office worker, to be precise the assistant chief of the top contract division of an important consumer co-op handling the manufacture of durable feed-stuffs and first of all

My three children, Svatopluk, Zdislava and Zaboj

I am taking the liberty of answering you. Please send me the precise dimensions of your apartment, i.e., including bathroom, WC

I'm 34 a yung felow you see and lively to. I'm surching for a lively girlfriend I've got a boy but they dont make me pay for him

I'd like very much to meet you and I'd like your picture. For the time being I don't enclose my own for understandable reasons. I'm big in build, the photo and a detailed description of the apartment with information on whether a garage can be built nearby

I too was deceived and I believed in her so much. I'd like to believe again, or at least hope, for what can life do to us now

still feel young and I'd like to try a third time if the apartment isn't on the top floor   We don't have anybody to do the cooking and the two children need warm food not yet forty   I'd be glad to move   two children also deceived and so   By a first-category apartment we surely both understand it to include central heating, a bathroom with hot water and a gas or electric They need a mama   in your apartment we fix our food all sorts of ways   in your apartment   with your apartment   your apartment

With a sigh Jacek classified the letters into acceptable, marginal, and discards, he transferred the sheets from one pile to another like cards and sighed more and more, at one point the acceptable pile had vanished entirely and everything was in the discards, the divorced, the retired, and the fathers of several children were only interested in a cook and someone to take care of their children, and all of them wanted to marry the apartment, what a pitiful squadron of mercenaries and retired paratroopers, Jacek drank strong coffee and with a cigarette he sat down at the blue-gray Zeta, he prepared 16 draft calls, first of all some recruitment slogans, From a hundred letters just your letter revealing real intelligence and an unusual you surely won't be disappointed, then a tactical comment, for reasons which you will certainly appreciate I am compelled for the time being to act for the woman advertising, and a Napoleonic ("Soldiers! I will lead you on to fertile plains...") conclusion: for contentment, happiness and a new life, and he dropped 16 letters into the mailbox.

Only 11 replies, of which 2 broke off the correspondence (is that office worker of yours literate? Unfortunately I have a lot to do with the authorities and I wouldn't be a bit surprised if, and I've turned your letter over to the police to check up on the suspicious circumstances), what poverty compared with the music of the women's offers, but the existence of a go-between had awakened fears even among eight of the nine acceptables, two had procedural doubts why doesn't she write herself, she wouldn't have to give her name does she really know you're acting for her in this rather important business, but one remaining one felt, on the contrary, joy I am a passionate adherent of psychoanalysis and find it a fascinating idea to penetrate through an intermediary who is an intimate friend, from all nine acceptables, however, came nine tidal waves of insistent questions

I'd like to believe in spite of this, but I'd be happy to find out more please write in more detail about her character, interests and preferences does she prefer company or being

alone? what are her ideas about marriage and does
she really want is she lively or quiet? the main
thing is her interests does she like to read and if
so which present-day Czech authors her character is she sincere? does she like classical
music and specifically what without using big
words describe her personality and inclinations
truthfully and specifically her attitude towards
nature about history and cultural monuments
specifically and in great detail describe her
character and her significant features more
about her psychic personality and in more detail
what she expects from her partner and what she
longs to give her ideals and her dreams what
more specifically she actually means by the slogan
"Live!" what she's really like—

the territory put up for annexation, what its mountains are
like, its lowlands and rivers, how it is populated and what
mineral wealth it has, what fauna and flora, what grain it
grows and what vegetables, how terribly little we know
about the evacuated territory—

In the bathroom an alternately hot and cold shower,
Jacek then unscrewed the shower head and turned the
swift stream straight on his body, hot-and-cold showers
whip you up to peak efficiency, and with his hair wet he
sat down again at his flying machine, Dear Sir, thanks
for your I assure you completely she is
fond of company, but not even while alone
does she she is lively and at the same time
restrained she likes to read and reads
almost exclusively present-day Czech writers
"What present-day Czech writers do you know?" Jacek
asked Mija over the telephone, "... what's that? *The
Dictionary of Czech Writers*... aha... in the town library,
many thanks and so long," you can't do it all in one day,
so then the next, Jacek pulled the sheet out of the type-

writer and again, Dear Sir, thanks for your   I can assure you completely   she has an intense interest in history and knows all about the Moravian rulers Jost and,   **hell, which other ones were there, how do I cross out the** and,   **and were they really rulers, wish I'd asked her sometime, but there wasn't time, Jacek pulled the sheet out of the typewriter and so let's just answer the things we know about Lenka,** classical music   **probably not, well, we used to listen to it, but not so much anymore,** attitude towards nature,   **she likes gardening, of course, and she used to go to the woods with me, good God, why did she give that up, of course it was the child, but then Grandma was always happy to,** is she lively or quiet?   **she's quiet and she's lively too,** in detail describe her personality   her interests   her character   truthfully and specifically   her character and her significant features   about her psychic personality more and in more detail   what she expects   **I don't know** what she longs to give   her ideals and dreams   **I don't know** what she really means   **I don't know**   what she's really like   **I DON'T KNOW HER AT ALL,** Jacek bit his cheeks and twisted the sweaty hair on his temples as painfully as he could, the damp of the shower had now been replaced by sweat, can I still give a profile of MY OWN WIFE, eat this paper if you can't do at least ten lines, Jacek pushed another sheet into the machine as if the last cartridge into a barrel pointed at himself, Dear Sir, thanks for your   I can assure you completely   and now for your question as to what she's really like   She's

The keys of the typewriter were like forty jeering eyeballs, for a long time Jacek pushed the space bar with his finger and finally he took out the sheet and began to thoughtfully chew it up.

"We can go to bed," Nada said in the room overlooking

the Decin harbor, "but even then you have to answer one very important question..."

"Truthfully and specifically...," Jacek whispered, and he shivered.

"The co-op I applied to wants to know our wedding date. If it isn't this year or next, they'll cross us off the list."

"But Nadezda, isn't getting married too conventional..."

"It's insane, but we'll sleep better in a first-category apartment than we do in this dump. I'll buy an apron for the first time in my life and a cookbook and a feather-duster and a vacuum cleaner—I'm looking forward to the first time I vacuum *our first carpet* as if it were my wedding night, those I've already had—you'll be amazed what all will pick its way out of me, why you're looking at me as if you were seeing me for the first time—oh Jacek, you still have so much to learn about me..."

"I can't catch the afternoon train, but *we* can still catch it—"

"But first that date—"

At last the Ford Taunus came out of Tina's room and unceremoniously Jacek squeezed into the still open door, "You were standing outside the door—" comb in hand, Tina was astounded, she was painfully beautiful and torturingly disheveled, "But you kept him here a whole eternity!" "Not at all, he flew out of here like a bat out of hell..." "Darling, couldn't you really give it up, I'll pay you out of my salary—" "With every cent you're paid we'd have to save for years to buy that gas station, lover boy!"

"... you're like a little boy, like a schoolboy...," Tina whispered, caressing Jacek's head on her lap, "but it'll soon be over, never fear, I want that gas station mainly so we'll be rid of this bar for good and rid of all this, believe me, more for that than for the money, someday I want to be the guest and not one of the staff, to have an honest profit instead of two-bit tips and crumpled hundred-notes, and most of all I want to have my peace of mind and like a banded middle-class wife go afternoons for my coffee with whipped cream and cake with a husband who has the same band I've got, two bands they take off only in the coffin—"

"They opened a new café on Strekov Hill last month," said Lenka, wringing a rag out into a bucket, "and if it stays rainy, we could go there sometime…"

"For coffee with whipped cream and cake!"

"That's it! So let's go?"

"But you could have gone there long ago, when I was away, with the little one, or Grandma could have stayed with her…"

"But I want to go with *you*—"

Jacek watched Lenka bending over, how little you have in common with that illegal hard-currency whore Tina, she should have a traveling husband, one who brings home lovers and suitors to her apartment—but what do we really know about you, behind the wall the vacuum roared in the bedroom and Lenka was singing to its roar, in the bedroom *our first carpet*—Jacek was afraid to go into the bedroom after Lenka, I AM NO LONGER SURE WHOM I WOULD MEET THERE—

V — eighteen

Out of the thickening dusk stairs ran up to our bench in front of the pink house and on all the tiny platforms in front of the houses with their shining facades quiet couples, "Happiness is such a strong feeling," whispered Hanicka Kohoutkova. "I've read many leading writers, Czech and foreign, but so far none of them has ever given an accurate description of... Jacek, which month will we hold the wedding?"

"Do you need the date this evening?"

"No. But soon. I have to have a white dress made and there'll be lots of shopping to do. Dad would like to combine it with a slaughtering—"

"That would probably be best..."

On the meadow in front of the forest ranger's Jacek pitched a tent with Arnostek, they snuck through the high grass to the garden, burst out with the battle cry of the Iroquois, and took Janicka captive, Lida tried to ransom her with a bilberry tart, Arnostek accepted the ransom but Jacek grabbed the little girl and ran off with her into the woods, she held on to him with her little arms and legs, "Cawwy me, Uncle, and we'll build a gingebwead house in the woods and we won't wet Mummy and Awnostek come—"

Jacek and Lida sat on the stump and the children's faces in the window above them, "Go to bed, children—" Lida called, "or Uncle won't come anymore," and the little faces disappeared at once. In a minute, though, Janicka's was looking out again, "Can Uncle come give me a kiss?" "You know he'll come." "And can Uncle tell a stowy?" "You know he will."

"She's so terribly attached to you," Lida whispered, touched, "Arnostek too, but he's a boy and doesn't show it, but Janicka— Jacek, she'll be going to school soon and

I'd be so happy… if she had your name, Arnostek can keep the Adalsky name, but Janicka could have yours, at least one of them would…"

"Today we've got to go to the publisher's," the beaming Mojmira called out in the Brno Main Station cafeteria, "and you don't know why, but I'll spill it to you: we're going to work together there, I'll do translations and you'll choose and edit them. Jacek, do you know what it's like to earn money every month on the dot, precisely on the day? It must be a fantastic feeling…"

Jacek and Mojmira walked out of the station in the midst of a hurrying crowd, "… it's fun to work for a publisher, you get to know a million terrific people," Mojmira was ecstatic, "and together we'll earn almost four thousand— month by month the whole year long and the next year and all the time—with our first paycheck we'll buy a suckling pig, for New Year's half a pig, and every summer we'll go to the seashore—Jacek, let's go get married right now—"

Right across the street the enormous airline building and out of its heavy chrome swinging doors came three officers in flight uniforms—friends, I've already sent out nine calls to mobilize and day after tomorrow I'll deploy my paratroops, a blue-gray airline minibus pulled up in front and the captains rode off, I am ready to go with you—

Of the nine, only five paratroopers heeded the mobilization order and presented themselves in the Zdar Café at 4:00 P.M on the succeeding specified days, "And otherwise it's quite simple," Jacek repeated to Tuesday's, Wednesday's, Thursday's, Friday's (Saturday and Sunday were days of rest) and Monday's paratroopers, "so let's go around to the development right now, without obligation you can have a look at the mother and daughter from a distance, and if you're interested I'll take you up to the apartment as a friend from the train…"

"I had a hunch she didn't know anything about it…"

Tuesday's whispered, a faded balding blond with fingers stained walnut-brown from nicotine, he drank up his Plzner beer and slunk away without paying or saying goodbye.

"So let's go!" Wednesday's said emphatically, a sweaty and smelly divorced guy with a large build and a forehead running straight back into a graying wire thicket, the whole endless trip on the streetcar he was doggedly silent and in mounting fear Jacek looked askance at his gloomy profile, wasn't it a bit crazy to bring this brute home to Lenka... and Lenicka—

"Excuse me, I've changed my mind, this isn't really the way to do it—" would have sufficed to call off the frightful deed, anyway it doesn't have to be this one, we have three more in reserve, Jacek thought feverishly, but he said nothing and already they were standing at the observation post behind the substation, between the buildings with their delicate pastel shades where the broad road leads past the playground to our home—

"So which windows is it?—" the fellow growled.

"There, over the left entrance on the third floor...," Jacek whispered in a choked voice.

"And when's she get home?"

"She comes home every day around five..."

"What?!"

"Around five... she comes home then..."

But today it was half-past five, the two figures, large and small, along the walk in front of the wall as if for an firing squad, "There—" Jacek pointed with a concentration of his last efforts, Lenka was dragging two heavy bags and Lenicka, with her doll, was holding on to one of the handles of one of the bags.

"The one with the bags and the brat?"

All Jacek could do was nod, Lenka bent her head to wipe her forehead on her sleeve and Lenicka ran ahead home...

"And now we're supposed to go and pretend we've just

come in from the train...," the fellow grumbled, Jacek just stood there, "—for that I ain't got the nerve," the fellow whispered, he turned and cleared out, Jacek took a deep breath and ran across the grass in the opposite direction, "Lenka...," he called from afar, "darling... wait for Daddy—"

A kiss for Lenka even before they were home, "You know what, let's go to that new café for coffee with whipped cream—no, let's make today a home day and not go anywhere..." "At least carry these bags upstairs," said Lenka.

And today we'll have a good romp with Lenicka, till evening or even later, she can go to bed an hour late for a change, "Darling, tell Daddy what you'd like and you'll have it—"

"I want a wowwypop!"

"But we'd have to take the streetcar again..."

"I want a wowwypop!"

"You'll have five of them, but now let's go home..."

Jacek set the little girl down on a step, he bent over and tried to take off her little shoe, it was terribly tight, he jerked a little and Lenicka started screaming, "It's too small for her...," Jacek told Lenka, "No it isn't, it's just that you've gotten out of the habit," Lenka sighed.

"So what do you want to play with Daddy tonight?"

"Opticle course and house."

"First let's do the obstacle course...," and already Jacek had laid two mattresses down flat on the floor and a third one vertically between them, the little girl climbed over it, fell down, and again climbed up, just then the bell rang and in the foyer neighbor Mestek's voice could be heard, he's come to change the washer in the faucet, "Uncle gwab me—" cried Lenicka, and she ran off after him, "Little one, stay here with Daddy—," but the little one was already off after Mestek and was working on the plumbing with him, "And now wet's go see Punchinjudy—"   "Where is it she wants to go?" asked Jacek. "Every Wednesday they have a children's theater here," said Lenka, "and Jarda Mestek has been good enough to take her when you're away." "We won't go today, Lenicka," Mestek said, "your Daddy's here, see!" "I'll give a show for you myself—" Jacek shouted, and already he was pulling out the puppets of the water-goblin, the princess, and the king, "I want to go with Uncle—" the little one screamed, and she smashed the poor puppets with her fist, the king's head and his crown flew off and out of his neck popped a copper spring, pitifully Jacek stood over the beheaded monarch, "You'll spend the evening with your Daddy," Mestek said sharply, and he went away, Jacek caught the girl and carried her to the living room, "Don't want opticle course!" she screamed, and she struck her Daddy on the face with her tiny fists, how strong she is for her age, she tore away from him and pushed with all her weight against the obstacle course until she'd demolished it, "—I want to go with Uncle!" "I'll take the kitchen spoon to you—" Lenka threatened, and the squealing Lenicka rolled around on the floor as if in a fit, struck her head against the carpet, and turned the color of raw meat, "... that's what happens when you're away all the time," said Lenka.

"Some jobs demand it, and what if I were a sailor or a pilot—"

"You've got it tough...," Lenka remarked, and Jacek tried for the last time to lift his daughter up, she scratched him under the ear till the blood came and then administered what was almost a kick to the groin, "So go along with Uncle—" Jacek said decisively, and Lenicka jumped right up and was running off, Jacek rubbed his groin over the ruins of the obstacle course, thanks, my clever little one, for this warrior-like support.

"... and otherwise it's quite simple," Jacek repeated on Thursday at four o'clock in the Zdar Café, "so let's go around to the development..."

"But it's a real horror story what you're telling me," Thursday's paratrooper said excitedly, curd white with goggly watery eyes (an interest in history and cultural monuments), "in essence you're offering your wife to me, though you're not even divorced yet and you're still living with her even!"

"That's only a question of time, you understand, I've been transferred to Brno and I'd like to leave everything in order here before I go."

"Does your wife know anything about the ad?"

"Of course not, otherwise she would have placed it herself."

"What makes you think she'd be interested in another husband?"

"What makes you think she won't need one?"

"So this is what I came here from Teplice for! I hope you'll at least pay for my round trip and for the waste of my time at the going rate for business travel. And my double coffee and the double cognac I'm about to order—I should have a whole bottle, tonight I won't be able to sleep—"

CAPTAIN, THE PARATROOP RECRUITMENT DRIVE IS COLLAPSING, enough reason to abandon it, but when wasted chances torment you so painfully, and after them neurosis and depression, "... so then let's go around to the development," Jacek repeated mechanically on Friday at 4:00 in the Zdar Café, "so that without obligation you can have a look at the mother and daughter from a distance..."

"I'm a passionate adherent of psychoanalysis," said Friday's paratrooper, Tomas Roll, a dwarf with tousled black hair which seemed to be fleeing in horror from his strangely crumpled face, "and I find it a fascinating idea to penetrate through an intermediary who is an intimate friend, even a husband—"

As if hypnotized Jacek observed his eager counterpart, but when the kind and fatherly Mestek and the elegant and perfect N. Hradnik have failed us, what hope can there be with this bungled imp, "It's awfully far away, it's the last stop on the streetcar, so let's let it go for another day...," Jacek said, "No trouble, I've got my car here—," the tiny man had a tiny bright red Fiat 600, he dragged Jacek into it and shortly before five they were standing at the observation post behind the substation.

"Sun, light, air...," croaked the dwarf as he greedily looked the development over, "you know, I've spent my whole life in a basement with a window looking out on a row of trashcans—and which are the windows of your dwelling, please?"

"There, on the third floor," Jacek pointed, now quite apathetically.

"It's a fine habitation...," Tomas Roll nodded.

"And here they are at last, the woman with two bags and the little girl running after her..."

"A beautiful, fascinating woman and a really charming little girl," the midget grew excited, "you know, I like women with good, sturdy figures and I'd never— and I'm awfully fond of children and I couldn't—"

Some of Lenicka's friends were playing in the sandbox, so Lenka let her play outside, Lenicka climbed up onto the concrete rim and leaped down, "Look how the nimble little girl climbed up there all by herself—" Tomas Roll sentimentalized, "and now she's going to jump, you'll break your leg, you little rabbit, hop—did you see her? And now she's climbing out again—hop! Boy, she's a real ballet dancer—you've got to let me see her closer up, you've really got to!"

And the tiny paratrooper ran out of the hideout by himself, he limped, and Jacek had to run ahead of him to keep him from climbing into the sandbox, "Little girl—" he called to Lenicka, and she came, today charming to the letter of the ad, she had evidently taken a fancy to the midget as to a new toy, they made faces at one another,

Lenicka made a curtsey and even sang a song "from kindagaden" *The Wittle Fish Swims in the Water*, Tomas Roll was thrilled and, "Come, little one, Uncle Roll will show you his car—"

Lenicka crawled through the red Fiat and sobbed with ecstasy, and she was even more ecstatic when the midget taught her to make honk-honk on the horn, "If you would be so kind, Mr. Jost, and show me how to pick the girl up safely and properly..." "Not that way, turn her face towards you, put one arm under her arm this way, the other under her bottom, you've got it, and there she is sitting in your arms...," Lenicka was sitting in the midget's arms, for his size he had surprisingly long, strong arms, like a gorilla's, he pouted with his lips to make a horrifying grimace and Lenicka ran her finger over his mouth to see how Uncle Woll did that with his wips, they both liked it so much that Jacek had to tear them apart and by sheer force stuff the imp into his car, but its honk-honk was still to be heard when the Fiat was no more than a speeding red dot far off down the highway.

"...the mother and daughter from a distance," Jacek repeated on Monday at 4:00 at the Zdar Café, rested and with new strength from the weekend, "and if you're interested I'll take you to the apartment as a friend from the train."

"Why not," said Monday's paratrooper, the last of the five to be mobilized, an obsequious, snake-like fellow with cruel yellowish-gray eyes, evidently an experienced, ruthless bastard, and when he'd obtained detailed information concerning the apartment, its furnishings, Lenka's salary, and Grandma's pension, he stubbed out his cigarette and grinned, "So what's keeping us?"

With mounting distaste, Jacek observed his so easily won-over counterpart, you've got the swing of it, you must be a real sharpie, too much so—

"It's five already—" said the paratrooper, and he tapped

on his watch as if impatient for the jump, but you're in too much of a hurry to climb into my bed, to see you there with Lenka, with my love, and as Lenicka's daddy—CAPTAIN, THE TASK IS BEYOND MY CAPABILITIES—

"So what's doing, mister?"

"Nothing," Jacek sighed. "Do you like cognac? Waiter!—A double cognac for this gentleman and for me soda and ice, and I'll pay for everything."

With Lenka to the new café on Strekov Hill for coffee with whipped cream and cake, the Josts exchanged news of the troubles that had befallen their two firms and their mutual acquaintances, of whom there were hardly more than five in all, and then they read the torn old magazines under the ugly, yellowed polyvinylchloride covers hung on the walls of this unsuccessful enterprise where you had to wait half an hour for coffee, they brought it cold and the icing on the cake was turning, "Daddy don't go way—" Lenicka babbled automatically behind her netting like a wind-up toy, then she yawned and fell asleep.

In the office a new plastic cover on the blue-gray Zeta and in addition to unanswered letters from Mojmira, Hanicka, and Lida, Anna had written:

Jacek,

You probably don't know—I didn't—what a certain man named Benoit did a hundred years ago with snails... He paired off fifty snails, left each pair together for some time so that they would get used to each other, then he painted identical letters on their shells and one of the pair he sent off to America, while the other one remained in Paris. After a certain time that devil Benoit exposed snail A in Paris to an electric shock—and snail B in America reacted the same way at the same moment... BE GLAD YOU'RE NOT A SNAIL!

Fists pressed to his temples and a tormented face, for three days now they walked through the technical division on tiptoe and better not to go there at all, "Jacek's got neurosis," and on the horizon the colorless prairie sky of depression, at 1:59 Jacek got up mechanically and at 2:00 the shriek of the siren propelled him out, right outside the gate a bright red Fiat gleamed and in a blue-gray waterproof jacket Tomas Roll leaped out of its little door, CAPTAIN—

"Climb in at once!" cried the dwarf, jumping around Jacek, and he shoved him into the door, resigned Jacek sank back in the cushioned seat behind the dashboard of the car sent for him, *Fiat* in Latin means *let it happen* and with fantastic acceleration the little car took off toward the highway to the mountains.

Lke a red beetle it went in and out of the mountainous dunes of yellowing late summer grass, while again and again the large man and the small one in agreement went in and then in disagreement went out of the waves of yellowing grass, "... we must know how to stimulate Lenka's interest, her rebirth, her conceptions, her desire," the importunate reader of ads insisted, "we must find someone who's succeeded at it and find out how he did it, we need a model, an example, a precedent..."

"Vitenka Balvin failed," Jacek whispered, "so did Mestek and Nora Hradnik..."

"Didn't Lenka love anybody before she married you?"

"It all went out the window the day we met..."

"She must have loved you very much, but no matter, we'll figure out how to bring this to a head. We've got one person left who didn't fail..."

"Who could that be?"

"You yourself! And now to business—how do you do it?"

"How do I do what?"

"Not fail. Let's look at the details: afternoons you come home from work, well—"

"Very rarely nowadays... Well, in the afternoon I come home from work, I say a couple of meaningless sentences to Lenka, I play a while with Lenicka, but Grandma does that more, then we eat, we watch TV, I go to bed and go to sleep before Lenka comes to bed, only on Saturday— and then not every week, well, and on Sunday we take Lenicka into bed with us and after dinner we go with Grandma to the zoo. Sometimes we go to the garden, the other day we went to that new café on Strekov Hill..."

"Don't tease me, you must give me all your techniques and recipes, your strategies and tactics, your dodges and tricks—"

"But I really..."

"Do you mean to say that you're loved just because you're you? It almost looks that way, but no matter, we'll simply imitate you. So let's go—what are you like, anyway?"

"Me?... Quite normal... though in some respects perhaps... on the whole... but then not quite... on the other hand, of course... to tell the truth... still... there are certain but it's hard... I think I'd... I don't think I'd... more or less..."

"You'll be forced to train me in your image," in the car Tomas Roll grinned and pressed on the accelerator, "but first, sir, what is that image made of, anyway, besides some canvas, a frame, and a hook for hanging up?"

V — nineteen

Jacek hurried across the excavated plain past the ten-
and twelve-story buildings shining above him with
their fresh facades, the first white curtain in our fourteen-
story has appeared on the eighth floor left, "We'll be the
last to hang ours up," Anna laughed in the white-and-blue
kitchen, in the corner an electric refrigerator purred
quietly, the apartment all ready to be moved into, only
by the door to the bathroom a big hole in the wall, "I had
them move the outlet higher so you wouldn't have to use
an extension cord when you shave... Just so I don't forget,
yesterday I got a call from the prime minister's office,
when are you going to take over the chemical department
at the information institute—"

"Anci, you know, I'm not really sure I'm up to that..."

"Don't be crazy, before you an ordinary druggist had the
position and he was in it eleven years... you just have a
little inferiority complex, right? Don't be afraid, Jacek,
you're really too good for a sinecure like that, usually they
sweep the worn-out big shots into those jobs, but you've
got something upstairs and you can make something of it,
you'll show them what you're worth..." TAKE IT DOWN,
DWARF, THERE'S MORE WHERE THAT CAME FROM.

"...and Comrade Dr. Mach was very satisfied with the
goose, though he didn't show it," Hanicka Kohoutkova
told him in the evening on the bench in front of the pink
little house. "Dad thinks you're going to live here under
his wing till you retire and he wants to have a serious talk
with you soon— Jacek, you haven't asked him for my hand
yet!"

"Have you thought it over well, Hanicka?"

"Very thoroughly. At the end of the school year we
always prepare reports on all the pupils, on their conduct,

personality, potential for development, talents, character traits, a complete profile. Every year over thirty reports, several hundred pages. I'm good at doing profiles."

"And what's mine?"

"You're an ideal husband. Mama says so too." NOTE IT DOWN, MIDGET. "Because you're mature now and you've sown your wild oats."

A cigarette on the stump in front of the forest ranger's, "Wait, I have to light up—" Jacek said, he extracted his hand from Lida's clasp and the cigarette gleamed in the twilight, "You said I'm a good man, but you also said that life here isn't easy, the house, the farming, the children... Lida, I'm beginning to think seriously whether I really..."

"You're a good man and life here isn't easy, but when you love children and the forest... and if you'll love me a little bit, too..."

"Uncle come give me a kiss too!" Janicka called from the window, "March to bed!" cried Lida, "I'll grab you—where it hurts!" cried Jacek, and he ran up the stairs to the children's room, of all the children all over the world Arnostek and Janicka went to bed the fastest, but on both their faces their eyelids quivered as they artlessly tried to fool their Uncle who comes to court their Mama, Jacek stroked the apparently sleeping Arnostek and gave Janicka a kiss on the forehead, the little girl tenderly took hold of his ear so he couldn't escape her yet, "When you go way, Uncle, I've got you here on the pitcher..." "On what picture, Janicka?" "On that one there—" and the child's finger pointed towards the well-known picture of an angel guiding a little boy and girl over a broken footbridge, "—that's Arnostek and me and you—" WRITE IT DOWN, IMP!

Tanicka Rambouskova rushed out of the Svitavy station to the door of the train car with an enormous suitcase in one hand, in the other two umbrellas and a parasol, "Move over, Jacek, I'm coming along!" "But I'm going to Brno!"

"Well, I'll find some place to stay." "But the trade fair's coming and everything's full up." "So I'll sleep in the waiting room at the station." "The police'll pick you up!" "Then I'll sleep at the police station!" she kept shoving onto the train and Jacek was forced to push her off the steps, the suitcase struck her on the knee, Tanicka let go of the suitcase and stabbed Jacek in the stomach with the umbrellas and the parasol, fortunately the train was already starting up, but the return trip from Brno would be safer on a plane, "On the way back from Brno I'll definitely stop off for you, my love—" "You bastard, you disgusting old billy goat—" "Darling—" "You fiend—" YOU NEEDN'T BOTHER WITH THIS, SHRIMP.

"... and you don't write, you don't answer, do you think that for you they'll keep a job like that on ice till Christmas?" Mojmira was getting upset, "I don't feel up to it—" Jacek said, weaving his way through Brno Main Station with his traveling satchel in his hand, "but can't you read and type, you ox?!" "And as for the two of us, Mojenda, you need at least thirty people to have any fun and there's only one of me..." "If you're going to give me the gate, say so right out—" "You know so many people, people more interesting than me, so why do you think I should be—"

Mojmira clawed at Jacek's satchel and violently pulled it toward her so that he had to whirl around and face her, "And if I'm fond of you?" "Who in Brno aren't you fond of?" "But they're—hell, OK, I love you!" "Why?" "Think I know? Maybe because you're somebody different, you're not just made of cardboard, maybe because you're simply a man—" WRITE THAT DOWN, YOU WHIPPERSNAPPER, in front of the airline building across the street stood a blue-gray airport bus and a man in uniform was dusting off the seats.

In a blue-and-white room a blue-gray electric fan was humming and five men in white labcoats were gazing across a wide table somewhere over Jacek's head, "It's easy to calculate according to the Gibbs-Helmholtz proportion," the sweat-drenched Jacek completed the last question of his fellowship interview, swallowed air, and glanced stealthily at Benedikt Smrcek, who was presiding, "Perhaps that will suffice," said Bena, and the men around him murmured something, "We'll inform you of the results in writing within a week," said the institute secretary, "Wait in the anteroom—" Bena added, and Jacek got up, bowed smartly, went out the door into the anteroom of aluminum and plate glass, and with a feeling of relief sank into a foam shell on metal legs.

From a pile of magazines on an asymmetrical table a recognizable face smiled out at Jacek from the cover of *Atomic Technology,* on a strange-looking little balcony in a forest of cables our château tennis player and the master of two billiard tables with the high-protein diet, Jozef *completing the preparatory phase for the final stage of thermonuclear synthesis,* we dined together that day and what have you accomplished in the meantime and what have I accomplished, but already now they're deliberating whether to take me on as a soldier in your Grand Army—

Five men in white labcoats passed through the anteroom, Bena came last and slowed down till the others had disappeared, "The Party, the Union, and the Scientific Council still have to give their blessing," he smiled. "That means—" Jacek took a deep breath, "I voted for you," replied Benedikt the Great, "of the seven you were the best. Now all you've got to do is bore your way in—" "Like a laser beam—" WRITE IT DOWN, IMP!

From under the daybed Nada pulled out a box as big as a suitcase and from under tissue paper a blue-gray vacuum cleaner gleamed, "... and it's got a whole bunch of attachments with brushes and without them, this nozzle is for sucking dirt out of cracks, see, and what a beautiful color..."

"A wonderful color—" "Don't touch it! It's for the new

apartment, for the time being we'll only look at it, a wet rag's enough for these rotten old planks, it isn't worth buying carpeting for this place...," and tenderly Nada wiped off the attachments and the body of the machine, covered them with paper, and pushed them back in again, kneeling as before a monstrance.

"Why you?" Nada grinned. "A woman's got to marry someone, so why not you?" IMPORTUNATE ADVERTISER. "Besides, I'll be twenty-four next year and my pelvis is beginning to stiffen—it hurts then, you know." ARE YOU TAKING THIS DOWN? "And now come to bed—you've only got a few months till the long intermission... with a child we can get an apartment faster!"

The bell sounded for the last funicular down, the tourists paid and left, the big white Mercedes 250S strolled right up to the tap, casually looked around the empty bar, and roughly pulled Tina toward him, by the window Jacek put his hands over his face, a noise, the white giant tried to pull the golden-orange Tina over the counter and Jacek jumped in through the open window, "Jacek—" Tina cried, "see this gentleman out!" and Jacek rushed through the bar to the counter, "Heraus, du Saukerl!" he roared with gusto, and then he corrected himself, even more cheerfully, "I mean—HINAUS!"

Tina tossed the keys into the office, in full stride she untied her apron and tossed it over a chair, she took Jacek by the hand and *on the double* let's catch the funicular, on the seat together they were borne aloft over clearings and forests and on each pylon a jerk up and then a drop down and on the next pylon the count was down one again, in Bohosudov they serve coffee with whipped cream and cake right by the bus stop, Tina carefully wiped her fingers and drew out a small blue etui, on the black velvet two golden bands, "Just take it," she smiled, "it isn't legally binding and for my business it's better to have one than not... carry it in your wallet with your change..."

"... and you're as insanely jealous as Othello, Jacek."

"But not a bit where Lenka's at stake."

"You trust her," Tina sighed, "and that's a greater sign of love than being angry that she's fooling around with someone else or afraid that she's enjoying it more than with you..." YOU DON'T HAVE TO TAKE EVERYTHING DOWN, MY DEAR SIR—

In front of our building on the rim of the sandbox Tomas Roll, dressed in a black sweater and black jeans, like a little devil in the circle of children having a wonderful time, in his hand a glass ball filled with water, in the water a mountain, and when you shake it up snow starts to fall on the mountain, Roll winked at Jacek and gave the ball to the ecstatic Lenicka.

"Who's he?" asked Lenka, pointing at the dwarf from the kitchen window. "He told me he knows you well..."

"He said that?"

"Those very words. When he tried to pull Lenicka into his car I ran out to complain, but he was very well behaved and he apologized, he said you'd given him permission to play with her. Did you?"

"I came close to hiring him for that."

"I hope you didn't, but he is touchingly fond of children and he's lots of fun—"

"Depends on how you take it. If you'd like I'll ask him in."

"Why not," Lenka laughed. "You know, Jacek, the wonderful thing about you is you're never jealous..."

MR. ROLL, MOST RESPECTED SIR, "I trust you," Jacek whispered, "and that's a greater sign of lo—" DON'T WRITE THIS DOWN and bring me back my child right away, "Lenicka!" Jacek roared out the window, "Come home!" the little girl was playing with the imp's glass ball and didn't want to come home for anything in the world, "You must always listen to your Daddy—" croaked the dwarf, deftly and easily he picked the little girl up in his gorilla-like arms, he was extremely easy to train, and he carried her to Jacek in the doorway, "Please come in—" Lenka smiled at him and Jacek had to introduce them, Tomas Roll kissed Lenka's hand and she took it very nicely, Grandma served him butter cookies on a tray and Lenicka pulled him away to show him her toys, it's a wonder the three females start a fight over him, and then the dwarf outdid himself, he turned somersaults and walked through the kitchen on his hands, the apartment turned into a vaudeville theater and Jacek himself yielded for a time to the charm of the little acrobat, the clown, and then suddenly he clapped his hands, "That's enough—"

With a cartwheel Tomas Roll again stood on his legs, bowed and scraped, and obligingly disappeared, Jacek stood by the window and pressed the warm little body against his own, the black imp jumped into his red car and drove off with a loud honk-honk through the pastel-colored buildings of the development, "Daddy, when will Uncle Woll come again—"

"Never, little one, never fear..." "But Daddy—," Trost appeared in the window across the way with his child in his arms, as if on purpose stuck into a denim shirt faded to a blue-gray, CAPTAIN, ARE YOU MAKING FUN OF ME, OR IS THIS A WARNING SIGNAL IN MY MIRROR—

Jacek walked through his office and impatiently looked at his watch, when will they come, alcohol is as necessary as milk today, finally Vitenka Balvin entered the room with Petrik Hurt staggering behind him, Jacek shoved at him, for his signature, a red issue slip for our 300 grams of absolute alcohol, Petrik's hand was shaking so that he couldn't hit the blank spaces, "What's the matter with him?" "He ran away from Verka and spent the night in the tow-cloth storeroom... he's been lapping it up since morning..." "But that isn't possible, from his Verka—"

Vertically, as with an engraving tool, Petrik wrote on the blank line Quantity: 3,000 and, rocking, he signed the slip, "I'm drinking my troubles away—" he said in a deep voice, "Once again I've got no place to stay..." "For the time being I've still got a place," Vitenka sighed, "but I may be worse off than you..." "You can't be worse off than me...," Jacek whispered.

"Today there won't be any sixty-forty!"

"Today no diluting!"

"We'll drink our alcohol straight!"

The murderous drink burned the throat terribly and without any delaying filtration or other detours it went straight to the neurons, "We won't be calling each other up anymore, 'Verenka darling,' 'Petrik darling,'" Petrik Hurt howled, "we won't go on the swings or for ice cream, you won't write poems about the two of us and you won't wait for me at the square by the column..."

"I can't go on like this anymore," whispered Vitenka Balvin, "one half of the apartment an amusement park and bordello, the other a cell for solitary confinement, that's how our improvement has ended up—you don't realize, Jacek, what you've got at home, every time you get up and go to bed you should kneel and pound your head against the floor in gratitude..."

"Vitenka, do you really think you'd get a kick out of playing dad and, instead of going to the woods with Milenka Cerna, taking Mom and the kid to the zoo every Sunday..."

"In three weeks Milenka Cerna's a bore, in four she's poison, and in five it's total despair—you've no idea, Jacek, what you've got in Lenka and Lenicka..."

"So I'll sign it all over to you with the apartment and the furnishings and all the papers!"

"Jacek, you're crazy—"

"I'm serious, I'd like to clear out for Brno and begin life over again. You see—I've been taken on there as a graduate fellow. Vitenka, on my knees I beg you, take Lenicka and Lenka off my hands, you aren't a midget, the apartment is first-category, it's got a balcony and a telephone, a refrigerator, a charming little girl, a TV set, and a grandma—and that's a treasure these days—wall-to-wall carpeting and in the kitchen linoleum at a hundred sixty a yard—it even goes under the sideboard where you can't see it—a thermometer and a cast of a red hippopotamus on the wall, ten Christmas neckties, all sorts of glass and china, I'll even leave you my slippers, my gardening jacket, the ficus plant, the funnels, mashers, glass spoons, saucers, spatulas, strainers, and pots... take it all off my hands or it'll drive me nuts—"

"Then why don't you get a divorce?"

"Why don't you?"

"It wouldn't do—I'm fond of Mija."

"Darling, the sun's shining here, it's shining on you too, it's shining on me as it's shining on you, let's hold hands and go for ice cream and on the swings we'll both fly right up to the sky, Verka, Petrik, Verka—the old goat, the fattened Danish cow—" Petrik Hurt roared as the siren sounded for lunch, and he banged his fist on the acrid drying puddles of alcohol, "Fellows, it was like puking to live with that cluck!"

"Talk if it helps, but you don't have to insult her..." "Why Petrik, you two have the finest marriage in all Usti..." "He'll sleep it off."

"I've slept it off already, I'm just pulling myself out of all this pink shit, fellows, you've got no idea what a hell it was, like two disabled soldiers when we'd meet and hook our artificial limbs together, we'd call one another up out of terror, we were worried the other might already be packing his suitcase, we'd both been divorced twice and all told we've attended six of our own weddings, what goes bang all of a sudden no one can patch up, but you can lie and go on acting till you're blue in the face, today you called up less than yesterday, today you came later than yesterday, you came over to me as if you didn't want to, your note wasn't as warm as the last one, and that terror makes you phone daily for an hour, jump off the streetcar before you reach the stop, and write poems about the two of us, more and more of them, phone for two hours, jump off the streetcar when it's still going full tilt, write operas about the two of us, phone for three hours, Petrik, she'd call, and she'd be looking at her watch, Verka, I would just be counting the minutes in terror— Jacek, you don't have the slightest idea what you've got at home..."

Jacek fled through the ridged mud of the Cottex court-yard, onto the bus and away along the highway, the monument with the lion, the linden with its sign, the clay path, and up the steps of stormy waves to the little beach of hotel Splendid Isolation, I HAVE NO IMAGE, BROTHER TOM, JUST BLOOD SAUSAGE—

V — twenty

Quick, down with the netting and the rough chin on her sweet little tummy, nothing's so sweet to kiss as our little one, "Uncle gwab me—" our pretty little girl calls, take her in your arms and rock her.

"Uncle don't go way—"

"I'm just going to give Mama a kiss."

"Uncle come back—"

"You know he'll come right back."

"Uncle tell a stowy—"

"You know he will!"

Lida was already warming milk for the hot cereal, "Look what I brought you—" "How wonderful, you're too kind, thanks—" and joy at an additional supply of Dutch cocoa, a water pistol for Arnostek, and a blow-up squirrel for Janicka, trampling her nightgown with her heels the little girl got all tangled up with the squirrel in the kitchen while

Arnostek liberally sprayed the walls, "To put that thing in his hand—" said Lida, "—means an immediate call to workmen to repaint the house!" Jacek laughed.

"And why did you choose to come today?" Lida asked.

"Uncle tell a stowy—" Janicka called from her crib.

"Chema made up its mind again it wouldn't raise the OMZ's balance allotment—"

"Just a second, please," said Lida, "I have to run and shut up the hens, the fox is making his rounds..."

"Uncle tell a stowy—"

"I'll just go put her to bed—" said Jacek. "So which one shall we tell, kids?"

"The sad pwince!" Janicka cried, "The sad prince!" Arnostek cried.

"Once upon a time there was a prince and he was very sad...," Jacek began.

"Because he had to wide the twain so much," Janicka whispered, and Arnostek: "Through eleven dark tunnels."

"... and in each of those tunnels a princess was walled up...," Jacek continued.

"In each of them they was one." "Eleven princesses in all."

"... and the prince rode from princess to princess..."

"And aways cwied." "Then where did he live?"

"... and he kept waiting until from the woods he would hear cwop-cwop-cwop..."

"And the auwochs'd come!" "Uncle, aren't there some aurochses in the Tatras?"

"Only in the zoo. Aurochs, little one, you're saying auwochs, aurrrochs..."

"And he was all golden—-" "But Uncle, I've seen a photo of a Tatra aurochs in the woods—" "and he said, pwince—" "But an aurochs wouldn't go into a tunnel!" and the children started to argue, "—here's your pwincess!" cried Janicka, "But which of the eleven was it?" Arnostek shouted at her, "And the pwince went boom like this!" Janicka squealed, and she hit Arnostek on the head, "And that tunnel went bang on top of him!" yelled Arnostek, and he jumped on Janicka and so because of the fairy tale fighting and tears.

Outside the window a mass of spruces pierced the morning sky with its Asiatic towers and from the wide dark-wood frame with the black ribbon the late Adalsky looked at them through the glass, on the other side of the wall a child crying, objects falling, and shouts.

"Uncle come today?"

"But he came last night."

"Uncle din't come!"

"But you've got that pistol he gave you, I mean, that squirrel. So hop into your pants!"

"Uncle put on pants!"

"Shh—Uncle's still beddie-bye and we mustn't wake him..."

"... and we mustn't wake him...," Janicka whispered on the other side of the wall, did we imagine it or did the face on the picture really move, the thirty-three-year-old forest ranger was grinning behind the glass and with horror Jacek hid his head under the pillow for his second sleep.

Outside the window the mass of spruces and across the strip of morning sky, above the Asiatic towers, a jet plane flew in supersonic silence, it disappeared behind the towers and shortly thereafter the empty blue-gray sky grew stormy, Jacek shivered, and again his head under the pillow.

"...and today I'd like to go somewhere we haven't been yet," Mojmira said as they left Brno Main Station, "Great!" Jacek agreed, "How about something sweet?" Mojmira proposed, "Coffee with whipped cream and cake!" Jacek said and burst into laughter, "Great!" Mojmira agreed, but Jacek suddenly stopped laughing, "What's the matter?" Jacek froze as he looked at the airline building across the street, did we imagine it or did those heavy chrome swinging doors really open all by themselves—

We haven't gone yet to Tomans' pâtisserie, Jacek ordered two coffees with whipped cream and Mojmira Parisian cake and cream rolls, "What's the matter now... Jacek?" "Nothing, I only imagined...," but he didn't imagine it, among the boisterous cluster of heads in the corner diagonally across, Nora Hradnik was reading the paper, now he put it down, drank his mineral water, and again vanished behind his paper sail, he couldn't have seen us—

"... and so it comes to six thousand," Mojmira prattled on and the crumbs from her cream rolls fell on her breasts, "I've taken care of the apartment, all we need is to buy a couple more things, I'd like a new rug and..."

"... and a vacuum for it..."

"Great, that would come in handy for dusting the pictures and the books...," Mojmira gibbered with chocolate-stained lips, and with greasy fingers she scratched her hair, Comrade N. Hradnik, how about this 29-year-old translator and editor, intell. no child. with own apart., take this one at least, let my holdings diminish a bit, "... do you know what we'll buy out of our first paycheck?" Mojmira whispered, "But it's plain as plain," Jacek said wearily, "wedding rings." "How'd you guess?"

Nora Hradnik suddenly laid aside his paper and got up, a pretty woman with two children came toward his table, she was maybe 28, they borrowed a fourth chair and all of them sat down at the round table, "But Jacek, you aren't listening to me at all and these things matter to a woman...," N. Hradnik had come back home and at his table the waiter was serving two coffees with whipped cream and four slices of cake, Lenicka was so fond of store pastry and so far she'd never been to a pâtisserie with her Daddy and her Mommy, "Jacek, what's wrong with you today..." "I forgot that I have to go back to Usti immediately, if I leave now I can just catch the R 7—"

Express R 7 from Bucharest, Budapest, and Bratislava was arriving two minutes early today on Platform One. "A reserved seat to Usti nad Labem—" Jacek shouted into the ticket window, he received his ticket at once and with relief rushed along the row of eccentrically numbered cars till he found his own car, No. 100, compartment G, except for two seats the whole compartment was taken, the trade fair had just opened, Jacek placed his traveling satchel up into the net, hung his beige iridescent raincoat beneath it, and as he was sitting down an air force officer entered the compartment, IS HE SUPPOSED TO GUARD ME, CAPTAIN, OR GIVE ME A MESSAGE—

The air force lieutenant, seat ticket in hand, gave Jacek a sharp look, he had the even number opposite, he placed his own light leather satchel—on duty, of course—into the net and hung his blue-gray raincoat beneath it, on his uniform the golden emblems of the air force shone, the train pulled quietly out, the officer took his seat, and he looked straight ahead.

"We're on time...," Jacek said casually, and he directed a smile of blandishment at his counterpart, the lieutenant neither returned the smile nor turned away, insolently he looked straight ahead and Jacek blushed, well, so a pilot's going by train, when you travel so often there's nothing mysterious about one trip with an officer, and angrily Jacek dug himself in behind his coat, today there's no view anyway and we know this whole stretch by heart.

In Svitavy Tanicka Jostova, in Pardubice Hanicka Jostova, Lida Jostova waiting in the woods and in Prague Anna Jostova is itching to see us, in Decin lies Nadezda Jostova, and then there's Tina Jostova in her tower, let's not forget Mojmira Jostova either, and then Jost the graduate fellow who's trying to conquer the world, you didn't stick in the two Lenka Jostovas yet, and the Jost

retreat in Ritin would make an even ten, but weren't these
ten Josts still too few, why not take out another ad—

Ta-ta-ta-dum the train went through meadows and
woods to the east and to the west, ch-ch-ch-ch it moved
slowly along the coast from beach to beach, ta-ta-ta-dum is
the dream of a man who's wide awake and ch-ch-ch-ch is
an awakening for the timid, ta-ta-ta-dum is the sign of a
weary traveling man in love and ch-ch-ch-ch is a boat
sailing to a fabled continent where one lives only for play,
hunting, and loving, ch-ch—close your eyes and repeat
after me: ch-ch-ch-ch—

At the terminal, Prague Main, Jacek waited hidden
behind his coat until the compartment was safely empty
and then he mingled with the hurrying throng, looking
around from time to time to see whether he was being
followed, outside in front of the station he stood for a
while, uncertain, we could try to ask for Lenka's white
plush, but trains don't wait and Jacek hurried by the shortest path through the park to Prague Central Station and
climbed onto the 4:45 to Berlin, as always there was time
to spare and in the corridor he leaned out the window,
behind the rail at the entrance gate a blue-gray air force
uniform seemed to flash by in the crowd, Jacek jumped
back into the corridor and banged the window shut.

Through the early Indian summer evening the train
rushed along past the sand and the white stones of the now
ebbing river, during droughts the river is at its lowest
point, beyond the empty harvested fields the copper-
colored woods of Varhost and below Strekov Castle the
first leafless trees, the first lights in the first houses of our
town, and on the express we've made it home—

Standing right outside the door were two air force
officers looking at the faces of those descending, Jacek
slunk back into the corridor and pressed his face against
the dirty wall, YOU WON'T LET ME GO HOME, CAPTAIN,

EVEN FOR A TWO-DAY LEAVE, and the train pulled quietly out along the bank of the falling river.

So the meeting with Speranza was ordained from on high, now the high command was taking responsibility for opening fire, Jacek was the first to jump off the train onto the Decin platform and he took a deep breath, but suddenly he felt the impossibility of leaving the station, minute after minute flew by, outside in front of the building Speranza was still waiting and inside the station Jacek ran back and forth, CAPTAIN, S-O-S, "This is a customs area," a man in uniform shouted at Jacek, "you have to exit that way—" and Jacek left.

Nada was waiting on the sidewalk in front of the station, just now her back is turned toward us, and the familiar air force lieutenant with the special light leather satchel, the one who got on at Brno, is looking right at us, of course it's me, the officer verified this with a short concentrated look, walked on in Nada's direction, and came up close behind her by the rail, both of them turned around and already they were walking back together towards us, he's really bringing her here, who'll fire first, all I'd have to do is press the trigger—

"There's no point in lying anymore, Nada, because I'll never marry you, I love my wife and daughter and besides them I've got six more women and two kids all along the line to Brno, why should I save up for years with you for a co-op apartment in this hole when I've got a better one in Prague, ready to move into, two more furnished ones in Brno, a family house is being readied for me in Pardubice, and I even have at my disposal a real forest ranger's lodge in the woods I love so much, why should I train as a case maker's apprentice at your Wood-Pak when I can be the head of a government office, amuse myself as a colorist or an editor, or rake in money like hay at a gas station, and besides I've been accepted in Brno as a graduate fellow, I have a girlfriend who writes poems about the two of us, and I've got two girlfriends with college degrees, I've got a simple, pretty girl who's younger than you and still a virgin and I've got an experienced Venus with skin like gold and like oranges...," all I have to do is say it, a jeep with a canvas top drove up to the sidewalk, the officer jumped in, and quickly the car drove off, CAPTAIN, WHY MUST I— "You're looking at me," Nada Houskova laughed, "as if you had something very special to say—" "Let's go to bed—" Jacek finally managed to articulate.

The next day, as if from the 4:45 to Berlin, Jacek hurried past the playground along the broad concrete road, the staircase to our apartment is once again quite a bit higher, perhaps with time it will grow up into the clouds and there will be peace and quiet, Lenka has the lights on, but what's with her that she doesn't come to greet me—Lenka was sitting in the kitchen with Grandma and the two of them were whispering with Tomas Roll.

The women didn't even stir to welcome Jacek, but the dwarf joyfully leaped up and greeted Jacek like a king, "I had to stop off in Prague...," Jacek whispered into the women's silence, "... and forgive me, Lenka, I didn't bring the white plush, but next time definitely—"

"I don't need it anymore," Lenka said softly, and behind her Grandma looked angrily at Jacek, the dwarf croaked merrily in the rude silence, and Lenicka was already asleep, don't wake her, "Get something in the pantry—" said Lenka, "we're going to the living room for a while." "You aren't even going to warm up my milk...," Jacek whispered. "Take it out of the refrigerator," said Lenka, "but it won't go very well on top of fried mushrooms!"

"On top of what fried mushrooms...," Jacek was confused, but behind the women's backs the dwarf put a finger to his lips and gestured zealously, what tricks are you up to here, Mr. Roll, what have you talked these two good souls into believing—but the dwarf was already being led by the women into the living room—or rather it

was he who was leading them, an unexpectedly efficient
paratrooper, in the living room whispers and smothered
laughter while in the kitchen Jacek drank his milk, frozen
solid as ice.

On his desk at Cottex several days' worth of mail had
accumulated, a pile of letters as if replying to an ad,
FOREST CONSTRUCTION 06 requests confirmation
your arrival by Oct. 1, by 10/1 KOLORA 04
PARDUBICE, signed *Dr. Biroj Mach*, Dear Comrade, we're
looking forward to your coming, **wrote the
TECHNICAL NEWS,** *A 20th-century Fortnightly,* it's a
great pleasure to congratulate you on your new
appointment, **Bena's RESEARCH INSTITUTE FOR
COTTON TECHNOLOGY** congratulated him, cable address
Brno RIFCOT, the 5th Citizens' Apartment Cooperative in
Decin requests the date of your wedding without
delay, **and THE COMMUNICATIONS OFFICE OF THE
CAPITAL CITY OF PRAGUE insists that** you fill out,
in your own handwriting, the enclosed application for telephone service, **from Brno his mom
and dad were inquiring whether** *they should get rid of their lodger
right away or by Oct. 1,* and I'm sending you this cargo
of memories and of my longing for the sun, may
it reflect at a sine angle and fall on your
shoulders as a hot and heavy mantle, **Anna wrote
from Prague, and Hanicka from Pardubice, that** *Mama is of
the opinion that it's good to have both children soon after the wedding,*

I am already
melted gold
which in your
hands finds
its own form

Tanicka wrote of her frame of mind in Svitavy and in
Svitavy, as in Usti,

The river in which
I drown is not enough
A deluge

a flotilla of lips come to attack like Hitchcock's Birds and
a terrifying siege one can only shoot his way out of, at a
distance it would be easier, Jacek tore the cover off his
typewriter, the blue-gray metal gleamed cold and the rattle
of its keys was like a machine gun:

```
Dear Madam:
    I can no longer deceive you. I have
concealed from you the fact that I have
been married for a long time, that I have a
good wife and a clever, pretty little
daughter. I won't leave them. Forget me and
try to forgive.
```

in six copies, the seventh to Tina by telephone, place an
order for an urgent call to the Mosquito Tower and, while
waiting for it to go through, type out six envelopes, Miss
Nadezda Houskova, Dr. Anna Bromova, Miss
Hanicka Kohoutkova, Mrs. Lida Adalska, Miss
Tanicka Rambouskova, Dr. Mojmira Stratilova
and seal up the letters and we're all finished with your
pirds, Mr. Hitchcock, and your tomfoolery, mudget, we've
fired off all the rockets and tomorrow—I'm sending them
special delivery—they'll thunder from Brno to Decin, in
Usti there's only a pygmy to deal with, DAMN IF I
HAVEN'T THOROUGHLY VERIFIED MY LOVE FOR MY
WIFE AND MY DAUGHTER—"Happiness isn't neces-
sary," the cardinal told Fellini in a film—AND MY
UNHAPPINESS.

Jacek jumped at the ring of the phone as if it were a shot,
CAPTAIN, —"Your call to Mosquito Tower is ready," the
receiver sounded and then, "Jacek—," Tina's familiar
subdued voice, "it's good you called, I've got the gas
station, it's near Harrachov, a marvelous area for tourists,

we'll live at the Hotel Belvedere... you must come and see me this evening!"

"I'll come," Jacek sighed, on the table the six blue letters, Jacek pasted a sixty-heller stamp on each of them and locked them up in his desk, he sat down, his fists on his temples and his face tormented, "Jacek's got neurosis," and the final symptom of depression— THE IMAGE COMMISSIONED BY T. ROLL IS READY TO BE PICKED UP.

INTO OVERTIME

*Everyone will eventually
find the sort of paradise
he is able to imagine.*
    —Armand Lanoux

Part VI — Flight — twenty-one

Jacek laughed till the tears ran down his cheeks, he poured out another cognac for himself and one for Tomas Roll: "...and what was that you told them about fried mushrooms, Tom?"

"I told them about that widow of yours in Teplice," the imp grinned.

"Who? I keep a file, but I can't remember any widow in Teplice..."

"She'll never see forty again, you often go visit her instead of going to Brno, all night long you two fry mushrooms and play duets on the ocarina...," the dwarf giggled.

"But why a widow of forty..."

"It has more effect on them than a broad from a hotel or a young eighteen-year-old chick," the imp explained, with his horse's teeth he clasped the thin edge of the glass and sucked the cognac out through a gap where once an incisor had been, Jacek laughed till he choked, a widow with an ocarina is in the last analysis only a dry advertisement in comparison with an illustrated Oriental fairy tale with seven naiads, Jacek poured again and raised his goblet in a toast, "Here's to freedom, Tom—" "to the two Lenkas, my lord Jost—"

The two Lenkas came home with Grandma at dusk, every day they come home later and later, "Uncle Woll, make a circus—" Lenicka cried, the midget jumped down from his chair onto his hands and somersaulted through the kitchen and the living room, with a single wave of his monstrously strong arms he swept the mattresses and cushions from the sofa onto the carpet, nimbly he arranged them in a semicircle and with his teeth he placed the kitchen chair in front of the audience, "And what will it be, little one?" he croaked, "A show," Lenicka gasped, and she clapped her hands in joy, the dwarf picked her up and tenderly seated her, Lenka and Grandma were already seated, and the imp was serving them full goblets, only Jacek didn't feel like sitting on the floor with his chin on his knees watching those silly puppets— "They aren't silly!" croaked the pygmy, for just an instant Jacek felt the clasp of his gorilla arms and then he too was sitting on the pillow-strewn floor with a goblet in his hand.

Holding the puppets' copper wires, Roll's hands flashed over the back of the chair and on the bright seat that acted as the stage, between a china mug and a box of matches, figure after figure appeared and greeted the public, the king, the queen, the princess, and the nice old lady, "She gets eaten up by the wolf—" Lenicka cried, "—and then Wed Widing Hood comes—," but Tomas Roll was enacting a new tale, the queen and the nice old lady jumped around the box of matches and stuck one match after another into the white mug, each match required tremendous exertion and the princess was jumping around behind them like a puppy, she wanted to play with them but there was no time for play, match after match followed the hard road and dropped with great effort into the mug, the king was lying next to the chair leg and going -zzzz-, now he gets up and enters the action—no, he doesn't get up but only turns over onto his other side and goes on snoring, meanwhile match after match went up and into the mug, the little princess climbed up to the very top of the chair, then she fell down on her back like a beetle and the dwarf faithfully screeched on her account, it's nothing, one more match and, with all their efforts, the last one—just then the king jumped up and snatch! there were no more matches in the mug (the dwarf had put them back in the box) and at once the weird ballet of the queen and the old lady commenced again around the box, the princess was once again clambering up to the top of the chair, she'll fall down again in no time and by the chair leg the king was snoring again, and again match after match up and into the white mug, the princess had fallen down boom! again and the dwarf had squealed again, this time Lenicka squealed too, and now Lenicka got up and went for the king, "...he's still beddie-bye and we mustn't wake him!" the dwarf croaked, "... and we mustn't wake him...," Lenicka repeated in a whisper and then squealed out, "—that's Daddy!"

Lenka drank her glass straight down and even Grandma took a mighty slurp, from behind the chair back two powerful arms reached out and filled their glasses to the brim, Jacek didn't get any, the dwarf threw the wires of the three female figures over his arm and just by jerking his elbow kept the three figures incessantly dancing, with one hand he grabbed the king's wires and with his other he fished for something behind him, the king sat up and traveled on his bottom across the chair seat, ch-ch-ch-ch went the dwarf, ch-ch-ch-ch and suddenly hop hop, a water-nymph leaped onto the stage, a new figure, she and the king grabbed at each other and hoppity-hop a dance together, they sat down together and shoveled it in, "They're eating fried mushrooms from the Black Forest," the dwarf commented, and again he raised them for a new dance, hop hop, hop hop, and hoppity-hop, Lenka drank her glass straight down and Grandma took a mighty slurp, quick as lightning the powerful arms had filled their glasses to the brim and quick as lightning they were back behind the stage, Jacek didn't get any, hop hop, hop hop, and hoppity-hop, exhausted from this hellish dance the king plumped down on his rear and again to the sound of ch-ch-ch-ch he traveled across the seat, ch-ch-ch-ch to the white mug and again made a—

"Gwab!" screeched Lenicka, "Grab," Grandma whispered, captivated by the story, "Grab!" said Lenka, and she drank her glass straight down, and Grandma downed the hatch as well.

The king was snoring again next to the chair leg, the queen and the nice old lady were carrying match after match to the mug, and the princess was lying on her back like a beetle, "Ith the king coming home today?" the dwarf lisped.

"But he came back last night," said Lenka, and this time she did the pouring for herself, for Grandma too, Jacek didn't get any.

"Daddy din't come!" Lenicka squealed.

"But you've got your third pistol from him and I've got my fourth cocoa," Lenka called, "so hop into your pants!"

"Daddy put on pants!" cried Lenicka.

"Shh—Daddy's still beddie-bye and we mustn't wake him!" cried Lenka, "I want to wake him!" cried Lenicka, ch-ch-ch-ch—the dwarf responded and already the king was riding again over the smooth surface and here again was the water-nymph and they grabbed each other, hop, hop, and hoppity-hop, the king exhausted on his rear and ch-ch-ch-ch back to the white mug, "We won't give you any!" shrieked Lenicka, she jumped up and grabbed the cup with both hands, the king kept trying to reach it, "Go way—" squealed Lenicka, and boom! she smashed the king with her fist so hard his head flew off, the head which had only been temporarily fastened on after that last trouncing, and out of his neck popped a copper spring, "Let him gorge himself," the half-drunk Lenka clamored, and she crammed the remains of the king into the mug, "Take that—" Lenicka cried, and she and the queen beat him down into the mug, and then the imp handed her the water-nymph, and Lenicka stuffed it into the mug as well, "And both of you take that—" and she thumped them around in the mug as if it were a mortar, the six female hands took over and the fairy tale turned into a bloody bacchanalia, Jacek put his empty glass down on the carpet and clapped his hands, "That's enough!"

Obligingly the dwarf pulled up all the wires and the puppets were borne aloft, the story was almost over, so sit down again, the queen and the princess and the nice old lady were kind enough to sit.

All of a sudden clop-clop-clop and the prince was here, he kissed the queen's hand and blew a kiss to Lenicka and Grandma, the puppets grabbed each other's hands and together hoppity-hop around the mug, hoppity-hop, hoppity-hop, hoppity-hop dancing around the porcelain grave, Lenicka must go beddie-bye now, hoppity-hop and that's the happy ending to our fairy tale.

Tomas Roll tossed the puppets into a box and took Lenicka off to her crib for beddie-bye, with Grandma he picked over the rice and with Lenka he made Swiss steak, he soaked some peas for tomorrow, at the next meal he told a dozen amusing stories, after dinner he sent Grandma to bed and went off to wash the dishes and wipe up the floor.

"He's beginning to get on my nerves," Jacek whispered when he was left alone on the living room sofa with Lenka.

"You're the one who brought him home...," she whispered, we have to whisper in our house now on Mr. Roll's account, and now the imp's back in here again.

"It was an awful lot of fun," said Lenka.

"Terrific," Jacek said.

"You can never have too much fun," croaked the dwarf, "and you have to have it, even if they hang your old man—

Just sit there, I'll turn down the covers for you," and he disappeared through the glass doors of the bedroom.

"What have you got to tell me, Jacek?"

"Tomorrow I'm going to Brno and please put two white shirts—"

"Can I help with anything, dear?" they heard from the other side of the door.

"Go to bed, you've had enough with your trip," Lenka called mechanically, and then she caught herself, "Excuse me, Jacek...," she whispered.

"OK. OK now," the imp continued his tomfoolery, "Beddie-bye and good night, dear."

Lenka stared fixedly at Jacek, Jacek avoided her glance and poured himself another drink.

"Tomorrow I'm going to Brno," they heard through the door, "pack two white shirts in my satchel, and don't give me any lunch..."

"OK," said Lenka, "and don't forget to bring me the white plush!"

"This time I really won't forget," the dwarf croaked through the door.

"It's just a trifle," Lenka said, "and I don't ask anything else from you..."

"I'll bring it, really I will," Tomas Roll promised.

"You've promised it to me for so long...," Lenka whispered.

"You know how it is, when a man has to travel...," the imp sighed insincerely.

"Then don't bring it," said Lenka. "Do you hear? I don't want to give you any trouble!"

"Ch-ch-ch-ch," came from behind the door. "I'm here now, my love—but I forgot that plush again!"

"I told you I didn't want it."

"OK. OK now," the imp mocked from behind the door. "Zzzz, I don't feel sleepy yet, yesterday she couldn't... come give me a kiss! Lenunka..."

"You even told him that?" Lenka hissed from the sofa.

"Lenunka, darling...," the dwarf croaked through the door of our bedroom, luckily he couldn't have anything left to lampoon, "It's never been like this before...," croaked the imp, "... and now I'm off to Brno. Pack two white shirts in my satchel, and no lunch..."

The best cure for depression is good cognac, the depression doesn't go away but it no longer bothers you so much, Jacek and Tomas Roll were drinking cognac in the living room while in the kitchen Grandma was beating the pans as a sign of defiance, dusk was just arriving at the balcony door when the pygmy left to get another pint, but suddenly he dashed back into the living room, "Come and look at something—," with a powerful tug he raised Jacek from the sofa and pushed him into the kitchen, Grandma was pounding the lids and directly beneath the window, on the playground, the two Lenkas with Trost.

Trost was actually trying to pick up those two dear creatures, he lifted Lenicka onto his shoulders and Lenicka laughed and grabbed him by his ears, he whispered something to Lenka and Lenka laughed and shamelessly leaned his way. "What are they up to with that slob...," Jacek whispered in horror.

"As chance would have it, he's a respectable man!" said Grandma and bang! with the lids.

"Let him talk to his own Mrs. and play with his own brat!"

"But he's got his little Pavel out there, too," said Grandma, and with her dried-up finger she pointed out some kid who was Lenicka's age, "and now he's the boy's papa and mama both, for Mrs. Trostova's taken to sleeping around."

"No wonder she's sleeping around, with a jerk like him..."

"He's a respectable man!" Grandma shouted, and bang! with the lids, "You could never touch him, Jacek! As those things happen, she was transferred out of her office and put on the road and she started sleeping around, they say she took up with some Ethiopian...," and Grandma crossed herself.

"Just so he doesn't hang around Lenka...," Jacek stormed dejectedly and hiccuped, "let him place an ad..."

"It isn't easy, Jacek," said Grandma, "you're always away and there isn't even anyone to help with the laundry, now Mr. Mestek's on vacation. And Mr. Trost fixed the switch for us and made us a key for the drying room and he knocked down those boxes on the balcony so Lenicka wouldn't trip over them—he's a crackerjack with his hands, O Lord!"

"I'll knock them off him...," Jacek muttered as he was seized by a powerful attack of hiccups, the dwarf hit him on the back until it passed, at last Lenka and Lenicka came home, but only for a second, Mr. Trost has promised to take them to see the monument with the lion, which they'd never seen though he said it was very close, "Uncle Twost's got a gweat gweat big motocycle," Lenicka pointed, "wif a gweat big sidecar on it—" "I'll take you to see the lion in my car," squeaked the dwarf, "Don't want any car, want motocycle—" Lenicka screamed, and she bit the imp on the arm.

"The gentlemen are having a good time—" Lenka grinned, and she tapped her finger on the empty bottle of Georgian cognac, Jacek received a perceptible whack on the back from the dwarf, he opened his mouth but only a mighty hiccup came out, "Huwwy, Mommy," called Lenicka, "We mustn't wet Uncle Twost get way—" and the door banged after the Lenkas, Grandma clattered the lids like cymbals on Corpus Christi, the dwarf planted cruel blows on Jacek's back, and down the concrete road past the playground Trost drove off with the Lenkas, if you ever bring him into my home I'll turn on the gas, but only till it makes an explosive mixture with the air, then I'll light a

match, IF NOT ALONE, CAPTAIN, THEN I'LL MAKE THE
FLIGHT WITH MY ENTIRE FAMILY—

VI — twenty-two

Stylish pearl-gray furniture on blue shag carpets and a
bluish-silver brocade on the king-size bed, Anna nice
and tanned in a silvery dressing gown by the illuminated
mirrored cavern of the bar, and just the right music
coming stereo from two speakers, the roar, muted by the
window, of the far-off capital, and on the ceiling the
shadow play of car lights, *stay here—*

DO NOT OPEN BEFORE THE TRAIN STOPS!

Reddening wild roses around the steps up to the house,
a pure kiss, a clean white apron, four heavy antique place
settings, the clean smell of roast meat and the glass jug
with the ten-crown note on the bottom, strong tan men in
clean white shirts on red garden chairs under a green
linden in the silence of an eternally blue canopy and clean
sheets for the clean strawberry loving of purity itself, *or
here—*

NICHT ÖFFNEN BEVOR DER ZUG HÄLT!

Arnostek and Janicka in Indian headbands took Lida
captive at the edge of the woods and led her through the
tall grass to her martyr's stake, Arnostek expertly tied his
mother up with laundry cord while Janicka approached
her with a box of clothespins, she attached the first one to
the hem of her skirt, she attached the second to her shin,
"That hurts—" Lida cried, "you're leaving again, don't
go—," *how 'bout here—*

NE PAS OUVRIR AVANT L'ARRET DU TRAIN!

Tanicka's eager face turned upwards toward the window of the car, the train stops here for just two minutes,

her slender shoulders and slim body at the very start of its life, hungry for instruction, eager to give itself and to go through the entire alphabet, "Everything is so terrifically wonderful—," *here*—

NON APRIRE PRIMA CHE IL TRENO SIA FERMO!

"I'm so huungry—" cried Mojmira from the exit of Brno Main Station, right across the street the heavy chrome swinging doors into the airline building stirred, for a moment a red No. 1 streetcar passed and hid the view, we used to ride that line to and from our school, that line goes past the theater and the Kiosk to the old Luzanky Park behind my home, I have a room there all to myself, a desk and a lamp that illuminates just the surface of the desk, and on the wall a wooden saber and a globe from Dad, with a briefcase in his hand an air force officer jumped off the platform of the streetcar and was running right this way, Mojmira drew Jacek to the left toward the Petrov Cafeteria and Jacek kept looking back, the red streetcar was pulling away, he had time to jump on, and across the way the heavy chrome swinging doors into the airline building stirred, "Watch where you're going!—" Mojmira shouted when Jacek, still looking back, banged into a passerby, "That's just what I'm doing," said Jacek, and Mojmira had to drag him by force into the Petrov and up to the second floor.

"Since when do you drink red wine?" Mojmira wondered aloud when Jacek ordered some. "I was once a commissary officer in the army, and each branch of the service had different levels of cuisine. The pilots had it best: they got game, chocolate, and red wine," Jacek explained to her.

Just then two noncoms in blue-gray uniforms stopped in the entry, they had submachine guns and red armbands, and Jacek stiffened, "A patrol," Mojmira said, the airmen gave a sharp look over the room, "An escort," Jacek whispered. "They must be looking for someone who's gone

AWOL," Mojmira laughed. "I know who," said Jacek, "definitely," and he rose, "I'll be right back," he said, and he smiled at Mojmira, "I'll be back again," and he went out of the restaurant behind the two men and downstairs and out into the street, the escort stopped in front of the Petrov and Jacek ran on alone, he made his way through the crowd and rushed through the heavy chrome swinging doors, down the corridor, through the doors with wings painted on them, and up to the counter, "A ticket, please."

"Where to?" asked a girl in a blue-gray uniform.

"To Brno!—" and Jacek bit his lips, we're *in* Brno—but the girl was not the least bit surprised, and quite matter-of-factly she asked: "From where and on what day?"

"From Usti, but no, there's no airport there. From Prague. The first of October, in the morning."

The girl turned a circular ticket holder and from one of the compartments she took out a ticket and stamped it. "Ninety-two crowns," she said, and Jacek paid, well, if you want to fly you have to buy a ticket, how magically simple it all is—

On the street Jacek remembered Mojmira and shrugged his shoulders, we've got less than twenty-four hours and many matters need to be taken care of, R 7 leaves in eighteen minutes so let's hurry and look for the white plush, Jacek bounded into the store across from the station, they didn't have any white plush, next door our toy shop's display window and Jacek bounded in, "No water pistols, no squirrels, something different—" and he bought a brand new novelty, Arf-Arf, a rubber dog that's supposed to bark, there was no time to try it out because in eleven minutes R 7 pulled out, the last train in our direction.

In Prague Jacek ran through the park from one station to the other and as usual he boarded the 4:45 to Berlin with time to spare, the white plush we can buy in Brno and send it back by mail, and the train pulled quietly out along the shallows and sands of the ebbing river.

And on streetcar No. 5 to Vseborice, to the last stop, and past the playground, neighbor Tosnar was waddling out into the road with his six daughters, there are as many conceptions of paradise as there are people, the staircase up to the apartment has turned into a tall barrier, Jacek took out of his pocket the ring with its flock of keys, it's this one with the letters FAB and the dog's head, on the way out toss it into the mailbox downstairs, on the door ENGINEER JAROMIR JOST, we'll have new business cards printed in Brno, day after tomorrow is the first of October and the flight—

A diminutive ghost emerged from the darkness of the quiet apartment, "They left me here so the water the giblets are cooking in wouldn't boil away...," Tomas Roll whimpered.

"Where are they all?"

"With Trost... She didn't even buy your milk..."

Every decision destroys all doubts with retroactive effect, at least there'll be quiet for packing, Jacek drew his suitcase out of the chest like a sword from its sheath, everything in it was long since packed and the space perfectly utilized to the last inch as with a cosmonaut's luggage, Jacek took off his shoes and for the last time picked up the suede shoes he'd been married in, still the same as they'd been five years ago, a sense of horror, how awfully permanent the LEAVE things are, he trembled and cautiously put the shoes away.

Outside the door a child's voice, the little one's here, and he fished out of the black traveling satchel—it's served us now for the last time, and Jacek trembled—the box with the new toy, Arf-Arf, he tore it open and couldn't wait to try it out, the white rubber dog had a label stuck to it—

WARNING: The balloon installed in our product is made of low-grade rubber, which stiffens in freezing temperatures. In severe cold Arf-Arf will not bark. In winter or other cold a strong pressure on the front paws can tear Arf-Arf apart. Do not use our product in severe cold.   Co-op Trendex

A rattling in the doorlock and Trost was the first to enter the kitchen: "Ah—Mr. Jost!" "Ah—Mr. Trost!"

"Did you catch the 4:45 to Berlin in Prague?"

"Sure. Of course."

"You make the trip often, don't you?"

"Too often for my taste."

"The weather's nice, isn't it?"

"It is now. Look, little one, what Daddy brought you— this is Arf-Arf, you see? You push it here—this way—and see how it barks!"

"I'll bark it—" said Lenicka, she snatched Arf-Arf up in her awkward paws, she pressed—crack! and that was the end of its barking. Now Arf-Arf was dismembered and Lenicka tossed aside the new toy from Brno with a great deal of contempt.

"I asked for white plush in Brno, but they didn't have any, but—"

"You didn't have to," said Lenka. "Mr. Trost's having dinner here this evening."

"I'm not hungry," said Jacek, and with his chair and a pack of cigarettes he went out on the balcony.

A minute later a scratching on the glass balcony door, Tomas Roll snuck out and whispered: "She bought him a side of pork and now she's putting it in the oven..."

"I wouldn't mind having some," sighed Jacek, "but I couldn't stand sharing a table with that— Tom, bring me something to eat."

Nimbly the imp ran off and in a while he returned with a bottle of Georgian cognac, "Lenka sent this, Mr. Jost, she says it's your favorite food, and Trost was laughing."

"Get a glass for yourself, too," said Jacek, the dwarf ran off and at once came back with a second goblet, "They're making liver and bacon," he whispered as he poured, "and roasted potatoes. I wanted to scrape them, but Trost took the scraper away and even shook his fist at me."

"So pour some more. And then bring me the sleeping

bag from the cellar and a blanket from the bedroom, I'm
going to sleep out here tonight."

Nine-by-twelve feet of squeaking planks, but the
squeaking's ours, and a roughed-up desk made of soft
wood, but the Germans weren't the ones who roughed it
up like that, and on the plant stand the new blue-gray Zeta,
to tell the truth it has a very hard action and this elite type
is so unpleasant to read, besides that you could still read
the seventh carbon from the Urania, Jacek sighed as he
wrote up his final travel report, pulled it out of the roller,
and inserted a blank resignation form

Name of resignee: Jaromir Jost
Born: Brno 1933
Reason for resignation:

and Jacek pushed down the space bar again and again with
his finger, Good God, what can I write on the spur of the
moment, failure is a perfectly adequate and valid reason—
Petrik Hurt bounded into his office and straight to the
phone, "Verka...," he lisped into the receiver, "of course
it's Petrik, Verka, the sun just began to shine in the color
room and I rushed here to tell you—" and already Petrik
was lying again, minute after minute.

Vitenka Balvin bounded into the office and straight up
to Jacek, Jacek tore the resignation form out of the machine
and threw it in the wastebasket, "You're the light-fingered
expert here," Vitenka Balvin roared, "tell me where I can
find some green paint." "Polak's got some in the workshop. Are you tired of that purple color in your room?"
"It's the most disgusting color imaginable," Vitenka
exulted, "I'm doing the entire apartment over in green, the
entire apartment, both rooms and the entire bathroom and
the entire kitchen and the entire WC as well, it'll all be
green as May—" "I'm amazed, Vitenka, won't Mija miss
her beautiful pure cerise?" "I found her out—" Vitenka

whispered ecstatically, "I suspected it all along..." "Found her out?" "She had taken one tile off my isolation wall and she was putting her ear to it, it wasn't really all the same to her what I was up to, nor was I really all that indifferent to her antics, and I caught her at it. She turned completely white, grabbed the scissors—" "That's the second time, I believe—" "I've still got the scar from the first time, look—but this time she didn't stab me. You say Polak's got some," and Vitenka ran off, "... and then let's go boating," Petrik Hurt was still on the phone, he glanced at his watch, "but first I'll buy you some ice cream..."

"Hooked up with that artificial limb again?" Jacek grinned when Petrik had finished the long conversation.

"Don't ever say that to me again!" Petrik Hurt said impetuously, "or to anybody else, understand?!"

"But excuse me, I was just quoting you..."

"You must have been imagining things, Jacek."

"Or you've been, no?"

"Perhaps, why not? Everything's relative, who knows where imagination ends and true... the true... Don't you ever imagine anything?"

"Right now, in fact: I've bought an airplane ticket to Brno for tomorrow."

"But the firm can't reimburse you for that," Petrik Hurt said in a voice suddenly that of an office superior.

"Just ninety-two crowns to get rid of a clown like you, it's a real bargain," Jacek felt like saying, but Petr Hurt's got to sign our travel order for tomorrow, no, now he no longer has to, but he does have to sign our resignation—

"They're saying in the director's office," Petrik Hurt began slowly, "that you're overdoing it a bit with those trips to Brno. I won't ask you about anything yet, but watch out, Jacek..."

Petr Hurt left and listlessly Jacek opened the drawer containing the resignation form, it wasn't getting any easier to fill it out like this in a rush, under it lay six blue envelopes, six cancellation letters to six unsuspecting naiads, the seventh Tina by telephone, just then the phone rang and there was Tina's familiar subdued voice, this really is telepathy or mysticism, "I can't come today, I'm about to go off on a big trip," Jacek said into the receiver, "I'll write you." We've already written letters to the others and all we have to do is throw them in the mailbox, the resignation can be mailed as well—Jacek filled it out, signed it, and put it in an envelope addressed to Cottex, seven letters in all, and he put them into his breast-pocket folder, in its soft black leather a white ticket:

Date: 10/1/66
Route: OK 035
Sector: Prague-Brno
Airport bus departs: 7:15 A.M.
Flight departure: 8:15 A.M.
Check all data at time of purchase.
No subsequent adjustments.
CZECHOSLOVAK AIRLINES

Seven blue envelopes are seven possible lives, seven freedoms taken together are no more than one aggravated solitary confinement with a crazy dream for every day of the week, but in the morning you've got to wake up and get to your feet—
"Express call to Prague, Czechoslovak Airlines," Jacek placed the call and before it came he shuffled the seven blue envelopes like cards, why not this one, that one, or these two, what a frightful risk it would be to waste another fifteen years of one's life, the last ones, then we'll be fifty already, why just these two, that one, this one, or this one here, and quite different ones would reply if an ad were placed on a different day and, perhaps, in a different paper, must DIFFERENT always be BETTER—

"Czechoslovak Airlines? Jost. I have a reservation for Brno tomorrow. Can I still get a refund?"

"If the passenger notifies us less than three hours and at least fifteen minutes before departure, he can claim a refund with a twenty-five-percent penalty. Does that answer your question?"

"Completely."

When a siren sounded, Jacek walked out slowly through the ridged mud toward the gate and toward the corner with the orange mailbox, he took the seven blue envelopes out of his folder and raised the first one up to the slot,
                    Miss Nadezda Houskova
on his last visit Nada had dragged her new vacuum cleaner out of the box under the daybed and for the first time she'd turned it on, its nozzle had rattled over the old planks of the floor and Nada had started to sing to its rattle, *our first carpet*, BUT I'VE ALREADY GOT ONE, AT HOME—

Jacek took a deep breath and dropped envelope after envelope into the slot, Miss Nadezda Houskova, Dr. Anna Bromova, Miss Hanicka Kohoutkova, Mrs. Lida Adalska, Miss Tanicka Rambouskova, Dr. Mojmira Stratilova, Cottex, Usti nad Labem — wait on the last one, that one we have to keep for a while and if we still make the flight, just for the fun of it, we won't come back from Brno until we find that white plush, hell, we've been in cotton for ten years, and when we can scare up three carloads of ethyl acetate from West Germany— and the seventh one, Tina by phone. Now only the white plush, a trifle, it's nothing actually—

It glows softly on our kitchen table, soft as the fleece of the most highly bred Australian merino lamb, how supple and delicate the cloth is, in fascination Lenka takes it in her hands and strokes it, Lenicka insists on stroking it, and Grandma strokes it too—in his blue-gray denim shirt Trost grins triumphantly over the entire scene.

"It was nothing at all," he blared, "by chance I was passing by and I said, Hey, they've got it here—where but in that new store right down the street—"

"Don't touch that with your dirty hands!" Lenka told Jacek, it would be a coat for Lenicka and because of it Lenicka "woves Uncle Twost!" and how unwilling she is to come and play with Daddy in the living room, she no longer wants to go through the obstacle course, "So wet's pway house, OK?" Jacek lisped ingratiatingly, "wet's put up our pway house—"

And right away, so that Lenicka wouldn't run off after Trost, pull the mattresses from the sofa onto the floor, Tomas Roll is an irreplaceable helper in all this, and Lenicka doesn't run off because Trost and Lenka have now come into the living room for her, the mattresses turn into the walls of our cottage, the coverlet into the roof, and the cushions into a balcony, "I'll build you a finer one, out of wood, a real one—" Trost wooed and pursued Lenicka.

"We've got our pway house all weady, cwawl into it, wittle one—," but Lenicka suddenly preferred "a weal one out of wood," "Just cwawl into ours, wook, Daddy's cwawling in and he's waiting for you there—" "Your feet stick out, Daddy—" the little one laughed. "And it's a bit flimsy, look here—" Trost brayed, and he smacked into the house with his knee, a mattress collapsed on Jacek's back, the second one fell under the weight of the coverlet, and Jacek was entangled in the blanket like a gladiator in a retiarius's net, above him guffaws and horselaughter, and with difficulty he crawled out into the light, "Let's do the obstacle course now, little one—" and with the dwarf's devoted assistance the two mattresses were laid flat on the floor and the third one perpendicular between them, quick, on the double, but Lenicka had already turned her back on the two frenzied builders and behind her Lenka and Trost brought up the rear of the procession, Jacek was left beside his obstacle course face to face with his pygmy. The dwarf croaked and walked over it on his hands, a somersault and he lay on his back like an overturned beetle.

Jacek took a pack of cigarettes onto the balcony, he lit them one after another and blew the smoke out toward the sky, at least there's the advantage that Trost won't be gawking at us from his window across the way now that he's safely within our own walls and behind our back, at least there's an unimpeded view of the eighty windows, let's have a look, but who's that on the fourth floor of section two in the fourth window from the left—some fellow our age is sitting there on his balcony, smoking and gaping straight this way, "Cognac!" Jacek roared into the apartment, and the imp brought some quickly, this time with two glasses, "It's the last bottle," he whispered, "they're carving the side of pork for him now and Grandma's opening some beer for him, they wouldn't give me any."

Jacek was drinking the last bottle from the warm slopes of Georgia and lit one cigarette after another, the dwarf kept running out onto the balcony with new reports, "He's taken your chair, Jacek, you shouldn't stand for it!" "So pull it out here!" and the pygmy ran back to the kitchen but soon he returned without the chair, "He didn't want to give it to me, he's already sitting on it," he announced, "and he's eating that side of pork with his fingers and Lenka's laughing at him, but not maliciously, and Grandma said: that's right, a man eats meat with his hands, and Lenicka's laughing and Trost is feeding her like you do an animal, with his fingers..."

"Go tell her that I don't think children should eat fatty pork. She'll get sick on it! And have them send out that ham in the pantry!"

The dwarf ran off and came right back, "They say the ham's for Lenicka's lunch and Trost says that you can easily buy your own when you have so much left over from your travel budget, he says the child needs it more than you do and Grandma says that's God's sacred truth and Lenka nods and Lenicka says we won't give Daddy any ham."

"Bring her here!"

The dwarf ran off and came right back, "She's eating now and they won't let her go and they said we shouldn't nag them anymore."

"This is my home—" Jacek stormed gloomily, and he took a swig straight from the bottle, "go back, Tom, and tell them…"

The faithful imp went on carrying messages and he kept bringing back worse and worse reports from occupied territory, Trost in the kitchen was like the Vandals in Rome and Jacek on the balcony resembled the last Byzantine emperor, "Bring me my daughter!—" he roared when he'd finished the bottle.

The dwarf finally succeeded in bringing Lenicka all the way through the living room and up to the glass door, throughout the journey she'd resisted with a fearful screeching and now Trost appeared, behind him Grandma and Lenka, without getting up Jacek opened the door from the balcony to the living room.

"Let the kid go, OK?!" Trost roared at Tomas Roll, but the dwarf went on trying to bring the child to its father, he seized it in his gorilla-like arms, but Trost stormed out in open battle and began to shake the dwarf violently and Lenicka fled, "We're fed up with you, up to the neck!" Trost thundered at the imp, "Uncle Woll go way!" Lenicka shouted, "It's high time now," Grandma said, and Lenka nodded, "Do you hear?!" Trost roared, "Clear out—" and he grabbed the pygmy by the shoulder, the imp jerked loose but Trost snagged him around the waist, the dwarf had powerful arms but his body was skinny and his legs were like a child's, laughing Trost picked him up and carried him out.

Jacek followed them slowly down the stairs, already

Trost was coming up the stairs and Jacek was forced to make way for him, out on the road Tomas Roll was dusting off his black sweater and his black jeans, "Forgive me, Tom," Jacek said sympathetically, "I'm terribly sorry but..."

"Go to hell, Mr. Jost!" Tomas Roll said firmly, he jumped into his red Fiat and this time without any honk-honk he drove quickly through the development, Jacek dragged himself toward the main highway, the Fiat was now no more than a red period at the end of a fairy tale, our *let it happen* is gone, what's next, right in front of Jacek a bus stopped and the door opened automatically, listlessly Jacek glanced at the tin stairs and mechanically climbed them up to the metal platform, "Last stop," he told the driver, and he paid three crowns.

Along the row of old chestnut trees, around the gas works and the pyramid of dead soil torn from the earth, the monument with the moldering lion, what time can do to metal, the linden tree with its sign and on the hill our yellow retreat, but it isn't ours, it's only rented, and Jacek rode on to the end of the line, tore his way through the underbrush and over rocks upward until a swift stream stopped him, the strong whirl of white foam over well-washed boulders, the water rushed over pebbles and was quiet only in the sandy shallows, once there were no valleys, only mountain chains, and their peaks sprouted up from the depths of the earth, but time and water had divided mountain from mountain and cut into them ever more deeply and wide, what fate was the water preparing for the rock, how systematically it carried out its fearful, patient torture, rock turns against its fellow rock, thigh-joint crushes collar-bone, rib pierces shoulder-blade, and the vertebrae mill themselves into bone meal, sand is the epilogue of the rigid mountain, sandstorms appease entropy with time, and duration is the highway to a desert.

Over the mountain stream it began to get dark, the

foamy water caressed the rocks and rubbed off molecule after molecule, the monotonous splash of the irreversible victory of water, but one thinking man with a pick and shovel has power enough to offset the division of mountains and the diversion of waters.

Jacek came back on the last bus and silently he walked through the apartment that bore his nameplate and out onto his balcony, to fly or not to fly, not to fly is the end, but how to take off, down from the mountains dark clouds covered the whole sky and suddenly it began to thunder, the first drops fell on Jacek's feet and he didn't bother to pull them in, after all a man doesn't dissolve in water, Lenka came through the door out onto the balcony, lightning and thunder again, now right above their heads, and Lenka fled the balcony, my wife is afraid of storms and inside Lenicka squeals with terror.

"It ain't nothing—" Trost shouted over the storm, and he led the frightened Lenka back onto the balcony, "rainwater gives you a pretty mug—," Trost neighed, and he leaned out over the rail, he let the heavy drops of water fall on his face, beneath the protecting arch formed by his body the now calm and laughing Lenka took the laundry down from the line and with cries of joy Lenicka caught raindrops in her hands.

"Come in," Lenka called onto the balcony late that evening, "he's gone."

Jacek put the mattresses from the obstacle course back onto the sofa and dropped down on it, late at night Lenka came for him in her blue-gray apron and Jacek went down before her on his knees.

"I understand, Jacek," Lenka whispered, "you're not happy at home anymore and you're afraid to admit it—we can't go on like this any longer. I won't drive you away, but it might be better for everyone if you were to go yourself."

CATAPULTED and in his soul there sounded forth a military anthem, CAPTAIN, TOMORROW I FLY—

"Tomorrow I'm flying to Brno, and please..."

"Two white shirts in your satchel, and no lunch. And this—" and Lenka pulled out of the pocket of her blue-gray apron a small clay monster with many pairs of eyes, the good-hearted imp had given us an ocarina.

"I'm flying with my suitcase, it's already packed."

VI — twenty-three

The unbuttoned iridescent raincoat shows off the suede leather of the jacket and the narrow stripe of the black leather tie highlights the dazzling whiteness of the nylon shirt, Graduate Fellow (today was October 1) Engineer Jaromir Jost clicked his tongue in the mirror, walked with his suitcase slowly up the steps to Platform Two at Usti Main Station, and at 5:14 he left on the R 10 express to Prague.

Sitting by the window, facing forward, Jacek read the headlines of the newspaper and glanced at the back page of the *Black Chronicle*,

> *Although 24-year-old Ludovit Feher did not know how to swim, he attempted to cross the fish pond near Turnanske Podhradi on a raft. He fell into the water and drowned.*

From Prague Central Station to the airline building, in the airport bus no one asked him for his ticket and by comparison with the sooty train station the airport was like a concert hall, on the other side of the red-and-white railing as far as the eye could see in all directions a concrete wasteland of runways for takeoff and landing, a yellow truck drives among the waiting planes and a red lead car with FOLLOW ME in big letters rushes toward the horizon.

Roaring, a giant Pan Am Boeing taxied in, slowly turned, and came to a stop, a motorized stairway pulled up and passenger after passenger stepped out, the first one looked familiar, it was the thirty-three-year-old atomic physicist Jozef, he jumped nimbly down onto the tarmac and already a cluster of people was bounding up to him, "Excuse me, please—" Jacek overheard his piercing voice, and now he was running up the stairs to a waiting Aeroflot TU-104A, immediately the heavy metal doors closed behind him, the TU-104A began to thunder, made its turn, and with a roar it taxied toward the runway.

"Passengers for Brno oh three five ready for boarding—" and impatiently Jacek ran toward his plane, we want to be first and get a seat by the window, he handed the stewardess his ticket and rushed up the motorized stairway to our highest beach, made of aluminum, the passengers took their seats, the door banged shut, and three men in blue-gray uniforms walked down the aisle, which of them is the captain—

The roar of the motors made the cigar-shaped cabin vibrate and outside the window the red warning lights were already flashing in the grass along the runway, signs lit up on either side of the captain's cabin, on the left PRIPOUTEJTE SE—NADET REMNI—FASTEN SAFETY BELTS and quickly Jacek threw the linen straps over his stomach and drew them tight through the aluminum safety catch, on the right NEKOURIT—NEKURIT—NO SMOKING and Jacek quickly put out his last Carmen cigarette, meanwhile we've already taken off, almost without noticing it, and Jacek glanced at his fellow passengers, no one had bothered to fasten his seat belt and a man across the aisle was even smoking a big fat cigar.

Outside the window the bluest blue-blue sky and below the blindingly bright wing that land a hundred times

traversed and conquered, a desk like a steamship, on the
first, glassed-in deck a regular library, on the upper deck
two telephones, a metal vase for a smokestack, and as a
mast towering above it all a magnificent *Palma areca*, a
morning cigarette in the colorists' lab, outside the windows
they've torn down a factory chimney which had interfered
with the clarity of the hues, in a hot bath a porcelain vessel
with our own creation the color of flesh, and drying on a
wooden stand Spanish moss, passion auburn, and Victoria
blue, the garlands, salvos, tricklings, tremblings, shocks,
and caressings of light among the gray fur of the lichens
on the trunks in the trampoline of wet pine needles, the
forest as recluse and the forest as multitude, the yellow
Parisian sky of tin over the narrow creaking bed of hungry
youth, ten times happy and each time in a different place,
how short a distance it is to Brno, how grotesque this
miniature landscape, cars like tiny grains and that line
below is the train line, are ten happinesses more or less
than one, today the Balvins are beginning to paint their
entire apartment green and Petrik Hurt goes on deluding
himself, but isn't a lifetime of self-delusion one of the
possible ways to take life firmly in one's hands, where
anyway, in this age of relativity, is the boundary between
certainty and self-delusion, obligation of course deprives,
but isn't freedom just the maximum degree of deprivation,
certainly also the maximum number of alternative paths,
but in the end one can follow only one of them, the
extension of a rabbit loose in other people's gardens or the
intension of a gardener at home, and Lenka has already
planted apple trees on our piece of ground, all three of us
have lain together on the grass and from every side the
scent of the hair of a loved one, on our own earth FROM
WHICH WE COME our daughter slept her beauty sleep
and on the other side of the wall we came together, our
longing contained within an order, how much happiness
will be left outside such an order— Into the frosty blue

space outside the window short lashes of flame from the two tubes on the wing and in his deep seat, in horror, Jacek pressed his hand to his throat, the hecatombs of the primordial ocean are buried deep in the earth under heavy pressure, locked between the Miocene and Carboniferous ages rest the masses of the detrital waters and their sands, and when hit by a bore through a seam they burst into a destructive flood which puts an end to all mining activity, in a second the wooden matchsticks and metal wires of presumptuous mining engineering are swept away, divinely, banally I love my wife with whom I live and have a child, and my image is only imaginary, an inconceivable cut-out from a family portrait, never with anyone else but you, Lenunka, my love, I must tell you WHO WE ARE, we Josts, Daddy only played for a time at being a traveler, a sailor, and a pilot, we're at Brno already, how terribly short a flight it was—

The plane was landing at the Brno airport, with a jerk Jacek unhooked his linen belt, got up, and started toward the aisle, "Are you crazy, fellow—" his neighbor snapped at him, but without ceremony Jacek stepped over his neighbor's knees and forced his way out, it was dangerous to delay, so quick, let's be the first to the exit and we'll be in time to buy a ticket for the return flight home on this very plane, everyone is hurrying home to his Lenicka and Lenka, I'll be the first and by the shortest route, down with the netting and the rough chin on the sweet little tummy, nothing's so sweet to kiss as our little one, and hold her hand till she falls asleep with her thumb in her mouth, this very afternoon we three can go to the pond and the movies and the swings, first I'll buy both of you ice cream and we'll take the little one to the pâtisserie, Daddy knows how much you love store-bought pastry, WHERE ARE WE FLYING— but Jacek flew on alone.

With the warning signs lit up PRIPOUTEJTESE—NADET REMNI—FASTEN SAFETY BELTS, with thirty-nine passengers seated and one standing, the plane was landing at the Brno airport and as it set down there was an insignificant retardation of the hydraulic system on the wheels, the wheels revolved only a fraction of a second late, and the plane was arrested for just a fraction of a second. But Jacek flew on. The unbelted passengers jerked slightly in their seats and then the plane glided along the ground in perfect order. But Jacek flew down the aisle, the tremendous force of inertia catapulted him forward towards the metal steps, and his face traveled up them as far as the metal platform in front of the captain's cabin.

The plane slowed down, turned, stopped, and its engines fell silent. The captain turned off the warning signs and came out of his cabin. From their seats the passengers lifted themselves and their terrified voices.

PENGUIN BOOKS

LIVE BODIES

Maurice Gee is one of New Zealand's best-known writers.
He has won a number of literary awards, including the Wattie
Award (twice), the New Zealand Fiction Award (four times)
and the Aim New Zealand Children's Book of the Year Award.

Maurice Gee's novels include the three books in the Plumb trilogy
and *Prowlers*, *The Burning Boy*, *Going West* (winner of the Wattie
Award in 1993), *Crime Story* and *Loving Ways*.
He is also an award-winning children's author, his most recent
book being *The Fat Man*, which won the Aim Children's Book
of the Year Award and the Esther Glen Award in 1995.

The author lives in Wellington with his wife Margareta
and has two daughters and a son.

Also by Maurice Gee

NOVELS

The Big Season
A Special Flower
In My Father's Den
Games of Choice
Plumb
Meg
Sole Survivor
Prowlers
The Burning Boy
Going West
Crime Story
Loving Ways

STORIES

A Glorious Morning, Comrade
Collected Stories

FOR CHILDREN

Under the Mountain
The World Around the Corner
The Halfmen of O
The Priests of Ferris
Motherstone
The Fireraiser
The Champion
The Fat Man

LIVE
BODIES

Maurice Gee

PENGUIN BOOKS

PENGUIN BOOKS

Penguin Books (NZ) Ltd, Cnr Rosedale and Airborne Roads, Albany,
Auckland 1310, New Zealand
Penguin Books Ltd, 27 Wrights Lane, London W8 5TZ, England
Penguin USA, 375 Hudson Street, New York, NY 10014, United States
Penguin Books Australia Ltd, 487 Maroondah Highway, Ringwood,
Australia 3134
Penguin Books Canada Ltd, 10 Alcorn Avenue, Toronto, Ontario,
Canada M4V 3B2

Penguin Books Ltd, Registered Offices: Harmondsworth, Middlesex, England

First published by Penguin Books (NZ) Ltd, 1998
This edition published 1998
3   5   7   9   10   8   6   4   2
Copyright © Maurice Gee, 1998

Designed and typeset by Richard King
Printed in Australia

For Emily

Acknowledgements

The early chapters of this novel owe much to the late
H. O. (Bert) Roth, whose activities in communist
underground groups in Vienna in the 1930s are recorded in
his papers, held in the Alexander Turnbull Library, Wellington.
I have several times quoted directly from Bert Roth.
I also made use of a published short story by Somes Island
internee and escaper Odo Strewe, and used material from
his file, and those of other interned aliens, held in the
National Archives of New Zealand.
The Oral History Section of the Alexander Turnbull Library
made several useful tapes available to me.

I am grateful to Mr J. C. Klingenstein for allowing me to read his
memoir of his days as an internee on Somes Island.
(This is also held in the Turnbull Library.)

Others I would like to thank are Mrs Anna Maria Tretter and
Mrs Maria Collins; Rhondda Grieg; Carl Freeman;
Henk Heinekamp; Michael Noonan and Nelson Wattie.

ONE

When I am a little drunk, and that is as drunk as I ever get, I lose my resentment and my fear and all knowledge of a social existence and know my being as molecular, like this wine in the glass, French wine, Swedish glass, or like the good cloth of my trousers that once was wool on the back of a Southland sheep, and grass before that, minerals in the soil, rain sucked from an ocean on the other side of the world . . . You see where I am heading? It is enormously comforting to make the journey into the universe and into time and understand that I come from there and will go there and that consciousness will be put aside. I look into the upheld rosy orb. It was the clay and gravel of Bordeaux and now it becomes part of my flesh and I will send it on somewhere else when my body decays: perhaps it will become grape again in the time that stretches like a field, and I shall be part of some man or woman in the twenty-first, the twenty-second, the twenty-third century. How one basks in that: to be forever, with fear and resentment put aside, and longing, gratitude, disappointment, love . . . I'll not make a list, it would become the dictionary. The social existence, affective existence, put aside and lids placed on the trashcans and honey pots of the past, and on that trashcan, future, too, and 'now' made safe by an arrangement of molecules, by the expansion that reduces . . .

It is a credit to me that drinking has not become an addiction.

A bottle lasts all evening and one evening a week is all I allow.

Tonight I am denied that escape. Consciousness has been digging a tunnel. It breaks out now and looks into the open air. You cannot intern, inter me, consciousness says. There is a thing that must be understood, or at least held in the light: Kenny's betrayal of all I have done. How it spoils my happy conceit, how it sends me scurrying backwards, looking for some other place to hide.

There are not many. Vienna? That is no place. Or no place I can rest in and make Josef Mandl free of care. My Nancy-life? Not there either, for Nancy, she-and-I, are all right for a time and then Kenny begins to scratch at the edges with his fingernails.

There is only one and, if I can, I'll go there, with the friend who keeps me company.

I look out the window into the night and it is dark. No moon, no stars. I cannot see. But I can *know*. Out there is my narrow place. It will not change and will not go away.

Willi and I dug a tunnel once. We burrowed for freedom in the ground, and it was a joyous enterprise, although I was terrified of collapsing walls and suffocation. To pass beneath the wire, that was a joy, scraping with my Dutch hoe six feet beneath the roots of the grass on an island in a harbour at the bottom of the world. I have read the note that betrayed us. It is fastened with a rusty pin in a file that carries Willi's name – Enemy Alien: Gauss, Wilhelm Theodor Georg – and it reads: Stope escappes. Socialist Gauss and dirty Jew diggen tunnel under House 7. I have taken the rusty pin from my file too: Enemy Alien: Mandl, Josef Maximilian. I was Willi's follower ('a simple-minded young man but untrustworthy and thoroughly unreliable'), so the note in mine is merely a transcription. Willi deserves the original for he was an 'original', although they never used that equivocal word of him. They allowed him nothing except his influence over me.

Where were we going as we lay on our bellies and scraped at the hard earth with our broken hoe? I had calculated how far we must dig, and drawn a map. I was the mathematician, the carto-grapher, and he the planner and the leader. He said 'there' so we went there, which was the YMCA hut forty feet outside the wire. We would break up in the night like moles beneath its floor and wait until the guard on the path strolled off for his cliff-edge pee – voiding into the void – and his squatting smoke in the lee of the flax bush (his hands cupping the cigarette were like a masked lan-tern), and we would free the loose base board and wriggle out. We crept bent-legged through the gap he left and climbed down to the water, using Willi's cat eyes and fox ears, and his nose for human stupidity, which was present on this island, he said, in greater con-centration than he had ever known.

I would do the next bit: make the canoe. Assemble the ribs Steinitz had made in the carpenter's shop, lash them with twine, fish out the waxed canvas from its hole in the rocks – Braun had placed it there while hunting for seagull eggs – stretch it and lash it to the skeleton, and we would have our two-man coracle. Which might, Willi said, hold only one. We would have to see.

'You go,' I said.

'That would be best. I am stronger, for the rowing.'

I think it would have held only one. I think perhaps it would have sunk halfway to Eastbourne, and Willi would have drowned in the black night, in the harbour at the bottom of the world. He had told us on our first escape, rowing to Petone beach, that he was afraid of bottomless water. How we cackled, Steinitz and I. Willi confesses to an imperfection. Our laughter increased, it bounced across the black water into the dark. Anything would have started us off, euphoric as we were with our easy freedom, and Willi dipped into the sea and splashed us with brine. 'Fools, they will hear. The night carries noise.'

Which escape do I write about? When they brought us back from the hills above the Hutt Valley and marched us into the compound, I thought, Well, it's over, we tried, but Willi said, 'Next time we will know what to do.' Next time was the tunnel and the canoe. I discovered another imperfection in him: he was terrified of being enclosed. His fear was different from mine. I was afraid the roof would cave in and suffocate me, he of being unable to stand upright and spread his arms. I heard him groan and heard his elbows thump on the walls as he tried to make himself more space. Once he screamed and came backing out, his boots in my face, and I backed out and we stood in the pit under my bed. I felt him gulping air and wringing his body this way and that and rising on his toes and flexing his arms above his head. 'I cannot be a worm, Josef. You will have to do it.' We climbed the ladder and spread our scrapings round the piles of the hut, and after that I was the one who worked on my belly. I dragged the earth back in flour bags and left Willi to scatter it.

The others in Hut 7 knew about our digging. Steinitz was not coming this time. He thought the tunnel too dangerous and believed the canoe would sink even though he had shaped the ribs himself. Moser pointed out that those who stayed behind would be punished for our escape.

'How can they punish you?' Willi said. 'Will they drag you into a cellar and shoot you as if you were in Munich or Berlin?' The lights would go out earlier, he said, that was all. Inspections would be held at 2 a.m. Even the rations would not be cut.

'We are escaping for all of you, to keep you alive. We are dying on this island. Measure yourselves. Every day you shrink a little bit. When Josef and I are free, you can stand taller.'

'And how tall will you stand when they bring you back?' Moser asked.

'We will be men who have escaped. We will hold our shoulders square.' He raised his fist – the red salute: 'And give this to the scum in Hut 5.' He perceived connections, read emotions, removed blocks; knew words and gestures; was a master of coarse acting and shifted us where he needed us to be; but knew we became private when the lights went out – was never surprised by the private life – and waited with his smile to be betrayed.

The tip-off came from Hut 7, although the letter was written in 5, the Nazi hut. 'Dirty Jew' is evidence of that, and 'diggen' rules out the Italians and Japanese. But only the inmates of Hut 7 knew about the tunnel.

So there at 3 a.m. were Lieutenant Dowden, swagger stick erect, moustache jumping, and Sergeant Pengelly (Scheisskerl to Nazis and Internationalists alike) and half a dozen privates with rifles and fixed bayonets rousting us nine half-naked wretches from our beds. Our feet scuffed the gritty floor, our eyes blinked at the silver blades aligned at us. Only Willi smiled. 'So,' he said, and left the rest unspoken: we are betrayed. They herded us into a corner and left two men like sheep dogs holding us while Dowden tapped and pointed with his baton, conducting the search, and Pengelly shouted orders – why do they shout, these sergeants?, they deny their humanity – and the privates overturned beds and manhandled trunks from under them and banged the floor for hollow sounds with boots and rifle butts.

I was the one sleeping over the hole. How cold it had made me in the night, that shaft that might drop to the Pole; and how I dreamed of wriggling to Vienna and breaking out on the Kahlenberg and sliding on my skis down to the city and meeting there, in broad streets, Mother, Father, Susi, Franz. An iron band fixed itself round my chest when I woke. My family had backed away as though from royalty, with large eyes and fixed smiles on their lips. A dream, only a dream, yet it hung on, squeezing me, while the men ranked in this wooden hut, snoring, farting, dreaming, were the dream.

The soldiers pulled floor boards up and shone torches down the hole at our Dutch hoe and pickhead chisel and hurricane lamp, our rucksack of sheep's tongues, condensed milk, herrings, dates. Plenty there to refuse to talk about.

'Whose bed is this?'

We would not say. Willi curled his lip at their stupidity in lumping all our gear in a heap.

'Mandl,' Pengelly said. 'Mandl was here.'

'Show me your hands, Mandl,' Dowden said.

I had dirt under my fingernails. So had Willi. Dowden already knew his prey, was simply demonstrating his British superiority to the Berliner and the Jew. He sent a private down the hole to hand up our gear, then sent him crawling round the piles where he found the ribs of the canoe, which Steinitz had numbered one to seven, and the interlocking sections of the spine on which the fool had written, Patented by Werner Steinitz, Somes Island Detention Camp, Wellington, New Zealand, 1942. (What a pleasant boy Steinitz was, a perfect blue-eyed Aryan who hated Nazis, and how he loved shaping wood and working out new ways of fitting this piece with that, of calculating stress and using weight against itself. He sank into a mind-deadening fear as the Japanese came down the Pacific. They would ship him back to Germany where the Gestapo would murder him. He tried to swim to Point Howard one night, and fought the policemen who picked him out of the sea, biting an ear, breaking a thumb, and earned himself a year in Mt Eden jail. He was a little mad when he came back, quiet and slow, and had forgotten how to work with wood. At the end of the war the Tribunal sent him home – was kind enough not to put him on a ship with the Nazis – and he became a labourer in Essen, a cleaner-up, but took to drink, his wife wrote, and died in a fall from scaffolding. Apart from Willi and Moser he was the only one I tried to keep in touch with.)

They marched us to the hospital and locked us in the operating theatre.

'It was Moser,' Willi said. 'It is their trick.'

'Yes, Moser,' Steinitz said.

I turned away from them, allowing these anti-Nazis their bit of Blame the Jew. I climbed on a chair and looked out a high window at the dawn lighting up the hills of Wellington. I was easy in my mind now that escape was done with. I don't have to go down that hole any more, I thought. I lay on the floor and went to sleep (Willi had taken the sick trolley) and remember waking up pleased that I had had no dreams. Steinitz was banging on the door, demanding to be taken to the lavatory. I climbed on the chair again and looked at the ragged hills and the flimsy houses and tried to think of a reason why people might settle in this vertical place – lean into the wind and rain, cling to the hills – and thought, There's an emptiness here I'll come to like, and a dumb stupidity, I don't mind that. If they'll let me off this island I might stay in their town. It was not simply relief at being out of my hole, for I remained in the larger hole and my sanity was under threat, but a recognition that bleakness and simplicity might be endured and a way found to a life in spite of them. I had come from a place with too much history.

Today, this very minute, from my desk, I look at Somes Island. A jewel set in silver. Cancel that easy metaphor. It is set in my forehead, a third eye through which I look at the other side; it presses like a thumb on the beating membrane, fontanelle. Was I so young, so unformed, when they took me there?

Perhaps on the morning when I peered from the operating room I saw my house. I looked towards Wadestown and Tinakori hill. The slopes black with pine trees under the hurrying sky were balanced like a stone that might crash down. I live now in one of the houses under threat, above the fault line on the tilted hill, and when the ground trembles in an earthquake I stand in a doorway and grip the jamb or I kneel under my desk, obeying the rules, but know it is the deep-rooted trees that hold me safe. Pine trees, my daughter says, have shallow roots, but that is mere botanical knowledge. They go deep enough for me.

I watch the island. My third eye, the island, watches me. Light narrows to an aperture; and light from the other side, where I lived in a great city between East and West, reaches me through that tightened place, giving each thing I see new lines and darker shades. The boys and girls marching in the Woods wear no merry faces, the fists they raise in the red salute are made of bone and their song goes nowhere, their song becomes a dirge.

The island was my war. It's nothing special. Others have their lens for looking at the other side – a better one, a worse one. I can be rid of mine by trying hard. That, as they say, is the way to go. I have no taste for retrospective prophecy or for the elegiac mood but am happier remembering matter-of-factly, thinking flat. Willi believed in that way of progressing too.

We compared our cities once, while sneering at this one. We had been at the wharf unloading coal and had washed ourselves clean in the sea. The Nazis had played at sabotage, letting sacks slip over the side, and Pengelly marched them back to the compound, leaving Willi and me to finish the job. We took our time and sauntered up the track when it was done, without a guard, and stopped to roll a smoke by the little graveyard above Leper Island.

'Look,' Willi said, 'they paint camouflage on the oil tanks there' – pointing at Seaview – 'but they leave the tops to shine in the night. The moon makes a target of each one. These British do not deserve to win the war.'

'New Zealanders,' I said.

'It is the same. They cannot decide to be who they must be but play their little British Empire games. There are no cliffs of Dover here.'

Sargoff the Russian went by with a dozen herrings strung on flax. (Why he had not been released when the Germans invaded Russia nobody knew.)

14

'He is more at home in this land than Dowden with his tippy-tap stick,' Willi said.

Sargoff would pickle the herrings in vinegar and sell them for sixpence each to whoever had the money – usually the Germans who had signed their adherence to the Reich and so received pocket money through the Swiss consul. I could have had it, being classified a 'German through annexation', but had refused, as all the anti-Nazis and Internationalists had. I made my few pence from working in the gardens and polishing paua shell for the shell-workers. Willi had his ducks, a more profitable business. He financed our escape by selling eggs, and had eight pounds in coins in a bag tied to his belt when we got away to Petone beach. They would have drowned him if we had sunk.

'I am more at home,' he said. 'Hey Sarge, I swap you one egg for one soused herring.'

Sargoff shook his head and walked on, grinding his black teeth. In our camp of angry men he was the angriest and we had learned to keep clear of him.

The *Cobar* pulled out from the wharf, past the buoy that marked the place where a bore was sunk for fresh water in the sea. It had been abandoned after striking rock, and a tanker still arrived a couple of times each week with an 8000-gallon load. Dowden had threatened to make us drink from the cattle troughs if we did not cut down on our use of water.

I described hillside meadows above Vienna and spring-houses built over springs, with streams winding through the grass away from them and running in little waterfalls among the flowers.

'Very pretty,' Willi said. 'It will take them a thousand years to build a Vienna or a Berlin here. Look at it, their capital city. You could scrape it off the side of the hill with your hand. Do they really think Hitler will come here?'

'There are Jews to kill, so he'll come. And Reds called Willi Gauss.'

'Yes,' Willi said, and ground his teeth like Sargoff. His hatred of the Nazis had more weight than his contempt for New Zealanders. 'When we escape we must learn how to survive in these hills. Make raids, that is what we must learn. Steal and live by our wits. And learn to kill.'

'Not kill,' I said, startled.

'Nazis, I mean, not these Dummkopf New Zealanders.'

'We should take Sargoff to bite off their heads,' I said, and mimed him biting the heads off herrings and spitting them into the sea.

'It's no joke,' Willi said.

I had expected to please him, for his humour was cruel – but it was scornful, sarcastic, satirical, emerging through his sense of better knowledge and greater worth. Sargoff was base coin; I should have known.

We watched stores from the *Cobar* travel up the tramway to the camp. The wire hummed and the wheels rumbled, while down at the wharf the Italians waiting to load up sang Neapolitan love songs, music that makes me hungry to this day.

'Coffee,' I said.

'Schweinewurst. Beer.'

We laughed sourly, knowing it was tea, and little of that, and sides of mutton dirtied with coal, and that the beer meant for our canteen would get no further than the guards' mess. We competed in tales of deprivation: boiled swedes, turnip jam, acorn coffee, bread with sawdust mixed in the flour, and clothes made of paper, shoes with paper soles (my 1919 Vienna tale, which came from my parents), and the scavenging children of Berlin, the ragged bands fed by English Quakers (Willi's tale). Then we left poverty behind and I eulogised my city – the cafes, the pastry shops, wine villages in the hills, the parks and palaces, the river with its barges, the streets with yellow tramcars sparking along. I cannot be lyrical any more, for they are places deformed by time, and other things, and this city on the hills that we swept into its harbour that day in an earthquake jumble of broken timber and bent tin, is richer than Vienna now. And Willi is dead in his Berlin of beer cellars and brandy shops.

The sun is shining. There's not a cloud in the sky. The new fast-ferry, heading out, makes a wide curve round a container ship. It is one of Wellington's rare windless days, with no threat from the south. The island lies flatter than it should, each of its three levels flat, and the quarantine buildings – no llamas now, no exotic sheep and goats – might be a cottage resort. Hut 7 was knocked down long ago, all the huts. The hole under my bed was filled in after it was found. No strolling lovers will tumble down when the island makes its next change into a picnic spot. But our thirty-six feet of tunnel remain. (That figure is exact. A nervous private inched along holding a measuring chain.) It begins nowhere and ends nowhere, our wormhole scraped out with a Dutch hoe. It is like a hollow in my brain, bending left at 30 degrees; but is not unpleasant, it brings no pain. I altered my shape in the tunnel; I passed from one life into another, changed hemispheres, and would have to pass through a similar wormhole to go back. We did not make our escape; were marched off by a clown with a pointed stick. But when I looked through the narrow window at the Wellington hills and the frail houses perched on them, it was as though I completed my passage and emerged in a place where I was free.

So I live in a house whose timbers grow pink in the rising sun, and I look from my desk at the island where I slept inside a barbed wire fence. I think of the boy I was in Vienna before passing through that narrow place, which did not break my continuity but made me dimorphous. They shipped me to the island as a 'live body', and delivered me back as a live body too; but my cells were differ-ent, my molecules were changed. Josef Mandl of the Rote Falken, marching in the Vienna Woods, singing the Internationale and rais-ing his fist in the red salute, is Joe Mandl (rhymes with handle) of Wellington, drawing dead to the jack at the Tinakori Bowling Club.

I stepped out of one world into another; emerged from my hole and watched the black hills turn to grey and then in a sudden burst let their colours out. The houses turned pink and the windows shone.

I never told Willi. He would not have understood.

TWO

Because I grew up in Vienna people expect me to be musical. 'Ah,' they say (always they start with 'ah')– ah, Mozart', 'ah, Mahler', 'ah, Johann Strauss –' and they ask me if I play an instrument. (It is like expecting all Australians to throw the boomerang.) I find it hard to answer civilly. I say that I went to the opera with my friends when I was young and stood in the fourth gallery where one could hear but not see, and they take that for enthusiasm – the poor student, thirsting for music, standing entranced above the moneyed throng. They say 'ah' again. 'Ah, *The Magic Flute*! *Don Giovanni*! Wonderful!' I don't disabuse them – that I went to be with a girl I liked – but turn the conversation to other things. And if they insist on staying in Vienna, I talk about subjects that did interest me, and still do – painting, architecture, politics. Most of them have not heard of Egon Schiele or Alfred Loos. Dollfuss and Schuschnigg raise a glimmer of recognition in the older ones. Herzl, no. I tell the story – I should not, I cheapen it – about Jabotinsky speaking at the Konzerthaus, four hours he spoke, and at the end holding up a suitcase and crying, 'Run, Jews, run.' They smile uneasily at that. They do not know how or when to say the word 'Jew'.

Freud they have heard of. It is astonishing how much they think they know about Freud.

I took Jabotinsky's advice in the year that he gave it, 1937. My father's boot was planted on my rear and I ran, leaning forward to keep my balance, across Europe and the United States, and sailed down the Pacific and entered New Zealand by way of Australia. It was my good fortune to arrive as a tourist not a refugee, then it turned into a misfortune. I had lived in a great city and crossed two continents, but my world narrowed to an island in a harbour enclosed by hills, and to a tunnel scraped in the ground. But enough of that. I glimpsed my wife on Somes Island. That's where I first saw the woman I would marry. She wore a Wren's uniform and her hair was pinned up, very smart, under a black and white hat.

Now if it's music that you want, *she* was musical. She played the piano rather well. Thanks to her, all our children learned: piano, cello, violin. Our grand-daughter is at the Juilliard School, thanks to her. Why haven't I written down her name? Her name was Nancy and I loved her very much.

She banged out easy tunes for me, things that gave me pleasure, and laughed and called me 'old rum-te-tum', which I didn't mind; and when we were in Vienna in 1982 I took her to the opera and enjoyed (sitting not standing) the way the voices climbed over me and up into the roof – acoustical experts will disagree – instead of coming round the corner like a train; but enjoyed her pleasure more. In the Kärntnerstrasse I waited patiently while she listened to students busking – violins and flutes – and when she said, 'I wish Kenny could have gone on with it,' I answered with an honesty I would have avoided in Wellington: 'He wasn't good enough.'

'I know,' she said.

In Wellington she would have been fierce: 'He could have been.'

Elizabeth, our older daughter, was nearly good enough. The piano was her instrument and I hear her playing now in the living room which still, in 'our family', is 'the music room'. Elizabeth has 'come home', at her own insistence, and is 'looking after me'. With her I have to use these quotation marks. There's a lot of her language I can't have people mistaking for mine.

To begin with, how can my house be her 'home' when she has been married and raised children in another town far from here, and made a garden that featured in 'City Gardens' on TV, and been a well-known hostess (prime ministers at her table), and partnered her husband round the world many times, to this conference or that, and been, as she claims, 'fulfilled'? Divorce does not alter it. The younger prettier woman at her husband's side does not cancel out 'all the good times we had'. Sometimes this seems healthy and at other times sick. I want her to be happy but I also want her to rage and break things – break him. She won't do it. 'I'd rather move on to something new.' What then brings her 'home' to this old man?

She says that she is getting out of her children's way and giving them a chance to get to know their father's new wife. That is too much self-effacement. It's self-abasement. 'If I can help them all to be happy I will,' Elizabeth says. She loves her husband still but does not want him any more. Is my daughter some sort of saint? I ask myself that question when I exhaust all other ways of trying to understand her. And I ask myself too whether it might not be that she is sly, she's devious. Perhaps she's just relieved to be free – delighted perhaps. The tunes she plays are merry enough. But if freedom is what she is after, why come here?

She's pretty still. She is a smooth-faced woman. There's not a wrinkle to be seen. Her body is plump – nice and plump, I almost wrote – and she dresses in a way that makes her seem rich and ripe, but also locked-up and unrevealed. Concealment is a good part of her style. She is a smiley person; smiles with genuine sweetness – I think it's genuine – but sweet has never been a flavour that I've liked: I much prefer savoury, in women as in everything else.

Elizabeth is contradictory. She's deep. One must not be taken in by her surfaces, yet she gives one little option but to accept what she presents, for she's vigorous in turning away exploratory expeditions – no visa granted – and subtle in her defensive shifts when the intimacies of shared experience, or of blood, bring about penetrations deeper than she wishes to allow.

A consequence is that she can seem shallow. She seems dim. People talk down to her or are too attentive and too kind. She lets it happen. Understands. Now and then she steps back and takes a deep breath to give her strength. As a hostess, as a dinner party or reception guest, she must have done better. Have I said that she is intelligent? Elizabeth has many interests and is able to converse wittily and sensitively. She's good at leading with little questions, and good at being quiet in a clever attentive way. It's a pity then that when she is happy and relaxed, which is most of the time, she lets her language lie so dead.

She's welcome here, in my house. She can, if she likes, make it her home. But she is not, definitely not, 'looking after' me.

I need no looking after. I am a spry old man. Before Elizabeth came I hired a woman to clean the house and iron my shirts and fold my sheets (I washed them and pegged them out myself, enjoy pegging clothes out in the sun), but I did my own cooking and the dishwasher did the washing up. I am a clever cook. I'm good at subtle tastes and various and competing flavours. Sauces, spices, herbs, with small cuts of meat and baby vegetables: these are the things I used to treat myself to. I am a better cook than Nancy was. I'm better than Elizabeth. But it's all gone.

There was never an ounce of fat in my cooking. There's not an ounce of fat on me. 'You need more weight on you, Dad,' Elizabeth says. Just a few minutes ago she brought me a cup of coffee and a sticky cake. Sticky cakes are another thing about Vienna that I do not miss. I opened the window and threw it on the lawn, where two thin sparrows tore it urgently before a gang of starlings arrived.

I must say that I like what she is doing in the garden. We will end up on TV.

❖

'What are you writing?' she asked me yesterday.

I made a defensive shift of my own. 'Putting a few things down before I forget.' I hoped she would think I meant things that I must do; or business perhaps, although I have no business left. I closed the notebook carelessly and yawned.

She had seen from her glimpse of the crowded pages that it was more than I said, and my bad acting reinforced it, but she's helpful and she let my deception stand.

'Do you draw maps any more?'

'Maps?'

'And charts? Diagrams?'

'No.'

'Whenever we had a map to do for school you'd always do it.'

'Did I?'

'Wonderful maps. You used to do little strings of barges on the rivers. The teachers couldn't understand.'

'It was a map that helped get me locked up,' I said.

'Locked? Somes Island, do you mean?' She looked at it incuriously. 'Spies draw maps. Was that what they thought?'

'It showed a naval base. It was there so I put it in. I was an innocent young man.'

'You must have been. With a German name.'

'I was a Jew so I thought I'd be safe.'

'Poor Dad.'

'A good many things got reversed down here.'

'Down here' made her blink, for she was not used to hemispheres in me. I had always pulled my accent straight – as straight as I could manage – before I spoke. My children were never much aware of having an Austrian or a Jewish dad. Later, when they were curious, I produced anecdotes and left them to find the larger history for themselves. They've not questioned me about it, none of them, ever. I shared the history with Nancy, as I shared my life.

'See, Dad, Vienna,' they'd say, pointing at the name on the page of a book, the way an entomologist's child might say, 'There's a beetle, Dad', and walk on. I walked on too. I did not stop to examine Vienna, and I take little notice now. I do, though, examine the Vienna that is gone. I used to draw maps of it, and I drew one after my conversation with Elizabeth yesterday. The Ring and the Kärntnerstrasse are the only streets marked in, and St Stephen's Cathedral the only building, although I included the ferris wheel at the Prater, and the river and the canal. Hills and woods stand around the margin and flat lands run away to Hungary. A tug with smoke rising from its funnel tows a string of barges upriver from Budapest.

My map is out of scale but no matter. I did not draw it for accuracy or to pinpoint this place or that, but to illustrate where the city stands. My family, generations back, came out of the East to the Vienna that, historically, guards the West. The hills and the woods mark a boundary. You can stand in Vienna – as I did once on a bridge over the Donaukanal – stand like a direction post with one arm pointing east and the other west, signalling a change at that point. From the wanderer to the settled man. From cart to motor car and plough to desk. From the communal to the social. Prayer to conversation. Dark to light. So it seemed to me. I had just walked up from Josefstadt, where Eastern Jews filled the Taborstrasse, people so foreign to me, so antipathetic and, it seemed, dangerous too, that I had walked fast out of there and not rested until I was on the Sweden Bridge and could see the hills in the west and the stars sprinkled in the sky. I turned myself into a signpost and sighted along my right arm into Europe.

This map I've drawn is part of my history. I'll keep it although I'll not show Elizabeth.

The streets where you could see large motor cars – Bentleys and Daimlers with chauffeurs at the wheel – and, through cafe windows, plump be-ringed matrons playing bridge; and nursemaids in frilly caps pushing baby carriages, and pretty girls fresh from class arm in arm with fathers carrying silver-headed canes; and more pretty girls (Vienna was a city for them) smiling from behind mountainous cakes in pastry shops – they were the streets where I belonged. It caused me some confusion, for I was a communist; but when I remembered I narrowed my eyes, observing the decadence, and curled my lip in a show of scorn. How these bourgeois would run from me if they knew the future I was plotting for them.

My father had a silver-headed cane. My father owned a Mercedes – but drove it himself. I did not scorn to go along for the ride. Mostly we went into Burgenland. A favourite drive was to Neusiedler See, where our goal was usually Purbach. Sometimes we crossed on the ferry to Podersdorf, and once we went to Illmitz, further south, but that turned out to be too long a trip for Mother, who liked to be home in Gluckgasse before dark. Franz sat in front with Father, while she was in the back seat between Susi and me. She felt safe there, and made us safe, and was queenly, dignified, turning her head to the left and right. She did not care for novelties and she never exclaimed. No craning to see out the rear window for her. She did not lean or point and would not allow us to hand things across her. I'm not sure that she saw much more than the back of Father's head as we drove. Father chain-smoked Turkish cigarettes, which Franz would stub out for him in the dashboard ashtray. Mother ate Leckerbissen, little sweets from a basket lined with frilly paper, keeping her right hand bare to pick them out. At intervals she offered one to Susi and me. Three on the outward trip, three driving home was the ration.

My mother and father seem like caricatures. I mustn't allow that. They died in Nazi concentration camps and I won't allow that either – I mean that I won't picture them there. I have dreamed their deaths many times but dreams have no place in my narrative. What I must do is see my parents straight. From my description so far you would expect Mother to be plump and greedy and vain, a complainer perhaps, and not to have much time for her children.

The opposite is true. She was tiny. I am not a tall man but the top of Mother's head fitted under my chin when I embraced her. I used to worry that her bones would snap if I squeezed too hard. Her hands were as light as balsa wood; she herself as light as balsa wood. Leaning backwards to lift her feet off the ground, I seemed to be lifting dry sticks. It did not come from ill health, for she was strong and agile and had a lovely pinkness in her cheeks. She was always busy round the apartment. Had borne her children easily. Had raised them in what today would be called a hands-on way, even though a nursemaid did all the grubby work. There was no fragility in her, but she had a nervousness that came from love, and from ambition perhaps. She was greedy for her children to succeed, and always alert; was cunning, ruthless, savage sometimes, against any person standing in our way. She was a snob. That accounts for her performance in the Mercedes. But there was also ceremony there and I can't see that as a vice. She was a little neurotic about physical dangers. That was fragile in her, I suppose. She did not want us killed in accidents. My father, who longed to drive fast, had to drive slowly, and not set our destination too far away. We must be home in the Innere Stadt before the sun went down. If the street lights flickered on as we arrived she would smile and say, 'There.'

Once out of the car Mother would allow herself to lean and point and stare. She became lively and curious. She fed us information, little facts, and so increased us. Father might wave his hand, leaving a trail of ash – the town, the lake: he did not need closer definitions than that – but Mother would tell us all. We got history, botany, politics, economics from her, as well as culinary tips and health information; we learned how to order in a restaurant and which foods complement which. I know the names of the waterbirds that feed in the rushes of Neusiedler See because of her. And so many other things I have not had to remember in sixty years: how the Roman legions formed for battle; the constitution of the Free Town of Rust; how to cook a goose. You felt her pat each piece of information into place. She hummed with satisfaction and looked to see how we had grown. Her pleasure gave her insistence a gentle quality, and put an excitement and lightness in our lives.

Father, on the other hand, was a bit of a bully. It came from carelessness not cruelty. A cigar-smoking capitalist: you would have him bloated perhaps? You would have him jowly and with a roll of fat on the back of his neck? Not a bit of it. He was spry, like me. He was trim and agile. He hopped like a flea and was too quick in his movements to keep track of. (I'm talking about the movements of his mind.) He changed direction at angles so severe that we, trying to follow, overshot, and were left groping in the dark while he sparkled somewhere else. It provoked me several times to bouts of rage, and reduced Susi to tears. Franz simply shrugged and yawned. Father laughed at us and gave us a push on the back of the head – something between a cuff and a caress. We were hopeless, he seemed to say, and had better run off and talk to our mother. He lit his evening cigar and gave himself up to his newspaper. With my father I always had the knowledge that I did not measure up. I wanted to please him but never could. I made him take notice in the end by outraging him.

I liked him best when he turned lazy, when he found nothing to interest him. He would have liked to screech round corners on our drive to Neusiedler See, but was not allowed, so he became as lazy as the car, as lazy as the countryside and the little towns. He waved his cigarette at the horizon and said, 'Yes, all this. Very nice.' Life reduced its pace and we ambled comfortably by the margins of the shallow lake, and Father, that sinewy man, became a little fat. So it seems. Things take a significance which they did not have – by the laws of consciousness, thank God. He gave his arm to Mother and held Susi's hand and let Franz row when we went on the lake. Sometimes he would walk between us, Franz and me, and offer us a cigarette, which we smoked like men.

Back home, in his smoking room, he would sometimes keep Franz back after pushing me and Susi out.

'What do you talk about?' I asked.

'Business,' Franz said – which was the coal business. Father's firm supplied the railways and the river tugs. 'He wants to start buying timber soon. And importing Bordeaux wine. Brandy too. He gave me some.' That was not a lie. I smelled it on his breath. 'We talk about politics.'

'He always talks about that.'

'Pan-Europeanism, that's what he wants. A continent of sans patries.'

'That wouldn't work.' I was much more a realist than Franz. 'Look how they guard borders.'

'But we've got to be Austrians first. That's what he says. Then we can think about all Europe. So we'll be safer.'

'We're safe now.' (My realism failed there.)

'He said some Jews tried to join the Heimwehr.'

'We don't have to be Jews.' (And there.)

'Maybe,' Franz said. 'He says the Zionists are the trouble.'

My father was an integrationist. He simply wanted to be Austrian. Perhaps he was, more accurately, an assimilationist. He was anxious to lose his racial identity – and indeed, like many Viennese generations removed from the ghettos of the East, wanted not to think of himself as Jewish at all. Politically there was nowhere for him to go, for he was a monarchist too. He looked back wistfully (and with a trace of desperation) to the days of Franz Josef, the old Emperor, who had been sensible enough to protect 'his Jews'. Try to protect. It had never been, never is, absolute. My father named his sons for that old man. I almost wrote 'old rhinoceros', but Franz Josef knew a thing or two. It's just that he seems centuries out of his time, although he died in 1916. My father took part in the war triggered by the assassination of his heir. He did not fight, although he wanted to 'serve Austria', but spent his time managing coal. It stood him in good stead when he was able to go into business on his own.

We were konfessionslos, which means without religion. Some Jews of our class converted to Catholicism, others became Methodists (I can't see what attracted them there), but Father and Mother had too much pride to take on a set of beliefs out of self-interest or fear. Their strongest belief was in their Austrian-ness. They wanted to take on the colour of Vienna, and be certain of their place, and no more noticed than any other prosperous citizen. They could not understand Judenhass (hatred of Jews) – and Father, seeking for reasons, came to believe that Jewish meddling in politics was the cause. He could not go deeper than politics. The Ostjuden, the Zionists, the Jews busy in the Social Democrat Party, and those few who found a place among the Christian Socials angered him almost equally. Arthur Schnitzler made the joke that anti-semitism became popular in Vienna only when the Jews themselves took it up. It's a bad joke but in a way it fits my father.

Being konfessionslos made no difference in the end. Nor did being Catholic or Methodist. Abseitsstehen – staying aloof – made no difference. The hatred was not political or religious but racial. I don't know why I bother to write that down, everyone knows. The Nazis used to chant a jingle and scrawl it on walls: Was der Jude glaubt ist einerlei. In der Rasse liegt die Schweinerei. Which means: What the Jew professes is of no account. Swinishness lies in the race itself.

I played bowls this afternoon and found Kenny waiting for me when I came off the green. He drove me up the hill to Wadestown and waited while I showered and put on fresh clothes.

'Now, what is it, Kenny? You've got a problem?'

He swallowed. Kenny is a capable and decisive man – his career in business proves it – yet he cannot be a man of any sort with me. I can't see how I've done this to him. I wanted him to be happy, prosperous, large in his mind, to be a man of courage and virtue, yet when I examine him he regresses to the child who had to be made to practise his violin.

It was not I who locked him in the music room, it was Nancy. I let him out when I came home; and when he developed an interest in cricket I took him to provincial matches at the Basin Reserve, and had him explain the rules to me, trying to make him feel important, trying to make him free. 'He's stonewalling,' Kenny said. I liked that metaphor. I began to like cricket, its elegance and futility: the men in white, hour-long, day-long, stroking a ball with a bat, yet finishing with a drawn game at the end of it. Kenny grew tired before I did. We took the tram to Thorndon and walked up the hill, and branched off the road at the Waterworks building, approaching our house by a path through the bush. (Still I want to write 'through the woods'.) Nancy was at the kitchen bench, preparing dinner and I stopped to admire her: so quick yet so dishevelled and impatient.

'I wonder what she's cooking,' I said.

'I'll see,' Kenny said, and he began climbing a tree growing just off the back of our section. He went up easily until he was fifteen feet from the ground and had sufficient angle to see the bench.

'It's meat.'

'I know that, stupid. What sort?'

He went a little higher, holding the trunk. 'I can't tell.'

'Come on down. We'll go and see.'

'Dad . . .' His foot groped. 'I can't.'

'Yes you can. Put your foot on the branch. Come down the way you went up.'

But his confidence was gone and with it all sense of where his hands and feet must go. He could only hug the trunk and close his eyes.

'Kenny,' I said, 'you're a yellowbelly. You went up so you can come down.'

It was no use. I recognised his state: the narrow box with closed lid, and consciousness restricted to what the arms are wrapped around. I went to the garden shed and wrestled the ladder from behind it. Nancy ran out of the kitchen.

'Kenny's stuck up a tree,' I said. (What an absurd name 'Kenny' is. Nancy is responsible for that.) I put the ladder into the branches and climbed up and tried to loosen his hold. 'Kenny, it's all right, it's me, Dad. I'm going to take one of your feet and put it on the ladder.'

'No,' he whispered.

'Open your eyes, Kenny.'

He would not. Nancy had climbed up behind me; and Susan was two rungs off the ground, bawling her eyes out.

'Kenny, just do what I say.'

'Josef, go down,' Nancy said. 'He'll do it for me.'

'If he'll just put his foot –'

'Get out of the way. Go and look after Susan.' She hooked her fingers in my belt and hauled me four rungs down, side-stepping into the branches – amazing grace – as I went by. Then she whispered at Kenny's ear, ten minutes long. I had to run for the kitchen, with Susan bobbing in my arms, to save the meat from burning. Called Elizabeth from her practice in the music room, left her in charge, took my post again at the foot of the ladder as, rung by rung, she brought him down. She bent outwards, was curved out, and he was safe inside her, as though he was in her womb again.

'Kenny,' I began, when his feet touched the ground, but her eyes silenced me. Hugging him, she took him inside while I put the ladder away and locked the garden gate. She was washing his face in the bathroom when I went looking for them. I heard their voices and paused outside the door.

'I can do it when he's not watching,' Kenny sobbed.

I have that effect on him still. It does not come from any pressure I can identify; yet he will say, 'Don't bully me, Dad', when all

I have done is look judicious or uncertain. Perhaps I was too insistent on pointing to moral standards, too ready with 'right' and 'wrong', but I found myself afflicted with watchfulness in the home, a place where I should have been free. I generalised too much, I see it now; gave too many lessons, and pushed my children off, without knowing it, from the transaction they wished to make with me. Transaction? From the hug or kiss they might have offered. But does that turn a boy into a nebbish? Does it make him unable to climb down from a tree?

I offered Kenny a glass of beer, which he accepted, although I was having lime cordial myself. Bowls dehydrates me, and I wake dry-mouthed and headachy at 2 a.m. if I do not fill up with water straight away.

'It's that bloody woman you put on to me,' he complained.

'Don't swear, Kenny. What woman?' I said.

'That Gummy. Gummer. That friend of yours I sold a mortgage to.'

'I don't know any Gummers.'

'The mother was the one you sent. She's senile now. The daughter's got power of attorney. She keeps on coming in and threatening me.'

'Mrs Lloyd's daughter, is that who you mean? Is Mrs Lloyd senile?'

'She's gaga, Dad. I went to visit her. She's lost her marbles.'

'I didn't know.'

'She calls herself Mrs Gauss and says she's learning German to go to Germany.'

'Has she forgotten Willi's dead?'

'Who's Villi?'

'Willi Gauss. He was on Somes Island with me.'

Kenny sent an impatient glance across the harbour at my third eye. 'How do I know what she knows? I couldn't get any sense.

32

It's the daughter I have to deal with. She's even crazier than her old lady is.'

'What does she do?'

'She says I cheated her mother. She says she's going to the police. She's laying charges.'

'Can she do that?'

'Of course she can't.'

'Did you cheat her mother?'

'Shit, Dad.'

'Don't swear.'

'I don't cheat anyone. I'm not in the cheating game. I sold her a mortgage, that's all.'

'The sort of interest you charge, that could be seen as cheating.'

Kenny slammed his glass down. 'I'm going.' Red-faced, upper lip bunched, white teeth gleaming. Yet his eyes were full again.

'Kenny,' I called, 'what is it you want me to do?'

'Just get those loonies off my back. You sent them in the first place.'

Then he was gone. His car made sounds of anger in the drive.

Poor boy, I thought. Poor Kenny. I wanted be at the cricket with him again, watching his finger point out fieldsmen on his home-made chart. 'Square leg. Fine leg. Third man.'

'Silly mid-off,' I said. 'Is that why you've made him cross-eyed?'

I would not call him yellowbellied again. I would not say, 'See if you can tell me, Kenny, why it's not right to behave like that.'

THREE

I feel the need for fullness and the rounding out of things. It cuffs and buffets me with 'not enough' and 'start again'. And I must try to tell no lies, for there's no one in a position to find me out. I need to know that I've improved.

Architecture comes into it. I mean the shape of the life I've made and how it may be built again, brick by brick, on the page. I am, above all, a practical man. So I must pull myself together. First comes Josef Mandl of Vienna. But each time I go back for my materials I must crawl through the tunnel. Direction and contour change. Air and language change. I must write those days in words that were not their own. Yet this language I write in is natural to me – I think in it, dream in it, and pass my daily life. Does it mean I can know that other time only at second hand?

I say no to that, even as I feel a dislocation, the little jolt that moves me outside natural understanding and hangs me with my feet several inches off the ground. The displacement is not only mine.

> Belov'd Vienna – dost thou lie on Ganges
> Or on the Nile?

The poet, whoever he was, asked a good question. There were no Nazis more eager than those of my home town. Once they were released they set to. Freud speaks of 'the deep abyss of

Vienna'. Stefan Zweig says 'the world fell back morally a thousand years'. It would be easy to proceed by quotation and accept this terminology which, in its context, is not wrong. It is just that I see the movement differently: a short step from one room into another.

These things are not mine to write about. I left Vienna in 1937, before the Anschluss, before the Blitzverfolgung, and my view does not have a place. I left on the point of my father's toe. It is strange how I persist in that – in seeing us like figures in a cartoon. In fact he hugged and kissed me and tears ran down his face. He pressed money in my hand and made me swear to write from every port. I did that; I wrote to my parents. I wrote long after they were able to reply.

My path to communism lay through the Boy Scouts. I enjoyed the marching in uniform and the saluting and the swearing of the oath. My parents were happy to see me there, following Franz, in an organisation so structured and Austrian. What they did not know was that many of the older boys were Reds and they used the Scouts as a recruiting ground. Vienna was a political city. It was a city for organisations, both legal and underground – for bomb-throwing and arson and private armies and bloody clashes in the streets. I was ten when the workers burned down the Palace of Justice. I stood in a park with my mother and watched them marching in from Ottakring and Floridsdorf. 'The hunger and the hatred of the suburbs' – men with pinched faces and starved eyes. Eighty of them were dead by nightfall, shot by the police. And when I was sixteen the Ringstrasse was blocked again, with machine-gun nests and barbed wire. I marched in my blue and yellow uniform to the Vienna Trotting Track and saw little Dollfuss, five foot nothing, prance up the steps to the draped rostrum, wearing a falcon feather in his cap. Columns of Heimwehr marched by, followed by the Tyrolese National Guard in sugar-loaf hats. 'Heil!' shouted the crowd. I shouted too, more in confusion than anything else. 'I announce the death of Parliament,' Dollfuss cried. Another year and he was hanging Social Democrats and turning his howitzers on the workers' model homes. That was the massacre of 1934. Dollfuss himself was dead a few months later, murdered by Nazis in an attempted putsch. So it went on. How could I not be political?

We camped among the beech trees, we sat around campfires singing songs, we slept in tents and cabins and learned skills that I was able to put to use several years later in the gorse-covered hills above the Hutt Valley. I was a listener and a watcher and something of a thinker too. I'll correct that: a reasoner. Nothing original came from me, but give me information to bend and fit and I made interesting shapes. I reached conclusions, and it was natural that in clerico-fascist Austria, and in embattled socialist Vienna (it's 1932 I'm talking about), I should come down on the left. I started listening to the German-language broadcasts from Radio Moscow and reading pamphlets slipped to me – I loved things clandestine and back-handed – by several of the older boys. The uplifting declarations and useful skills of the Boy Scout movement began to seem childish and I looked for a place to go where my new-found political wisdom might be put to use. I'll have to examine that as well: did I wish to be useful? The most truthful answer is that I wished to be active and wished to be free. The desire was a vehicle that rolled without direction until I was able to steer it on to the Marxist highroad. Then it went along at an exhilarating pace. And indeed my beliefs were sincere. Some of them I hold to this day.

Again I hear a voice saying 'not enough'. All right, go back.

At the Gymnasium I took English as my optional language and found that I had an aptitude for it. I liked its simplicities and its suppleness. It seemed to me a language made for forward movement. The mind-filling certainties of German were like good food, served with ceremony, but English was a stand-up feast; it was plucked from the table and eaten as one stretched across for something of competing flavour on the other side.

Is it only now that it seems so? I could not have made these judgements then. My father held that German was the greatest of all languages and that it was our natural tongue; felt perhaps that, mounded over us, it hid our ancestry from view. He saw no reason for me to know any other language, but chose Italian when I insisted, out of his admiration for Mussolini. I rebelled – one of the luckier rebellions of my life – but would not have had my way if Mother had not supported me. She had spent several years in England as a girl and spoke the language rustily and wanted someone to practise it with. As well as that, she wanted to share with me. For several years we sat knee to knee in her little parlour or strolled arm in arm in the parks, exchanging formulaic pleasantries and cramped information. Gradually I became proficient in the language and far more confident than she. 'And how are you this afternoon, my son?' she might begin, and I would reply, 'I am very well thank you, Mother.' But it was not long before 'Top hole, old fruit' became my response (I had bought a novel by P. G. Wodehouse in an Austrian Railways lost property sale), and we laughed in our second language and I began to chatter in it – albeit with an accent I still hear every time I open my mouth today. There are tricks my tongue never learned to do.

On the political level I took Wodehouse's novel for realism. How strange that in Dollfuss's Austria I should pledge myself to destroy Bertie Wooster's world: that in a police state, with the workers crushed and the peasantry under the thumb of savage priests, I should see a dinner-suited drone as my foe. It did not last for long: 'discussions' with the agitprop committee put me right. But I jump ahead – and I do not mean to write about that side of my 'education'. How futile it seems now. Enough to say that Trotskyism was portrayed as our greatest enemy.

With fellow students from my class (I'm in the eighth class now), fellow members of the KJV, I delivered illegal leaflets in tenement blocks in Döbling. The method was to go to the top floor, break open the packet, and come down fast, leaving a leaflet in each letter box or under the mat. I loved doing that. I was quick and neat and cool – was out of there wearing a little smile and on my bicycle pedalling home while the others were only halfway down. It was part of our discipline that we must ignore each other and not try to help if someone got into trouble; must 'fade away like smoke', our leaders said. We were like smoke in the streets of our city and soon we would be a fire burning old structures to the ground. I've no doubt all the underground groups felt that, and there were enough of them: communist, socialist, Nazi.

We heard them on Sundays in the Woods, singing their songs, as we, in our clearing, sang ours. The Woods were outside the city boundaries and although we kept an eye out for the mounted Heimwehr, illegal groups were safe there from the police. Several years ago I exchanged letters with Trudi Prager, who was my girl-friend in the summer of 1935, and she, in Miami, looking back more than fifty years and writing in a bouncy style that reminded me, wrenchingly, of her way of walking and of hugging and of kiss-ing, yet also, I imagine, with a tear in her eye, recreated those after-noons of sun and comradeship and hope and singing. 'Remember the little clearing,' she wrote, 'and how we came to it over the stream and how you boys offered your hands to the girls on the stepping stones. That used to offend us modern misses. "Get your paws away." Do you remember me saying that? And Wolf trying to carry Gretl and slipping on the rocks and dropping her to save himself? Some swain! But weren't those good days, Josef? They were our spring, and although we lost our summer, we can look back on some happy times.'

We put our food in the common pile, each what he could manage (I, from a wealthy home, was clever enough to see that quantity not quality served me best), and sat down obediently, although with a serious iconoclastic glee, to our morning of discus-sion and political study. Each of us had to lecture at some time.

When my turn came I spoke about the struggle of the Chinese communists, a talk based entirely on Malraux's *Man's Estate*, which I'd just read.

I was there as much for this, the serious part, as for the socialising and the flirting, the singing and the games that we moved on to in the afternoon. Some people came for that alone, and sat hiding yawns through the talk sessions, and we had our sexual opportunists too – couples dropped out and were not seen again – but a core, perhaps a dozen, were dedicated Marxists, and among that group I was perhaps the most ardent. Ardent, though, for revolutionary air more than tyrant blood. I felt myself uplifted on the swell of history. I was borne along by inevitability. How does this translate into everyday speech? How did it set me stepping through my days? I was an eager, bright boy, tumbling out his words – too many words. I see myself not with flashing but with darting eyes. Excitement moved me rather than passion. Nervous movement, in mind and body both, kept my insecurities from fastening on me. 'Yes' was my word – interrogative and affirmative – and 'we must' my declaration. I was a bit of a joke, but being laughed at seldom offended me, for it acknowledged, in a curious way, my purity, and turned me into the conscience of our group. Trudi Prager does not mention it. She simply says that it was hard to stop me from exclaiming. She says I sat there nodding and turning like one of those mechanical dogs that say 'Yap, yap.'

In the afternoon we played games, some of them introduced by the ex-Boy Scouts among us. Instead of 'Der Kaiser schickt Soldaten aus' we played 'Der Lenin schickt Soldaten aus'. Through the trees, across the stream, the Nazis were marching, their white socks flashing like rabbit tails and their leather pants gleaming. We raised our fists and roared at them, little roarings in the Vienna Woods – how sad and terrible our games seem now. We finished the day standing in a circle, singing the Internationale, all three verses, with our fists raised in the red salute, and then marched back to town in ranks, to the tune of our fighting songs, 'Die Arbeiter von Wien' and 'Roter Flieger-marsch'. People cheered us in the growing darkness and some joined our ranks and sang with us. At the tram terminus we broke up and went our ways, but little groups, carried away, would sometimes march on singing into the suburbs.

That, for several years, is how I spent my Sundays in Vienna. It worried Mother and enraged my father. Keep your head down, do not be seen except as a Viennese gentleman going to work or going home – that was his prescription for safety. Schuschnigg gave him hope for a while. He was no less a fascist dictator than Dollfuss had been, but was at least a lawyer and not a peasant. His policy was to keep Austria Austrian and Hitler and his Germans behind their frontier, and while he had Mussolini's support there seemed some hope that he might do it. His anti-semitism was a tactic – he used it only when he felt it would do him good. Schuschnigg had not understood, any more than my father had, the Judenhass of the Austrian.

I argued with my father that the best way for Jews to assimilate and not be seen was to join, join, join – Boy Scouts, I said, chess clubs, Esperanto groups, barefoot walkers. The argument would not extend to the KJV or the GRSV (United Red Student's League), which I joined when I went to the university, or to the Hilfzentrale, a pacifist organisation we began to infiltrate. The Hilfzentrale too was declared illegal. 'Everything you are in is underground,' my father cried. At times he recoiled from me as though I was unclean, as though I brought dirt and slime with me from down there. But to me we seemed creatures of the upper air. Every Aktion, every Treff, secret though it might be, took place in a glow of excitement and righteousness. The Nazis were earthbound, monochrome, while we were spirited and free, we were the future. I saw it in the long swinging stride of our girls, in their mannish haircuts – the Bubikopf – and in our red scarves which we sometimes wore pirate fashion round our heads.

Did I not glimpse the thing that uncoiled and opened its eyes and moved on its heavy sinuous path to crush and kill us? The answer is, no I did not. I saw violence, bulging faces, bulging eyes, and heard shouts and screams and saw blood and broken teeth, and heard, more than once, bones crack. I was a player in a dangerous game and brought home, two or three times, blood on my face to prove it. I had no doubt that it was an important game. Yet I could not be deep and could not scheme, could not be ruthless, and must have seemed light and unreliable to our bosses. I never became a boss myself.

Franz obeyed my father, he kept his head down, but Susi wished to follow me. She tried to join the Red Falcons, an underground children's group I had been in for a few months between the Boy Scouts and the KJV. Like me she was trying to be free, she wanted to be bobbing her hair and wearing a dirndl and marching in the Woods and running in the streets. I told her how we fought the Nazi students at the university and each side tried to throw opponents down the steps to the waiting police, who were not allowed inside the buildings. I told her about meetings closed by detectives, and friends of mine questioned and beaten in the cells, and how once, at a Hilfzentrale meeting on The Economic Causes of World War, the speaker had barely started when the police commissioner himself jumped up and cried, 'You're a pacifist organisation, you must not talk about war.' So one of the young KJV members, Herbert Roth, read a pamphlet instead, and it came much closer to sedition than the official speaker would have dared. The commissioner snatched it: 'We're confiscating this.' 'It will cost you three Groschen,' Bert Roth said, and the commissioner paid up.

That was a triumph just right for a girl of fourteen. Susi beat her feet on the floor in excitement. I told her how we wrote slogans on glass windows with fluoric acid, and how a group of students hid a red flag in the neon lighting tube above a blackboard. A time mechanism unrolled it slowly behind the professor during the compulsory lecture on Catholic Doctrine of the State. Susi laughed and beat her feet again. I did not tell her that there were bitter quarrels about this action because although it was supposed to be joint only the hammer and sickle appeared on the flag and not the socialist three arrows.

How shall I write of Susi? She escaped the Nazis but died in Paris of an asthma attack before even Father and Mother were dead. Franz, whom I loved as one loves a brother but did not like, buried her there and carried on to America where he – the coal factor's son, destined for wealth – worked behind a counter in East Side New York until he died. And that is a brief history of my brother and sister. It will not do.

I can only say of Susi that I loved her. I can only see her as she was for me. How can I pretend to know how she was for herself – a girl-child in the Vienna of the thirties, raised in a non-Jewish Jewish family, given everything she needed, and more, but little of what she wanted, and asking her brother to make her free? How do I say who that Susi was without spilling over her all that she was for me? I can only choose an incident, describe what Susi did, and hope that some part of her is contained in it.

Father would not allow her to join the Red Falcons or go to the Woods with me on Sunday. So now and then I took her to the Kuchelau, a sandy beach on the Danube north of the city, a popular picnic place at the time. The Alsergrund YCL met there, as well as Nazi and socialist groups, but Mother and Father did not know that. There was little chance for organised activity because the beach was crowded with ordinary Viennese enjoying an outing, but fierce impromptu debates went on between the communists and the socialists, and now and then Nazi groups tried to march. Sometimes we would sit cross-legged around some wise man and listen to his experience and advice.

There was a communist lawyer there the last day I took Susi, a worn-looking but lively man who had done time in the fascist concentration camp at Wollersdorf. Susi had not heard of concentration camps and could not believe we had one here, in Austria. In Germany perhaps, in Hungary. The lawyer smiled. He was taken with her. (Susi had the same features as me, but some shift in growing had turned her away from the foxiness I retained into a sharp-edged prettiness.) He gave us a short course in modern history, which I didn't need, although I sat there patiently, cross-legged. The sun, the crowds, the company: I'm happy, I thought. The meadows on the far side, the running of the river, and the city quiet in behind, while he spoke of Hitler, Horthy, Franco, Mussolini, made me think of longer histories and – it followed naturally – of the importance of this moment, now. I want nothing more, I want no change, I thought – and grinned at my sinfulness: a communist wanting to keep things as they were. Meanwhile Susi drank in his lesson, and when he moved on to police interrogation and how we must behave in court her eyes began to flash with a foxy light. 'Always sign your statement close to the last line,' he said. 'Yes,' Susi answered, knowing the reason before he explained. 'The accused must turn accuser,' he went on, and 'Yes,' she said. I smiled at her, and thought, This moment, now.

I took her swimming in the brown river, in the safe band between paddling children and young men sporting in the current far out. While we were there a German tug came down, towing barges. This was a regular event (and how discordant, unnatural, the hooked cross flying above the toy boat with its red funnel and tip-tilted nose). Each of the groups – communist, socialist, Nazi – gathered at the waterline and shouted slogans, sang their songs as it steamed by. A few of the stronger swimmers swam right out and cried, 'Down with Hitler' and 'Freedom for Thälmann' only a yard or two from the string of barges. Susi and I, up to our necks, screamed and shouted too. She bobbed on her toes, submerging as far as her mouth, then springing up until her throat was bare. I can still see her small fist dripping water while she smacked the surface with her other hand. We sang, or tried to sing, the first verse of the Internationale.

The Germans on the tug ignored us usually – the captain smoked his pipe and the bargees went about their work – but on that day a man on the stern of the last barge answered with a clenched fist, the red salute, which raised a roar of approval from the beach. The Nazi group there, white-socked, leather-buttocked – they kept to their 'uniform' in spite of the heat – exploded into rage and charged, wedge-shaped, at the Alsergrund YCL. They knocked them flying and set about them with their boots. That was all I saw of the larger battle: it became close and personal. Forgetting Susi, I ploughed from the water and found myself wrestling on the sand with a Nazi thug – his breath in my throat, his saliva smeared on my cheek. He rolled on me and crushed me with his weight and rose on one arm to beat my face, but two young men from the socialists pulled him away and threw him in the water and pushed him under when he came up.

Then I saw Susi. She had a double-fisted grip on the belt of another Nazi who was lifting and throttling the lawyer from Wollersdorf, and she tried to jerk him away. She was like a terrier in a dogfight swinging on the tail of some huge hound. He turned and punched backhanded, clubbed her with his fist, and she went tumbling on the sand with her hair (she should have been allowed her Bubikopf) twined round her throat. I scrambled to her and picked her up and did not see the end of the battle (people ran from all over the beach with their boots in their hands and clubbed the Nazis into retreat). I cleaned her and dried her with her towel and took her to a water tap and washed her bleeding mouth. For a few moments she was dazed; then she wept; and then grew happy. We had beaten them, she said. Yes, I agreed, and now we had to go home and face our father. Susi, brave Susi, made a grimace of mock fear with her wounded mouth.

Parental rage – I have felt it myself. And I sympathise with my father's extravagance, for he was afraid. He struck me; he gave me a full-handed slap that made my mouth bleed the same as Susi's. And when my mother, examining her, cried that her tooth was broken, he rushed at me for a second blow. Franz stood in his way. 'Father,' Franz said, 'we're a family.' It was a powerful word and it stopped him, although he continued to shout at me – using, among other terms, meshuggah and ganif: the only time I ever heard Yiddish from him.

He banished me from the supper table but someone, Mother or Franz, must have used the 'family' argument again, for Franz came to my bedroom door and thrust his head in. 'You can come.' And when I was at the table, Father said, 'We'll have no more talk about it now. Josef and I will talk in the morning.' Mother kept her eyes down and would not look at me; Franz, plump and waxy-skinned, ate in his orderly way; and Susi, white with pain from the nerve in her broken tooth, managed only a small agonised grin. I was resentful. I felt I had done well and should be praised – but enough. Enough of me. Before I set off on the tour that has lasted the rest of my life I want to say how they, Susi and Franz, made their escape from Vienna – and so be finished with them and let them rest.

This I put together from the letter Franz wrote from Paris to poste restante in Auckland, my only address. He told me about Susi – the girl of sixteen dying in a shabby Paris room, with her un-favoured brother, who had saved her, at her side. I'll talk about the saving, not her death, for I cannot, no matter how I try, make it mine. I've wept over her and wrung my hands but she won't be mine.

Anschluss. Hitler. Seyss-Inquart. Communists and socialists herded on trains to Dachau. It happened in a night and a day. Still Father would not leave. He did not try until it was too late. Austria, Austria, must have rung clear in his head like a bell. Persecution and murder in full swing – it was a German sickness, and Austrian good health would soon come back. All this while trucks full of

45

brown-shirted Viennese shouting, 'Juda verrecke' rumbled by in the streets, and the friendly caretaker, wearing a swastika armband, knocked him sideways on the stairs and spat in his face. But one part of my father's brain stayed unconfused, and the message was clear: Susi and Franz must go. Now, now, now. They must escape. Franz too was clear-headed and quick and smart. If Father made the decision, *Go*, and put the money together from bits he had hoarded here and there, Franz was the one who worked out how it must be done.

They both had passports, Susi's secured just a few months before, on her sixteenth birthday, because Franz had persuaded Father it would be wise. But after the Anschluss Austrian passports had to be validated with a swastika stamp and if you were Jewish you could not get one. So most escaping Jews were turned back at the borders. Many got free – went through tortuous channels, bribed their way, some to safety, others to countries soon to be occupied. Franz had a friend who skied out over the mountains. He might have done that himself, he said in his letter, but he had Susi; so he tried an even braver thing, he went into Germany. The border officials were not concerned with Jews crossing over. From Munich he might have taken the train round Lake Constance to Switzerland, but there the guards would be alert. The other way, across the lake, had more chance of success: news of the swastika stamp might not have reached a smaller post. So he and Susi took the steamer, and it worked. The Swiss border guards let them through (the Germans closed that loophole a few days later), and my brother and sister had escaped from the Nazis. In Basel they tried to take the train to France but were thrown off because Austrian passports were no longer valid. They crossed the border on foot, paying their guide, and found another train – two young Jews with a suitcase each, with their useless passports, with their bit of money next to their skin – and reached Paris, where they could not work, where they were stateless. Susi died.

Franz buried her. Somehow he got himself to New York – I never asked how – and there his energy ran out. Franz, who is the hero of this story, Franz, my brother, whom I never liked, found a job and rented a room and never left either; grew fatter and paler (I visited him, for an hour, in 1967) and died after thirty years of it. He left me the few dollars he had, and Susi's Austrian passport, with no swastika stamp, and a folder of research into our parents' death. There was also a framed studio photograph of the Mandls, taken in 1935. Father is looking proud and Mother dignified. Susi and Franz are smiling. I wear a twisted mouth that might pass for a smile. I did not want to be part of this bourgeois ceremony.

When I went into Father's study in the morning I was surprised to find Mother there. I disturbed them in an embrace. I had never seen them do more than formally kiss, or her take his proferred arm when they were out walking and rest her gloved fingers on his sleeve. Now they comforted each other, and held hands when they moved apart. It frightened me. It told me that my fate would be severe.

'It's not as if the university is doing you any good. You've wasted all your time there. You've not done any study. Life is not . . .' Father said, and could not go on.

'Life is not a game, Josef,' Mother said.

'And Susi must not . . . you will ruin her life. Don't you under-stand, we must not be seen.'

So, that old argument. I managed to insulate myself. But Mother, seeing my face harden, ran to me. 'Josef,' she cried, 'listen to your father.'

'We cannot have it, Josef. We cannot take the risk.'

'There's no risk –'

'Listen,' she cried.

Father wet his lips. I understand how hard it was for him. I understand how much family meant. All that was most precious existed in this little compound inside the compound of our street, and forces he could only half see – turning, my father, this way and that – pressed in and threatened to destroy us. I see him in a trap, not understanding the mechanism. He hardened himself, this kind-hearted man, to expel me and make the rest of them safe – and perhaps make me safe as well, in the world outside.

'We cannot have you here any more,' he said. 'We cannot have you putting her in danger.'

'For your own sake, Josef,' Mother said.

'You are old enough. And when you've seen it – seen the world – you can come back. We will be waiting for you here.'

'You will understand then, Josef. You will be a man.' She embraced me – her fragile bones. Father, standing close beside us, with his hand on my shoulder, turned his head away so that I should not see him weep. But I had no pity except for myself.

'I don't want to leave Vienna.'

'You must, Josef. You must.'

'The police will come. Police are everywhere. They'll come and find you.'

'Franz found all those papers you had hidden in your books,' Mother said.

'Papers?'

'Communist,' Father said.

'They're only pamphlets.'

'They're illegal. Josef, what are you doing? Don't you know they'll hang you?'

'What did you do with my pamphlets? They were mine.'

'Stupid boy,' Father shouted. 'You're a stupid boy.'

'We burned them,' Mother said. 'Josef, in these days, we have to be safe.'

'And you are going away,' Father said. 'Right away. You can come back when you're sensible.'

'Darling, darling, you can see the world.'

For me there was no world outside Vienna. And when I left –

visas, tickets, money, suitcases, even skis – I believed I would find nothing there. I reached New York on a forward slant, propelled, as I've said, by my father's boot, and did not stay in that unnatural city. It rose so high. We in Vienna were ground-clingers, although we might live in apartments four flights up. Thirty, forty, fifty storeys – 101 the Empire State – filled me with dismay. I felt my dislocation from my place, felt myself turn giddily in the thinned air; and I ran, leaning forward still, across America, and let gravity tumble me down the oceans into a country where, if the proportions were wrong, at least they erred on the side of smallness; where, although things remained unrecognisable still, at least I might shift along close to the ground.

FOUR

My senses have always been sharp and my memories are precise, and when I recall smells, sounds, textures – the smells of chocolate and coffee and cigars and marsh mud and hot leather and river water, the sound of creaking suitcases, the grinding of tram wheels, the textures of silk and lace and hair – then I experience a kind of suffocation as time stops and breathing is held still and one small part of an existence becomes the whole. My mother's scarf slithers cold, a snake, across my wrists – and that, for a moment, is all of me. The rude smell, the savoury smell, of Father's cigar wraps me round and I am in his study once again. Then there is taste and flavour – and almost always it is bread that stops me in my tracks. Colour of crust and firmness of bread-flesh, grain and texture of crumb, loaf-weight, weight on the palm, and the shape of it, mounded, coiled, plaited, smooth – these become a part of bread in my mouth, of its presence on my tongue. I experience a transference; it is almost synaesthesia, magical. Time and place slide across their natural boundaries and become a function of consciousness. For a heartbeat. For a breath. Regulators are not to be denied, for which I'm grateful.

Elizabeth is baking now and although she uses something called a bread-maker, the smell is genuine enough. Warm yeast, rising dough, how ancient they are. There must be ancestral memories – hot stones, fermentation – going back into times of which there can be no other record. If one day there is to be an obituary of Josef Mandl it must say – I demand it says – 'He taught New Zealanders to eat bread.'

The kitchen, Nancy's kitchen, from which I've just returned, is no longer a place in which I'm welcome or at home. Elizabeth turned the oven light on and let me look through the glass and I saw with disappointment that she had made rolls instead of the cob loaf I had hoped for. She was brusque with me and snapped off the light. My interest in bread is an affectation, she believes. The other woman, smoking at the table, thinks so too, although she has nothing to base an opinion on. She took a dozen rapid puffs to occupy herself.

'If you don't mind, Julie,' I said.

'What?'

'No smoking.'

'Oh, shit, the nicotine mafia,' she said, and stubbed the cigarette out in the peanut butter lid Elizabeth had placed as an ashtray.

'Thank you,' I said, courteous, although I trembled briefly in a rage. 'I don't mind if you smoke on the porch. How are you, Julie?'

'OK. Why?'

'I was hoping that you're better. Kenny said you'd had some sort of setback.'

'Did he now?' A strange unseeing glitter in her eyes.

'Julie and I were talking, Dad,' Elizabeth cut in. 'I'll bring you a hot roll when they're done.'

'As soon as I turn my back you'll let her smoke again.'

'Let me have the kitchen, Dad. Give me one room, please.'

'Your mother never smoked in the kitchen.'

'I'll go on the porch,' Julie said. 'I'll go in the garden.' She went, with a jangle of tin jewellery and a waft of sweat.

'Now see what you've done,' Elizabeth said. 'She's your granddaughter, Dad. You could at least be polite to her.'

51

'Call her in, then. Call her back. I'm going.'

I sit at my desk and watch them walk up and down the lawn – Elizabeth using her skill as a listener and the girl animated, sliding her bangles up her arms, running her hands through her hair. More trouble, I think; she only comes here when she's got points to score. I see how sharp her lips are and how pointed her teeth.

I've never liked her, even when she was a child. A thin, demanding, screeching, whining, querulous small girl. She had bones that hurt me when her mother parked her on my knee – where, to my relief, she never stayed. She had Kenny's padding as a baby but seemed all joint and angle by the time she was four, and shed even more of her meagre flesh as she grew. I'm aware that this is selective and I see the easy damage a description can do, yet when I cast around for something nice to say – her brown thin hands, how they express; her finely made ears – I come up with bits of prettiness. I would do better to leave her alone; but there she is, centred in my view, imparting – I am sure of it, see her lips work – spites and dissatisfactions to Elizabeth.

The rolls are firm and tender and spread with the home-made blackberry jam sent to me across the strait from Nelson. Blackberries. Another taste that brings a memory – but I'll leave it now and concentrate on what's before my eyes. Not that girl eating berries from her tin billy in the sun all those years ago, but this one on my lawn, with her hair shorn up one side and weighted on the other, and rings, half a dozen, ruining one ear, and a silver stud like a pimple in her nose. There's a tattoo on the point of her shoulder. That is new. Please do not let her put tattoos anywhere else.

I'm surprised that I care enough to ask. It comes not from love, for love is rare, but close connection; from shared blood, which binds with a knot I can't unpick. My son's daughter, my grand-daughter, hurts me and concerns me and I am shaken by the depth of it.

❖

52

Elizabeth is grave but there is broken glass behind her smile. She sees Julie into the little pink Honda, the toytown car, that is, I suppose, a present from Kenny (he tries to win Julie's love with expensive gifts). She lets her hand rest on the girl's shoulder as though trying to hide the ankh tattoo, and kisses her, which is a surprise. She whispers to Julie, prompting her, and Julie flashes a false smile at me, 'Goodbye, Grandpa. Thanks for letting me visit.'

'You're welcome, Julie. Come back and have a talk some time.' For I want to help, I want to like, and I'm curious. How, why, has her life turned into a path without direction, when not much more than a year ago she moved ahead so surely to her goal? I had been able to see it in her feet – another pretty part, high-arched and expensively shod (shoes from Kenny). They pointed forward, tapped impatiently to be gone. All the same there was a day when she sat with me on the veranda – I in my canvas chair, she on the top step with her toes slightly turned in – and talked in a way she never had before, easily and happily and with a flicking of her hair. She leaned back on her arms and her elbows turned double-jointedly, and I almost cried, 'Don't, they'll snap.' The stretched skin of her inner arms was white and pure.

She said, 'I'm good at it, Grandpa. It's nice to know you're good.'

'Congratulations. What comes next?'

'After the juniors? The seniors. Next season.'

'And what do you do?' I said. 'Do you bat or bowl?'

'I do both. But batting's my best. I scored fifty-one last week.' She sighed with pleasure, remembering it, and I thought what a difference happiness can make, plumping out a skinny girl into a fat one. (She was not fat of course but gave a round impression on that day.)

I asked her what she meant to do with her life, apart from play cricket.

'Oh,' she said, 'the law. I guess I'll do law. I'll switch next year. Dad wants me to go in with him.'

'Property law, then? Business law?'

'Yes. Why not? I want to be rich, Grandpa. There's nothing wrong with that.'

'Be rich and score centuries?'

'Centuries and millions,' she grinned. 'Centuries first.'

'Does Kenny need a lawyer in his game?'

'Oh, the law's a base. You can stand on it, Dad says, and jump whichever way you like.' She sighed again, reversed the painful angle of her elbows and massaged the insides with her palms. 'I love your house, Grandpa. I've always loved your house.'

'I love it too.'

'I want one like this. Up top. With a view.'

'You'll get one, no doubt.'

'But first I want to enjoy myself.'

'You'll do that too.'

'Nobody better try and stop me.' She touched the inside of each wrist with her tongue and rubbed the saliva in as though it were a lotion: an innocent self-love, it seemed to me, although a little strange, a little too removed from the world. 'Come and see me play,' she said. 'Dad's coming.'

A wasp was buzzing round her face and she flicked her hand at it. Some hard part, fingernail or knuckle, sent it tumbling senseless into the garden.

'You're quick,' I said.

'Gotta be.'

'Have you ever played table tennis? You'd be good at it. I played once. We had tables in our youth clubs and I played for Döbling against Alsergrund. Won easily.'

'What's Döbling?'

'A suburb of Vienna. I was beaten in the final by a fellow from Josefstadt.'

'Germany,' she said.

'What?'

'In Germany. That war.'

'Vienna is in Austria. And it was before the war.'

'Well, whatever.' Julie yawned and stood up. 'Gotta go, Grandpa. Gotta go to practice.'

'In the war,' I said, 'I was interned. Out there.'

'Where?' she said, looking.

'On Somes Island. For four years. I was an enemy alien.'

'I heard about that. No one ever told me they used Somes Island though. You're not kidding me?'

I felt my balance slipping and I put my hand on the porch rail to hold myself still. 'It's not important. Only to me.'

'An island must have been a picnic, eh?'

'It was,' I said, 'yes.' For at the word picnic some gigantic weight in me, an iron screen, rolled aside, and I saw the camps at Chelmno and Dachau, and what went on there; and I repeated, 'Yes,' and said, 'I'm tired, Julie. Good luck in the match.' And managed to close the screen again and think instead of her ignorance, which surely crippled her, and crippled her generation, and yet might be seen as a blessing.

I had reasons after that for liking her more and liking her less; but saw her in her round persona only once again, as she walked out to bat for the Wellington Junior Women's Cricket team against Canterbury.

Kenny and I sat on the bank – Kenny and I at the cricket again! – and watched her take centre and face up and tap her bat on the popping crease, and oh how frail she suddenly was, with head up and bottom out and bony legs strapped in man-sized pads. She scored nineteen (which was her age) and stayed at the crease while other batsmen came and went.

She was wristy, she had style and finesse, but no strength. She never drove but scored her runs in cuts and deflections and scampered in her flapping pads up and down the pitch, while numbers six and seven and eight slogged away until they were skittled or caught. Julie was mathematical. Angle and gap, pace, turn, bite of ball on the grass: she read them instantly. Clever batting. She might have won the game for Wellington but ran out of partners and her captain sent the order out for her to slog. Which she tried, and suddenly her timing and her competence were gone. They should have trusted to the skills she had. Instead she aimed for the mid-wicket boundary and popped a catch straight back into the bowler's hands.

I understand cricket. I like the game. Patience, skill, formality, not too much brute strength. I would go again if it weren't for the beery thugs who infest the grounds. If it weren't for the memory of Julie. She did what no one must ever do: disputed the umpire's decision. Her clear indignant voice rang across the ground: 'That was a bump ball.' Turned to the square leg umpire: 'Bump ball. You saw.'

'For God's sake, Julie,' Kenny whispered.

She made a furious turn and scythed down the stumps with her bat. Then she walked off, eyes hot, leaking tears, while the opposing team made way for her as though she'd scored a hundred.

'Cooked her goose,' Kenny said, driving me home. He gnawed his lips. 'Jesus, Julie,' thumping his hands on the wheel. He would not come inside but dropped me at the gate. And Julie had, as he'd said, cooked her goose of course. She would never be chosen to play for Wellington again.

And she'll not, it seems, do law or go in with Kenny. She won't get her house on the hill or a million dollars in the bank. Ankh tattoos and nose studs and Doc Marten boots are now her way. There's more than a mistimed stroke responsible for this, more than a temper-flash driving out judgement. I must believe that it connects with things that came before.

And now I have the connection, although I won't accept it, I refuse.

'Does she even know what an ankh is?' I said.

'Maybe. She's going to put a scarab on her other shoulder. Or Anubis.'

'Why him?'

'Egyptian things are in.'

'Why not Isis?'

Elizabeth looked at me sharply. As I've said, there was broken glass, a cutting edge in her, so far removed from her usual softness that I asked, 'What, Elizabeth? Is something else wrong?'

'You didn't finish your roll.' She opened the window and threw it on the lawn. 'Blackberry jam. We're spoiling those sparrows.'

'What else did she say?'

Elizabeth sat down and gripped her knees. She seemed to want to twist her kneecaps off. 'She's been going to a therapist.'

'What sort? Why?'

'Trying to get her memories back.'

'Has she lost them? What sort of memories?'

'They've discovered that Kenny abused her as a child.'

I did not understand. Had he shouted, called her nasty names? He was too easy with her, far too soft for that. Then I heard 'abused' in its modern sense.

'No, that's impossible,' I said.

'Her therapist is a woman who specialises in that sort of thing. It's called repressed memory syndrome,' Elizabeth said.

'I've heard of it. Not Kenny, though. It's out of the question.'

'I don't know what to believe. Julie's sure. She's *sure*. She says she *remembers*.'

'Nonsense. Repressed memory is a hoax. It's a modern form of witchcraft. It all goes back to Freud, who was a charlatan. I know. I come from the same town.'

'Stop being stupid, Dad.'

'You're not saying you believe her? The girl's always been just a bundle of resentments. She has to blame someone because she's herself.'

57

'Be quiet. Let me think.'

'She's like a room that's been locked up too long. Open it and bad smells come out.'

Elizabeth leaned forward and hissed. I was afraid she'd bite me. 'You know Kenny. He's always been a weakling.' It was him she wanted to bite.

'Not that weak.'

'And sentimental too. "My girly girl." Can't you remember the way he used to stroke her? I thought even then something was wrong.'

'That's being a father. That was love.'

'It was . . .' Elizabeth said, and could not find a word.

'Elizabeth,' I said, 'it's fantasy. Things that bad you don't forget. What does she claim he did to her?'

Elizabeth shook her head. And perhaps it was her grief and anger and her helplessness, the loss of her usual placid self, that made me turn as though to another window, another view – a betrayal of the mind? a revelation? – and see Kenny and his child: a scene I'll not describe.

'God, no,' I said.

'What can we do?'

'Stop her,' I said. 'Don't let her go to the police.'

'Why not? If it's what he did? And he probably did. You know it, Dad.'

'I don't know it. Why did you tell me this? It spoils everything. I'm going to telephone –'

'No.' She held me in my chair: surprising strength. 'I told you because I thought you'd help, not make things worse.'

'How can I help?'

And I still say that. What can I do? We cannot stop Julie if what she says is true. And if it's true, how can we help her? Is it normal in me, isn't it perverse, that I want to help Kenny even more?

❖

I've had time to think about it now. Elizabeth and I ate our meal and she let me help with the washing up, although it's only stacking the machine. We talked into the night and went to bed when the hour hand started downhill – the first time I've been up so late for years. Kenny was only a part of it. We came back to him, could not help coming back, but our grief and fear had found a course to run – the best I can call it is 'do nothing yet' – and I told her about my life; I used my past as a kind of slowing-down and stepping-aside device. She received it like a gift, with liveliness and pleasure, and it pained me to see how Kenny put a shadow on her face as he returned.

In the morning – this morning – I played bowls. Now there's a game Julie might be good at. I wonder if it might hold a cure and get her on her chosen path again.

A cure from delusion or abuse?

I walk down. The road winds with the contour of the hill, turning on the edge of a gorge filled with trees, where, after rain, you can hear the running of a hidden stream. The cuttings on the high side are bright with Cape daisies at this time of year, and huge pines, purple and scaly, bend their arms like old men and make a soft hissing like the sea. High in the trunk of one, where it bifurcates, is a small native tree with shiny leaves, growing as though in a pot. Needles strew the slopes, as slippery as ice, and give way to lawns with rhododendrons at the edge. One day I saw two parakeets, yellow and red, conversing in the branches of a tulip tree. Between my suburb and the city, this magical place. I end my walk with fresh blood in my veins, ready for the live weight of bowls on my palm and their lovely progress on the green.

I play for the bias, for the curve. When I come down to it, past the companionship and the pleasure of winning, that is it: the turning of the bowl on the green. I hold each one a while in my palm, the way one holds the back of a baby's head, and then with an easy step send it on its way, its built-in imperfection measured to the fraction of an ounce. It rolls, it progresses, as heavy as a mastodon and as smooth as oil, and breaks left or right into the head. I rest on my opponent's bowl and kiss the jack! Let me have that two or three times in a game and I will go home happy, win or lose.

I play, Dennis once said, with Jewish subtlety. Dennis is a Catholic priest. He's retired, as much as a priest can be. Clive, who makes up our trio, is a one-handed man, but one hand is sufficient for bowls. He's a returned soldier – strange to retain that name fifty years after the war – and a socialist and rationalist. Unlike some amputees I've seen, he covers his stump. Religion, race, politics, nationality – all four are present in our game. We never speak of them. Dennis's remark, made long ago, is the closest we have come. He writes letters to the paper. So does Clive. They play another game, or fight a war, in the correspondence columns, and I'm pleased to be out of it. On the green there's a battle too, but each of us enjoys moments of isolation when the well-played bowl is enough. And we're saved from gladiatorial confrontation, man on man, by the fact that we play a game called sixes, where each is against the other two. It stops things from getting personal.

Dennis is a flashy fellow. He grins a lot, showing his nicotined teeth. He lays his smoking cigarette down when it's his turn to play, leaving brown scorch marks, like freckles, on the grass; then sets off, bent-legged, tracking his bowl, and stops halfway, repudiates it with a fling of his arms, comes back hissing and takes his cigarette from Clive, who has picked it up to save the green. Or, now and then, he'll follow it into the head, high stepping like a swamp bird, and cry, 'Yes, yes, yes,' orgasmically. I'm easier with him than with Clive, who turns his mouth down at his good shots. Perhaps he has learned to smile that way. He grunts when I say, 'Good bowl, Clive,' and will not let his eyes meet mine. Yet he'll pick my bowl up in his hand and, perhaps, clap it to his ribs with his shortened forearm and wipe it clean with his cloth. There is, I think, shy good feeling in it. Now and then I'll reciprocate, hand-ing his polished bowl to him. 'Lovely, Clive,' I say as he runs my shot bowl into the ditch. I don't say things like that to Dennis. 'You're a tinny bugger,' I tell him – as non-Jewish in my idioms as I can get.

I won this morning. The draw player comes out on top. It was my fourth win in a row and that was too much for Dennis, who had chipped one of his bowls with a drive that jumped out of the ditch and hit the base of the drinking fountain. Clive had finished ahead of him too. We have a lingua franca that gets us through our game and allows our differences to be hidden and even some liking to be expressed, but now and then one of us speaks in his proper tongue. Jewish subtlety, there's an example.

We locked the mats and jack and scoreboard in the shed and went into the locker room to put our bowls away. 'The Irish like to come at things head on,' Dennis said. 'You won't find us sneaking in at the side door.'

'Bowls,' I said, 'is mostly about the side door, Dennis. They wouldn't have weighted these things on one side if they were meant to roll straight.' But I was pleased with him for speaking out and allowing me to speak out. I thought, He's a man I could talk to if he'd let me. Not about bowls, which should finish on the green, or about his faith. I would have to say that I think it's nonsense. How his eyes would light up at the challenge. Dennis has been, in his time, a teaching priest and I would be easy meat for him. I mean just talk easily about whatever subject raises itself, and then perhaps about our different lives, I'd like that. I'd like it with Clive too. How did he lose his hand? Was it the Japanese or the Germans? He takes me for a German, although he knows I'm Jewish.

Dennis must have heard many thousands of confessions. I'd like to ask what men who abuse their daughters have said to him. If Kenny is guilty of it, I want him to confess. I'd be prepared to see him turn Catholic and sit in the box with some nicotined old sinner to get it done.

◆

Usually I call a taxi to take me home. This morning I telephoned Kenny and told him I had to talk to him. I did not mean to talk; I simply needed to look at my son. I felt that the sight of him would tell me yes or no. He came willingly, expecting to hear that I'd sorted out his trouble with Mrs Lloyd and her daughter.

'Stop here, Kenny,' I said, as we drove up the hill. There's a parking bay just past the Waterworks building. It looks over the tops of trees at the harbour. Lovers meet there. They kiss, and perhaps do more, in their cars. Office workers drive up in the lunch hour to read books or listen to music and be alone. I've seen a woman crying and one talking fiercely to herself, and a man punch his girlfriend in the face and then drive away with her before I could even think to take his licence number. It seemed a good place to look at Kenny.

'So, Dad?' he said, facing me.

'I won,' I said.

'You didn't ring me for your chauffeur just to tell me that?'

'I haven't had a chance to see Mrs Lloyd. I've been busy, Kenny.'

He saps my strength. It's his plumpness does it, as though he has somehow fed on me. It's the gaining and getting that fills his days. He has built himself a little room and occupies it in his plump white way and he can no longer fit through the door to the outside world. I try not to see him like this. Disappointment, fear too, makes me extravagant. He's just a greedy man, of limited interests and poor intelligence. He has no curiosity. Kenny cannot wonder. I've never seen him stopped in his stride by some strange or beautiful unexpected thing.

Weak, susceptible, poor specimen myself, I looked for some fold about his eye, some fall or contour in his cheek not present before, something new as evidence of his degradation. I half expected a fetid smell – but no, it was only Kenny, pink and plump, blue-eyed, bulbous-eyed, and ready with his juvenile impatience.

'Shit, Dad, I'm busy. You can't use me like this.'

'I wanted to talk to you. It's about Julie.'

At once he was suspicious. 'Yes?' Was he afraid too?

'She came to see us yesterday. I'm worried about her.'

'I'm worried too. I've been worried about Julie since she was that high' – demonstrating with his hand. 'But there's nothing you can do, Dad. She's my responsibility, not yours.'

'What's happened to her, Kenny? Why this change? I can't say –' and almost went on 'that I've ever liked her', but changed it to 'that she and I have ever got on –'

'Not her fault,' Kenny said.

'– but now she's gone right away. She's turned herself into some sort of outlandish creature.' This was not what I wanted at all. I wanted, 'Did you, Kenny? Did you do what she says?'

'It's that fucking cricket match,' he said. 'She was all right until then. It really knocked the stuffing out of her. I tried . . .'

'What, Kenny?'

'I tried talking with her. Cricket's not, you know, the end of the world – that sort of thing. But she was already waitressing. And getting in with this feminist mob. I couldn't believe it when she didn't go back to varsity. I was frightened she was turning into – one of those.'

'A lesbian?'

He made a sound with his mouth, as if to spit out something bad. 'But she's not. I don't think she is. She's got some bloody female therapist though, messing up her head. That's why she left home. You can't live with your parents, that's the dogma. There should be some law so you could prosecute these bitches.'

He seemed to tell me, with his anger, that he was innocent.

'They've got her sticking rings in herself.'

'Yes, I've seen.'

'She's got them here.' He jabbed his nipples with his thumbs.

63

'How do you know?'

'Her mother saw. Do you think I looked?'

The thought of rings in that knob of flesh made me feel sick. And I became convinced of her delusion and that Kenny had not done to her what she claims.

'You've got to hate yourself. It's mutilation,' Kenny said.

'I want to get out now. I need some air. I'll walk from here.'

'It was you that started this. Don't blame me.'

'I'll talk to Mrs Lloyd. I'll telephone her.'

'Get her off my back. Are you all right? Can you make it home?'

'I'll make it.'

Relief was making me dizzy. My son was not a monster after all. I went back down the road and up the path by the Waterworks building. It was steeper than I remembered. Several times my feet slipped on the crumbling earth and I almost tumbled into a gully. I was exhausted by the time I reached home.

Elizabeth was waiting lunch for me.

'It's all rot,' I said, 'what Julie says. You can put my lunch in my room.'

I showered first, and ate a little, then had a sleep. Afterwards I spoke with Elizabeth and told her what I had found out. Julie's pierced nipples convinced her too.

So I can write that my son has not abused his daughter.

But how can we cure that poor sick girl?

FIVE

I did not choose this country and nor did it choose me. I arrived by accident, but after the accident came necessity. I am tied. There are bonds I can never break.

I did not like the place at first (and do not always like it now) but it was as far as I could run. If there had been lands further south I'd have gone there. In Auckland I slowed down the headlong rush of mind that had carried me into this new hemisphere. I held myself still and looked around. Sea coasts increase the inlander's sense of being lost – of being cut off from the certainties that have sustained him. I was not used to moving waters, not on this scale, or to such intimacies between the elements. It seemed indecent. Neusiedler See was nowhere more than two yards deep. If you tipped out of your boat you would stand in water up to your chin until someone rowed along to save you. And at the Danube there was always an opposite shore, fields, vineyards, houses, trees, a hundred yards away, no matter how the water rushed between. In Auckland the sea and land lapped at each other or they contested.

Willi and I drove in a borrowed car out to a west coast beach called Muriwai, through hills that had no buildings or people on them, and that was bad enough; but at the beach waves as high as houses rolled in half a mile apart. Spray streamed from the tops as they mounted higher. They turned their shoulders into their laps and made the coastline tremble. This went on, I could see, for twenty, thirty miles, into the haze. A beach, they called it. I felt it suck the breath out of me and weaken my blood. Yet there was no disharmony, although water beat and land withstood. And nothing was disproportionate. Only me. I did not want to go there again. So we lay, Willi and I, on the brown beaches of the other coast and I watched him pull young women into his orbit by a combination of boldness and physical charm. Once they were inside he drugged them with his personality. I saw their eyes glaze and their mouths droop open as though they had forgotten how to breathe in the normal way. Several, of course, grew shrill at his outrageousness and got up and stalked away. Others stayed. But I must not make it sound wholesale. They were only two or three. And I was explaining the land, the sea, and the intertwining, the pawing and soft melting, that goes on between them on that coast. People who belong there do not see it. It made me uncomfortable, just a little mindsick in a way. I have lived in Wellington and have learned its severities well enough to be easy there, but I would, I think, always have been uneasy in the north.

We rowed one day, Willi and I and two young women, up a mangrove creek at high tide. Yellow water lapped into the trees; and trees of a larger kind, whose names I had not learned, grew on the banks, overhanging that khaki garden rooted in the mud. I tried to understand that everything was natural, that these were natural forms, belonging here, but half expected some wide-mouthed beast to surface in the tepid water and swallow us all. The women were strange too. They spoke an English I could barely understand, full of strange expressions and loose ends and with a disturbing deadness of intonation. I could not work out who they were. Shop girls? Factory girls? Secretaries? One dark, one fair, one plump, one thin. They were sticky with lipstick on their lips, but were not cheap, I thought, in spite of it. Willi did not go for easy conquests. I tried to understand what went on in their minds.

66

Dulcie was one, Phyllis the other – names I could not place on a social scale.

'Dulcie,' I said. 'That's unusual. Where did you get it?' She was the plump one. Willi's little half-nod had told me she was mine.

'From my mum,' Dulcie said.

'But where does it come from?'

She shrugged and looked at me strangely, as though I meant to criticise her. 'It's just a name.'

Willi rowed. Then he took his shirt off and rowed some more, glancing along his forearms to see the muscles shine.

'Are all German boys big like you?' Phyllis asked. She was in the bow, watching his back.

'They've got blue eyes and blond hair,' Dulcie said. I understood I was to be left out: black-haired, brown-eyed, I was not foreign but alien. It would have been a waste of time to explain that I was Austrian. And a Jew. They would not have known what 'Jew' was.

'I'm not a boy,' Willi said, offended. He was a man of twenty-eight.

'Mmm,' Phyllis said, and wrapped her hands round his upper arm to feel it work. Drugged, I thought. Just his physical presence was enough. He winked at me, ignoring Dulcie at my side, and nosed the dinghy into the mangrove trees.

'Time for a swim.'

'We didn't bring our togs,' Dulcie said. She knew she was not chosen. 'Togs' – a new word, I filed it away – had an ugly sound, expressing her resentment.

'No need,' Willi said. He clambered out of the dinghy and climbed away through the branches of the mangrove trees.

Dulcie leaned at Phyllis and said through her teeth, 'If you do.'

'There's no harm.'

'Without any togs?'

Willi came back, walking waist deep in the water. He put his clothes on the seat. 'Come on, girls. You get no prizes just for sitting there.' He sank, went under the dinghy – we heard him knocking – and came up at the stern, where he put his wet hand on Dulcie's neck, making her scream. Then, with a kick, he went backwards into the river: a flash of white hips and silky penis and he was gone, deep down, along the mud.

Phyllis stood up, looking away from her friend. 'Turn your eyes,' she ordered me. I obeyed, and felt her, a moment later, sit on the edge of the dinghy and lower herself. She went soundlessly and when I looked I saw her and Willi, two blond heads, bobbing away along the mangrove fringe.

'You can have a swim if you want,' I said to Dulcie. 'I'll go somewhere else.'

'No,' she said, crumpling Phyllis's clothes in her lap.

'I'm going in.'

'You try it.'

I saw her dislike of me, and knew she would have swum with Willi if they'd been alone. So, I thought, she doesn't want me, but on the other hand I don't want her, that makes us even. I felt too, or seemed to feel, something sliding, slippery, something anarchic here, and did not want to be part of it. So I climbed away through the mangrove trees; felt the water, did not care for its blood-warmth; climbed on to land and into trees that seemed to me more natural, although too close and dark, and spent half an hour there, wandering and gazing and thinking that Willi was fortunate and unfortunate both and that I must not let him take over my life; then went back and found Dulcie sitting in the dinghy still and holding it in place by gripping a mangrove tree. The tide had started out. There were tears on her face.

'They haven't come back,' she sobbed.

'They're swimming,' I said, climbing in and letting her free her hold.

'You know what they're doing.'

'Well,' I said, uncomfortable, 'it's their business.'

She rubbed her face, smearing lipstick on her chin. I gave her my handkerchief.

'I was the one who saw him,' she said.

'It's like that.'

'She always . . . she always . . .'

I let her cry. Later, as we waited, I tried to talk with her. I asked what she did for a job.

'I'm at school.'

'I thought you were older.'

'I'm sixteen. She's not yet. He could go to prison.'

'You're both too young for this,' I said, adding silently that Willi was too old. But I thought it likely that he too had misjudged their ages. Prison, I thought: impossible, he has to stay free, he's a natural man. I overlooked, for some time, that I was implicated.

He swam back, strong against the current, and gripped the dinghy and grinned at Dulcie as though it might be her turn.

'Where's my friend?' she cried.

'Waiting for her clothes.' He took them, took his own, held them bunched in one hand, high out of the water, and floated away down the mangrove fringe.

'Bring the boat down and pick us up,' he called to me.

I wondered whether they had lain on mud or grass. I could see nothing wrong with what they'd done, in spite of Phyllis's age, but that was a judgement influenced by sun and water, and no doubt by my concupiscence (no small thing), and I knew, when I thought coolly, how the world would see it. They clambered aboard from the mangroves and Willi took the oars from me by right and guided us to the river mouth. He treated Phyllis casually but was kind to Dulcie, which I thought clever. Kindness was not easy for him. He walked on the beach with her a little way and patted her like an older brother. Phyllis grinned at me.

'She's a dope.' I was learning words. 'A real sap.'

When the girls had gone I said, 'You know how old Phyllis is?'

'Sixteen.'

'Fifteen,' I said. 'She's still at school.'

Fifteen brought a frown to his face. He was not pleased that she had lied to him. 'I know about school. She's going to wear her uniform next time.'

'She'll tell on you. You could go to prison.'

'Not me. I made her happy, Josef.'

'The other one will tell.'

'Dulcie?' He liked the name. 'I'm meeting her on Wednesday night. We're going to the pictures.' He bared his big horse teeth at me. 'You are not trying. We must stop these little girls from being virgins.'

'I'll bet your Phyllis wasn't.'

'No. And nor's the other one.' He patted me the way he'd patted her. 'There is nothing wrong with fucking, my friend. It is one of the main things we're here for.'

He had his way with me as surely as he had it with those girls. I'll leave it so, although it brings a bad taste to my mouth. But that was Auckland, where, as I've said, things melt and become promiscuous. In Wellington, on that cold harbour, he was still the boss, but there I learned to stand on my own.

The other main thing was politics. Willi was being political, in his way, on the night I met him. I had been in Auckland several weeks and could see no reason to stay longer, or to explore further south. I thought I might go to Australia and then perhaps to India and Egypt, and creep home to my parents by that route. I drew a map for Susi, showing the places I would stop, with a likely date alongside each, and drew myself woeful on an elephant, then a camel, and looking happier at the Parthenon. I would be home in Vienna by March, perhaps in time for some skiing, and then, in summer, we would swim at the Kuchelau but this time keep out of the

70

Nazis' way. My money (Father's money) would last until March, I said.

Then, having decided, I began rushing about like a tourist. I went to Rotorua on the bus and saw the geysers and the boiling mud and Maori children diving for pennies under a bridge. Why am I not where I belong?, I thought. I went to Taupo, the rapids and the falls and more steam hissing and mud plopping, and saw a mountain smoking far away, and thought, Interesting, interesting, but Vienna is where I should be. Back in Auckland, I needed to hear my own language. I needed, for an hour or two, not to translate but just to let my ear hear and my tongue speak, and meet the lost native part of myself again. So I went along to the Deutscher Verein, the German club.

As well as need in this there was bravado. Although I had been propelled by my father (by Mother too), I also felt that I had run away. Walking through a door into a room where I might not be welcome, where indeed I might be insulted or attacked, appealed to me as a blow I might strike for the cause I had left behind: as, perhaps, an Aktion. It might define me in a place where definition was lost. I did not expect real trouble, perhaps only veiled hostility, perhaps even, from a few, a civil welcome, civil enquiry, this far from home – and, whatever else, words in a tongue that brought a dampness to my eye when I spoke aloud to myself.

I walked from my hotel through a park and stopped to view the little city from the top of a hill. A red and yellow tramcar passed through an intersection. The sight of it, the sound of it, said 'home', and I thought, I'm going and this place will be as though it never was. A ship, all lights, was steaming into the harbour. I wondered if I might be on board when it steamed out. Tomorrow I would make enquiries.

In a dark street I found a narrow stairway and went boldly up. A green corridor with a brown lino floor – was everything in this country green and brown? – led to an open door with light streaming out. I heard voices murmuring and although I could not make out the words it was my tongue. They stopped as I reached the door in my creaking shoes. Four faces, four white moons, shone at me; but it was the fifth, and the thing beside it, that stopped me in my tracks: Adolf Hitler and his flag, the Hakenkreuz. The space and time between me and Vienna rushed away and I was there, I stood entrapped, swaying in the lighted door of the enemy. Now I felt the slimy crawling thing, here on the wrong side of the world.

Let me name those three men at the table, sitting underneath their leader and their flag. I was to know them on Somes Island: Geissler, Hoch, von Schaukel. Geissler with his narrow head and flattened ears and a slug moustache copied from the man on the wall; Hoch with beer face, sky-blue eyes, glass-marble eyes (yes, I am aware of it, Hermann Goering); von Schaukel with oiled hair and a curling mouth and pince-nez at the end of his thin nose – bored, aristocratic, above the fray, that was von Schaukel, but Prussian above all, and willing to pass the orders on.

The fourth man? Willi Gauss? I'll come to him.

They knew me. While my eyes stayed fixed on Hitler with his holstered pistol and black stare, and the black hooked cross on its red ground, they knew me in that time. There is no place to hide, anywhere.

Geissler nodded. He smiled and, I don't imagine it, beckoned me. Von Schaukel curled his mouth and turned away. Willi Gauss watched with interest. It was Norbert Hoch who spoke. So I heard the language I had come for.

'Run, little Jew, before we squash you.'

It was a large room. Benches stood around the walls, stacked three and four high. Inside the door was a wooden chair with a white heavy blue-ringed porridge bowl on it, meant for coins, just like in church.

I had no clarity of purpose. I was armed with rage and loathing. And quickness too. I stepped into the room and gave the red salute. I seized the bowl by its lip and pitched it underarm at the man on the wall. Hit, I think, the flag instead. Turned and ran.

I can see them rise: Geissler, Hoch, Willi Gauss. Then I was in the corridor, sliding, running, bouncing off the walls.

'I'll get him,' cried a voice. I flung a backward glance from the head of the stairs and saw the big man, the perfect Teuton, burst into the corridor and fend himself off the opposite wall and come at me.

I was too quick for him. I went down the stairs four at a time and into the street, and ran for the lighted end of it where cars might pass and people walk – although in this city which closed down for the night that was hoping for too much. I heard his steps come after me, but was confident, I was elated, and turned long enough to throw another clenched-fist salute at him.

'Stop,' he cried softly, 'I'm your friend.'

'Ha!' I responded. 'Mörder! Schläger!'

In the lighted street I slowed down, to play with him and let him think he gained, then I kept ahead a dozen steps, calling Viennese insults over my shoulder.

'Look,' he said, stopping, 'come back. I'll put my hands in my pockets. I'll give you a free hit. You can have two. But we must talk.'

'What would I talk to a Nazi thug about?'

'I'm not a Nazi. I hate them too.'

'Hands off Austria. Free Thälmann,' I cried. A strange conversation for an Auckland city street. It struck us both, and we laughed, but singly, not with each other.

'Ah little Jew, I love you,' Willi said. 'You are so brave.'

'Don't call me Jew.'

'Why not? It is what you are.' I had let him come close, confident I could dance away. 'But I don't care. It's your politics I'm after. You can keep your race.'

'What do you know about my politics?'

In answer, he gave a slow, half-mocking salute – strange too for an Auckland street, that upraised fist.

'You're up there with a gang of Nazis,' I said.

Willi smiled. 'Ah, but you see, I am infiltrating. I am finding out their game.'

'They can't do anything here.'

'No, not much. Propaganda, that is what they do. Painting pretty colours on the Nazis is their game. The German consul helps. He brings pressure on us, all the Germans here. I will write an article when I have enough.'

'Who are they?'

'Those ones? Little cur Berliners and Müncheners, that is all. They love their Führer, he has made them feel so brave. He tells them, Go out in the world and show your teeth. So they piddle on all the lamp-posts here.'

'They're not spies?'

'No, not spies. They're businessmen. Chemicals and cutlery and suitcases. That is Hoch and Geissler and von Schaukel. Geissler is married to a New Zealander. She is a worse Nazi than him.'

'What's your name?'

'Willi Gauss. Journalist. At your service.' He gave a satirical click-heeled Prussian bow.

'How long have you been here?'

'We cannot talk now. They will be expecting me back. With blood on my knuckles. Can you spare some blood?'

'No,' I said, stepping away.

'Very well. I will say you were too fast for me. They like it when Jews run. You dived down a rat hole like a rat.' He raised his hand. 'Do not punch me. I am too strong. What is your name?'

'Josef Mandl. And I'm not a German, I'm an Austrian.'

'I can tell that from your Geschnatter. A Viennese. How long do you think there will be an Austria, Josef? No, I do not want your slogans. Do you have a family in Vienna?'

'Yes.'

'Tell them to get out. Tell them now. And don't go back.' He stepped away. 'You see, I have put myself in your power. It is not recommended. But here at least there is no Gestapo. Come and see me and we will talk. Come on Saturday.' He stopped and pulled a notebook and a pencil from his pocket. He wrote and tore the page out. 'That is my address. You take the ferry.'

'You'll have a gang of thugs to beat me up.'

'Ah' – he smiled sadly, and yet mockingly, and let the piece of paper flutter to the ground – 'come or not. As you please. And be careful, Josef' – raising his fist. 'They like communists here much less than Nazis.'

I watched him walk away to the street light at the corner: a tall man, shabbily dressed (although I knew it later for carelessness), looking – how did he manage it, through confidence, through arrogance, through knowledge of a history and a cause? – looking German. He was unhurried and in charge. It made me shiver. I did not want to trust him, and yet he had said 'trust me' in a simple way that belied arrogance.

I picked up the piece of paper and saw that he lived in a place called Milford. Back in my hotel room I looked at a map. It would take a bus as well as a ferry ride to get there. And Saturday – by Saturday I wanted to be on a ship heading away from this dull little land.

Yet I let that ship go, and I took the ferry and the bus. Why was that?

We walked on Milford beach from the reef at the southern end to the creek and the saltwater baths at the other, then back again, five or six times, exchanging histories; yet when it was done I had said everything I'd ever wanted to say and he, although he used many words and was large in his ambitions and his hatreds and his cause, had given me, once again, just his name and trade. His evasions, which I did not recognise fully on that occasion, came, I think, from habit; or perhaps he simply practised for the time of more strict interrogations to come. He told me lies as well. That was practice, and for fun. It pleased him to deceive, it was his nature.

I shall put down the facts that I gleaned over the years. He was born in Berlin in 1909, of lower middle-class parents. His father was a clerk and a drinker and waster and wife-beater. His mother, from Swabia, was the daughter of a magistrate, which may sound grand, but in the Germany of that time a magistrate, a country magistrate, although he had great power in his court, was no more than a legal drudge, poorly paid and with little hope of advancement. Willi's grandfather was, as far as I can tell, a failed bitter man trapped in a small town. His daughter married beneath her and escaped to Berlin, where another failed man reduced her to a frightened kitchen drudge. Willi had beatings too and was hungry most of the time. His father went to the war and died there in the mud or on the wire – and good riddance, Willi said. His mother sent him to his grandfather in the country. In the collapse, the hunger, at war's end, the old man gave legal advice in the inns and taverns of the town and was paid in bits of bacon and sausage and bread. Sometimes he took the boy with him. The wheat and rye still ripened, the pigs grew fat and cream turned into cheese in the same old way, and Willi, thin and hungry as the farmers chewed their sausage and drank their beer, boasting of fornication with the dairy maid – yes, he was selective, like me – Willi began to ripen too for his life in the politics of the back room and the street.

When the old man died he returned to Berlin and was in a rat pack roaming the alleys. The food they got, these scavenging children, came as often as not from charities. His mother drudged and slavvied for people who had just a little more than her, and, he hinted once, turned to prostitution for a time.

How did he get his education, the book-learned sort? I do not know. Communist youth groups had him soon enough – a natural progression. He was at a Marxist school on the Frisian Islands at the age when, eight or nine years later, I was passing my Matura at the Gymnasium. Then journalism, always in Berlin. Berlin was the centre of the world; even Moscow was a province. He worked for the communist press, wrote pamphlets and broadsheets, and was in, as well as reporting on, every street action of the time – against the SA and the republican Reichsbanner both. Four years of that. After 1933 he went underground. The Gestapo took him in for questioning. They broke his jaw and cheekbone and several of his ribs, and beat his kidneys with a rubber hose – 'pissing blood, Josef, have you ever pissed blood? You feel as if your life is running out.' Somehow he kept his teeth intact. He must have them for grinning at girls.

They expelled him from their Reich – two days to get out – and he went looking for Germans in the world, looking for Nazis, and found them in every place he stopped. Found them in the south seas: Samoa. Found them in Sydney and Melbourne. Auckland too. His cover here, he told me on the beach, would soon be blown.

'I am making a dossier, Josef. All their names. One day it will be their turn. They stand before us in their underpants in a little room. We are the ones behind the desk. I will make von Schaukel shit his pants.'

I asked him what he had meant when he told me not to go back to Austria. Why must I get my family out? I believed it was to hear his answer that I had stayed in Auckland – but of course it was more than that. I was drawn to him like some light metallic thing, pin or paper clip, to a magnet.

'I know only what Hitler means to do,' Willi said. 'He will have all his Germans, every one. And then – you heard his man, Hoch – he will squash his Jews. Austria will be first. You must read the papers, Josef. Get your family out.'

'Yes, I will,' I said. 'I'll write today.'

'Bring them to New Zealand. You must stay here. I need your help.'

What he needed was a translator. He must have someone to turn his articles – his stories too, his plays – into English.

'I have met a man,' he said, 'who is just back from a visit to Germany. Two weeks, that is all he had, but he tells these Schlafmützen here how wonderful it is. He stands on a stage and describes the German miracle, and soon he will print it in the paper. I must write and say what lies he tells, and you will translate. We will talk to him, Josef, this afternoon. Roy Cooksley is his name.' He switched to English. 'We will cook this bugger properly.'

'He'll know I'm a Jew.'

'No he won't. They think it is all caftans and long hair, it is Shylock here. You will be Josef Mandl from Berlin. A rich young man who travels to see the world. You are in love with our Führer, can you do that?'

We called on Mr Cooksley and his wife for afternoon tea. He lived one beach away, at Castor Bay. He was not a Nazi; a common or garden fascist, that is all. The ground was thick with them (and they are still around: my son Kenny is one). Willi was not entirely right. Cooksley smelled something wrong in me, even though he could not say Jew. I was, and still am, surprised by it, for I was more convincing than Willi. He played the journalist proud of his country, eager for praise, and hammed it dreadfully – but Cooksley's puzzled looks were all for me. His wife and daughter simply seemed offended by my manners. What is it about these people, I wondered, that they respond more to a buffoon than a gentleman?

'Your parliament,' Willi said, 'has passed a new trade agreement with Germany. That is good. We must be friends. The Germans are a very friendly people.' (And I stepped in to translate most of that.)

'I found them so,' Cooksley said. 'We found them,' remembering with a little nod, half resentful I thought, to include his wife.

He was one of those thick-necked, backward-slanting men, whose front, including his belly, seemed all chest. He reminded me of a farmer of the Upper Austrian sort, but he was, he told us, in insurance.

'We are now most-favoured-nation,' Willi said. 'That means you like us, we like you?'

'As far as trade goes,' Cooksley said. 'But we like you all right, the wife and me. We like the spirit in Germany, and the discipline. We beat you fair and square twenty years ago, but you're up and running now and not so far behind. Everybody there thinks alike, that's the thing.'

'We like the way they look up to Herr Hitler,' Mrs Cooksley said.

'And the way they train their children. Hitler Youth. No snivelling there and no cheek either. But the best thing was the women, we thought.'

'Ah yes, the women,' Willi smirked, turning French.

'Don't get me wrong, Mr Gauss.' Although he named Willi, he glared at me. 'What I mean is, they weren't painted up. They kept their self-respect, didn't they Myra?'

'Yes,' said Mrs Cooksley, looking at her daughter, who kept her eyes fixed on her hands in her lap.

'Healthy-looking women. Wholesome is the word. They looked as if they could march all day with their men. They'll be good for babies. Having babies. Big strong girls.'

'The men were fine and healthy too,' Mrs Cooksley said.

'Not a weed among them,' Cooksley agreed, looking at me. 'I never saw a single pair of round shoulders there. We went to a meeting in Dresden. Thousands of people. Uniforms, wonderful uniforms. Oiled boots. They all saluted Herr Hitler, their arms came up like they worked on a spring.'

'Wonderful,' said his wife.

'And one voice. Sieg Heil. Why can't we do that?'

'The Führer in his book calls it Pflichterfüllung. Josef?'

'Duty,' I said. 'Readiness to obey the call.'

'We could do with some of that here,' Cooksley said.

'So if you lived in Germany you would be a Nazi?' Willi said.

'Now just a minute, I didn't say that. It might be there's too many policemen on the streets. And Germans have to watch what they say. They're not British after all. But if I was there – the Old Country, I mean – I might just find myself supporting Sir Oswald Mosley.'

We ate pikelets with jam. The daughter rolled the tea trolley in and handed round the cups while her mother poured.

'Did you go to Germany too?' Willi asked.

'I stayed home with Aunty,' she replied.

He smiled at her. How friendly he seemed. 'Have one of these,' he offered, tapping a pikelet with his fingernail.

'When it's my turn.' She pushed the trolley to me, with red cheeks but a disapproving mouth. I thought what unpleasant small unlit eyes she had.

'These camps they talk about,' Cooksley said, with half a pikelet swelling his cheek, 'we never saw them. The people we talked to hadn't heard of them. The wife and me reckon they're propaganda. They're all lies.'

'Did you see any Jews?' I said.

'Not many. Not in the places we went. Because there's laws. "Jews not admitted". "Jews strictly forbidden in this town". Say the words, Myra.'

'Juden Verboten.'

'That's it. Plain language. It's best if inferior races know where they stand.' He gulped some tea and washed the pikelet down. 'Herr Hitler says it in his book. I've got it underlined. "With Jews there is no bargaining – there is merely the hard Either-Or." Not that I know much about them, Jews I mean, except money-grubbing. It's just that "Either-Or" I like. Straight talking. And the salute.' He stood and flung his arm up. 'Sieg Heil! Wonderful.'

Willi jumped to his feet. 'This,' he cried, 'this is the way.' He clicked his heels, tightened his buttocks, gave a perfect Nazi salute. 'Heil Hitler!' Then he grinned at me, frozen in my chair, and said to Cooksley, 'Do not ask Josef to salute. He hurts his elbow playing tennis with Baron von Cramm. It is sad for him.'

We walked back over the hill. Willi let me tremble for a while, then let me rage.

'Never mind, Josef,' he said. 'I shall fuck his daughter.'

'Her,' I said. 'She's a Nazi too.'

'She is nothing yet. She is green fruit. But you will see how she ripens up. Leave it to me.'

'We must write the article,' I said. 'Straight away.'

'I must write it. You must translate. Do not worry, Josef, there is work that you can do. You will come and live with me. I have room in my house. And for both of us, plenty of girls on the beach. We will have fun. But what you must do first, write to your family, get your family out.'

I wrote that night. I went to share his house. And he was right: before long the Cooksley girl was in and out of his bedroom. She never passed me without blushing and turning down the corners of her mouth.

Willi and I were busy and 'had fun' too – he more than I – until March of the following year, when the Anschluss came.

SIX

When my money ran out I hunted for jobs. There were none on my level that I could do. My English was not good enough for clerical work – and was certainly not good enough for translation, as Willi found out. I could only labour at unskilled jobs. So I worked in canteens and kitchens, in bakehouses, on assembly lines, lasting nowhere more than a few weeks. I worked in a sawmill, where I saw a man killed by an overbalancing stack of timber. His hand, three-fingered from some previous accident, was all of him that showed, reaching out from the sawn planks. My own hands, ruined by two days' stacking, would not allow me to continue there, but I should not have gone on anyway. I was not ready for that casual kind of death.

I went down the road and started at the tanneries, which made me smell like a man who scrubbed out sewers. There I was allowed to take home scraps of leather, and I sold them to a refugee whose wife sewed them into purses. These people were from Vienna too. They were Jews and were, like me, konfessionslos. For a while I fancied myself in love with the wife, but that was because she knew my streets, she spoke my tongue. Her husband, older than her, had been a doctor. Now he worked in the brickworks at New Lynn, and worked at his English half the night – not to study medicine and qualify again, that was finished with, but to get the essential thing done and stand, he said, upright and make his way.

He had seen, quicker than most, that business was where the refugee would succeed – making things, providing goods that we had taken for granted but that New Zealanders had not felt the need of yet.

His wife went into the local grocer shop and asked to buy sour cream. The scandalised owner shooed her out. Everything was fresh in his shop, how dare she ask for sour? I was to remember that. There came a day when I made them eat sour cream in this country.

Rosina was the woman's name. She was clever and well mannered and had expected to find a welcome among the established Jews of Auckland, but they were upset by the influx of non-religious Jews and moneyless Jews. They told Rosina she must learn her place, which was not to come in by the front door. They found a job for her as a cleaner. Her husband too, doctor or not, must start at the bottom and make no fuss and not be seen. For a time it seemed to this couple that they were back in fascist Vienna, but then they learned the huge ignorance of Jewishness in New Zealand and they rested in it and found that poverty was their greatest burden.

There were many of them, Rosinas and Karls, putting aside their largeness, making their narrow start; saving their inner wealth for a day that was still far off. I was one of them and yet not one. Leave aside that I was not a refugee. Leave aside that I was single while they, almost all of them, were married. And leave aside my secret life with Willi. My difference from them was that I believed I would go home. They understood that there was no home. They had seen a change in nature. I still thought Vienna was there. I had had Franz's letter and knew of Susi's death and I heard, each day, my parents' silence, yet I had only seen the Nazis marching, I had seen nothing else.

I knew that my parents were almost certainly dead. I knew that I would never return to live in Vienna. Yet I passed my days in expectation. Deeper than all else lay expectation. I was like the drowning man who does not accept until the last second that he is dead. I had not yet known that darkening in my consciousness.

The Weisers shared a house with another couple in the side streets of New Lynn, next to a muddy river called the Whau. On Sunday afternoons their house was a magnet that drew the Austrian refugees of Auckland into the west. It was not the conversation, not even the food, that took them there. (Rosina baked bread, pastries, Kipfels; she was a marvellous cook – but had lost her job in an Avondale tearooms because she could not do pikelets and scones.) It was Karl's gramophone and his five hundred records that drew those busloads of silent or discreetly murmuring foreigners out through the barren suburbs to the edge of the farms. Silent? Silent Viennese? They had learned quickly not to speak their language in public places.

The garden at the Weisers' house sloped down to the river and there on a table on a piece of lawn surrounded by bean rows and radish patches Karl set up his concert, when the weather allowed, and his guests sank down on blankets or sat straight-backed on kitchen chairs and dreamed and wept and thought and conducted the afternoon away, however the music and their histories took them. The volume had to be low or the neighbours complained. They complained of the 'screeching' of Lily Pons and the 'bellowing' of Martinelli, of violins like, one said, 'a gang of bloody tomcats in the night'. They would not have minded hymns, said the woman on the other side. So the refugees drew in close and sat with arms interlocked and sometimes faces touching.

Those of us who were unmusical – there were a few – gathered at the water's edge and discussed politics and the state of the world and our hopes of finding more suitable work and this strange land we found ourselves in. We meant, we said, to join its army and fight in the war that was now only two or three months away. We meant – every one of us was passionate – to fight against Hitler. I remember all that passion with deep sadness. It had no bluster or loudness in it. There was so much defeat we had already known.

Autumn and the blackberries were ripe. Several of the young men and women took basins from Rosina's kitchen and went out to harvest them along the river bank. I had not seen such blackberries before. They were as large as plums, and perhaps, I said to Rosina, they fed on the sticky river mud and so grew plump. She and I left the others and crossed the bridge to the Avondale side of the river, where there was a special clump of vines she had saved for us. This was the Rosina I fancied myself in love with, and perhaps she fancied herself a little in love with me, unlikely though it seems, for an infant swelled her womb, a lovely melon shape that plumped her out and made her ripe and rosy. We went along between the blackberry vines and the mangrove trees and heard Martinelli complain across the tide-swelled river and saw the amphitheatre of the lawn, with table and gramophone and audience. Karl waved at us and we waved back. He mimed the singer, down on one knee with arms outspread, which made Rosina laugh. 'Isn't he a lovely man?' That persuaded me not to kiss her, which I had been set to try when we should be hidden, baby or no. I said, 'This reminds me of the Kuchelau,' although it was nothing like, and the semi-rural countryside nothing like the Woods. What was like was the happiness I felt, unspoiled for the moment by all that had happened since I had been there with Susi.

A shallow bank rose on our left and I saw an expanse of promising blue through the trees, while in the west, over the ranges – out where those long waves curled and crashed – a purple blackness intensified. The blackberry vines tangled with the mangrove tops and although fat berries hung over the water there was no safe way to harvest them. I was all for rolling up my trouser legs and climbing, for hanging upside down like a monkey if it would make Rosina admire me, but she forbade it and followed the vines up the bank, where she found a patch of sun on yellow grass and sat down to eat our juiciest berries from her billy. That, I said, was cheating, but I was eager to join her in the dishonesty, to set up a bond and share guilt – of which, of course, we had none, excepting comic guilt. And I kissed her on her berry-stained mouth, but it was, like our guilt, more comic than serious. It was – how shall I put it? – occasional. It seemed that we would sin against the hour, would somehow leave it incomplete, if we did not kiss – it would be like a sunny landscape with no artist's signature.

Then we talked of this and that – of her baby mostly and, a little, of Karl's ambition, which she shared almost to the end, where it frightened her, and of our horrible jobs – among other things she cleaned lavatories – and her holidays in the east, in Galicia, and of the cafes of Vienna, mine the student sort, where one could read the afternoon away over a single cup of coffee and then play cards until dawn, and hers those marble-tabled halls inhabited by furred sweet-smelling matrons filling their afternoons with bridge, and sighing and saying, ah, no, ah, yes, at the monstrous, the impossible cakes. She had, she said, served her pre-nuptial apprenticeship there, in the Vindabona – but preferred, she said, eating berries from a tin billy with me.

Thunder rolled distantly, hundreds of miles out to sea, and we imagined Karl's anxiety for his records. 'We should go back.'

'Yes, but first I'll show you something,' Rosina said. 'Up here, help me up.' I took her hand and hauled her up the slope, watching her, admiring her, and thinking regretfully of the love I could not have, until I felt the top bar of a fence pressing my back and a great expanse of light swelling behind it. I turned and she said, 'There, have you ever seen any place so empty?'

Had she understood me or was it simply chance? She had knowledge, of course, through her circumstances and her history, that duplicated mine and perhaps shadowed forth the ways my mind had taken and perhaps showed plain where I stood. She seemed to know, yet could not have guessed, that bringing me to this place would overturn me and, again, set me on my feet.

'It's a race course,' Rosina said.

'Yes, I see. I didn't know there was a race course here.'

'I discovered it one day out walking.'

And it had been, I understood, for her a little bit like a blow, coming from the trees to the edge of this vast unexpected place; and it was for me a hole in nature. It was all that had been mine and was mine no more. It was all that I had lost.

The white rails made their way by geometry round to my right, to my left, and off into the distance like skeleton arms, past a grandstand hollowed out, and closed their embrace over there, a mile away, in front of toy houses where the world went on – but in the centre was nothing. Flat green grass, with here and there a goalpost for rugby reaching up. It was – how can I say it? – it was the emptiness Vienna left. It was Vienna stolen from my life and never to be mine again.

'Josef,' she said, 'are you all right?'

I wanted to say that I had joined them, the refugees, and that I knew there was no home, but I said nothing, for it was not sayable. All I could do was hold her hand and walk down with her to her house, and say, 'It was pulling you up that bank too hard,' to explain the whiteness of my face, which she remarked on, and smile at her to concede that all she imagined might be true. She held my hand as though she were holding me up.

The thunderstorm broke and wet us through, and Rosina made blackberry pie for the several who stayed on, and I rode back to Milford – bus, ferry, bus – wearing clothes borrowed from Karl and thinking, I shall wear these clothes for ever now. Tears? On my own, late in the night, on the still beach. I wept for my parents and for Susi, but made a gravelly sort of moisture, for although I came close to them there was no way of touching, no bathing them in grief, no mingling I could achieve. I wept dry tears for myself. I stood in this place, on these two feet, a refugee, and in a way the whole empty world was mine. Off in the distance a door opened, a door closed, as Willi let Norma Cooksley out. Her footsteps sounded on the path as she went unescorted home.

What can I do now?, I thought, and there was nothing except stay on and join their little army and when the time came go back there round the world and fight against the Germans – and against the Austrians too, the Viennese.

It seemed enough, although it was thin, cold, airy – enough to fill the rest of my days.

I said to them, 'Give me a gun. Put me in your army. Send me over there, I can fight,' but all they did was look at papers on their desk, and say, 'Who are you, Mr Mandl? What are you doing here?' And they said, 'Do you have a camera? You must hand it in. And you must have your radio sealed.'

They did the same with Willi, for we were not refugees. We were all – tourists and temporary residents and refugees alike – aliens, that was the blanket term, but Willi and I had arrived before the Anschluss and before Crystal Night, and in any case he was not a Jew. He had not begun to publish his anti-Nazi writings until the start of the war, had stayed in the German club – happily, the Tribunal implied – until then. It was useless for him to claim that it was part of his cover, that the deeper he infiltrated the more damage he might do. And useless for him to claim that having a Jew share his house – the risks he took doing that – proved his anti-Nazi sentiments. They put Willi on the island quick. He was one of the first to go, with Hoch and Geissler and von Schaukel. Me they classified C and sent to the State Placement Service, which found me a job on a farm, and when my uselessness with cows was sufficiently proven – it took, surprisingly, four months, during which time I shivered and complained and broke things and was butted, kicked, trodden on, shat on and once, I am ashamed to say, was discovered frostbitten in the corner of a shed, hidden underneath a pile of sacks – they sent me to a joiner's shop where I made mouldings and skirtings. I became quite good at that.

In June 1940 a ship called the *Niagara* was sunk by a German mine in the Hauraki Gulf. A great upsurge of spy hysteria started in New Zealand, fuelled by the weekly newspaper *Truth*. There were tales of lights flashing mysteriously in the dead of night from high on hills, and other lights that answered from the sea and then vanished, then *sank*; and of people passing packets on street corners, with no word, and hurrying away to cars that waited out of sight; and women in phone boxes speaking German; and strange men digging at the edge of public parks; and others with binoculars who watched the channel where the ships went out. *Boys' Own* paper stories, Schmidt the Spy. Now I learned not to be seen, as my father had wanted. Now I learned to creep and defer and not open my mouth. I hid myself as a German not as a Jew – I who was an Austrian; but blazed, I am pleased to say, on the two or three occasions when I was cornered. I told my persecutors exactly who I was and challenged them to hate the Nazis more.

'Hey, Fritz,' they answered, 'Fritzie, have a swim,' and they swung me, two on my arms, two on my legs, back and forth, and threw me in a great arc off the ferry wharf into the harbour.

I stayed away from Karl and Rosina, from the refugees, for they began to make their way. They made this step, that adjustment, and although they were uncomfortable still, and on an angle from most things taken for granted by these rudimentary New Zealanders (who seemed to me, at times, several steps behind us on the evolutionary ladder), yet they were a little more snug and I did not want my troubles disturbing them. I haunted offices that might give me something useful to do; I explained who I was, a man whose country had been invaded, whose property had been looted by gangs of Brownshirt thugs, who belonged nowhere any more, and please take me, train me, give me a gun, let me go back there and let me fight; and when none of this impressed the man behind the desk, I was, I said, a man whose parents had been murdered, which made him blink at least, and ask what evidence I had.

None. That was the worst of it. I had no word or report, how-ever roundabout. No fibre in me twitched: they are alive. No great hollow opened: they are dead. Yet I never, from the time I learned of Susi's death, had any hope.

I looked at the face over the desk. It took its health and colour and humanity from some blissful territory on the far side of the divide, its ignorance from there, and its patience with me – a place where my words and knowledge would never penetrate – and it maddened me, and I forgot my deference and invisibility and leaned clutching at collar and hair and cheeks to drag him over, and had to be held a while, down in a corner; and then, amazingly, he gave me tea and a biscuit and sent me home.

That was kind. That was more than I could have expected. Yet he must have made a complaint, for the following day a policeman from the Aliens Department turned up at the joinery factory and asked me to accompany him to my room, which he had a warrant to search. From that moment I was in the camp.

He found books in German left in my care by Willi and, alas, *Mein Kampf* was among them. He seemed puzzled by it, but pounced on Marx and Engels like old friends and asked me what I did with them, as though perhaps they served as instruments in some secret vice. 'So,' he said, 'you're a communist?'

'Yes, I am,' I said, 'although I'm not a party member any more. What I am is an anti-Nazi.'

He nodded as though it were of little interest. But the next thing he found made him shiver with delight. I'm sure he thought he'd changed the course of the war. Among my letters, which were from Franz, from Willi on Somes Island (heavily censored), from the Red Cross saying that nothing was known of my parents' whereabouts, was one I had been writing to Susi on the day I learned of her death. It was in German, so he could make nothing of it, but on page two, for her entertainment, I had drawn a map of

Auckland, with its volcanoes blowing and little ships loaded with butter (bread and butter and jam and sailors picnicking on the decks) departing from the wharves and sailing up the Rangitoto channel, and little toy warships at the Devonport Naval Base, their guns shooting corks that went 'pop!', and a ferry pulling out from the bottom of Queen Street, and Josef Mandl making a despairing leap for it and landing with a splash in the sea. He looked at it a long time. He turned it upside down and held it to the light.

'What would this be?' he said at last.

I explained that it was a letter to my sister, written more than two years before and never sent because she had died.

It was in a writing pad, waiting to be torn out. I saw how fresh it looked, so I showed him Franz's letter telling me she had died, and said, 'I'd hardly be writing to someone who wasn't alive.' I turned away from him to hide the wetness in my eyes. 'It was written before the war started. It was June 1938.'

'Susi could be a code name.'

'No.'

'I'll have to take all this for translation. Come with me.'

He took me downstairs and used my landlord's telephone, gripping my forearm all the time. He asked for a car and two more men. They sat me in a chair in the middle of my room – have I said that I had moved from Willi's house to a bedsitter in Grafton? – where I could reach nothing, and they lifted the mats, shifted the furniture, felt in my bedclothes, they pried a loose skirting board off the wall (which my landlord charged me for when they had gone); they searched the bathroom and lavatory and kitchen, which I shared, and one of them, young and keen, fetched a step ladder from the back yard and climbed through the manhole into the ceiling, where he found a stack of magazines specialising in health corsetry which I could not persuade them were not mine.

They loaded every book and scrap of paper into butter boxes, they checked the seal on my radio, went through the Aliens Regulations with me clause by clause – had I changed my abode, had I left it at any time for more than twenty-four hours, had I travelled more than twenty-five miles away from it? – but I must say that when I had settled down, when I had my indignation under control and was simply waiting for them to load me into their car and take me away, I found myself overcome with respect for them, and with pity for their decency. They called me Mister, they never laid a hand on me more than was required. And I thought, They will either win the war because of this, or lose it. They don't understand what they're fighting against and that's either a weapon or a huge handicap.

In the end they gave me a receipt and said goodbye – advised me to learn the regulations by heart – and they left me sitting only slightly rumpled in my chair. I should have been a bleeding ruin whimpering in a foetal ball down in a corner of the room.

That night I lay in bed thinking of my map. It was a naval base and shipping lanes; and Susi, with whom I'd been joking, seemed long dead: she was dressed in strange clothes which our grandmother might have worn – crinolines, skirts that reached the ankle, a fur boa. Susi, who had fled the Blitzverfolgung, suddenly belonged in an age of innocence. I made an enormous shift in time from her, and was so close she seemed to sit on my bed, which sank under her weight. She held my hand and I could love her without grieving.

Three days later I was summonsed to face the Aliens' Tribunal at the Supreme Court. Nothing now surprised me except the leisureliness of the procedures for locking me up. I felt, perhaps because of Susi, fatalistic and peaceful, ready for what might happen and angry only in a wistful, partly humorous way at the absurdity of these New Zealanders in refusing to use a willing able-bodied man.

The Tribunal had three members: one I believe a retired judge, one a pensioned-off army officer and the third a civil servant. They were sharp and courteous. The procedures lost their leisurely pace. There were chairs, a table, a general air of dowdiness in the room. There was formality but no ceremony – which suited the civil servant and, strangely enough, the judge, but made the officer querulous. He seemed to want someone to salute him. They did not at first ask to hear my story but took a version of it from papers supplied by the police.

Several years ago I visited the National Archives in Wellington and read my file which, because of my attempts to escape from the island, is rather fat. Only Willi generated more paper than me. I read the Tribunal's report and discovered that all three members were struck by a feeling of 'great uneasiness' about me. Someone underlined in red the word 'Jew' every time it appeared. 'Mandl presents unsatisfactory features,' they wrote, 'and might well be pliant under the offer of money. He has not the straightness and honesty of others who have appeared before this Tribunal.' (I looked up Hoch and Geissler and von Schaukel. They admired the straight-ness of von Schaukel.) 'He exhibits the shiftiness and the free way with the truth already noted in others of his race who have appeared before us.' So, without knowing it, I encountered anti-semitism, and part of their reason for locking me up was that I was a Jew.

I find it hard to think about this coolly.

Elizabeth works in the garden. How busy she is with her trowel and how intimately she feeds pellets of fertiliser – slow release, she tells me – into the worked loam about the roots of her seedlings, which will, I imagine, as it's autumn now, fill our winter flower-beds with colour. She is like a young mother feeding spoonfuls of pudding to her child, and yet is unlike, for she is removed from the danger of immediate response. She would be appalled, I think, at the emotions running free in my room, and if she came through the door – if she had come in a moment ago – would have backed out with a cry of alarm.

But I have myself in control again. They were not bad men, they were simply stupid. And seeing that word, I cry no, that lets them off too lightly. How is one to know that they would not have stood jeering in the street as Jewish matrons, down on their knees, scrubbed the pavements of Vienna clean? That they would not have killed my father in Dachau and my mother in the Chelmno death camp? This one yes, that one no, how is one to judge? Let me just record: someone underlined Jew in red, and the three of them locked me up.

I gave them other reasons, gave sufficient cause. The map was one. My sharing house with Willi was another.

'Were you aware of visits paid to Gauss by a young woman called Norma Cooksley?' the judge asked.

'Yes,' I said, 'they were friends. But surely . . .' Was my shrug a Jewish shrug?

'Were you aware of the immoral nature of the relationship between Gauss and this unfortunate young woman?'

'I knew,' I said, and my English began to let me down, 'I knew that they made some sex together. But she is surely old enough . . .'

'Did you also have immoral relations with young women in Gauss's house?'

'I had,' I said, 'yes, one. But I only touched her on the outside of her clothes. She was afraid.'

'Was that young woman a schoolgirl?'

'No,' I said, 'certainly not. I would not have relations with a schoolgirl. I do not understand these questions.'

'Who was that young woman?'

'I do not remember her name,' I lied – and they heard it. 'She was a . . .' I tried to explain the concept of 'Du süsse Wiener Mädel', which translates as 'the sweet Vienna maid' – a shopgirl, I said, with whom it is all right for the young student to gain his first experience of love. My young woman had been, I joked, 'a sweet Auckland maid' who had allowed me scarcely any liberties at all.

What stony faces. They would have locked me up for that alone. But there was more.

'Did you help Gauss compile for the German consul a list of Jews working in Auckland businesses?'

'Yes,' I said, 'but he must have told you.'

'Told us what, Mr Mandl?'

'That we made them up. We even put Spinoza in. We put in Jew Süss. He worked for the city treasury.'

'Are you telling us that the whole of the list you and Gauss made was a lie?'

'It was a joke. Willi didn't care by then if they knew he wasn't a Nazi.'

'You gave the *consul* a list of made-up names?' Our crime was lèse-majesté, I saw.

'Mr Mandl,' said the judge, 'these actions that you claim you were engaged in against the Nazis, is there anyone you know who can substantiate them?'

'No,' I said, 'no one here. I suppose most of the people are dead. Some got away to America. But there are refugees here who were communists. They could tell you that those things went on. Those battles in the streets. And at the university.'

'Who are they? These people?'

'No. I don't remember.'

'It will help you if you give us their names.'

'I will give you the names of New Zealanders who are Nazis. Wouldn't you like to have those?'

'This attitude doesn't help you, Mr Mandl. If you have the names of communists you must make them known.'

'Is New Zealand at war with Russia?' I asked.

They became angry and I was angry too and grew careless. So that they should know I had spilled my blood fighting on the streets

95

of my home town I described a running battle with Schuschnigg's fascist police, how the student groups armed with batons and stones had thrown themselves in waves against armed men, mounted men, and how we had retreated, bloody but in good order, to the safety of the university.

'We led that,' I said, 'the YCL. The socialists and Nazis were only hangers-on.'

'One moment,' said the civil servant. The judge had picked it up too. 'The Nazis were joined with you in this brawl?'

How could I explain to them the street politics of Vienna in the mid-nineteen thirties?

'You have to understand,' I said, 'the enemy on that occasion was the fascist government. So all of us, all the underground groups, joined in the fight. It happened sometimes. It didn't make us hate the Nazis less. We made use of them, that's all. That was before we had seen what they really were.'

'So what you are saying is that you fought in collaboration with Nazi groups?'

'No,' I cried.

'It seems to us, Mr Mandl, that you are a very shifty customer indeed.'

I made up my mind to be quiet. Their report does not use 'shifty customer'. It says that my allegiance appeared to bend to whichever side might serve my interests best and this had led, in one instance at least, to my collaborating with Nazis. It says that I refused to name individuals who might become enemies of the state. It says that my morals in sexual matters were lax. It says that I kept a store of smutty magazines in the ceiling. It underlines that I was a Jew. For good measure it adds that I made the members of the Tribunal 'deeply uneasy'. But they used another reason for locking me up.

'There is no evidence that your parents are dead? You have no documentary proof of it?'

'No,' I said.

'Believe me, Mr Mandl, you have our sympathy for the treatment meted out to members of your race by the Nazis in Vienna, and elsewhere, but it places us in a difficult position in relation to persons in your situation.'

'I don't understand.'

'It is possible, is it not, that your parents are alive and held prisoner in a camp? You must surely see that the Nazis could use them to bring pressure on you.'

'Pressure?'

'Would you remain loyal to this country, Mr Mandl, if threats of harm were made against your parents?'

'Would you supply information if you were asked for it?'

'Would you draw more maps?'

They gave me no credit for the straightness of my reply. 'I'd draw as many maps as they wanted,' I said.

I waited in the corridor, sitting on a chair, while the soldier, the judge and the civil servant decided my fate. When they called me back the judge said, 'We feel very strongly, Mr Mandl, that your continued freedom would constitute a danger to the security of New Zealand. Our recommendation to the Minister is that you be re-classified in Class A.'

'What does that mean?'

'It means, Mandl, that you will be detained at the Minister's pleasure for the duration of the war.'

'You're locking me up? I want to fight.'

'You are free to appeal. The procedures will be explained to you. Remove the prisoner.'

Prisoner! That's a word like an iron bar. It locked me out from everything I knew. If Susi and my parents had walked in at that moment we would have been invisible to each other. It was grief for my lost life, and theirs, that made me sob into my hands – which went down very badly with the judge, the soldier and the civil servant. But they were done with me and did not have to witness it for longer than it took the policeman to get me out of the room. He walked me to a lavatory where I could wash my face. I have always been grateful for that.

Prisoner or no, they let me go back to work. I suppose I could have run away and hidden in those three days. It crossed my mind. I could bed down in a bramble patch beside the Whau creek and swim across each night for bread and sausages with Rosina and Karl. My fantasies were of that sort: I turned in an imaginative circle that, translated into space, would have been no more than three feet in circumference. I reported daily to the police station and on the third day the sergeant said to me, 'I'll come back home with you and get your gear. You'll go down on the Express tonight.'

'What is this place?'

He shrugged. 'An island. I've never been there. They used to use it for quarantine.'

We went to my bedsitter and I packed a suitcase of clothes. I had sold my skis. I had sold my overcoat with the fur collar. I dressed like a New Zealander now – although not like a workman, like a clerk. (And was clerkish in my manners; had said, 'Thank you' each time someone handed me a plank when stacking timber in the lumber yard.)

'Take warm clothes,' the policeman said. 'It's bloody cold in Wellington.'

'How many men are there?'

'I don't know. It's mostly Eyeties, I think.'

He took me by tram to a military depot, shook hands with me, which made the receiving officer grunt with annoyance, and went away. So I became an object for delivery: a 'live body' was the term.

A corporal and a private took me down. One sat in the aisle seat, locking me in. They took turns in fetching food (it was a pie each time, and a cup of tea) at stations whose names filled me with apprehension and dismay – Taumarunui, Taihape. My two years in New Zealand had got me used to outlandish names, but now, on this trip, they were new again, and I seemed to be heading into Africa or Peru. There was enough moon to show the emptiness of the country we passed through. Miles, miles, and not a single light, not a house or car, only trees, mountains, streams so deep in folds in the earth that they simply winked, a silver flash, and were gone, and a sky whose emptiness seemed of a different order from that of northern skies. I should not have been surprised if someone had told me that astronomers had proved there were fewer galaxies here and greater stretches of empty space. I could not sleep. The soldiers called me Fritz and were cheerful enough at first but grew surly as the night went on and one, at last, as the other slept, refused to take me to the lavatory. 'Shit your pants, I don't care,' he said.

It was early morning when we reached Wellington. Sky, hills, water, that was my impression as the train burst from the tunnel on to the harbourside. I looked for buildings that might make a city and found them at last huddled at the foot of hills and looking, I thought, shrunken to be in a place so inhospitable.

The corporal and the private smartened up and managed good salutes, Prussian salutes, as they handed me over to an officer – a lieutenant, I think – who looked too young to be called sir. He led me to a truck full of soldiers and I took a proffered hand and was jerked, lightweight, off my feet and into the middle of a platoon, where I rode twenty minutes among feet and rifle butts until the truck stopped and someone said, 'This is your stop, Fritzie.'

I jumped down, caught my lobbed suitcase and was left alone, I thought, beside a beach. Then I saw the lieutenant standing on the sand, watching a man with a pair of oars on his shoulder walking towards us along the water's edge.

'He's a slow bugger,' the lieutenant said.

'What is this place?'

'Petone beach. That's Somes Island out there.'

The sea was pink. The water seemed as thin as air. The island, on the other hand, appeared to be made of granite, although I was to learn soon enough that it was clay and sandstone eroded by the sea.

'Mountains all around,' I said. 'Mountains everywhere.'

'Oh,' he said, 'these are only hills. Come on, Wishart. God, he's slow. We might as well have a cigarette.'

'What I need is the lavatory,' I said.

'Dunny in the changing shed,' he said, indicating a little wooden building. 'There won't be any paper, take some grass.'

So, unguarded, I sat on the lavatory. Then I washed my hands in the sea while the lieutenant practised handstands on the sand with his cigarette in his mouth. Perhaps he was just a lieutenant in the school cadets. I could run away from him – but where would I go? It made me shrug and laugh, and he laughed too. The boatman was rowing towards us and I studied Somes Island as he approached. Although it taught me nothing I had time to assemble myself and say, This is what comes next and I can handle it. So I reached the island in an adult frame of mind.

We had to wade to the dinghy. The lieutenant was not pleased. He was wet up to his knees. I was startled by the coldness of the water. The sky was clear, the morning windless and the sea calm, but the water came from deep in the south, from iceberg seas. Wishart rowed to his launch, climbed aboard, secured the dinghy and headed out towards the island. The trip took twenty minutes, the distance measured less than two miles. The lieutenant stopped being friendly. He took off his shoes and dried his feet with a rag Wishart tossed to him. He wrung out his socks over the side. All right, I thought, I'll show him, and I opened my suitcase and found dry shoes and socks and put them on. He was, I think, close to ordering me to change back. When I looked up, the island had grown taller and spread its boundaries. Figures on the wharf waited for me. I saw a track turning right and left up the hill towards low buildings on the second level, and a tramway running straight up like a parting in hair. On the right a smaller island covered in bush had detached itself – Leper Island.

'That's where they put you if you play up,' the lieutenant said, but was too much a boy to make me believe him.

Wishart brought the launch in at the side of the jetty and held it with a throttled-back motor while the lieutenant and I stepped ashore. Pengelly, the sergeant, was there to – I was going to write 'welcome me', but no, to take possession, accept delivery. I stood between two privates, both armed with rifles and bayonets, while he and the lieutenant exchanged papers. From up the hill, from a working party hidden in the trees, a call came in Italian, 'Hey, amigo . . .' followed by words I could not understand, but welcoming me perhaps, or perhaps just asking if I was German or Italian.

'Silence,' Pengelly shouted. 'Identify that man.'

Laughter came from the trees, then cows mooing, dogs barking, birds calling – the Italians were especially good at bird calls. Pengelly turned away, red-faced, signed a paper for Wishart, then strode off, leaving the privates and me to follow. We took a path leading away from the Italians.

'Tell the bugger to slow down,' one of the privates said. 'Hey Fritzie, say you've got a sore foot, eh.' But we maintained Pengelly's pace all the way to the commandant's office and I was pleased to find myself breathing more easily than the soldiers.

On the way I had taken a better look at the city; no city, I thought, but a settlement, a huddle of low buildings where perhaps a fishing village should have been; and looked south towards the harbour mouth and the reef, black and sharp, and beyond it the sea that ran on until it reached the polar continent; and, warmer, for one needed warmth after that emptiness, the yellow cliffs of the island with, at the foot of them, a party of men guarded by a soldier, making a sweep with a fishing net in the sea. I saw too, down a long slope, a group of men waist deep in a pond, clearing weed. One of them had the look of Willi.

I saw cows and sheep, which made me smile, for no prisoner of war camp I had ever heard of had those.

Pengelly marched me into the commandant's office, and that silly man, although he had his clerk ready with pen and paper at a side table, ignored me and Pengelly, and pretended to work for five minutes – behaviour that never fails to make a man ridiculous. Pengelly kept himself at attention all the while and I could tell how he hated Dowden. When the man looked up I thought, Oh no, a comic-opera soldier, he's a joke, and I never had to revise that judgement.

'Mandl, yes,' he said. 'I've read your report. You're a bad egg, aren't you, Mandl?'

I made up my mind not to understand his English but look half-witted if I had to, and so have as little to do with him as I could.

'You're an Austrian aren't you, Mandl? And a Jew?'

I shrugged.

'It says here you speak English, so don't play dumb with me.'

I kept quiet. I spoke single words when I was sure that they were wrong. I was more alert with Dowden than at any other time during my stay on the island. It is hard not to be stupefied and enraged by such a man but I managed to stay ahead of him, and stay calm. He gave up trying to question me after a while and ordered Pengelly to search me, which Pengelly did roughly, taking my pocket knife and straight razor and box of matches. He made me take my shoes off and felt in the toes and asked why the pair tied to my suitcase were damp.

'No smutty magazines?' Dowden said. 'I don't like grubby-minded Jews, Mandl. I've a good mind to confine you when the Wrens come ashore.' But he got nothing from me and grew bored and went off to his morning tea in the mess, leaving his wry-necked clerk to deal with me.

'You understand some English, don't you?' said the clerk.

'Yes. Some.'

'It's better if you understand me. You'll find life a lot more comfortable.'

'All right.'

He read me the camp rules, which I did not try to memorise. Willi would tell what to do.

'Do you want the German government to be notified you're here?'

'God, no,' I said. 'Why should I want that?'

'You're a German subject.'

'I am not. I'm Austrian.'

'Austria has been annexed. You're a German by annexation.'

'Not if I say I'm not. I'm stateless. Would you record that? I declare myself stateless.'

'Declare all you like if it makes you feel better. But unless the German government is informed you'll get no pocket money. It's thirty-five shillings a month. You must want that.'

'No, I don't.'

'How will you live?'

'I dare say you'll feed me. Or will you let me starve?'

The clerk laughed. 'The grub out here isn't too bad. The money,' he added kindly, 'comes through the Swiss consul. You could argue that it's neutral money.'

'No,' I said. 'I'd have to sign myself Reichsdeutscher, wouldn't I?'

'Yes.'

'No.'

'Good luck then, Mandl. Sergeant, take him to the quartermaster and get his issue.'

So, with Pengelly, who made up for the clerk's friendliness by speaking to me loudly when civilly would have done and making every instruction an order, I went to the quartermaster's store, where

I received two shirts, two singlets, two pairs of underpants, two sets of denim trousers and two pairs of socks. I received a tin plate, a mug, a knife and a fork and a spoon. All these I carried away on my second trip, for on the first I was loaded down with a wooden bed, a kapok mattress, a pillow and three blankets, two sheets and a pillow slip. It was like settling in at a Boy Scout camp.

There were three barracks in the compound as well as a number of huts. I hoped that I would be in the same building as Willi but knew it would be pointless asking favours of Pengelly.

'In here,' he said. 'You'll be with the Jews.'

'How many are there?'

'No questions. You speak when spoken to.'

I saw from photographs of wives and families and one of Stromboli volcano that the dormitory was Italian. The Jews were housed together at one end. At least, I thought, they haven't put me in with the Nazis. I made room for my bed and made it neatly, stored my suitcase underneath, and when Pengelly had gone put my shoes out in the sun to dry.

So my life on the island began. Wearing my new clothes, I sat on a bench and waited for the working parties to come in. The cooks were busy in the kitchen making lunch but everyone else was out. I saw the farmhouse down the hill, the farmer on his tractor, saw his wife carry a bucket of slops to the pigs, and his children ride a home-made trolley in the yard. A cluster of official buildings stood outside the wire. I wondered what a Wren was – surely he did not think I was dangerous to a bird. I wondered what work could be found on a small island to keep more than a hundred men busy. A guard, far off, walked a path beside a cliff, and I made out men in his charge, stripped to the waist, working with hoes and shovels and wheelbarrows. Others worked in gardens, which were luxuriant with vegetables. I saw a little swastika flag flying on a stake at the end of a bean row and wondered if I would make a good start by tearing it down. But Dowden might see me from his office so I stayed on my bench. The sun seemed cooler. And I became aware of the boundaries of the island. Although it sat in the great basin of the harbour and only a tiny city and its tinier satellite stood on the shores, and the mountains climbed row on row beyond, I began to feel hemmed in. It was more than the wire. It was more than guards carrying rifles. Nazis were here. It pressed on me and made the flesh shiver on my bones.

Why can't I go away somewhere and fight?, I thought.

At midday the working parties marched back to the compound. I had been right about Willi, he was one of those working in the pond. He went into a barracks and emerged a moment later in dry clothes. He saw me and we strode at each other, and although I had been ready to embrace him we made our greeting with a formal shaking of hands.

'What took you so long, Josef?' Willi said. 'I have been waiting here. There is work to do.'

SEVEN

Somes Island. On the outer path you can walk around it in less than an hour. Its area is 120 acres and its height above sea level 200 feet at the highest point. I use these imperial measures because they are natural to me, they fit my times, and I stay with 'Somes' (an official of the company that colonised Wellington) for the same reason, even though I think it only just that some at least of our place names should change back to the original Maori. But Matiu Island would not be mine.

There are beaches on either side of the wharf. The rest of the coastline is rocky, and broken cliffs rise from the sea. The island is ideal for confinement – people and animals have both been kept there. It has been longest used for animals but its most intensive occupation was by human prisoners in the two wars. Many people believe von Luckner was there, but no, von Luckner was held on Motuihe Island near Auckland and made his escape into the Hauraki Gulf. Four of his crew members were held on Somes. But I do not mean to write a history of the island, even of the years when I was there. I'll simply say that its cruellest story does not concern a German or Italian, or one of the Japanese who arrived after 1941, or one of the Thais, the Samoans, the Tongans (German Samoans and Tongans), or the Russian Sargoff, or the Pole, the Finn, the Norwegian, the Frenchman, the Spaniard, the Czech who were there – the worst story is that of Kim Lee, the Chinaman who was quarantined for leprosy on the little island off the north-western tip of Somes in 1904 and lived there alone, some say in a hut, some in a cave, until he died. Leper Island. (Mokopuna, properly.) The people on Somes Island sent him food on a wire.

It was not certain that he had leprosy: the suspicion was enough. They took his body away and buried it secretly.

Willi was healthy in his body but excitable, even violent, in his mind. He seemed to have grown inches taller, and had lost the fat that used to soften him at the waist and plump out his hips in a way that was almost feminine. His skin had turned the brown of light-tanned leather. He was leathery and bony in his hands. It was mid-December when I arrived but already Willi had the colour that people lie all summer long on beaches to acquire. His muscles shone and looked as hard and supple as an athlete's. Some of the puffiness was gone from his face. (Willi was not handsome and it always puzzled me that he attracted women so easily.) His great horse teeth were yellow not white – because, he said, he could not get soda to clean them on the island – and his blue eyes, always prominent, seemed to have an added pressure making them bulge – the pressure of ferocity and contempt.

He was full of contempt for Somes Island as a prison. 'I could swim ashore any night,' Willi said. He was contemptuous of the discipline. 'These Nazis are their enemy yet they do not punish them. They let them sing "Horst Wessel" as though it were "Jingle Bells".'

'Who are all these brown men?' I asked.

'Nazis from Samoa. At least they suffer. In the winter the cold makes them cry.' He grinned at me. 'Wait until you see a southerly storm. The wind will freeze your balls off. Little Moser has to creep on the ground.'

I told him I was in a dormitory with Italians and asked him what they were like.

'Italians are the same everywhere,' Willi said. 'It is Mama mia all the time. But some of them are old men. Sixty years. They are crazy, these New Zealanders. They must have spies, they must have a prison or else they are not properly at war. Hoch and von Schaukel, those ones should be shot, it would be cheaper. The rest should be put in jobs somewhere. They do not know economy in this country. They would rather salute and say God save the King.'

He told me the Italians did not like sharing with the Jews. 'But it is better than at first,' he said. 'They put you with the Nazis in the same hut and could not understand why there was trouble. They are still in nursery school. Listen, Josef, the Italians will make it hard, but soon I will have you out. I am making an Internationals group and we will have our own hut, wait and see. Then we can go to war with the Nazis. They are more than a hundred and we will be ten, but we will make their life for them hell on this island.'

What did I feel for Willi? Admiration. I was always pleased, always a little excited, when I was with him. Love? I suppose so, of the sort that is friendship taken to that extreme. But I found, in my first few days on Somes Island, that I did not believe him any longer. Too many of the things he told me were distorted by his wish that they were so. He would not allow me to disagree with him, so I did not disagree. I needed Willi. But I stood on my own feet and looked my own way, unknown to him.

I saw how things were: men struggling to survive. Others competing for a little importance. The mad ones – and Willi, I came to see, was a little mad – were those who thought the war could be fought here. The mad ones remained in the grip of their idea. They collected followers; but following was, for most of us, just something to do. (I leave aside those who would murder Jews. I leave them outside all description.)

Occupations had to be invented. Pastimes too. Braun, a fellow Austrian, was a lucky one, using his sport, rock-climbing, in a hunt for seagull eggs, which he sold. (They did not have the salty taste

I had expected. Their yolks were rich and red, like little suns.) Willi had his ducks and sometimes let me have an egg free. Sargoff jagged herrings and soused them in vinegar. The Italians hunted birds with horse-hair snares, and smoked fish in a smokehouse by the shore. They asked for rabbits to be released so they could hunt them too, but Dowden turned down that request. They (the Italians) were the best fishermen, but everyone tried netting and we all caught a few flounder and snapper. Sometimes we pulled a penguin in by accident. Nobody cared for the taste.

The vegetables we grew would have satisfied a professional gardener. I spent a good deal of my time in the gardens, but in winter my chief occupation was polishing paua shell, which I sold to the men who made ornaments. For recreation I tried my hand at painting but I have no colour sense – strange in a Viennese. I admire Klimt and Kokoscha, and love Egon Schiele, but the artist I should like to have been was the Berliner, George Grosz. He would have found men to draw on Somes Island.

Working parties cleared the maze of tracks about the island, and when they were finished cleared them again. They painted the huts, they laboured for the man who ran the farm, they built cow byres and chicken coops, repaired fences, they kept the little quarantine cemetery tidy, they scoured the rocky shore for driftwood for the stoves, they unloaded stores from the *Cobar* on its visits, they dug an underground tunnel to a waterhole until the engineer gave it up, they cleaned the pond, and cleaned and shifted cattle troughs – but still there was not enough work to keep us busy. We cooked, we scrubbed the kitchens, scrubbed the tubs and benches and the meat block. Not enough. We scrubbed the latrines. We counted days and marked off weeks and months and wrote our endless appeals for release; and read the reply, which we knew by heart: 'I am directed by the Minister to inform you that he has considered your case and is not prepared to release you from internment . . .' It was signed R. Bartram, Under-Sec. None of us ever saw this man but our hatred for him became as personal as our hatred for Dowden and Pengelly, whom we saw every day.

Willi was often punished, often locked up, but he almost always had his way. He set up fights with the Nazis – the first one that I saw was provoked by young Steinitz taking the paper swastika off the bean row and pretending to wipe his arse with it. Willi gave the signal. He wanted a fight that evening so he could convince Dowden that the Nazis and the Internationals must be kept apart. (Or perhaps just to impress me.) Two men, then three, then four, rushed at Steinitz, but if we had had a boxing tournament on Somes Island Steinitz would have been the champion. He knocked the first man flat on his back with a single punch. It was only when the others pulled out stakes to attack him that Willi gave a nod, sending several of his men to join the fight. Two guards arrived a moment later and knocked the sides apart with rifle butts.

'So you see,' Willi grinned at me, 'we have our bit of fun.'

Apart from the half dozen who sided with Willi, the Germans in the camp fell into two groups: the Nationals, who were simply Germans interned, and the hard-core Nazis, the Vaterländische. While the war was going well for Hitler the Nazis were strong. Later their numbers fell away.

Hoch had made himself leader. The camp was not a place where von Schaukel could thrive and Geissler, for most of the time, was dispirited or sick. (He was released in 1942, for what reason I do not know, and perked up enough to give the Nazi salute before getting on Wishart's launch.) Hoch made impromptu speeches and sometimes broke into song. Moser, who knows about music, told me his voice had been trained. He stood in the moonlight outside his hut and sang arias. But usually it was:

> *Heute gehört uns Deutschland,*
> *Morgen schon die ganze Welt!*

He organised a rebellion of sorts – smashed beds, smashed tables, and sent a stove his men were shifting tumbling down the cliff into the sea. He led a hunger strike that Willi predicted would not last more than a day. (It lasted two.) He refused to let his Nazis work until Dowden signed a declaration that nothing they did helped New Zealand's war effort. He was clever at small acts of sabotage and expert at harassing the guards. Hoch fancied himself a hero of the Reich.

What heroes must do is persecute Jews. But the worst of it was over by the time I reached Somes Island. Moser, who had more courage than Willi gave him credit for, had taken his blankets outside and slept wrapped in them on the grass – 'under the stars'. It was this demonstration, he claimed, that persuaded Dowden to shift the Jews out of the Nazi barracks. I arrived only a week after the change and perhaps have Moser to thank for avoiding the worst of the bullying.

Hoch spotted me straight away and bared his teeth. He had his thugs rough me up several times, and he knocked me into the sea himself, in mid-winter, while we were unloading stores. (But that was nothing, I mention it in no personal way.) He had swollen in confidence and importance in those days when the war was won, and could not restrain himself. He was always saluting and looking for occasions to put his swastika on. We heard them Sieg Heiling in the German barracks on Hitler's birthday and after news of victories, which came thick and fast in 1941 and '42. They cheered when Geissler read New Zealand casualty lists from the paper. Hoch started up 'Horst Wessel' and 'Deutschland über Alles', which he had told Dowden were folk songs, although it was plain to anyone what they were. (The Italians, from their barracks, replied with 'Giovinezza', and sometimes we struck up the Internationale, standing outside the German door, behind Steinitz armed with a lump of four by two.)

'Come with me,' Willi said one day when he and I were

confined to the compound. It was in the late spring of 1941, before we escaped. We had strolled up from unloading coal and had squatted for a smoke in the bracken above the graveyard: having matches was our crime.

'Come with me. I'll show you a comedy.'

He took me upstairs in one of the empty huts and beckoned me to a window.

'A seat in the gallery,' he said.

We looked down into the Nazi end of the main German barracks and there was Hoch, confined for sabotaging coal. He had pinned up his photograph of Hitler and was busy saluting it, practising salutes that grew more violent and correct.

'Wait,' Willi said.

We watched, he with huge delight, I with a feeling of nausea, as Hoch moved from worshipping his Führer to being Führer himself. He had hung a mirror beside the photo and he began to practise faces in it, determined, thoughtful, lofty, visionary, trying for Hitler – but looking more like Mussolini to me, il Duce of the ludicrous poses. Then he took a smaller mirror, ready on his bed, and studied his profile. He made more faces, using his mouth especially, pushing out his lips with his tongue. His eyes did not please him (he was plagued with styes on the island, but had no stye at this time) and he pulled an upper eyelid out, delicate with his fingers, and let it snap into place. I wanted to stop looking. I could not see the game Willi saw. He held me still; must have watched many times and knew the entertainment to come.

'How can they win the war, a party of Hochs?' But I knew (and Willi knew) it was not as simple as that.

Hoch laid his small mirror aside. He took the larger one from the wall, arranged it slanting on his pillow, stepped back to give himself more room, and began to do poses, from simple hands on hips, addressing the rally, to enunciating the Vision, with eyes wide, fingers splayed on breast, fist raised to the sky. It was his favourite, he returned to it several times, stepping back to get as much of himself in the mirror as he could. It was too small and he had to pull his arm down, which spoiled the effect.

'He likes to make a big cock,' Willi said, showing his own fist.

'I've had enough of this. I'm going.'

'No. He gets a big cock in his pants. See the lump. He likes to have one of his bum boys standing by. How sad for him he will only have his hand today.'

'You can watch.' I went away and later tried not listen as Willi entertained his Internationals by describing Hoch bare-bummed and doubly at attention, offering his Führer the tribute of his seed.

I wanted to know nothing about Hoch. He was never a joke to me.

'I have a surprise for them next time they sing,' Willi said.

'Not before we go' – for we were planning our escape.

'I have the stuff. It should not be wasted.'

The 'stuff' was some chemical or other, and I must say how he came by it, if only to show how insecure Somes Island was. Visitors came once a week – three for the Italians, three for the Germans. Willi had a woman whose name I forget. She was middle-aged and had a crossed eye, but Willi cast his net wide and was not put off by plain looks. He must have pleased her mightily for her to take the risks she did. This woman – it comes to me that her name was Joan – worked in a chemist shop. And let me digress – there was other 'stuff' she brought him and I can name it: strychnine. Willi procured it for the Norwegian, Strand, who, though a rabid fascist, had grown depressed at the German invasion of his country and, he said, wanted to kill himself. He must have meant it (or perhaps he wanted strychnine for some more sinister purpose), for he paid Willi three pounds, all the money he had, and a wooden longboat he had carved, a clumsy thing. (Joan took it away as a present the next time she came.) Willi would not hand over the strychnine until he had the money in his pocket, then Strand became suspicious at the colour. He exchanged a pair of shoes for a sparrow caught in a snare. The Italian held it while Strand forced a few grains of strychnine down its throat – and now I take 'strychnine' back, for the sparrow did not die. The Italian killed it quick enough and threw it in the pot. He would not give Strand back his shoes, and Willi, pulling himself up to his six foot two, would not return the money or the longboat when screaming little Strand came for them.

'What was that stuff, Willi?'

'Who knows? I asked for something to make him shit his pants. I am not mad. Strychnine for fascist scum like that? He would kill us all. It is a pleasure to swindle him.'

Strand could not complain to Dowden, or to the Nazis, who would not like Willi's victory. He became more and more withdrawn, uttering no words at last, but lying on his bed curled in a ball. They took him off the island and put him in a mental hospital somewhere.

Is this a memory that enhances Willi or dulls his light? Sometimes it is one, sometimes the other. I must leave it and get back to the other 'stuff'.

The prisoners met their visitors in a cabin on the top deck of the *Cobar*. They faced them over a table, with one guard at the door and another circling. Joan passed the chemicals in little tightly sealed paper packets. As she and Willi smiled and chatted and looked each other deep in the eye, she slid the packet down her thigh and let it fall – and Willi gave a great laugh as it hit the floor. She slipped off her shoe and found the packet with her foot, and picked it up and fitted it – clever toes – into his fly, where he had left a button undone. Willi told me this. But when did they work the system out? And how, for that matter, had he told her what he wanted while a guard was listening?

'They yawn. They sleep,' Willi said. 'Besides, we have a way of whispering. With women you must learn everything.'

After she had passed the chemicals they had sex. Again she used her naked toes. And Willi eased his shoe off and gave her pleasure too. They laughed, exclaiming loudly, as they came. So Willi says. If all this activity disturbed the packet of 'stuff', it slid into his trouser leg.

'That is why I wear my trousers in my socks,' Willi said.

Did he? I can't remember. All I know is that Joan brought him two packets of chemicals. The second came in a little bottle which, wrapped or not, must have made a clunking sound as it hit the floor. He used it late in November. The Germans were singing again. Watching from the Italian door, I saw Willi and his half-dozen anti-Nazis slip out the far end of the German barracks and stand in the shelter of the wall. They scattered, and Willi strode off with a small open-topped can held at arm's length and his head turned away from the smell. Steinitz ran ahead of him to open the main door. The Nazis sang 'Horst Wessel', Hoch leading in his tenor. Perhaps they cheered themselves up, for the Russians had stopped Hitler's drive on Moscow and the winter snows had set in. Moscow by year's end, Hoch had boasted, but they saw it was not to be.

Steinitz threw the door open, Willi flung the can in, shouting his message. They both ran. I could not hear what he said above the singing, but he told me later it was, 'Here is Joe Stalin's present to Adolf Hitler.' The Germans boiled out shouting and found the compound empty. Some tore off their stinking shirts while others set out on an aimless hunt. Guards were running up, and Willi, clever Willi, emerging from the dark, set Steinitz on one of Hoch's bully-boys, and wrestled on the ground with one himself. Separate fights. More guards. Dowden himself. Half-naked men ran looking for water to wash themselves. Others rolled in the grass. Willi's aim must have been good, for von Schaukel had taken a splash. He ran in circles, tearing at his clothes. He screamed like a girl. By the time Dowden had control he no longer cared about reasons, punishing everyone who made a move was all he could do. He was so angry, shrieking like a soprano, like von Schaukel, that I don't believe he smelled the chemical.

'I did not do it just for fun,' Willi told me next day. He claimed it was tactical. But he could not stop grinning and gleaming. Recollecting all this, I am reminded how important he was to those of us who stood against the Nazis. He kept us moving, thinking, on Somes Island; and he gave them for a moment their proper smell, those ones who would kill me for being born.

I've always wondered why Joan did not smuggle in a packet of soda for Willi's teeth.

Moser was angry with me for joining Willi's escape in the caretaker's dinghy. It was a waste of time and energy, he said, but I had plenty of time, and nothing to spend my energy on. It is something to do, I argued, and I can be free for a day or two, outside this wire and off this island.

'You can get shot,' Moser said. 'Or you can get drowned. Can you swim?'

'I learned to swim in the Danube,' I said.

He agreed to answer for me at the 10 p.m. roll call. He was not afraid of that. Kuhn answered for Willi and Riedl for Steinitz. By that time we were through the potato garden, which we had planted down the gully to hide us as we crept, and over the wire. We squatted on the beach, halfway between two duty posts. A guard had just passed on his round and the next was not due for thirty-five minutes. On a warm night such as that they would yawn, they would sleepwalk, and perhaps even lie down in the bracken for a snooze. Steinitz had retrieved his improvised oars from their hiding place. He had made a pair of wooden rowlocks and muffled them with cloth and I carried those along with my rucksack of food and spare clothes. Willi was ahead, scouting on the beach. We should have brought some Italians along to signal with bird calls, I thought. The night was dark, no moon, and only a few stars showed through the cloud cover.

Willi came back, too noisily, and told us the dinghy was in its usual place, tied to a ring by the boatshed. It was only on stormy nights that the caretaker locked it inside. 'We could break the lock and get some proper oars,' Willi said, but Steinitz insisted that his would do the job. And they did, perfectly, with no noise but a muted rumbling that could have been taken for water sucking round the jetty piles.

Steinitz rowed, strong and careful. It was a big dinghy and could have taken eight or nine escapers. I knelt in the bow, keeping watch ahead. We meant to get Leper Island between us and Somes to dampen our noise and allow Steinitz to row freely. But already we were elated. The roll call must have passed without alarm. No lights showed on the island except for a crooked line in a badly drawn blackout curtain in the caretaker's house. Once, looking back, I saw a red pinprick in the dark by the cemetery and guessed it was a guard having a smoke. Then we were round the northern tip of Leper Island and Steinitz leaned into his rowing. The crossing would take an hour and a half. By midnight we would be on Petone beach.

Then Willi confessed his fear of bottomless water and Steinitz and I laughed, which made him angry. He splashed us with hand-fuls of brine. They could flood this harbour with searchlights, he said, and we would be sitting there like a cockroach on a tin tray. So we carried on in silence to Petone beach. Steinitz rowed non-stop. I told him he should be in the Olympic Games.

We came ashore fifty yards from Petone wharf; which was dangerous, Steinitz thought, but Willi insisted. We pushed the dinghy out to make it float away.

'Wait here,' Willi said, and was gone, and Steinitz and I crouched on the beach, hidden from the road by a ridge of sand. The wharf glimmered faintly against the eastern hills.

'We're too close. Someone could be out there,' I said.

'It is the place to take a girl,' Steinitz said sadly.

We heard a car start and drive away. Willi came back, wearing a pack and carrying a fat canvas roll on his shoulder. 'A tent,' he said. 'And we have blankets and more food. We will not have to go into shops.'

'Who was it, Willi?'

'A friend.' He never said more than that, but it must have been Joan – there was no one else. Willi could have gone with her and got well away.

He gave Steinitz the tent to carry. We walked along the beach towards the western hills, and cut across the road and the railway line and went up a dirt road into scrub and bush, which leaned towards us, making fists and heads. We climbed a farm gate, which creaked so loudly it seemed the sound would carry to Somes Island. Petone was hidden, Wellington was hidden, and soon our piece of harbour withdrew behind a hill.

'There will be a moon in half an hour,' Willi said.

We had agreed that we would travel by night and hide by day, but had not known that the country above the Hutt Valley was as gully-hatched and scrub-covered as this. The paddock we had climbed into ended in a wall of tea-tree, with water running in it, deep in a cleft. So we followed the fence line north, with sheep galloping out of our way. Soon we found another fence cutting steeply down towards the east, and knew we would end among houses on the valley floor if we went that way.

'It is supposed to be a farm,' Willi complained.

'But the farmer is away fighting Hitler,' I said.

'They should have used us out here cutting down trees instead of locking us up on an island,' Steinitz said.

We sat down for a while and worked out what to do. It was plain we could not cover the fifteen miles a night we had planned. I did not mind. I knew we weren't going anywhere; we were out for a trip in the country, a holiday. My hope was to stay free for a respectable time. But I kept that to myself. Willi meant to last until the war was over, while Steinitz hoped to escape from New Zealand. His plan was to steal a yacht and sail north into the Pacific and find an island and stay hidden until it was safe to come out. He dreamed of turtle steaks and coconuts and dusky maidens.

We climbed the fence and broke through tea-tree scrub. A half moon came up but was of little help, apart from giving us our compass points. North was the way we meant to travel, between the Hutt Valley and the coast. Willi wanted to go inland after a day or two and cross the mountains into the Wairarapa, and Steinitz wanted to stay close to the sea, where we might find a yacht moored. I voted with Willi. Sailing blind into the Pacific was crazy, I thought. None of us knew any navigation. I wanted to find open bush and catch eels in a stream and sleep on a hillside in the sun. I wanted the scrub to turn into the Vienna Woods; but instead it smothered us and drove us left and right, with Steinitz cursing the heavy tent on his shoulder. Before long the tea-tree gave way to gorse. There was no way through so we angled to the east, back towards the Hutt Valley, and found more gorse that way, old man gorse. I left the others resting and crawled on needles through the scurfy trunks; I wriggled on my belly a quarter mile towards a growing lightness, and tangled at last in barbed-wire fencing off a paddock. Sheep went skittering away. The moon gleamed on water in the bottom of a valley and lit tree faces on the far side. There was my bush, there was my stream. I felt myself grinning.

I crawled back and found the others by calling out – more noise than we had wanted to make – and we battled with our gear to the fence and went down to the stream, which was narrow and still and possibly dirty. We drank and filled the empty beer bottles we had brought and corked them tight. Then we zigzagged up the other side of the valley. We had taken four hours from Petone beach. The sky was lightening. It was time to find our cover for the day.

We climbed the fence at the top of the hill and went into

the bush. Soon the understorey opened out and we walked more easily, keeping the open valley on our right. We were going north again and we kept on until the sun was up. Then we went deeper into the trees and found a hollow with trunks closing it off and foliage hiding us from the air. We did not put our tent up, there was no need. We made a little fire of twigs – a fire with no smoke, I promised Willi – and opened cans of beans and corned beef, and boiled water in a pannikin. We ate slabs of bread cut from a loaf; and Willi looked at his watch (an illegal watch) and said, 'Now they find out we are gone.'

The earth was damp in the hollow so we opened the tent for a groundsheet and wrapped ourselves in blankets and settled down to sleep out the day. But midday was the best we could manage. We were too keyed up. I scouted round. The bush seemed to go on north and south. I did not try west, wanting to keep away from the coast and Steinitz's yachts. Sheep grazed in a bare valley, which turned out of sight, running north. There were no houses, no roads, no farm tracks. I thought we might as well stay where we were for several days and let the search go by us, and went back to put that to the others. They were quarrelling. Steinitz was determined to head for the coast. I took the pin I kept in the point of my shirt collar and started digging gorse prickles out of my palms. Willi would do better by himself, I thought. Steinitz too. But I did not want to be alone.

'What we should do,' I said, 'is find the railway line and follow it over the mountains. Then we can work our way north. There are farms all the way up there, as far as Napier. We can do that all summer, live in the bush and kill sheep on the farms. And then in Napier,' I said to Steinitz, 'you can steal a yacht. That way you can sail straight out into the Pacific, you don't have to go into the Tasman Sea.'

It was a good plan for keeping us together. Steinitz would fall for being an outlaw and stealing into farms at night to kill a sheep.

As for Willi – I told him the hunt would die down and he could work his way north from Napier and hide in Auckland with one of his communist friends. The police would not think of looking there.

A plane flew over, banking and circling, but our tree cover was thick. We heard no other sound except the calling of birds and, far off, the bleating of sheep.

'I will kill one tonight,' Steinitz said. 'We can have fresh meat.'

Willi winked at me. He recognised how I had captured Steinitz; but did not see that I had caught him too. He was a city man, a Berliner. He needed streets and buildings and a room to sit in while he worked out plots. His eyes had made a flash when I said Auckland.

We travelled north for another night. Steinitz chased several sheep but all he came back with was a handful of wool. At dawn we crawled into a patch of scrub high on a hill and ate our food cold and drank cold water. Again we could sleep only half the day. The plane flew over, and once we heard men shouting back and forth on another hill. Willi was worried that they would use dogs to hunt for us. He had armed himself with a tea-tree club. 'Any dog that comes at me, I will knock his brains out,' he said.

'We will eat dog liver,' Steinitz said.

I was startled by them. They were turning savage. Yet half an hour later Willi was calculating and afraid, for we went scouting through the scrub, trying for a view of the land we would traverse on our third night. The harbour opened up and there was Somes Island, bright in the sun, and only a dozen miles away, which deflated us; and then we found a new valley with a marshy stream in the bottom and, hunkered down on clay plateaux beside a gravel road, four squat buildings with grey asbestos walls and frowning roofs. A soldier, pacing back and forth, guarded each one, while men unloaded boxes from army trucks and set them on their shoulders and carried them inside.

'What are they?'

'Magazines. Ammunition storage,' Willi said.

'We can blow them up,' Steinitz said. His life had become us and them and he had forgotten that the Nazis were the ones he should fight.

Willi had gone pale. 'We should not have seen this.'

The buildings made me frightened too. 'Those soldiers will shoot us,' I said.

'We will go to our camp. Be very quiet. And then we will go the other way,' Willi said.

We crawled and slunk, watching out for twigs that might snap. Those grey squat buildings seemed to press on our backs, forcing us closer to the ground. It took an hour to work our way through the gullies to our camp. Then Steinitz wriggled off to scout at the edge of the scrub. In a moment he was back. 'Come. Look.' We crouched at the edge of a paddock. 'Soldiers. Over there.' They were spread out in a line, several hilltops to the south. 'They are hunting for us. We must go a different way. We must steal a yacht.'

Then we heard voices, so close I thought they were at my shoulder. Two soldiers walked towards us along the line of the fence.

'This is a waste of bloody time,' one of them said. He was panting and unhealthy, perhaps a reservist, perhaps Home Guard.

The younger one, a boy, knelt and sighted his rifle across the valley. 'Pow! Fair up Jerry's jacksie,' he said.

'Cut that out,' the older man said. 'You're on charge if they see.'

'All I want is a shot at them,' the young one said.

They walked by, ten feet from us, and we squatted like barn owls on a rafter, watching them go.

'There are soldiers everywhere. They're in the trees,' Steinitz said.

'They'll find our camp.'

'They'll shoot us if they see us. These are the ones who can't go to the war. We are their only chance to kill a German,' Willi said.

'What shall we do?'

'Hide,' Steinitz said.

'They've got us cut off.'

'We have come too close to their magazines. They will think we want to blow them up,' Willi said. 'So we must go into the open and sit down. We must play dumb Fritzies.'

'Not me,' Steinitz said.

'You go that way, then. Head for the coast and get yourself shot. Josef and I will go out here. Josef, take some dry branches. And some green leaves too.'

I gathered them quickly. The soldiers had gone round the hill and the ones further off had dropped out of sight, but soon they would come up on the skyline in a row.

We slid under the fence. We ran down the paddock into a hollow. Steinitz came too, frowning and sullen. I made a pile of tea-tree branches, dry at the bottom, green on top, and Willi lit it with his matches. He tipped the whole box on, and white smoke went up in a plume.

'Now we sit like Dummkopfs,' Willi said. 'We warm our hands.' We sat cross-legged round the fire. In a moment the line of soldiers came over the hill. I saw the man in charge raise his hand and they fell still. Half a dozen knelt and aimed at us. The rest came stepping quietly down.

'What are they doing?' Willi said. 'Will they shoot?'

'They are keeping us covered. They're coming down.'

'Pretend you see them now. You tell us and we put up our hands.'

We raised our arms over our heads.

'Sit still. Do not move,' Willi said.

The soldiers walked down the hill. Their rifles were ready. They gathered round us in a ring.

'Dumb buggers,' one of them said.

'We are the winners here,' Willi said.

Soon an officer arrived with two policemen, who handcuffed us. Willi said in German, 'Say nothing about the tent.'

'Don't talk that fucking lingo,' the officer shouted.

They marched us round a hillside, heading further away from the magazines, and put us in the back of an army truck with a guard of six men, and drove us into Wellington, which I was pleased to see – streets and buildings, women, children, a tram like a Viennese tram. They questioned us in a blind cell for an hour, and that was the end of our escape. Theft of a dinghy was all they could charge us with; and no place to put us but back on Somes Island.

By roll call we were in our huts. Moser gave a sour grin to see me. But I had been two days in the bush, walking free. I was pleased with that, I was refreshed. I was grateful to Willi for managing it, and for thinking clearly at the end. It still seems to me that he saved our lives.

EIGHT

When the winter storms came I thought our huts would blow off the island. Southerlies, carrying chips of ice, came through the harbour mouth, over the black reefs, and struck us blows that seemed personal. The hump of the island gave no shelter. The wind came down with a greater weight. We hid inside by the stoves and felt the huts shudder and groan. Rain and hail on the roofs made a roaring like huge waterfalls.

Moser and I and our fellow Jews did not get a place by the stoves. When I wrote 'we' a moment ago I was thinking of everyone, all forty men, Italians and Jews. Now I separate us, as they separated us and kept us out. The old Italians were harder, more violent than the young; and harder physically too, although several had to be invalided off the island when the cold weather came. I do not know if they survived somewhere else or died. We shivered in our beds and slept curled in a ball even though we had two extra blankets for the winter. Working, we ran from job to job, close to the ground, and did not dare shelter in the groaning trunks of trees. I watched the tiny city. It had turned grey and silver and looked like a broken shelf of stones at the edge of the sea. It did not seem possible that people lived there, only creatures that had learned to lie flat with the wind and rain. I asked Willi if he had seen it properly, but like me he had come to the island straight from the train and only glimpsed it from the truck after our arrest.

Moser had lived on a central city street called The Terrace and told me there was no building over five storeys tall. He had walked about one day counting them. The houses in the suburbs were made of tin and wood. I could not understand why their roofs did not fly off, and I looked with respect at those Italians who had worked as fishermen on the south coast, at Island Bay. How could they sail their boats in a place like this? The ships that came in between Somes Island and Point Halswell seemed too small to survive out past the reefs. Only the battleships, lead-coloured and spiky with guns, seemed to belong. They came from the war, which was fought in countries I no longer recognised. The place I could know was Vienna, and Vienna was gone. Somes Island and the storms were mine.

One thing was normal. One thing went ahead as though a world might exist. That was the life of the caretaker's family. How avidly I watched his wife pegging out clothes to dry. (And once, in summer, in a northerly, a blouse tore from the line and floated like a gull to me over the wire. I plucked it from the air and was overcome. I buried my face in the cloth until Pengelly ran up and snatched the blouse away. He hauled me in front of Dowden who prodded my trousers with his little stick and told me to keep what I had in there for Jewish girls.)

The children sometimes walked with their father down to the shore. A boy, two girls, aged about fourteen, twelve and ten. The girls grew friendly with some of the Italians but I kept away. I was frightened I would touch them; feel a cheek like Susi's, feel an arm. I watched from a distance. The boy made his sisters lob a tennis ball at him and struck it with a bat in a game I had never seen. (Cricket it was.) The wife dug a flower bed, then worked the earth with a trowel. She knelt and planted seedlings and stood and pressed the soil firm with her toe. I waited through the weeks to see them flower, and when they came they were white and yellow. One of the daughters picked a bunch and carried it gravely inside.

I came to need rather than to love them, and when they chugged away on the launch for a holiday, leaving a temporary man in charge, I felt the island darken and something die, even though the sun burned down that day.

Battles, atrocities, things I do not think of even now, were happening, but my world was 120 acres in size and two miles around. My feelings went lancing out from it, then sheeted in the sky and flickered away, like the aurora australis we saw one night. There was nothing out in the world for them to fasten on. All the same, I kept petitioning to go out there and said each time that I wished to go away and fight. The answer came back no, and in the end I wrote only to practise my English. I had no one else to write to in that language. I requested permission to buy a grammar book and a dictionary, and Dowden said yes – my only yes. The volumes that came were tattered but complete and I set myself to learn them from cover to cover. There was also a library that sent books to the prisoners on request, charging a fee. I asked for novels by P. G. Wodehouse but none came. Dickens came, just one book, *Nicholas Nickleby*, which I struggled with but increasingly enjoyed. It seemed to me that he wrote about a fantasyland and I was willing to go there. The Society of Friends also sent books – no charge. Willi asked for *Soviet Communism* by Sidney and Beatrice Webb, which Dowden, though he searched the pages muttering, allowed. Willi muttered too as he read it. He was a pure Marxist, and Russia sullied his ideal. I had to help him out with words and meanings now and then, and I read the book as an exercise when he was finished. Communism was done with for me; it was out there in a world I could not make exist; it was a book of words, no longer an action and a history – but I was after words so I got through to the end, and even read a bit of it to Steinitz, translating into German as I went.

Books helped save me on Somes Island. (That's a fourth thing, with Willi and our escapes, the caretaker's family, and my morning vision of Wellington.) And they saved me, my grammar book and my dictionary, in that cold hole, Pahiatua. We transferred there in 1943, after the Swiss consul reminded the authorities that under the Geneva Convention internees must be kept away from possible fighting zones. With the Japanese advancing down the Pacific, Wellington was likely to be bombed. It took the authorities almost a year to change the racecourse at Pahiatua into a camp. They shifted us up by train in March 1943. I want to say nothing about the place. (I wish the consul had kept quiet.) We stayed for eighteen months and I've never been back. The cold there soaked through our skin like muddy water. It took up residence in our bones. The rheumatic old men groaned louder. They wept and wanted to die.

We worked for a time in great flapping tents. We looked out at nothing but low hills. I longed for the island that was the centre of my world. I longed for the city and the ships. My dictionary, my grammar book, lay beside my pillow where they might transfer words into my brain as I slept. I kept them whole with pieces of string. The wind, coming in the door, tried to flip pages away. When Hoch, walking by, snatched a front cover and sent it skimming at waist height along the barracks I did not know whether to run after it or leap at him and tear out his throat. 'Jew,' he said, which was the most he said to me up there. I retrieved the cover and then looked up the word. 'A person of Hebrew descent,' my dictionary said. It wiped Hoch out.

The books had belonged to a girl called Avis Greenough. Her name was printed inside the cover Hoch threw away. She went to Wellington Girls' College and was in the sixth form in 1928. Avis, I said. Avis meant bird. Greenough, I said, pronouncing it Greenuff. The name was strange and wonderful but I kept possession of it by using the ordinariness of school and form and date. There was a girl who used this book, I said, and I laid my cheek on it almost as I would have laid my cheek on the caretaker's child. It meant more to me than the rules of grammar – although by the time we left Pahiatua I believed I knew English grammar well.

We left because Polish refugee children needed the camp. They would have enjoyed Somes Island more. I came back to it like a home. I looked at the city with an intimate knowledge even though I had only been in the railway station and the cells.

There were fewer of us as the year went on. The Japanese were taken away for prisoner exchange and the Italians, allies now, were released. The Finn went to work on a coastal freighter and Moser in an electronics repair shop. (None of us knew he had those skills.) Germans were let go every week. Even one or two of the Hitlerites were freed, which drew a spate of letters from Willi to every Minister of the Crown he could find the name of. I no longer asked for my release. It would come. My aim now was to stay in New Zealand, by which I meant Wellington. I did not even mind the southerly gales on Somes Island but was simply happy not to be in Pahiatua.

I washed myself in the moving air and once or twice in the cold sea. There was a new commandant, Blaikie, a courteous man who preceded most of his statements with a nervous 'Aha!' I learned from him 'Goodness gracious me!' and 'Well I never!' and used them for many years until Nancy shook them out of me. Pengelly was gone. The guards were more relaxed. I began to learn their idioms and slang. I wanted all of English, its vulgarities, formal phrases, greetings, metaphors – every word. So I learned 'go to pot' and 'clip on the ear' and 'belt on the lug'; learned 'skite' and 'barmy' and 'you bet!'. I could say, 'Keep your eyes peeled' and 'Don't give lip.' 'Strike me pink!', 'God strewth!', I went about exclaiming. (For many years I thought 'strewth' was a word even though I could not find it in my dictionary.) 'Rooting' and 'shagging' were in my range if I should need them. I learned 'yellowbelly' too.

One of the guards said to me one day, 'Grab a hold of me rifle, Joey, I need to take a leak.' I held it as he peed against the trunk of a tree, held it as though presenting arms. The war must be over, I thought. Goodness gracious me!

Karl Kraus used to talk about the moral function of language. And Wittgenstein, another Viennese, was seeking, among other things, its ethical dimensions. I don't know about all that. I know that language, a new language, helped put me together after I'd been broken apart. English was sometimes fast and then was slow; it put its shoulders up and groaned and twisted at the lumps it must smooth out, and the sprinting it must do when it was already out of breath. It was not the easy language I'd once thought. I did not mind. I was used to knuckly, gristly, meaty, nourishing constructions. And English became more, for there were places I could go that I'd not gone in German. Perhaps all I'm saying is that English was my language as I came to life again, even if I had to put it first by an act of will.

'Good as gold,' I learned to say. I stood on top of the island and shouted, 'Good as gold!' without any belief that it was true, but hoping that the words would carry me with them by some magic. It was like smiling in order to be happy. Willi, learning too, coming on me there, told me I was 'off my rocker'.

Most of the time we spoke German, of course. And life on Somes Island was not suddenly 'hunky dory'. We saw men leaving all the time. The Samoan Germans, no longer a threat as the Pacific war went back the way it had come, were shipped home. Fewer than fifty men were left by November – and what threat were we? Willi said they punished us for what we had in our skulls. 'For our brains,' he said. 'They are frightened of us.'

'They don't know what to do with us,' I said. 'They can't send us back to Europe yet.'

'As long as they send Hoch and von Schaukel,' Willi said. 'I want them to see the Russians string Hitler up.'

I might have said, 'I want them to see extermination camps', which we were beginning to learn about. But I could not make the words, in English or in German. I could not make them part of my conversation. So I complained that there was enough stupidity about for the Nazis to stay in New Zealand and Willi – although I said it under my breath – to be shipped off to Germany. It made me angry to think of, but I could handle emotions of that size.

The Nazis were a shrunken band by the end of the year. They knew their war was lost and their thousand-year Reich would not last another six months. The Ardennes offensive may have had them singing and saluting again, I do not know. I was off Somes Island by that time. Blaikie had told me to appeal again. It would help my chances of staying in New Zealand, he said, if I were in some essential job and seen to be working diligently. 'Diligently' – the first time I had heard the word, although I knew it from my dictionary. I smiled at him and took his advice.

I left Somes Island early in December, wearing the clothes I had arrived in, carrying my suitcase with my books inside, wrapped in a shirt. I took away a few polished paua shells which I hoped to sell. We had been forbidden to make ornaments because we might compete with returning servicemen, so I had only a few coins in my pocket. I did not mind. My first stop would be the National Service Department, which would direct me to a job.

'You will not,' Blaikie said, reading from a paper on his desk, 'do or assist in anything helpful to an enemy with which New Zealand may be or remain at war, and not in words or writing discuss the war against either Germany or Japan, or put forward sentiments –' and so on. I loved the words, and admired the style, and I sat down and signed the promise, smiling.

'Attention, Mandl,' he said. 'You're to understand that you are –' he read again '– still subject to the Aliens Emergency Regulations so long as the Regulations continue in force . . .', which was likely to be as long as New Zealand remained at war. I could be re-interned whenever the authorities thought it necessary.

'Yes,' I said, smiling no more.

'That's all. You can go.' And he added for himself, 'Aha, Mandl. Good luck.'

His decency was a sign that I was almost free. I wanted to shake his hand – almost gave it a try – but went out into the spring air and felt the sergeant push my back to send me on my way. There was, though, an hour to fill in, so I said to Willi, 'Come and have a walk with me. I can't sit around.' He was writing another letter – this one to a politician called Holyoake. Willi was trying to get an official declaration that he had not been locked up for Nazi activities and that he had opposed the Nazis in the camp. I have read some of his letters in his file at the National Archives: 'Before el Alamein, before Stalingrad, I stood up in this camp against two hundred German, Italian and Japanese fascists and the mob of cowards who were turning their coats to the victorious signs of Swastika and Rising Sun, stood and was manhandled, abused, boycotted by this mob . . .' I would have admired Willi's style too. But what he says is true, largely true. If the camp had a hero it was Willi. When the Nazis paraded in their swastikas after the occupation of Paris and Dowden and his guards failed to disperse them it was Willi who charged their ranks, armed with a leg torn off a bed. 'My reward, a Deportation Order.' He told Prime Minister Fraser, 'For the sake of New Zealand's and our good name', that he must release the anti-Nazis before the hard-core Nazis, but left Somes Island on the same launch as Hoch and von Schaukel. He pleaded for a letter that certified he was anti-Nazi to take back to Germany for his credit there, or just to make himself safe, and Bartram, the Under-Secretary, wrote to his minister: 'I think it would be a mistake to arm him now with a letter signed by a responsible Minister of the Crown to the effect that he was not interned because of Nazi activities. Gauss is a glib-tongued opportunist and has the continental's capacity for distortion and making mischief. He would be almost certain to misuse it. He is, I have to add, a libertine and a seducer of women.'

Willi had his letter though. There is a copy on his file. It came from Holyoake, a member of the party on the right. 'National? They are National Socialist,' Willi had sneered. How Holyoake's letter must have surprised him: 'It is definitely recognised that you are, in both outlook and activity, anti-Nazi. If you desire it a certificate will be issued to this effect.' No Labour Party politician showed such a sense of 'fair play'.

Willi said no to my invitation, so I left him writing in the sun and walked around Somes Island on the clean path we had made. At the south end, under the cliffs, a pair of shags stood like black crosses on the reef, drying their wings. Above me, out of bounds, anti-aircraft guns waited in concrete pits for Japanese bombers that would never come. The shags, I thought, were more threatening – and then I thought, No, they're birds, that's all, only birds. So I looked again and saw shags being shags, and I have loved them ever since.

I walked anti-clockwise, losing my view of Wellington city but meaning to end with it. A naval launch was tying up at the wharf and two Wrens from the degaussing station were waiting to go aboard. I stopped on the beach path and pretended to tie a shoe lace. If I could time it right I would pass the foot of the wharf as the replacement pair stepped on to the path. It was a long time since I had seen a woman close. I felt my fingers tremble as I fumbled with the lace. I did not want breasts and legs and hips – though Willi's talk was frequently of those, and other parts. I wanted to see a woman's face. The new pair stopped on the wharf and chatted with the ones they were relieving. I could not risk standing in the open any more so I moved behind a tree. The charge would not have been spying: the war had moved too far away for that. It would have been – I do not know the word, so our modern 'perving' will have to do; and useless for me to claim that my desire was pure. Blaikie would have blushed as he dealt with me.

I waited there five minutes, in great danger, for still there was a guard who walked the paths. I watched for him on the clear stretch coming down the hill, and pleaded with the Wrens: Come on, come on. Surely they should salute and pass. But these were easy days and discipline was gone. I heard them laugh – clear laughter on the sea. The two who were leaving did a quick amazing dance, no more than a step or two – the jitterbug – showing perhaps how they meant to spend their leave. Then, at last, the new ones broke away: a large woman, a small one, in black uniforms and black and white hats. They walked along the wharf in step, as though some order were now restored; and I came from behind my tree and advanced to meet them, whistling through my dry lips unconcernedly. They saw me as they stepped on to the path, and the smaller one, startled, flung up her arm and shied away. Then she recovered and spat at me, 'Shoo! Scat!', flicking her hand. She was dark and pretty, china white on her brow and as pink as candy in her cheeks. 'Go away,' she said. The larger woman held me with her gaze. 'He's harmless, Moira.' She was brown-haired – brown and blonde – and broad in her cheeks and full in her mouth, full in her chin. Her eyes were blue and mild, mild, mild. She quite wiped the other out. I did, with her, look at breasts and hips, they were so round, so very much presented in a natural way – made nothing of. She saw my look and gave a little smile. Slanting down her finger, she drew a quarter-circle I might walk around her on my way, and I followed it; and at the end a guard, coming down the hill, shouted, 'Clear out, Joey. Double quick.' When I looked again the Wrens were chatting with him and lighting cigarettes. I did not mind but went on up the hill towards the barracks. She had made me easy. It was as if she had finished Somes Island for me and started up my life outside.

I fetched my suitcase from my bed, took no last look at anything, called Willi from his place in the sun and walked with him down to the wharf.

'I'll write, Willi. It won't be long. You'll soon be out.'

'And on a ship going to Germany.'

'There aren't any ships yet. You'll stay. Wait and see.'

He would not let me cheer him up, for he was left with only Steinitz now for company. The rest were Nazis, although they were, most of them, denying it. I told Willi they were frightened of him. 'They think you'll go back there and tell the truth and get them shot.'

'No one will believe what I say.' It was the only time I ever knew him pity himself. But he recovered: 'Have a girl for me, Josef' – and could not resist a sneer: 'Even if you can't have one for yourself.'

We sat on the wharf and waited for Wishart's launch, and Willi surprised me. I had thought he hated Somes Island but he said, 'I would like to buy this place.'

'You can't own property, Willi. You're a communist.'

He smiled and turned away. 'I can be anything you like.'

The launch came round the tip of Leper Island.

'I'll take your place,' he said. 'You stay here. We can go in the bushes and change clothes.'

For a moment I thought he meant it. He saw my fright and laughed with his old malicious glee. 'Enjoy yourself, Josef,' he said, and jumped up and walked away before I could shake hands or embrace him. He trudged up the hill past the graveyard.

But Willi was not the person I watched as I left Somes Island. The two Wrens had come out of the degaussing hut. The small one stood on the beach and the large woman with the mild blue eyes climbed a short way up the grassy hill. Each had a pair of flags, red and white halved diagonally, and they began sending semaphore messages to each other. I suppose it was practice. Perhaps it was just fun. They were fast. Their red and white flags darted, then fell into a neutral place, crossed on their thighs. The small woman signalled, the tall one replied. So the last thing I saw as I left Somes Island was Nancy talking on the side of the hill.

NINE

I found a room in Thorndon in the back yard of a house. It was one of a pair in a lean-to shed beside a vegetable garden. The doors opened into the dark like the mouths of caves. At the end of the building was a room containing a hand basin and a bath. Two cubicles opened off. The smaller contained a toilet, the larger a set of tubs and a copper for boiling clothes, which also boiled water for the bath. I cooked on a gas ring in my room. I cleaned with a broom and brush and shovel and washed the lino on my knees with an old pair of underpants and a bar of sandsoap. Fetching water from two doors down was easy after the camps. I learned to keep a bucketful in my room for cooking and drinking.

Washday in New Zealand was always Monday but I was a working man so I boiled my sheets and shirts and underclothes when I got home from work on Saturday afternoon. My landlady in the house tut-tutted me and said I should get up early and do my washing on Monday morning before leaving for work. I pointed out that Wilf did his then, starting when the sun came up, which left me no time, and she agreed that it was difficult and allowed me Saturday in the end. 'But don't you try on Sunday,' she said.

I admired Wilf's washing. I could never get my sheets as white as his. When I asked the secret, he said, 'Boil 'em hard', and when I told him I already did, he said, 'Boil 'em harder.' Wilfred White was his name. He lived in the next-door room. The vegetable garden was his and it took all his time except for late afternoons when he walked down Mulgrave Street to the Thistle Hotel and drank two or three beers with a mate – and got away before the six o'clock swill. I liked Wilf – liked his industry and quietness, and his seventy years which somehow made him neutral in a world that was largely hostile to me. He had been in the Boer War, which I had never heard of. 'You fellers wasn't in it,' he said. I had explained that I was an Austrian but the only Austrians he had come across were Dalmatians and I plainly wasn't one of them – so German I became (and Austrian Dalmatians remained), and although I did not like it there was nothing I could do. But where I came from 'didn't matter a damn' to Wilf. I became his friend when I showed that I understood gardening. So my work on Somes Island and in Pahiatua won me a good neighbour straight away.

He let me do some weeding when his back was bad. He let me pick peas and now and then a tomato after he had told me which one. I learned to hang my clothes on the line so they would not flap against his beans – his runner beans on bamboo poles shaped like a wigwam. Then I sat in the sun outside my door and watched him work until pub time. The garden was the size of a bowling green and produced enough vegetables to feed a barracksful of men. Wilf gave them away – some to our landlady, who perhaps reduced his rent, some to neighbours up and down the street, some to me. I never had to buy vegetables, even potatoes. I think perhaps he sold some in the pub. Once or twice he went off with a wheelbarrow full of pumpkins and marrows and came back with it empty and I heard coins jingling in his pocket as he went by.

Horse racing was his only interest outside the garden. (His unit in South Africa had been a mounted one.) He placed his bets with a bookmaker in the pub and when that man was arrested took the tram to Newtown on a Saturday morning, where another bookie worked in another pub. He left the door of his room open and turned his radio up so he could hear the race descriptions, but dug on impassively until the horses entered the straight, when he would stand up and face the door. If he won he gave a little nod and went on digging. If he lost he made no sign at all. I tried to follow racing too but could not work an interest up, and Wilf did not want horse talk with someone like me, so I gave it away. I sat on my kitchen chair while the copper boiled and read a book, deaf to the commentator's voice until the climax of the winning post, when I watched to see if Wilf had won. I rinsed and blued my sheets and put them through the wringer and hung them out to dry with my shirts and socks and underpants; came back to my chair, read a page or two, looked up at Tinakori hill and down again at Wilf among his silver beet and corn, and realised that I had reached a sort of contentment, although the war went on, although my parents had died horribly. Sometimes I seemed monstrous to myself, at other times no more than natural. I developed a passion for innocent uncomplicated things which I need do no more than stand and watch. I did not want to be, for that time, any more than a man who lived in a lean-to shed and went with a basin now and then to pick runner beans. I walked to the end of the potato patch and stood one-footed on an upturned bucket, which raised me to chin height against the wall, allowing me to look down into a bowling green. Men dressed all in white rolled heavy black and brown balls in a curving line on the smooth green grass and made them cluster far away about a smaller white ball. It seemed futile and beautiful to me. The clicking of the balls and the calling of the players made a small music, as much as I could bear.

Was I sick? In a way, but not mortally. And there was a sort of cure when one day I recognised Dowden playing there. He stood on the rubber mat and wiped his bowl with a cloth and bent his knee and sent it on its way and I made an exclamation of disgust and the world fell into focus again. I stepped down from the bucket and saw Wilf crush a snail between his finger and thumb. He wiped his hand on his trouser leg. I went into my room and closed the door and sat on my bed. 'What do I do now?' There was no answer except Keep going and Wait, which brought me no comfort, but allowed me later in the afternoon to go outside and feel how my sheets were drying. I made myself a cup of tea. Wilf made one for himself. (We did not offer each other tea because of rationing.) We drank silently, he sitting on his doorstep, I on my chair. Now and then I'd say, 'Those marrows are looking good', or, 'Do the snails eat much?' and he'd answer yes or no.

I did not stop watching the bowls but I never saw Dowden again, although I saw men who looked quite like him.

My work was at a joinery factory in Petone. I might have been forced to take a room out there, but the clerk in the National Service Department did no more than raise his eyebrows when I told him I would sooner live in Wellington. I did not mind going to work on the train, I said. I did not tell him Wellington was where I meant to spend the rest of my life. It would, I guessed, have annoyed him rather than pleased him. He reminded me at the end of our interview that my performance would be watched and reported on. I was still up for deportation, he said.

I walked to the station and sat with other workers on the train as it side-stepped through the shunting yards and turned along the harbour front to Kaiwharawhara and Petone. Soon Somes Island came into view and I watched it with an easy knowledge that it was mine – and with puzzlement that Willi should still be there, behind the cliffs, behind the wire. When would they let Willi out?

The train turned away and stopped at Petone, and I got off and walked to the factory. There were nine other men but no production line. Each tradesman finished what he began, whether window frame or door or set of cupboards or shelves. One made scotias and cornices on a moulding machine, an iron monster running half the length of a wall. There was a planing machine and a lathe and

139

circular saws and band saws, which I tried to be away from when they worked. My hearing was damaged at Barton's Joinery. The other noises, hammering, hand planing, panel sawing, I could stand. I did not mind the thump of the mortising machine. And noises that I made, they were mine.

I grew expert at filing saws and sharpening planes and chisels. Most of the men liked to do their own – it was a skill and part of being a joiner – but one by one they began to bring them to me; and tested them on their wrist hair when I gave them back and never complained. One or two even let me reset their planes. I swept the floor at night, rolling the shavings ahead of me like a wave. I helped unload the trucks that came with timber and load the ones that took the finished joinery away. Keeping my eye on each job, keeping the men supplied, was a skill I learned. Soon no one had to shout at me; I was there with the gluepot when they wanted it. 'Thanks, Joey,' they said, 'Good on yer, mate.' So I grew confident, and stronger and quicker than I'd been on the island. I wanted a good report, but also I enjoyed doing something well; and I began to hope that I might train as a joiner.

Only one man gave me trouble. He was a Joe like me but no one called him Joey. A thickset man, bald-headed, middle-aged, with bushy eyebrows that turned white with wood dust from the sander. Joe was a Christian – but I suppose they all were, more or less. I can't say what his church was, but something off centre, fitted with the Bible, buttoned in. 'Language, tut tut,' Joe would say when someone swore. He had a picture of Jesus tacked over his bench and he wiped it clean several times a day with his hand-kerchief.

Joe would not take his timber from me. He never let me help him carry away his finished work. If he saw me coming down the shop he would turn and go by on the other side. How did he know I was a Jew? If he had had a sign to make, he would have made it against me as I passed.

'Don't take him serious,' the other men said. 'You just do your job, Joey. Keep out of his way.'

I managed that for several months, and tried not to meet his eye. But it seemed the more I ignored him the more he became aware of me. I began to hear a sound between us, a buzzing underneath the screech of the saws. I felt his eyes pass over me, simple and certain and half blind, and knew I should not be working with him in a room full of tools for cutting and hitting.

We had a new man, Wally, just back from the war. He bubbled with soldiers' slang, shufti and bint and kaput, and stories of Italian girls he'd had. He puzzled me, repelled me, for I could not see how a man who had been in the war could be so cheerful. I kept clear of him, although he did not seem to mind working with a 'Jerry'. Joe was the one he could not take: 'I'll clobber that stupid bastard if he says tut tut once more.' I hoped he would take Joe's attention away from me – but no, Wally might blaspheme and mock and swear but Wally was not a Christ-killer, not a Jew.

One morning when Joe was in the yard fetching his timber Wally drew a speech balloon coming from Jesus's mouth. 'Well bugger me, tut tut,' Jesus said. As soon as I read it I knew that Joe would fix on me. I considered walking out and not coming back, but I liked my job and, besides, I might be deported; so I moved to the far side of the workshop and stood with the foreman and Barton, the boss.

'Yeah Joey, what is it?' the foreman said.

'We'll need to get a truck here for the sawdust,' I said.

He looked at me impatiently – I'd told him the same thing earlier in the morning. Then Joe came in and saw the speech balloon. He dropped his timber on the floor, and the clatter helped save me, for everyone turned to see what the accident had been. Joe looked for me and found me. He chose from the tools on his bench and started across the shop with his two-inch chisel pointing at my face.

'Hey, Joe. You stupid bastard,' Wally yelled.

I remember best his eyes that never left me, and the dust that puffed from his eyebrows as the other men wrestled him to the floor. The chisel sliced Wally's palm wide open. And quickly, with an abnormal quickness, Joe was still.

'Let me go. I'm all right now.'

'Keep sitting on the bastard,' Wally said.

'He was going for young Joey,' the foreman said.

'I'm quitting,' Joe said. 'I won't work with a Jew.'

'It was me that wrote that stuff on his picture,' Wally said.

'I forgive you,' Joe said. 'Let me go.'

Barton wanted no trouble. He told Joe to get his tools together and clear out, even though some of the men wanted to call the police. Wally went off to the hospital for stitches. And Barton was sour with me for a week or two. He'd lost two good tradesmen 'because of that little kraut', I heard him say.

I walked between the factory and the station keeping a look-out for Joe. I expected him to come from a sidestreet with a knife. His madness was not the sort that would go away. Then I saw him on a train travelling into Wellington, where he must have taken a job. It pulled up opposite mine at Kaiwharawhara and we looked at each other from facing windows. He turned away. He took out his handkerchief and spat on it and polished his scalp. I shifted to a seat on the other side of the carriage and never laid eyes on Joe again.

Willi was released in September. He had gone to Somes Island nine months before me and stayed nine months longer at the end. There was never a more violent anti-Nazi.

I got off my train from Petone and found him waiting in the station tearooms. He was at a centre table eating a pie, and he greeted me without getting up.

'Look who I found waiting,' he said.

The woman turned her eyes on me and turned away. She was Norma Cooksley, whom I'd last seen six years before, walking off into the dark along Milford beach.

'She's been coming out to see me,' Willi said. 'She can't keep away.'

'Speak in English, Willi.'

'Sure. OK. You have been out a year, Josef, and Wellington is as far as you have got?'

'I like it here. Where are you going? Have they put you in a job?'

He scowled. 'Forestry. I have a brain so they send me somewhere to thin trees. I have always told you they are mad.'

'Are they going to deport you?'

'Maybe not. They have won the war, they are getting lazy.' He gave a wolfish grin. 'Hoch and von Schaukel, they will go.'

'What about Steinitz?'

'He is gone already. He wanted to go home and find his girl. I always said he was wrong in his head. Lopsided, eh? There are plenty of girls.' He made a contemptuous nod at Norma Cooksley.

'Why didn't he come and see me?'

'Ah, still sentimental? You wanted to hug and cry, perhaps?'

'We were friends,' I said. 'But never mind. Where is this forestry job?'

'I get off in . . .' He looked at Norma.

'Frankton,' she said.

'And go to a place called . . .'

'Kaingaroa.'

'Another camp. These New Zealanders are trying to dig a hole and bury me. They have no chance.'

'So you're going up on the train?'

'In –' he looked at the tearoom clock '– two hours. It will be like Pahiatua, it will freeze my balls off. I think when it is done I will go up north. Into the mangroves and the mud. Find little

Phyllis and Dulcie, eh? Listen, Josef, how far do you live?'

'Up the street in Thorndon. Ten minutes.'

'So, we can have an hour. More.' He spoke to Norma Cooksley, not to me, and although her cheeks reddened she gave a little nod and sipped her tea.

'We can use your room, Josef. You can guard the door.'

'No,' I said. I felt my eyes shining, hot and sore. All day I had thought how Willi and I would take up our friendship and tell each other what we meant to do – and all he wanted was that I should stand guard at the door while he fucked his girlfriend in my bed.

Today I don't find his behaviour outrageous. He had not had a woman in six years. He reminded me of this soon enough – in a savage rattle, in our tongue, while Norma Cooksley wiped lipstick from the rim of her cup with a hanky.

'I don't talk German any more,' I said.

'Bourgeois, Josef. You are a little bourgeois Jew.'

'I've got a landlady,' I said. 'I've got a friend in the next-door room. And I don't want people fucking in my bed.' It was the first time I had spoken that word. 'If you call me Jew again I'll knock your bloody block off.'

Willi laughed. 'You are swearing in front of a lady. Listen, Josef. You know how I am. Will you make me hire a room?' He went on in German: 'She is dying for it. See how she has to let the cold air in her crotch.'

'I'm sorry, Willi. Not in my room.'

'So.' He made himself smile. He raised his palms. 'I will find a hotel. It is not the first time.'

'They don't have Stundenhotels here.'

'You want to bet? I'll bet you a pound.' He lifted Norma's face with his finger under her chin. 'You look like a nice girl, you can get the room. And maybe I will let you have some sleep on the train.'

'Is she going with you?'

'Why not? She will find a job in Kaingaroa.' He switched to German again. 'It is not for ever, Josef. The world is full of women. Still you don't learn.'

I stood up and said, 'I'm in the way. Let me know when you've got an address.'

'You're not his friend,' Norma Cooksley said.

Willi laughed again. 'Freunden für immer, Josef,' he called as I walked away.

And of course he was right. I was not ending our friendship, I was just letting him know I was a different person now.

He wrote to me from Kaingaroa, his first uncensored letter in six years, asking for the pound he'd won. He told me Norma Cooksley was 'a pain in the neck' and he would 'send her packing before long'. Polite language for Willi, but he wrote in English – practising, he said. He no longer thought the government would deport him. He would stay in New Zealand and 'make a big splash'. 'One day,' he wrote, 'I will be the boss. You wait and see.'

In politics? In business? In crime? He did not say. And why do I think of crime? I'll say right now, Willi did not go in for that.

Elizabeth said, 'Does it help remembering this stuff?'

I gave a sharp answer: 'It's not stuff, it's my life' – and might have asked, 'Help with what?' But I apologised when I saw how my impatience wounded her, and I tried to explain: that memory is in nature, not in history (nature, where I tried to put myself in my early days in Wellington). 'We're not only here,' I said, and went on to declare that tomorrow would not come unless yesterday had been. It seemed true at the time but I've lost its meaning now. Elizabeth answered, 'Ho!', which meant that she had heard enough of that, I should climb down. So I asked her how she was getting on in the garden and she said it needed a couple of years before any real improvement showed.

'You can take all the time you want. I like having you here.'

'What I'd like,' she said, 'is someone to do the heavy work. And mow the lawns. I can't push that rattletrap out there.'

I can't push it either when the grass has got away, and I won't have one of those filthy machines with a motor, so I said, 'Hire a man. As long as he's quiet.'

'Of course,' she said, and went away. I drank my coffee and returned to the thing troubling me: the reappearance of Norma Cooksley in my story. As soon as I remembered her with Willi in the tearooms I knew I could no longer put off talking to Mrs Lloyd. I wanted to go but did not want Kenny's business muddying things. It was bound to be taken as my reason for a visit – and my proper reason, how could I explain it when I did not know myself? All I can say is, I felt a kind of hunger for Norma Cooksley; and a fear of seeing the old woman she had become.

I drove out in a taxi yesterday. Miramar is a suburb I have no liking for. No sea view in spite of its name, nothing except low hills and the house next door. Mrs Gummer answered my knock.

'Is it about that mortgage?' she said.

This is Willi's daughter. I saw Willi in her face. And how could I see other than a Willi degraded and debased? Degraded almost in a biological sense. But that's a judgement I arrive at now; while then, at the door, her face, her Willi face, assaulted me, it gave me a slap that made my ears ring and my eyes water.

'No,' I said, 'the mortgage is none of my business. I used to know your mother years ago. I'm a friend of a friend of hers.' That was the best I could manage. This woman might know Willi was her father or might not. She might scream at me and slam the door.

'You're the one who got her into it,' Mrs Gummer said. 'You and your son.'

'I didn't exactly "get her in". She rang me one day –' I did not say to borrow money '– and I gave her his number. I had no idea

146

she'd take that sort of mortgage.' Still I had not got my foot inside the door. 'Lots of people have them. They're legal, you know.'

'They're a legal way of robbing people,' she said, and I saw her tremble. She stamped on the carpet with her woolly shoe. My forehead began to sweat as I saw she might attack me.

'Perhaps,' I said, 'I'll come another day.'

'I want some satisfaction. You're a bunch of crooks.'

A person shuffled in the gloom down the hall towards us. I thought it was Norma Cooksley and my heart gave a double beat.

'Leave the man alone, Deely. It's mother he wants to see.' He came into the light – a shuffler, a man melted down to his bones – and gave a twisting smile. 'You'll have to excuse my wife, she gets worked up. Deely, you shouldn't go to the door wearing that.' He turned her round and untied the apron she was wearing. 'Mother,' he said to me, 'lives in there', pointing at a door. 'You can see her if you like, but don't stay long. She can't talk long.'

'It's not that Alzheimer's either,' Mrs Gummer said. 'She gets mixed up, and that's no wonder with her life.'

'Come in, Mr Mandl. We're losing all our warm.' He drew me inside and closed the door, then tapped on a panel and opened the hall door. 'Knock, knock, Mother. A visitor.'

I obeyed his pointing hand and found an old woman sitting in a chair by a gas heater. She swivelled her head and looked at me – eyes that had always turned away. I advanced towards her.

'Hello, Mrs Lloyd. Hello, Norma,' I said.

'You're that Josef Mandl. I don't forget.'

The door closed behind me, darkening the room and somehow thickening the air.

'No,' I said. 'The last time we met was in the tearooms at Wellington station. Can I sit down, Norma?'

'Sit,' she said.

I took the second chair after moving it back from the heat. A scorching smell came from the soles of Mrs Lloyd's slippers. I considered calling her daughter, and I said to the old lady (old but several years younger than me), 'It's hot today.'

'Winter is coming,' she replied. 'I feel the cold.'

The smell of overheated wool – most unpleasant, a lavatory smell – came from the blanket on her knees. She herself seemed neat and clean. The habitual redness – her easy blush – was gone from her cheeks. Her grey hair was combed close to her scalp and pinned in a plait from ear to ear, as flat as a belt tied round a trunk. She did not see well; there was a milkiness in her eyes, even though they fastened on me hard. I wondered what she did in this room all day. It was furnished with a bed, two chairs, the heater, a sideboard with china rabbits, pink and blue; but there was no TV set, no radio I could see, no books, not even a newspaper or a magazine. Would her life have been different, I thought, if Willi had not walked into her father's house on that afternoon in 1937? He was her luck: good or bad? Useless speculations – but I could not doubt that she was in this room, and in this state, because of him.

'Auf Wiedersehen,' she said. 'You'd know that. It means hello.'

'No,' I said, 'it means –' and stopped myself, tried to smile. 'Yes, hello.'

'I'm learning German. Goebbels. Goering. I'll be able to speak it soon. I'm going to Germany to be with Willi. My husband is dead.'

'I'm sorry,' I said.

'Willi is waiting for me.'

She pronounced his name with a W. The schoolgirls in the dinghy, shrieking with laughter, had managed V. I remembered him taking Norma by the shoulders one day on Milford beach and shaking her softly, then harder and harder, her poor cheeks flaming, her head jerking back and forth. 'Villi, say Villi.' Her mouth refused to make the sound, although she could say 'very' and 'vulgar' perfectly well. ('Perfectly well': I've an idea I heard that first from her.) Tears streamed down her cheeks, and I, hearing her jaws clack, said, 'Willi, you're hurting her.'

He pushed her away. 'The stupid cow. She's only use for fucking.'

'It's "good for" not "use for", Willi,' Norma sobbed. It was the only time I ever liked her.

'Willi used to talk German to me,' Mrs Lloyd said. 'I used to answer, Auf Wiedersehen.'

'Yes. Hello. Mrs Lloyd, do you remember being in Kaingaroa?'

'I lived in a house there. Willi and I were married. Delia was born in Kaingaroa.'

It was the truth for her, but the facts are different. They never married. Willi sent her away after a month or two. He found other women in Kaingaroa, and claimed later on not to have known that Norma was pregnant when she left. The baby could be anyone's, he told me in a letter.

'And what about after you stopped living there?' I said.

'Willi had to leave. They persecuted Willi, the Jews, so he had to escape. He dug a tunnel. Willi is sending for me soon.'

She seemed not to remember that for more than ten years as she lived in Auckland Willi was in the same town, going about his affairs.

'Your father,' I said. 'I met him once. And your mother too.'

'I don't know them any more,' Mrs Lloyd said. 'I only know Willi. He had a name for them . . .' She frowned. 'I forget it now. My father died, you know. Quite young. He was a disappointed man. And disappointing.'

'When you visited Willi on Somes Island –'

She looked at me fiercely. 'That is where we were man and wife.' She thrust her hands at me, both hands, with the fingers stiff, as though she meant to peck me with her nails. 'Man and wife.'

'How . . . ?'

'Willi paid the guard and he stood at the door. We were married there. Our honeymoon.'

It is possible. Visitors came to the recreation hall in the last days, and perhaps he bribed the guard and took Norma Cooksley to his cubicle – so I am wrong in supposing that he had not had a woman for six years.

'Then we went on the train to Kaingaroa. That was lovely. Willi was lovely to me there. But he had to go to Germany to be in the government. It won't be long before he sends for me. In the mean-time . . .' She looked at me with sudden clarity and her eyes filled with dislike. 'I won't hear a word against my husband. I won't have people like you . . . He loved Delia like his own child.'

'Yes, of course.'

'We bought this house in 1960. I'm telling you this because you were my friend. Before you and your son stole it from me.'

'Mrs Lloyd,' I began, but she cut me off.

'I'm going to tell Willi what you did. What sort of friends. I used to tell him Jews only wanted money.'

I did not say goodbye. I got up and left the room and she said after me, 'That's right, run away. The Jews always run.' I closed the door and at once Mrs Gummer appeared at the other end of the hallway.

'She's sitting too close to the heater,' I said. 'She'll catch on fire.'

'And then your house will burn down. What a tragedy.'

'Listen, you stupid woman,' I said, but her husband shuffled round her and came along the hall.

'Please, Mr Mandl, there's only damage here. Go away.'

'Yes, she's not dead yet. You can't have it yet,' Mrs Gummer shouted.

'Deely, love, go back in the kitchen and sit down. I'll see you out, Mr Mandl. If you don't mind.'

He came on to the porch with me and closed the front door, locking her in. 'I suppose Mother said her stuff about the Jews?'

'Yes, she did.'

'I'm sorry about that. I try to stop her. Delia too. But you can see how upset they are.' He helped me down the two steps to the path, and I helped him. 'This house isn't worth that much,' he said. 'And nearly all of it belongs to your son.'

'But the money she's had . . . ?'

'All gone. Don't ask me where. It was going to be Delia's. The house, I mean. Mother promised it to her if we came and lived, so we did. We didn't find out about the mortgage until then. I'm not blaming you or your son, Mr Mandl, I understand it's quite a common sort – but someone should have advised her. I really think you might have, being a friend.'

'I'm not a friend. I've always disliked her. And she hates me.'

'Well, I'm sorry.' His smile was more cheerful than apologetic, as though he had learned that things must be as they are and humour was the only effective response. 'I wouldn't worry too much about here, although if there's any way of easing . . . no, there's not. Mother's had the money after all.'

'I've got no connection with my son's business.'

'Oh?'

'But it's called a reverse annuity mortgage.'

'Names don't make things better. But never mind, we'll get by.'

'I suppose she gets a pension?'

'Yes. And I get my benefit. I can manage as far as the gate with you, that's all.'

I asked what his illness was and he told me asbestosis and gave his smile: 'Another joke.'

We stopped at the gate.

'In the meantime,' he said, 'it's a lovely day. And I'm out of the house. Tell me, Mr Mandl, did Mother talk about Willi Gauss?'

'Yes. He's why I came. To see what she remembered. But we didn't get far. When her mind's clearer, does she know he's dead?'

'That's as clear as she gets. We used to say he was, but we've given up. So I just say Auf Wiedersehen and she says it back.'

He surprised me by pronouncing the words correctly. 'Does she know any more German?'

'Just what I say to her. Wiener Schnitzel, stuff like that.'

'And Goering and Goebbels.'

'Yes, that. Himmler too. I don't say those back so she thinks I'm dumb. Tell me, Willi Gauss – he's Delia's father, but we think he must have been –' he shrugged '– a very bad man.'

'No, he wasn't. He was a complex man. He . . .' There was so much I could say, but marshalling it was impossible, so I said, 'He treated women badly. But they loved him. She loves him, in there.'

'Yes, she does. Delia – she doesn't look like Mother so I wondered, is she like him?'

'There's a resemblance.'

He swallowed. I saw that he loved his wife, and that she, not the mortgage or his illness, was the cause of his back-handed cheerfulness, and of his desperation too.

'I've wondered,' he said, 'I know he's been dead a long time, but maybe he left something, some property . . . ?'

I told him I did not think so: that Willi had died in an East German prison and any property he'd had would have been confiscated; and his wife in the West would have had first claim on anything there.

'Ah,' Gummer said, 'Mr Moser didn't tell us that.'

'Moser?' I said. 'Has he been here?'

'He comes a bit.'

'I thought he was in Auckland.'

'No, he's down here now. He wanted to be close to his grandchildren.' Gummer smiled. 'He brings Mother chocolates. He's a very nice man.' Again he smiled, perhaps with nervousness. 'So you see, we know all about you. And Willi Gauss too.'

'Moser doesn't know about Willi.' I was shaken, I was angry. I wanted to be gone. 'Where can I get a taxi?'

'I thought you'd have a chauffeur-driven car.'

'Is that a joke?'

'Yes. I'm sorry –'

'You're mistaken about me, Mr Gummer. I'm not a rich man. Don't let Moser tell you lies.'

'He doesn't talk about money. He just says how he liked you on Somes Island.'

I could not answer that, it confused me, so I opened the gate and went out.

'I'll phone you a taxi,' Gummer said. 'If you wait along there, there's a seat in the sun.'

He shuffled away and I walked to the seat – perhaps shuffled too – away from Norma Cooksley in her over-heated room, and Willi's daughter with her Willi face and her pop-eyed hatred, and from the strange fellow Gummer, who loved one of them, perhaps loved both. Well, I thought, he shares a house with them: he has to love or he'll go mad.

I sat in the sun. Presently a taxi came and drove me to my house; to my daughter and my room, where I was safe.

To my notebook, where I've written it all down.

TEN

I have dreams. They're not exactly nightmares although they are filled with anxiety. Always there are people I can't reach. I can't reach Willi. I can't reach Franz.

I say to Willi, 'Wait for me,' but he is gone. I sit down to eat with him, Viennese meals, and cannot reach the food, something intervenes and holds me away; and then they fade, Willi at the table and Franz, huge-faced, at my sleeve, they become uncoloured and other dreams emerge from the side, like a stroke crossing the eyeball, filling it with blackness or with light.

Somes Island appears. It turns as though I'm in a helicopter and I see the grassy slopes, the reefs and beaches, and Braun suspended on the cliff. I cannot tell whether he is climbing in or out. Dowden then, sillier than he was in real life. He stands with his megaphone above the strait separating Somes from Leper Island and moos at a launch full of women rocking there: 'You are entering a restricted zone. Go back or you will be fired on.' Norma Cooksley is on the launch but oh thank God not Nancy.

And now the bull is servicing the heifers and we – but not Willi, where is he? – stand with our fingers in the wire, watching as he mounts them one by one. All of us tumescent – and I wake; and lie remembering the bull, how he lost his footing and floundered in the sea, then walked polished, dripping, in the sun, with the caretaker leading him by the nose; and his rolling gait; and his prancing as he sniffed his herd. We followed. We hooked our fingers in the wire. Men without women, watching animals copulate. Some of us, embarrassed by arousal, had to turn, hands in pockets, and walk away.

I'm not troubled by desire any more, or lack of desire, and yet I dream of things like that, and lie awake reconstructing them – the barracks at night, the whispering and panting of solitary men. My subject is hardly sex at all, it's being lost. That must be why Nancy isn't there, for she was a finding. And Susi, I found her. Found my parents, in a way, although where they went to is a place I'll never look. But Willi and Franz, I've never found them, and will not now.

Our new handyman is mowing the lawns. Our handyman is Julie, Kenny's daughter. Where the grass has tufted she squats like a coolie and saws at the edges with a sickle. There's less temper in the girl than there used to be; but still she demands a weed-eater, Elizabeth says. Tell her no, I answer. Her grandma used that mower. She got down on her knees and worked with sheep shears, trimming up. They're still in the shed if Julie wants.

I haven't spoken with her yet. I've spoken with Kenny; told him there's nothing I can do with Mrs Gummer and Mrs Lloyd but that he might find Gummer more receptive. 'He seems a rational sort of fellow.' I kept his asbestosis to myself.

Kenny did his usual amount of squawking. I'm the only one who's heard that voice. He'd be out of business if he used it there. I told him not to get in a twist, and said that Julie was doing a bit of work in the garden and living in the spare room for a while – which, more than my admonition, calmed him down.

'Well, that's good. That's really good.'

Kenny has not seen Julie for several months. He wants to know how she is, how's her health, her mental health, and after that her physical. He questions me with urgency, but love and pain keep him level-voiced. This is real business, the business of nine-tenths of our life, and there's no room for squawking here.

I say that she looks thin, but she's always thin, it doesn't necessarily mean that she's not eating. As far as I can see she still has a stud in her nose, but the row of rings – the golden caterpillar crawling on the curl of her ear – is gone. I can't tell about her other parts. And she wears a skivvy because it's cooler now, so I can't see if her left shoulder is tattooed.

'You'll have to ask Elizabeth about her mental state.'

'Dad, will she see me, do you think?'

'I can't tell, Kenny. But whatever's happening, easy goes' – and I call to Elizabeth in the kitchen that her brother wants to talk with her, and hang up when she comes on the line.

And now I watch my grand-daughter working. The lawn is finished, the tufts of grass that grew, I don't know why, like those rich tufts in paddocks where cowpats have lain, are sickled away. She's trimming the hedge – and will, no doubt, want electric hedge-clippers soon. Thin, I said to Kenny. Her arms are as thin as the handles of the clipper; but she goes snip snip energetically, and leaves and twigs fall about her feet, where she tramples them with her big boots.

And now she has a plank on two boxes and stands on it, tests it, making it bounce. I have hope for her. She cuts the top of the hedge as level as a haircut, and when she needs to rest her arms she lets the clippers lie there and leans on the squared-off wall she has made. She looks into the harbour at Somes Island – or perhaps beyond it, at the Orongorongos, which soon, with winter coming, will have snow on them.

She spits over the hedge into the road. I don't like women spitting. But I have hope for her.

I haven't written here since last week. It's Friday now. Julie is still with us. Her little pink car stands in the drive with rain beating on it and water flowing inch-deep round its wheels. Her washing tumbles in the drier with mine. Elizabeth unpicks scanties from my shirts. It seems like family so I don't mind.

'How long will she be here? How long will it take?'

'Maybe for ever.'

'What I mean is, she can stay as long as she likes.'

'Have you told her that?'

'No. But I will.'

Her door stays closed today; she's lying down with, Elizabeth says, PMT. Women are frank about these matters today and although I'd just as soon not hear I suppose I can look on it as family too.

Julie is sick. She's very sick. That mental state I did not know I know about now. But she is free of the therapist who led her there, and that's good news. It was Elizabeth who got her away. She has been busy while I looked somewhere else. Julie goes to a new woman, who works to clear all the septic clutter from her mind, and it will be long. Part of her prescription is my house, my garden, my long view over mountains, which Julie is said to like; and Elizabeth, who is essential. I would like to add, me too, Josef Mandl pottering about. But nobody has suggested it.

She does not seem all that different to me, except that she's more patient and more soft. That may be because of her medication. She can still be sharp and sudden and ugly with her tongue. I make her frown with my old-fashionedness, which I see clearly now she's in the house, although I've always tried to move with the times. She exclaims softly, 'Jeez!' Once or twice she's had to get up and leave the room. Does not slam the door though, closes it with a moderate bang.

'You made a good job of the lawn.'

'I would have done it better with a decent mower.' Then she smiled. 'I oiled it. If you've got a file I'll sharpen the blades.'

'How much should I pay her?' I asked Elizabeth.

'Job by job. Some days she won't want to work. I'll get some money from Kenny if you like.'

'No. I'll pay. Did you tell him all of it? What did he say?'

Elizabeth is changing too. Her blandness is eroded; her efforts to please take a sideways shift and she doesn't always pull them back.

'I told Kenny not to come here. I told him he can see her in six months, if he's lucky. If she's lucky, I should have said.'

'What did he think about . . . ?'

'What would you have thought about something like that?'

I can't answer. I can't imagine. The 'something' Kenny was supposed to have done, created by that woman whispering there, grew into multiple rapes of the six-year-old by all his friends and business partners, standing in a circle, taking turns: devil masks on their faces, wives in the shadows, twittering. It was sometimes in a room and sometimes in a garden, and always at night, with candles burning, and Kenny capering, phallus erect, and Priscilla coming with a glass of raspberryade and wiping Julie's brow with a flannel at the end.

The woman, her therapist, believed it was true. There is ideology in this. And Julie believed it was true once she had 'recovered' it. But she is not to blame. Julie must be held innocent.

'Was I . . .' I said, 'was I . . . ?'

'No you weren't,' Elizabeth said. 'There's only room for so much. She wouldn't be here, Dad, if you were one of them.'

'How can she stand it? How can Kenny?'

'I didn't tell him some of the worst. The only bit of luck we had was getting her away from that wretched woman. Once that stuff is in there it's hard getting it out, but Helen thinks she's got a good chance.'

Helen is Helen Henly, a psychologist. Elizabeth persuaded Julie to her rooms, I don't know how – and she is a woman good at seeming soft and slow. Julie sinks into her like a feather bed, and although it's still dicey, she will stay.

'I can see why looking across the harbour might help.'

'Just be friendly with her, Dad. Not too cheerful, not too bright.'

I play my part adequately. I smile and frown and cogitate and pass harmless opinions. Now and then I disagree with Julie, use a strong expression now and then, but it's never about anything important – and lack of a subject becomes a strain. Often I can't do better than just stay quiet. Elizabeth takes up the job of nothing-talk, or she turns on the TV set. They laugh. I laugh. I almost fall off my chair when Mr Bean, in the Queen Mother's presentation line, finds his finger poking out of his fly. Julie frowns. She wants American sit-coms with smart young people in apartments wise-cracking endlessly. I can't take more than two or three minutes of that – or of the endless advertising. I did not invite these hucksters into my living room but here they are. I pretend I'm tired, I play grandpa needing his bed, and say my goodnights and go to my room, where I turn on the heater and sit like Mrs Lloyd, with my slippers scorching. I try to believe that Julie is better today, she gets a little better every day, even though Elizabeth has told me Helen Henly will not say yes or no. If Julie sharpens the mower blades and laughs at TV and asks for more pudding at dinner, she must be getting better, isn't that right?

The sun broke through the clouds this morning and the wind died away. I took a cushion out to the porch and sat on the top step in a pool of warmth. The mountains were dark and the harbour spar-kled. The trees on Somes Island turned from black to green and the Cook Strait ferry, heading out, leaned into a curve that would send waves breaking on the reefs and easing between the large island and the small. One can be satisfied by this as if by food. There need not be anything transcendental.

Julie came out of the house and sat beside me. 'Have my cush-ion,' I said.

'Thank you. I've got sharp bones in my arse.'

So have I these days, although I would express it differently. We talked for a while, I shifting forward and back and from buttock to buttock, and she seeming perfectly comfortable. I asked her how her car was running – remembering too late that it was Kenny's gift.

'All right,' she said. 'I hardly use it except when I'm seeing Helen. I should try to get into town more.'

'Why don't you?'

'Well, I don't want Bonnie grabbing me.' Bonnie is her former therapist.

'No,' I said.

'She would, you know. She'd kidnap me. Grab me by the hair.'

'We can't have that.'

Julie looked at me sharply. I need to be more careful.

'She was putting some bloody awful muck in my head.'

'Yes,' I said, not wanting to hear; and Julie closed her eyes and turned up her face and worshipped the sun Swedish-style. She leaned back on her arms in her double-jointed way and rested her booted heels three steps down. I took cautious glances at her face: so thin, so sharp. Her hair is growing out on the side that was shaved but she has cut the other to even herself up. Bonnie would have trouble getting a handful to drag her with. I hope she lets it grow long everywhere.

She opened her eyes and smiled at me. 'Lovely sun.'

The mountains lit up as the clouds floated south. Snow from last weekend's fall gleamed in creases under the tops. I asked Julie if she had had her second tattoo done.

'Yes,' she said, and tugged her loose skivvy off her shoulder.

I was pleased not to see a beetle. 'It's a caduceus,' I said. 'You've got Greece on one shoulder and Egypt on the other.' And I could not help showing off – explained the caduceus and the ankh and told her that with these symbols she was bound to get well.

'I thought it was just a stick with snakes around it. I like snakes.'

'Now you know the meaning.'

'Stuff meanings. Why do you always have to know so much?' Her face began to pucker, her mouth went down. 'You've spoiled them now.'

I apologised. I tried to pat her, but she gave an electric jump.

'Don't touch me.'

She clattered away down the steps, then clumped back to the top against the rail.

'Don't you ever touch me.'

'I'm sorry, Julie.'

'I know there were no masks. And all those men weren't there. Bonnie made that up. But the rest is true. Mum and Dad. Don't you try and make me say it's not.'

I sat there in the sun after she had gone. I heard her radio playing in her room – rock music, cheerful enough – and tried to take hope from that. I must creep about the house, move with care and smile like an old man, and try to believe that she has improved. The devil masks are gone, and the circle of men.

Now there is just Kenny raping her, and Priscilla bringing raspberryade.

I have a place to go where I can be away from this – but I have been silent (silent in my book) for more than a week because I do not want to retreat to that early time but go there with a recollective mind and hold each thing, when it is found, in a steady light and turn it in my two hands like a vase.

Elias Canetti (these Jews, these Viennese!) has described his childhood as 'rich in displacements'. I think of my single displacement, from Vienna to Wellington by way of Somes Island – which seems to me now like the narrow neural pathway things must pass through after a stroke, from one wide place to another. (But

Vienna has been displaced too; mine has not been the only shift. Vienna passed through its narrow place in 1938 and found a new location and can never be the same.)

Canetti, describing a forced move, says that, like the earliest man, he came into being only by an expulsion from Paradise. I too was expelled from my paradise and I came into being in the hard world of the island. I thought, I have had my nose rubbed in this place so I will stay and make it mine. I will stay here and keep what I find. That moment of euphoria – that epiphany – when I looked through the hospital window at the city lit up in the dawn was judgement too, was decision too.

In the beginning what I found was a room in a back yard and a job sweeping wood-shavings in a draughty shed. But there's more than that when I turn it round. There's Wilf's garden in summer and autumn and spring. There are wigwams made of leaves and bees in pumpkin flowers and tomatoes going through their colour change, green, orange, red. There are butter beans, radishes, rock melons, silver beet; corn whose leaves clatter in the breeze coming pine-scented from Tinakori hill. Wilf throws a cob across potato rows and I jump and catch it over my head, strip its jacket off, pick away the threads of silk and plunge it into boiling water for my lunch. This sweet taste is Wellington. I have found it and it's mine.

Then winter comes – so let me turn the tense back from present to past. I had two hard winters in my room. I was used to winters from Somes Island but each one takes you unprepared. I crouched over my heater – first came across the scorching of leather soles there – and wore two pairs of socks and woollen gloves, even in bed. I wrapped my scarf about my ears, pulled my hat down low and walked down Molesworth Street into a southerly sharpened with chips of ice. I climbed with a tarpaulin on to the roof at Barton's Joinery and tied it over the hole where the storm had torn off a sheet of iron and flung it into a back yard two streets away. The rain, at work and home, deafened me, but I thought, This is their noise, these iron roofs, so it is mine. Wilf brought me cups of tea and bowls of porridge when I had flu, then it was his turn and I did the same, but had to leave him in the day and came home to find him shifted to the hospital with pneumonia. I visited him on Saturdays and told him the winter jobs I had done in his garden. Both of my winters he was in hospital but he came home in the spring and carried on as though he had not almost died.

Some days I walked out, huddled in my raincoat, exploring the city and the suburbs and the hills. In little parks on plateaux or in valleys I came across rugby, that barbarous game, and stood on the sideline trying to understand the butting of heads, the savage assaults, and the ball that would not bounce true, and thought of Hakoah, the soccer team I had followed for a season in Vienna, and tried to find a connection between that game and this. Could not. Did not want Hakoah anyway, those memories, and so left the rugby players grunting, steaming there, a part of my new home I could not make mine. I walked along to the next ground and watched a hockey match. That was more civilised and more to my taste.

On a fine Sunday – the sky turned inside out – I walked up to Wadestown by the lower road, explored the long ridge of Tinakori hill, and came down on the high road that turns off at the shops. I leaned on a railing for the view of the harbour, as fresh that day as on some first morning of the world, then looked across a shallow gully of scrub and saw my house. And I'm stopped dead. I stopped on that day, and I stop now, to clear my head, get rid of the dizziness caused by a crossing of time lines. I've only to leave my room and walk a hundred yards along the road and I'll meet him, my young self, Josef Mandl in his second-hand jacket and cracked shoes looking with a silly glazed grin at the house I'm sitting in now.

Red roof of corrugated iron. Overlapping weatherboards. White concrete chimney. (Barbarous, most Viennese would say; but I like it better than anything Alfred Loos ever built.) I walked on and saw how comfortably it spread on the headland jutting into the road. A wide deep porch took up half the front wall, with bow windows on either side. They looked over a hedge at the top of a bank. I climbed up and grabbed roots and hung one-handed, looking out; and there, where I had known it would be, was Somes Island. The sun flashed mirror signals from a barracks window.

A woman's voice called from three feet away, 'Harold, come quickly. There's a man in the hedge.'

I dropped and slid, ending on my knees in the road, yelled, 'I'm sorry', and ran away, under the cuttings, above the gorge – and I run out of that uneasy connection with me, which threatened my balance for a while. I came to my room in the lean-to by the garden, where old Wilf, pretending not to work too hard on a Sunday, left his spade upright in the soil and invited me to share a bottle of beer with him. We brought out chairs to enjoy the last ten minutes of the sun. We drank and smoked cigarettes.

'I saw the house I want to buy,' I said.

'What's wrong with this place?' he replied.

Wilf is almost fifty years dead.

I ran into Moser in a restaurant in Manners Street where they served a main course of meat and three veg, followed by jam roll or treacle tart. I walked there after working late, up Lambton Quay and Willis Street where the only places open were a greasy spoon or two, and came with a steaming sigh out of the cold into the warmth, took a table by the window, ordered roast mutton with cabbage and potatoes, looked down as I waited into the street – this street in the capital city at seven o'clock on a Wednesday night, with only a tramcar each half hour, and no pedestrians, no life, now that the shops were shut and the pubs closed. Only two cold shufflers in black coats along by the Willis Street corner. I looked at them again. Jews, I thought. How is it they are so unmistakable?

My meal came. The third veg was a slice of beetroot bleeding into the gravy. I put it on my bread and butter plate, concealed beneath a slice of white bread I would not eat, and transferred my dob of butter to the mashed potatoes, where it melted greasily. I had eaten better on the island, I thought: thicker slices of mutton (when the coal dust was wiped off), fried sausages, lamb's fry, mince stew. At Pahiatua the Italians had made spaghetti, with a delicious sauce of anything they could get their hands on, and sometimes I bought a leftover bowl of that.

'Josef, it is you,' Moser said.

They had hung their coats on the stand inside the door and stood by my table in pre-war suits from Germany. I shook hands with Moser and asked him and his friend to join me at my table. Like me they had come for the warmth rather than the food – for whatever this dismal place could provide of a coffee-house atmosphere.

Moser was in his thirties, older than me. He was a lugubrious fellow, living at a low temperature. Yet he had done that brave thing on the island, taken his blanket out under the stars and won the Jews their freedom from the Nazis. I was pleased to see him, pleased to see him well, with his cheeks fattened and a pleasant sharpness in his eye.

'I did not know you were in Wellington,' he said.

I explained that I lived quietly; went to the pictures on Saturday night for my social life. His friend was an older man, reserved and courteous, who came from Hamburg, where he had been a music teacher. His name was Benjamin Ascher. Moser was his boarder in a little house in Berhampore.

I saw that Benjamin's eyes were on my bread, which had a red stain, so I raised it and showed the slice of beetroot underneath and told him it came with the mutton and that he should order something else.

'It is the bread I am frightened of,' he said.

They chose shepherd's pie and had their coupons clipped by a waitress blushing at the old man's courtesy.

'And a pot of tea, if you please.'

'It's a cup of tea.'

'A cup then. For two.'

'The coffee's better. It's nice and sweet.'

'Thank you, Miss. The tea will do most . . .'

'Adequately,' I supplied.

We smiled at each other as she went away. Coffee in this place was hot water poured on goo that came from a bottle. We talked about good food and how it went hand in hand with art and civilisation – but fell silent, all three, remembering the history of the lands we came from; ate, when their shepherd's pie came, without much talk. Then Moser asked about Willi and I told him that he worked in a forestry camp.

Moser made a sour face at 'camp'. (We spoke in English, not to offend diners at nearby tables – and softly to keep our accents hidden.)

'It is his proper place. He can be the bully there.' He turned to Benjamin Ascher. 'Willi Gauss was our big boss on Somes Island.'

'Samuel and Willi never got on,' I said. 'They were chalk and cheese.' Proud of the idiom, I almost went on to claim that Willi was the hero of Somes Island and if he bullied us it was for our own good. He helped us keep our shoulders straight, I almost said, but heard Roy Cooksley, the insurance man, in that, so I said lamely, 'Willi was my friend. And so was Samuel, of course.'

Moser grinned. He had learned to grin. 'Willi was a big friend. The rest of us were little friends.'

'Willi was the man who got way?' Benjamin Ascher asked.

'Josef too. Josef got away. He was the one who dug the tunnel.'

'But did not escape that time?'

'No, someone wrote a note . . .'

Moser gave another grin as I trailed off. 'Willi said I wrote it. But I have worked out who. It was Willi Gauss.'

'That's a lie,' I said, then paused and was silent for a time while Moser and Benjamin looked away. It is not pleasant, perhaps, to see a man understand the truth. But they were mistaken: it caused me no pain. It turned Willi – turned him like a vase, revealing a part I had not known. How shall I put it? Willi became more dear to me.

'Well,' I said, 'he hated it down there. That pump of Steinitz's didn't give enough air for him.'

It did not give enough for me, and on my last night at the tunnel face the hose got a twist in it and no air came through. When Willi worked the bellows the nozzle blew out. He jerked the rope tied around my ankle, calling me back. I was close to fainting by the time I reached the pit. Willi pulled me upright and stood me on the ladder with my head in the cold air under the hut, breathing deep. 'I can't do it all, Willi. You'll have to help.' 'We will widen the tunnel for me,' he said. I worked on that the next night and got half a yard in from the mouth – easier work, plenty of air, with Willi lying flat among the piles, spreading the bags of earth I heaved up to him. Later, as we slept, Dowden and his men burst into the hut.

I smiled at Moser. Willi should have found a Nazi to blame. 'It wasn't a very good tunnel,' I said.

'I would like to meet this Willi Gauss,' Benjamin said.

'He's going to Auckland when he's finished in Kaingaroa.'

'Then Samuel will meet him. They will shake hands, perhaps, like New Zealanders after they are fighting in the pub.'

I smiled at his joke. 'So you're heading for Auckland?' I asked Moser.

He was going to join a friend, he said, who had a little factory for making furniture. I was jealous.

'I could do that.'

'You will not steal my job? Start a factory in Wellington.'

'I didn't know we were allowed to leave the jobs we've got.'

'Ask,' he said. 'Perhaps not Willi Gauss, the dangerous one. But you and me . . .' He shrugged. 'Do not wait, Josef. Anyone can be rich in this God's Own land. A little bit of comfort, sell them that.'

'Their god forgot to order it,' Benjamin said. 'Just as he forgot the bread.'

Perhaps because I smiled at his jokes (although his cheerfulness pleased me more) he said to Moser, 'Samuel, we will give him some. Will you bring my bag?'

'It's for Mrs Steiner,' Moser said.

'Mrs Steiner will do without. A piece off the end. Shall I go?'

'Sit, Benjamin,' Moser said and stumped away as though detailed to scrub out cattle troughs; fetched a bag hanging with the coats and brought it back. Benjamin put it on his knee and lifted something out. I knew the smell: new-baked bread. He put it on the table and unwrapped its cloth, revealing a loaf eight inches long, four inches high. (I knew the size exactly from my timber-measuring eye.) It was brown and firm, elastic a little when I pressed. Using the cloth, I weighed it in my hand.

'German bread.'

'Rye bread,' Benjamin said.

'It is his hobby,' Moser said. 'He has a big oven and he bakes. He plays his violin to make it rise.'

Benjamin smiled at him, then raised his finger for the waitress.

'My dear, can we have a knife to cut this loaf?'

'You can't have that in here,' she said, and looked around alarmed. 'Wait a bit.'

In a moment she came back with a bread knife in her apron. 'Do it quick. Don't let the manager see.'

Benjamin sawed the loaf in half.

'Which is the piece off the end?' Moser said.

'Half for Josef and half for the young lady here. Eat it in the kitchen, dear, and give the chef a piece for his excellent shepherd's pie.'

'What is it?'

'Bread.'

'You could have fooled me. All right. Ta.'

She carried her half away and Benjamin wrapped mine in the cloth. Then we had treacle tart.

In the street, huddled in our coats, we said goodbye. I wished Moser luck and he told me not to stay too long in my job.

'Now we go to tell Mrs Steiner that her loaf of bread grew some wings and flew away.' He pointed at Benjamin. 'Visit him. He will be lonely when I'm gone.'

I carried my half loaf home in the leather schoolbag I used for my lunch and library books. I walked down the Quay and up Molesworth Street, past the building where parliament sat – and this, with its steps and columns, this little low place, pretending there, told me more clearly than it ever had before that I lived in a land without a history. Against my wish to be at home in this town, I yearned for Vienna – where Marcus Aurelius had died, where the Turks had laid siege before turning back from Europe, where an empire lasting five hundred years had built its parks and palaces. Where, I thought, you can go into a cafe at midnight and find the coffee-brewer at work, smell the scents of mocca and sausage and brandy, sit at a table for three hours playing cards or reading the papers from Zurich and Milan, while a continent talks outside the door in a dozen tongues, and murmurs for a thousand miles away in every direction. Then I thought, No, Vienna does not exist any more. All that remains of it I carry in my bag. And anyway, he is a German, it is German bread.

The weight of it in my satchel helped keep me in place. In Vienna I had lived in a bowl, with two thousand years pressing down and holding me firm; but in Wellington I was on the outside curve of a ball, even when I walked in gullies underneath the hills;

I was clinging on and might be swept off. This wind, this rain, were certainly enough to sweep me off.

I ran into the garden and saw the light shining from Wilf's window – and thought, He's the history of this place, Wilf and all those soldiers home from the war. They go far enough back.

I took off my raincoat and changed my wet shoes. Then I knocked on Wilf's door and offered him a piece of rye bread. He liked the look of it and liked the taste, but apologised for not eating more than a bite. It hurt his teeth.

ELEVEN

I shifted into Benjamin Ascher's house at the end of winter. Wilf was home from hospital and watching over Tinakori hill for the spring. He gave me some seeds to make a garden in my new place. There had been a time when I had thought I would stay with him, live in the lean-to, work as a joiner if I could train, and take over the garden when he died; but Moser, it was Moser, elbowed me past that; and Benjamin with his loaf of bread. Now there were things I must think out, and things that I must work at hard.

I visited Benjamin shortly after meeting him, inspected his house, which was no more than a two-bedroomed cottage: tiny bedrooms up a flight of stairs where the walls made you clamp your elbows to your sides, and a living room and kitchen down-stairs. The kitchen was the largest room in the house. It had a long wooden table and an iron stove in a brick alcove, and it was there that Benjamin spent most of his time. Baking was not the hobby Moser had said. Benjamin enjoyed eating his bread but did not enjoy making it. His wife had been the baker, had baked all day long in the kitchen, four loaves at a time in the oven, and had sold them for eightpence each to refugees about Wellington who could not stand the local bread – 'white pap' she had called it. Benjamin made the deliveries on a bicycle. He sold a dozen loaves a week to a health shop in Cuba Street. When Mrs Ascher died he let that contract go and gave her recipe to her private customers, trying to get them to make their own bread, but felt he must keep baking for those who could not manage it. He made four loaves three days a week and still rode about on his bike delivering them.

Benjamin wanted me to move straight into Moser's room. I told him I had grown used to Thorndon. It was handier than Berhampore for catching my train. The truth is I could not leave Wilf until he was well again and busy in his garden. I've learned in this country not to talk about loving friends, especially men, but in my notebook I'll say what I like. I loved that old man, perhaps even more than I came to love Benjamin. (Was it because he came from 'here' and Benjamin from 'there'?) I had to make sure he knew that I had found a job that I might do to make a life. I said, 'I'm going to bake some more of that bread you can't eat. I'll build a factory for baking bread.'

'Come and we'll drink a beer to it,' Wilf said. He took me to his pub for the only time, and the next day I packed my bags and shifted by tram to Berhampore.

I found Benjamin kneading dough in a wooden trough on the kitchen table. He wiped his hands, rolled down his sleeves and took me to my room, eager to show how he had made it ready – a hand-made quilt on the bed (payment for her weekly loaf from a Viennese lady) and a bunch of freesias in a vase on the chest of drawers. Their scent reminded me of the Woods, which moved me in a way I did not want, but I said, 'It is nice, Benjamin. Behaglich, my friend.' He went back to his kneading and I unpacked, thinking, I am here and I will work. I get my house in Wadestown or the dump. Now I will not think of 'there' any more.

I went downstairs and said to Benjamin, 'Let me do that.'

'Wash your hands, Josef,' he said.

'Lesson one.'

'Then put on Maria's apron and roll up your sleeves. Do you have plenty of . . .'

'Elbow grease?'

Benjamin sighed. 'You will be the New Zealander, not me.'

We agreed that I would speak English, and he use German only when he was tired – which turned out to be almost never. He kept running upstairs to find words in my dictionary. I told him to bring it down and leave it on the table. Before long though he used me as his Wörterbuch and we rarely opened Avis Greenough. It became a game with us to hunt for words – but the language I was after was the language of bread. Benjamin saw soon enough what my purpose was. I kept on at Barton's Joinery but spent more and more time, my weekends and whole evenings, baking and delivering. Sometimes I worked until two or three in the morning. I wanted the skills and I wanted the base. I picked up sacks of flour – rye flour, hard to get – from a mill in Petone and carried it home on the train and tram. I bought timber at the joinery and built larger troughs – three feet long and eighteen inches deep – and carried them home in the same way. Benjamin kept his old customers. I found new, starting with the Cuba Street health shop, bringing in another in Kilbirnie, and then trying dairies and suburban grocer shops. Only one in ten was interested but one in ten was enough while I stayed small.

Benjamin came down one night at two o'clock. 'Josef, this is no good. You will burst a pipe.'

'Burst a gasket,' I said.

'Whatever it is, you will soon go bang.'

'No I won't. I'm getting ready to stop.'

'Stop?'

'Finish at Barton's. Benjamin, I'm going to need your help.'

I meant that I would need whatever money he had. I would need him as a partner, sleeping partner, I said, and I think it was his pleasure in the term as much as his faith in me that made him say yes. So I sent him out on his bike hunting for a building where I might install an oven, and he did better than that: found a little bakery in Newtown with a shop in front. The owner made white bread and brown – which as far as I could tell was white dyed brown – and sponges and seed cake and lamingtons. There were two ovens and a mechanical mixer and all the utensils and furnishings I would need – and it cost too much; but Benjamin bought it with the help of small investments from his friends. He never doubted that I would make money, and he make some, and when I told him there was a man in Auckland baking bread just like ours, and that I had seen it for sale in a Wellington shop, he said, 'Leave your job, Josef. Leave it now. We cannot let someone else . . .'

'Beat us to the punch?'

'Is he a refugee?'

'He's got a Jewish name.'

'Leave tomorrow. Quit.'

I told the clerk at the National Service Department that I had been offered a job in a little business started by a friend, and that I hoped to own a share of it myself – thinking it better not to lie. What sort of business?, he wanted to know. Would I be competing with returned servicemen? I told him I meant to bake pumpernickel bread (not exactly true, but I wanted a word he could look down on), mainly for refugees, and he made a spitting sound, adjusted his teeth and signed a paper releasing me. So I left Barton's Joinery and became a baker. I hired a man to help me, one of the Dutch immigrants who were starting to arrive. They would be making bread themselves before long. I told Benjamin we were lucky to 'get the drop on them', and he practised the idiom, adding it to others I brought home. He was happy in those several years before his death: baking no more, teaching violin, which he loved.

We called our bread Ascher's Bread. There was no secret recipe, no hocus pocus like that. It was plain bread, made with yeast and flour. It weighed like bread and looked like bread and tasted like bread, but it would never outsell 'white pap' on the market. I worked hard to get it known and liked. I did the marketing and advertising – and I baked it too, with my Dutch helper, working from 3 a.m. to 11 a.m., and again, alone, from 5 p.m. to eleven at night. I made some smaller doughs, kneading by hand in my wooden troughs, but most of the mixing was done in the old cast-iron machine I had bought, five feet long and five feet high, with a long horizontal mixing arm that had to be wiped every ten minutes or oil dropped into the dough. Its noise sent me home deafened and I slept my three hours, half past eleven to half past two in the afternoon, without being able to hear Benjamin taking violin lessons in the living room. He had one of his lady friends make me some ear muffs, and I wore them to block out the Dutchman's cheerfulness. I was not cheerful at that time; I was obsessed. Wilf's seeds lay on a shelf in my bedroom and lost their life there. I would not make my place in my new land by planting things but by making people eat my bread.

Selling from the shop did not succeed so I let it to a radio repairman and bought a little van on time payment; then a larger one able to climb hills and get Ascher's Bread to the towns of the Wairarapa and the Manawatu. Inside a year I was employing three bakers and a driver, and selling in Taranaki and Hawke's Bay; and I was still in debt. I thought, Either I grow bigger or I go back to baking bread for Benjamin's friends.

I woke in my room, shook paint flakes from the ceiling off my quilt, and heard, far away, a child scraping dolefully on a violin. My future seemed no brighter than hers. Then Benjamin struck with his bow, and the sound, full of light and life and authority, made me sit up in my bed and swing my feet on to the floor and stand up and stretch and fill my room. It was as though he had goosed me, to use an Americanism, and I thought, I'll either be a bankrupt or a millionaire. So I gulped some food and rode my bicycle back to work and mixed a new dough in my wooden trough, with wholemeal flour and cracked wheat and honey, while Henk watched cheerfully and wanted to try it too, and Ron and Fred shook their heads and said it would never sell. It sold, never as much as my rye bread, but it sold; and so did my almond bread and my pumpernickel, and I was a little less in debt. I started shipping Ascher's Bread across the strait – it was like exporting to another country – and I sent Henk to Auckland to set up a bakery there, and soon (is four years soon?) I was able to pay off Benjamin and his friends. I moved to more modern premises and I put another van on the road. Ascher's Bread had found its place. I had climbed the dangerous mountainside and reached a ledge where I might stop a while. And now I could choose: stay and be safe and comfortable or set off again and climb the rest of the way.

I talked it over with Nancy – but who is Nancy? I must step back into that narrow house in Berhampore and to an afternoon when I sat at the kitchen table drinking tea before riding over the hill to Newtown. I heard Benjamin playing a little concert for a pupil, a practice frowned upon by most teachers, he said, but without it how could he convince these children of music while they still struggled to make sounds? I pushed away my cup and rested my head on my arms, giving myself a moment. When this pupil left at the end of her half hour, it would be time for me to go. I went to sleep, and woke with my arms numb and my face pushed out of shape – dribbling on the table too. Benjamin's pupil was gone and he had been creeping about for over an hour trying not to wake me.

'Do not be cross, Josef,' he said as I jumped up. 'I sent a note to Henk with my poor girl.' (All his pupils, except for one boy, were his 'poor girls'.) 'I told him you are sleeping and you will be along when you wake up.'

I went to the bathroom to wash my face and he followed me.

'I told him that tomorrow afternoon he works overtime – and I will pay,' he added, seeing my astonishment. 'You will come with me and see that there are people in the world, it is not all bread. I am playing a concert, and you will sit in a chair and be quiet or else

I will go to the beginning and start again. Josef,' he pleaded, 'you must have a rest –' I saw with even greater astonishment that his eyes were wet '– or you will curl up in a corner and die.'

I told him I would come, even though music was wasted on me. I told him that my view was Settembrini's, that music made for inertia and stagnation; and he grew angry, as I had known he would: who was this Settembrini? He had never heard of the man but plainly he was an imbecile.

'I'll tell you one day,' I said, and put on my trouser clips and rode off to work.

The next afternoon, a Saturday, I went with Benjamin to a house in Brooklyn owned by that Mrs Steiner who had lost her bread to me. I sat on a hard chair in her living room and listened to Benjamin on his violin, Mrs Steiner on viola and Nancy Brisbois on the piano. 'We are, today, the Steiner Trio,' Benjamin said, and everyone laughed – a room full of Jewish refugees – so I guessed that I had heard a joke. (Which was that they were usually the Ascher Trio. 'Steiner' meant that she had won an argument over the order in which the pieces would be played.)

I can't say what those pieces were. I knew her at once. I knew Nancy. That was the music I heard. And I do not mind the Hollywood violins playing here, for it is true; I knew that I would marry Nancy Brisbois and we would live in my house on Wadestown hill. It is not knowledge, of course, but a kind of wishing. There could have been a weeping of stringed instruments that day and a crashing of discords on the piano – but no, she was not married, not engaged, and she had no prejudice against small men. When I had the chance I said, 'We've met already,' and she didn't mind my cheek. 'You sent me a message with your semaphore.'

'I don't remember you. Were you a prisoner there?'

I told her I had been interned for four years, almost three of them on Somes Island, and had watched the Wrens come and go and they were the only women I had glimpsed in all that time.

'But you can't have been a . . .' Remembered not to say 'Nazi' in this room full of refugees.

'No. I come from Austria. I'm not a German.'

She smiled at me. 'I love the Jews.'

'I didn't say I was one.'

'I think you are though, aren't you?'

'Yes.'

'I think you're so musical.'

I forgave her that. And she forgave me for being a baker, and for being non-musical, although she did not find that out till later. She asked if she could visit the bakehouse. She had seemed a practical person at the keyboard, sitting square, although in her body she was round, and playing her notes without the usual high-jumping with her hands, and I thought I might impress her doing practical things; so I said yes.

'Come tomorrow if you're free.'

Then I slipped out the door at the back of the room as the Steiner Trio prepared for the second half of its concert, and walked home to Berhampore, looking in at the bakery on my way to see how Henk was getting on, and I lay in my narrow bed while soft rain fell on the iron roof. It played a private concert for me. I slept until Benjamin called me at eight o'clock. He had made bread dumplings, with Kaiserschmarrn for pudding, and he behaved as though our meal was a celebration.

'Be quiet, Benjamin, or I'll go to work.'

'Miss Brisbois will not make music her career. Her playing is too square.'

'Have you told her that?'

'I am not her teacher.'

'Don't tell her anything. Button your lip.'

He smiled with delight.

'And I'm sure,' I said, 'that Miss Brisbois could be a concert pianist if she liked. I just don't think it's the life she wants.'

'I think she will learn baking bread,' Benjamin said.

Nancy came to the bakery next morning. I had the mixer going and we could not talk. I sat her in a warm place by the oven, put my ear muffs on her, and went on with kneading a small dough. She watched for a minute, then came to my side. 'Can I do some?' she shouted.

'Wash your hands. Lesson one.'

She laid them for inspection on my palms when she came back, and I felt their weight (like bread) and saw their strength. Then I watched as she worked dough in the trough, a large young woman, taller than me by an inch or two, and perfectly made: rounded, muscled, sinewed, strongly boned – breasted too, hipped too; and I thought with no concupiscence but only recognition, a woman who was open not closed, and moist not dry, and was ready to be loved. I told myself, She'll do; and several months later, when I confessed it to her and she'd laughed, she said that her feeling as she worked had been the same – he'll do. We did not understand that we were falling in love, for we were both of us unromantic. Romance did not come into our lives till later on. We remained practical and excited; and that I recommend as a course, even if now and then you hear violins play.

She walked home with me to Berhampore and we ate lunch with Benjamin at the kitchen table. He talked about music, trying hard not to embarrass us, and so embarrassed us a little.

'He's a lovely man,' Nancy said as we went back to work. 'His wife gave him a hard time with all that baking bread.'

'I've saved him from that. But I should tell you, I don't like music much myself.'

'Hmm,' Nancy said.

'But of course I can learn.'

I timed things so I could see her home to Island Bay, where she boarded with an aunt. We walked up past the rugby ground, then I sat her on the bar of my bicycle and doubled her all the way down the long road to the sea. She did not ask me in to meet her aunt, or the friend who boarded with her – that little sharp Wren with the porcelain cheeks who had ordered me to scat. (She, Moira Williams, never liked me and thought Nancy mad for marrying me, but Aunt Alma came on to my side once she had decided I was 'a Christian Jew'.)

I rode back up the hill, fit and strong, and coasted down to Newtown, where I worked till 2 a.m. I put on my ear muffs because Nancy had worn them – and that is romantic, I suppose – but soon took them off because they turned my ears hot. I had given her two loaves (she had earned them) and I thought, Nancy is eating my bread for lunch tomorrow. That, I see, is romantic too.

She worked as a clerk in a government office and she began to catch an early tram and get off in Newtown and spend half an hour each morning in the bakehouse with me. I put gloves on her, armed her with a paddle and let her take loaves from the oven, her favourite job. She turned them from their tins and set them to cool, then with a grin was off to work – and came back scarlet one day because she had joined the tram queue wearing her apron. I kissed her cheek to feel its warmth and thought with amusement when she'd gone, I'll always be kissing uphill.

I make a joke of that time because it is too much for me. I do not wish to peel myself, or reveal Nancy, whom I knew then and cannot know again. I would simply make her pirouette. Anecdotes are another matter. I could talk about her till the cows come home.

She borrowed a bicycle to ride out with me and one Saturday afternoon we pedalled along the Hutt Road, with a southerly wind pushing us into the base of the hill, and walked to the end of Petone wharf. I pointed out Wishart's launch and the part of the beach where Willi and Steinitz and I had come ashore. She remembered the escape, she had been in her last year at school.

'There was a man, I can't remember his name . . .'

'Willi Gauss.'

'His photo in the paper was so good-looking. We didn't want him to get caught.'

'What about me?' I was trying to put aside the fear that if Willi met Nancy he would steal her from me.

'I don't remember you. Was your picture there?'

'Yes. They said I had thick lips. But Willi's got thicker lips than me.'

She looked at me, startled. Then she laughed. 'Yours are thin. And rather mean-looking at the moment.' She touched my mouth. 'Smile. That's better. Tell me about your escape.'

I told her; and for a moment she joined the other side. Germans had to be captured, good-looking or not. Then, hearing me, and seeing me, she swung, quick and easy, on to my side. I told her how we had been caught, and then how, next spring, I had dug a tunnel.

'You could have been killed.'

'I was pleased when someone pimped on us.'

'I bet you were. I'm glad too.'

I kissed her. It was the first time we had kissed, and I thought, We should do this lying down. I pulled off her woollen gloves – in the southerly! – and we held hands with naked palms.

'Can you still talk in semaphore?'

'If I tried. It's just the alphabet. We used to say some rude stuff – about men we liked.'

'Did you like some?'

'Of course I did. I'm a normal girl.'

'What's degaussing?'

'Oh, it's for repelling mines.'

'I know that. But how does it work? What did you do?'

'Well,' she said, 'when a convoy came in –' and she talked non-stop for ten minutes – F coils and Q coils, plus and minus settings, and calling ships on the radio for length and beam and draught –

and I saw how she had enjoyed being in the Wrens.

'We didn't know what you were doing,' I said, not telling her Willi's joke that the degaussing hut was a brothel for the guards.

'We had to keep away from you prisoners,' she said. 'They told us you had some baddies there.'

'Hoch was bad. Von Schaukel was bad.'

'I met a bad man,' she said. 'He wasn't on Somes Island.'

'Who? Where?'

'He was a Yank. A sailor. I didn't know Wrens were only supposed to go out with officers. He was just an enlisted man. I'm sorry, I don't mean just.'

'What did he do?'

'He wasn't even drunk. And he said, "Come on, baby. Let's increase the population of the coming generation." I mean, what a way to talk to a girl?'

'What did you do?'

'I punched him.'

'Slapped him.'

'No, I said I punched. I broke one of his teeth. The Yanks are very careful with their teeth. So he punched me back. He knocked me over.'

'Good God,' I said.

'He tried kicking me on the floor but I got behind the sofa. I think he would have killed me if his friends hadn't come in and stopped him.'

'Is this the hand you punched him with?'

'Yes. See the little scar there, on my finger.'

'Did you ever have to punch anyone else?'

'I know what you're asking. I don't believe in it till after marriage.'

We rode home, away from Somes Island and the war, into a gale that very nearly stopped us dead, and although we had not used the words, or kissed more than once, I had asked her to marry me and she had said yes.

I had learned that Nancy was not always mild.

Benjamin sacked her from the Ascher Trio and gave her place to a girl of fifteen. She wasn't offended.

'I wasn't good enough for them.'

'Don't give up the piano.'

'I won't. But I'm going to spend more time baking bread.'

'Why don't you spend your whole time?'

'What?'

'I need someone to look after things. Do the buying and the orders and accounts. Could you do that?'

'I suppose I could.'

'And manage the place when I'm not here. You can even do some baking. Henk's going up to Auckland next week.'

'If I come you've got to keep this place a bit more tidy.'

I smiled at her. 'You'll get what you're earning now. Plus as many loaves as you can carry. But you've got to start this morning. Right away.'

'What about my notice?'

'Take a sickie. And then take leave. One of my drivers isn't in. I've got to go on the road. So, you start.'

'I like bosses who say please.'

'Please,' I said.

The missing driver came in ten minutes after I'd gone. He had been at an all-night party.

She said, 'You're late. And you stink of beer. And you're not shaved. Do you really think I'm letting you deliver bread like that?'

'Where's Joe?' he said.

'Joe's out on the road, doing your job. Which you don't have any more.'

'Like hell!'

'Go and see your union. Right now. While you're drunk.'

Something like that. Henk described it, laughing all the while. The man spat on the floor and walked out, and Nancy ran a bucket of hot water and got down on her knees and scrubbed him away.

'She is good wife. Marry her,' Henk said.

We travelled by train to Masterton to meet her parents. It was no small thing for us to take the whole Saturday off and we were cross, thinking about the bakehouse, as well as nervous and edgy about the meeting. They were not going to like me, we knew that. Already they had called on the telephone to say how appalled they were that she should leave her 'nice job at the ministry' to be 'some sort of slavvy in a baker's shop'.

She played a jumpy tune on her knees all the way along the harbour front. I put my hand on hers. 'Stop it,' I said.

'You'll hate them.'

'Are they so bad?'

'They're pretty awful.' She looked at me and grinned and whispered in my ear, 'They eat white bread.'

'How did they have you, then?'

'They found me floating in a basket in the reeds.'

'Ha,' I said. 'You know I'm not a Jew by religion. We don't have to have a rabbi marrying us.'

'That will really please them. Josef, before you meet, I want to know about your parents please.'

I told her about our apartment on Gluckgasse, a good address, only five minutes walk from the Graben. I could look out from my window over the roofs and see the flying buttresses of St Stephen's Church. I described growing up with a maid and a cook, and driving in a Mercedes, and walking in the parks, swimming in the river, camping in the Woods – and none of it was alive for me. We reached the hill, where Fell engines coupled on. 'Yes, Josef,' she said, 'all that's very interesting. But what about them, your family?'

I said that I had a brother, Franz, who lived in America. We wrote to each other once a year.

I felt Nancy's hand grow slack in mine, and I thought, I'll lose her unless I tell. If I know hers she's got a right to mine.

'I had a sister called Susi,' I said. 'She was fifteen when I left. She and Franz escaped from Vienna when the Nazis came. But then she died in Paris.'

'Died of what?'

'I don't know. Franz said she just couldn't breathe any more. He went to New York and he's still there.'

She swallowed. I saw her throat swell and wanted to touch it with my hand and feel the passage of her blood.

'What about your mum and dad?' she said.

I had never called them that. It moved them so close I felt they might sit down in the seat across from me. I said, 'They're dead.'

'Tell me about when they were alive.'

'Yes, all right.' I swallowed too, and she said, 'Only as much as you want to, Josef.' She said 'Josef' with the proper Austrian sound.

'Their names were Anna and Benno,' I said. 'He was a coal merchant and she played the piano, but not as well as you. They were . . .'

I talked about my parents all the way to Masterton, and when I came to their deaths I said, 'My father went to Dachau. They sent all the socialists and communists there. And anyone else they didn't like or wanted to rob. Lots of Jews. My father went so some Nazi party man could steal his business. They didn't murder them all in Dachau, only some.'

'Don't,' she said. 'Don't tell me how.'

'They starved them and shot them and made them work sixteen hours a day. Old men too. It wasn't an extermination camp. Not till later. They sent his ashes to my mother and made her pay. She – I don't know how she lived. She stayed in Vienna three years. Then they rounded them up and sent them to a ghetto in

Poland, at Lodz. She must have been too sick to work. She was only there a few weeks and they sent her to the death camp at Chelmno.'

'That's enough, Josef. No more please.'

'They gassed them in trucks on the way to the graves.'

'Josef.'

'You started me.'

'And I'm stopping you. Here's Masterton. It's my parents now.'

They were more awful than she had prepared me for. Mrs Brisbois had a false-teeth smile and eyes that hated me on sight. She hated Nancy too, for 'doing this to her'. I could not believe that there had ever been love. As for the father, he was Roy Cooksley again – the same pumped-up belly and oxblood cheeks. He had been a great rugby player in his day and photographs of him in his black jersey adorned the walls. Huge hands. Shoulders huge. Ears cauliflowered from locking the scrum. 'Brisboy, none of that fancy stuff.' He was in insurance, he let me know in the five minutes before we broke our news. Insurance, bloody Cooksley, I thought. And because I must say something: 'That's what Kafka did.'

'Who's he? Some wop?'

'A writer,' I said – and Nancy stared at me, amazed. 'He was a Czechoslovakian. And a Jew.'

'So, they'll have got rid of him,' Brisbois said.

'We're not too keen on foreigners in Masterton,' said his wife. 'But if you're a friend of Nancy's . . .'

'There's a good halfback in Auckland called Tetzlaff,' Brisbois said. 'They're little jokers, most foreigners. Do you know what I weighed in my playing days? Sixteen stone. I could pick Vi up under my arm and run the length of the field with her. What you think of that?'

'What for?' I said.

Brisbois grinned at me, or bared his teeth. 'To score three points. You're some sort of baker, Nancy says.'

'Yes, I am.'

'Do you make any money or just dough?' It was a joke, he'd thought it out, and I was so startled that I laughed.

'I'm doing all right. Nancy brought a loaf of bread for you and Mrs Brisbois.'

'Yes,' Nancy said, and took it from her bag, wrapped in a cloth.

'Give it here,' Brisbois said. 'Jesus – sorry, Vi – that's a weight. Enough of these and you could build a house. You sell this stuff?'

'Lots of it,' Nancy said. 'You're behind the times, Dad.'

'What's your part? How much does he pay you?'

'More than I used to get. I do all the buying and the accounts. I do the books.'

'It's not as nice as working in the ministry. That was a salary,' Mrs Brisbois cried.

'Yeah. You chuck it, Nance. Monday you get your old job back.' He turned his eyes on me and I saw I was wrong to suppose that joking made him capable of good humour. 'I think this feller might be stringing you a line.'

'No, he's not,' Nancy said. 'Mum, Dad, there's something you should know. Josef and I are getting engaged.'

'No, we're getting married,' I said.

Mrs Brisbois leaned at her husband. She broke in the middle like a stick. 'Brian, tell them no,' she cried.

'You don't marry a German,' he said.

'Dad, I marry who I want. Can't you be nice about it? Can't you just say congratulations?'

Mrs Brisbois hissed. 'I knew that music would get you in trouble.' ('That' is demonstrative here.)

Brisbois – Brisboy – sat back in his chair, making it creak. 'I'll have you deported, son.'

'I don't think you can.'

'If you deport him, I'll go too,' Nancy said.

'We'd want you out of the country, married to a Jerry,' he said.

'In that case we'll go now. Don't try and stop me, Dad. I'm more than twenty-one.'

'If you go out that door you're gone for good.'

'He's not even a Christian,' Mrs Brisbois cried.

'Then nor am I. Come on, Josef.'

'Goodbye,' I said.

'Hitler did a good job on you lot,' Brisbois said. 'It's a pity he didn't get round to you.'

I wanted to hit him and it wasn't fear that stopped me – he would crush me in one hand – but Nancy standing in the door. If I don't get her out of here she'll die, I thought. I took her arm and pulled her down the hall, out into the front yard, out the gate into the road; and Brisbois, on the porch, with his wife held in one hand, yelled, 'Take this German muck with you.'

He heaved the loaf of bread overarm. I thought it would hit Nancy, and pulled her out of the way. It struck the footpath where she had been standing and made a crooked bounce into the street.

'I've got other kids. I don't need you.'

'Run,' Nancy said, 'he'll follow us.'

'Walk,' I said. 'Walk with me. Just hold my arm.'

Nancy wobbled. Tears ran down her cheeks. 'I'm never going back there,' she said.

'No, you can't. You can't have people like that in your life.'

'They're Mum and Dad,' she wept.

'Now we're round the corner. Now we're out of sight.'

'How can they be like that?'

'Sit here, love. Here's a bus stop. Sit.' I gave her my handkerchief to wipe her face.

'I love you. I should have told them that,' she said.

'They don't know love.'

'Can he? Can he deport you?'

'No, he can't.'

'He knows all sorts of people.'

'Nancy, he can't.'

'I feel so empty. I feel torn. He was so good once. He loved me once.'

'Maybe.'

'I want to go now, Josef. I want to go away from here.'

We walked through strange streets – strange to her now as well as me – into the town. We ate food, such bad food, in a cafe. Then we caught a train that stopped and started, and made our journey back to Wellington. Nancy, exhausted, slept on my shoulder for most of the way.

This is more than anecdote. And I make Nancy do more than pirouette. When I started I did not think I could write it down. Now it's done. We married in a registry office, not common in those days, and had our reception at Mrs Steiner's house. Aunt Alma came. Moira Williams came – and I wasn't much fonder of her than of Nancy's parents, who did not come. Not invited. Wilf White, in hospital although it was summer, sent a telegram wishing us a long and happy married life.

I didn't invite Willi. To tell the truth I wasn't sure where he was. A letter I wrote to him had come back marked 'Gone no address'. As well as that I thought, I don't need Willi to tell me it's all right to get married. So I left him out.

Franz sent a letter. He said he was glad the Mandl name would carry on.

Mrs Steiner's lawn was filled with light. The sky was deep blue. There was no wind. From our Brooklyn hillside we looked across the harbour. Somes Island, shining there, was not invited here but was not unimportant all the same. I would not have stayed in Wellington if I had not been locked up there. I grinned at it, then turned my back and ate from the tables with my wife. The Austrian cooks of Wellington had come to life. We had Florentiners, Marillenstrudel and Lebzelt Bäckerei – too sweet for me but I smiled and pretended to eat, for Mrs Steiner had smuggled Nancy and me into the kitchen and given us a meal of meat dumplings and soup all to ourselves. The Ascher Trio played. Elinor Cleghorn, the Wunderkind, sat at her piano inside the french doors while Benjamin and Mrs Steiner stood like gypsies on the patio, and Nancy, teaching me, whispered what was well played and what was simply amazing. The music ran down the hill into Wellington, and I thought, We belong here, this will be our place. Then Nancy played, and said she was sorry for her mistakes, and Benjamin replied that there could be no mistakes on a day like this.

And now I am back where I began, talking over with Nancy whether we should sit still and be comfortable or set off again and climb the hill. She was no longer Nancy, my bride, but Nancy Mandl with a daughter five months old dozing in my office in her pram while I jigged the handle with my thumb to keep her from waking up. They had walked down from our rented house in the Aro Valley so Nancy could eat her lunch with me.

'How big?' she said.

'There's a limit to bread unless I start baking white.'

We had, by that time, raisin bread and almond bread, honey bread, oatmeal bread and three sorts of rye, all selling to the market called niche today. Unless I went into cakes and sticky buns there seemed nowhere to go.

'You don't want to do white pap, do you?' she said.

'No. But listen, Nancy, I don't have to stay a baker. We'll keep this place for our bread and butter,' I joked, and gave her a pencil and a piece of paper – 'but here, do this. Write down all the things you haven't tasted.'

'Like what?'

'Coffee. Proper coffee.'

'I've tasted that.'

'All right. All the food you've ever read about that you can't buy. And I'll write all the things I'd like you to taste.'

'Do I get a prize?'

'You might get rich.'

She wrote 'Dutch cheese'. She wrote 'Salami sausages, all sorts'. Then it grew harder and she had to joke: 'Frogs' legs, Snails, Bird's nest soup'. Meanwhile I filled half a page.

'Swap,' I said, and laughed at hers.

'All these?' she said, reading. 'You want to start importing them, don't you?'

'Some of them we can get made here. Sour cream. Cottage cheese. Why not?'

'Do you really think New Zealanders will eat yoghurt?'

'Some do already.'

'And sauerkraut?'

'Of course they will. We don't have to import that. Cabbages grow here. Nancy, would you like to own a delicatessen?'

'Yes.'

'Or two or three? And a restaurant selling proper food?'

'What do you want to be, an importer or a restaurant owner?'

'Both of them. And be a coffee-brewer. And make salamis.'

'Choose.'

'We'll start with importing. Only food. And open a delicatessen for you.'

'Can you get import licences?'

'We'll see.'

'Swiss chocolates?'

'We'll see.'

'You'll never get New Zealanders using olive oil. I'll make a bet.'

'But shall we do it? Will you help?'

'Of course I'll help.'

Elizabeth woke and Nancy fed her. I took them out to the yard and commandeered a van to drive them home, but turned away from the Aro Valley and drove through Thorndon and up the Wadestown road. At the top of the hill I turned into the upper road and coasted down until I reached the spot.

'That's the house we'll live in when we're rich,' I said.

Nancy smiled. 'I like it.' She held Elizabeth up. 'See, baby. That's where you're going to grow into a great big girl.'

TWELVE

I did not become a restaurateur. Nor did I become a coffee-brewer, alas. But we had, in our time, three delicatessens, and Nancy managed them – even with three children she managed them, working late into the night. It was not until the sixties that they started doing well. But our real success did not lie there. The food importing business was where we prospered. We called it Mandl and Ascher, not because Benjamin took an active part, he did not, but because he helped us with another loan at the start.

I do not want to write a history of the firm: how it grew and grew and how I sold it in the end; or how I sold Ascher's Bread to a big company, a giant. Many people think I was merely clever – a Jew – and do not know how hard I worked, how hard *we* worked. I am not interested in proving them wrong. I say, as a Kiwi, to hell with them.

If I can untangle it, I'll tell our story, not the firm's.

Benjamin died. That is first. Or perhaps it is second, for Wilf White was dead too, in Wellington Hospital. Neither of them was as old as I am now. I went to the garden, which had run to seed, asked permission of the woman in the house – the men in the lean-to didn't give a damn – and found a few tender little self-sown potatoes, which I took to the hospital and showed Wilf on the palm of my hand. He was too far gone to know what they were, but managed to whisper, 'I need a beer.' I gave him water, which he sipped; then he tried to wink at me. 'Thanks, Joey. That's a good drop.'

There were five of us at his funeral: two bookmakers and a jockey and his drinking mate and me.

Benjamin had several happy years before he died, watching, listening to, Elinor Cleghorn. He stayed on in his Berhampore house when I left and took her as his boarder at seventeen, which raised a few eyebrows round town – but no, she was his marvellous child, only that. He put a piano in the living room and she practised all day long – a sweet girl, too sweet for the hard life of the concert halls, I thought, which shows how little I know about music, and perhaps about character.

I visited him in hospital, in the ward where Wilf had died.

'Settembrini, Benjamin.'

'It is Elinor who proves him wrong.'

'He's a character in a novel by Thomas Mann.'

I had not known Benjamin could be angry. Two red spots showed on his cheeks.

'You should not cheat, Josef. From a book of lies.'

I asked him to forgive me; then Elinor came and his cheeks flushed with happiness, diffusing the red, and I went away. Neither of us mentioned Settembrini again.

We had no service for Benjamin, no eulogies, no memorialising. A few of us went to the cemetery, then we drove to Mrs Steiner's house, where the crowd filled all the rooms and spilled out to the patio and lawns. Moser was down from Auckland. He was doing well, working hard like me: 'You fill their bellies,' he said, 'I will build them sofas to park their bottoms on.' I asked if he had seen or heard of Willi and he made a sound of disgust.

'I hear. I don't see. I make sure of that.'

'Where did he go? He seemed to vanish.'

'He is still vanished. He went up north to live on beaches. He has a little house, it is a shack with broken walls, and he lives in the sun without his shirt. I hear all this and read it in the *Truth*. They say without his trousers too. Doctors' wives and lawyers' wives visit him there and everyone swims naked in the sea.'

Oh yes, Willi. He grew a beard, he grew his hair – but we had seen him long-haired on the island. It was for *Truth* a deadly crime. They wanted the government to ship him away. We must get rid of this man's evil politics, they said. Not communism now but being friends with Maoris and telling them to make a republic in the north.

'It is hot air,' Moser said. 'Everything with Willi is hot air. Always he is out for what he can get.'

'He believed in communism.'

'Communism now and free sex later, but me first with Willi every time. It was King Willi on Somes Island. You remember that. Or commissar.'

I walked away. I did not want to quarrel on this day, but it seemed to me that Willi would never get a fair hearing anywhere.

Nancy found me at the bottom of the section, muttering in a corner to myself.

'Come on,' she said. 'It's our turn to talk to Elinor.'

'What's wrong with her?'

Nancy looked at me with disgust. 'Oh. Yes,' I said, and followed her to Mrs Steiner's bedroom, where Elinor Cleghorn lay on the bed, weeping and weeping, unable to stop. Her parents, from a mining settlement deep in the bush, sat on chairs and watched her, waited for her. They were sad, silent people who loved their brilliant daughter but could not have her any more. Proud of her, so proud – and frightened now that her music would all go away, and then perhaps she would die. They leaned forward and patted her from time to time.

Nancy and I could do nothing. Elinor did not hear us, and what could we say to bring a halt to weeping like this? Then Mrs

Steiner took her by the shoulders and sat her up.

'Elinor,' she said, 'it is time for you to play a concert for Benjamin.'

Nancy and I went out and I said, 'She's mad. That girl can't play today.'

But in half an hour there she was, professional: clear-eyed, strong-fingered, straight in her back, playing as she would play in later years in concert halls in London and Vienna and New York. She went on longer than her teachers would have allowed – and I don't know the pieces. Nancy would tell me if she was here.

Nancy said, 'Won't it be wonderful when Elizabeth can play like that.'

Four years passed before we were able to buy our house. We had stopped driving past it because our insistence had begun to seem foolish and our longing neurotic perhaps. But when I bought a house in Karori I said to the agent, 'Wadestown is where I want to live. But not just any house. This one.' I gave him the address and made him promise to let me know if it ever came on the market. Did not say, They are old (which I knew from spying), they're bound to die. I stopped myself from even thinking it, from a superstition that someone I loved would be taken from me in punishment. This fear came with marriage, which put me into life in a way I had not been since Vienna, and made me observant, attentive, practical, but allowed demons and harpies a place in the night. For each thing given there is something taken away? No, I don't believe it, for it implies that Someone tots up an account. Or plays a game. But for each cruelty committed, for each failure in sympathy, for every sneer something taken away? Oh yes, that is true, and we are responsible for the process; but in the night, and when good sense is low, harpies come and tear away parts of you that are the ones you love.

I lay beside Nancy and heard her sleep, and I breathed stupidly,

'Be safe, my love.' I crept to the children's rooms, crept in like a murderer, and laid my hand on each warm brow: 'Be safe.' Afraid for them, afraid of myself who, in the daytime, busy, busy, was an admirable provider of love and cash.

I was, by temperament, a daytime man, and not in the least bit then afraid of myself. My fears were of a different kind. In 1951 the waterfront troubles – strike or lockout, according to your view – almost brought my new-fledged business to an end. I was angry about it, but not afraid. Fear came when I saw in this land I had believed innocent – primitive yes, but innocent – movements, stirrings that had the shape and colour of fascism here and Stalinism (without Stalin) there. It was the fascist stirrings that frightened me more, for I had grown up in Vienna and this man Sid Holland was making sounds like Dollfuss – and I'm frightened today, for aren't there fascist stirrings to be seen and sounds to be heard, with a new dictator, Market, standing in for The Man? And my poor Kenny is a follower.

This is not to my purpose, which is story. I must go back. The land agent rang me in 1954 and said, 'The owner of that house you want is dead.' (Refreshing language. I had learned to say 'passed away'.) 'The Public Trust has got it so it's going to take some time, but I know my way around there. It's a matter of being ready with the cash.'

We gave him our Karori house to sell the same day. We were ready with the cash. Early in 1955 we moved in. I sat down with a Ha! – the Ha! of arrival – in the room I'm sitting in now. Nancy came and plumped down on my knees, a lovely weight. Then the children piled on: five of us tangled in one chair. Across Nancy's shoulder, over their heads, I saw Somes Island, green, black, three-levelled, in the sun. 'We made it,' I said.

I've been living here for forty years. Our children grew up. Nancy died. I will die. I hope to say Ha! as I depart.

❖

What can one say about a house? It encloses one as naturally as the air. But there's a daily magic about doors that lead to other rooms, where your books sit on shelves, your food bakes in the oven, your wife, in steam, towels herself dry, and your bed is turned down for love and sleep. Time is the air you breathe in rooms that branch, unfold and welcome you. Open another door. A girl with her hair in a plait plays 'Für Elise'. She is the one who, yesterday, in another house, was sitting in a highchair gnawing a piece of twice-baked bread. And the boy squatting on the floor making his pet snail retract its eyes was dozing on his mother's breast at 2 a.m., while she breathed softly for fear that he would wake with his colic again.

House and family and time intertwine. And earlier houses are swallowed by this one and smaller times are subsumed.

Elizabeth, Kenneth, Susan were our children. Nancy was determined that each should have the chance to be a great musician. Her mildness, which was a form of laziness (and which I loved), gave way to ruthlessness as each practice hour began. 'Nancy, you'll make them hate it,' I said. I am non-musical but years before she would recognise it I saw that none of them would make music a career. Elizabeth enjoyed her piano – still does, she's playing now – and Nancy never had to bully her. But there was a curious looping turn, a kind of back somersault, at some place between Elizabeth's brain and hands; and her music, even when she was a five-year-old, gave a bounce, which pleased Nancy at first and then began to worry her. She tried to see it as lyrical, but I think it came from a neural tic, or a connection not made, which the child overcame by enthusiasm – and the woman today by dreaming as she plays. Nancy shifted her from teacher to teacher and in the end took over herself.

'Nancy, she'll only be unhappy if you make her think she's better than she is.'

She would not listen. Brian and Vi Brisbois had tried to turn music into a suitable hobby for a girl, like flower arranging; so Nancy would make sure of its proper place in her children's lives by practice and more practice and when it was done by praise and praise.

When Kenny had had enough of bowing and fingering he cried. I thought it sensible of him, although I'd have been more pleased in the end if he'd broken the back of his violin on a chair. He never had the slightest gift – how could Nancy not hear? – and the only desire he had was to stop. Susan, on the other hand, was good. She was the best of them and might have gone on, perhaps played cello in an orchestra or chamber music group, but – how else to say it? – Nancy knocked that future away. Susan wanted all sorts of other things – basketball, hockey, climbing mountains, parties, reading, boys – and Nancy would allow her none that got in the way of cello practice. So they fought, and Susan was away in a flat at eighteen, and married at nineteen; a mother at nineteen too. She left her cello behind, but came for it one day when Nancy was out so that her own daughter might have a bit of music in her life, 'just for fun'. That is Bea at the Juilliard School.

I don't feel bound to recall how we 'fucked them up', as the poet says. I feel more inclined to say how we loved them and, mostly, made them happy too. But there's no clear dividing line. And I didn't start writing here for this sort of thing. I'll just say, in fairness to Nancy, that I too put a burden on them, and its name was 'right and wrong'. Willi sneered once about my 'Jewish passion for justice', and how it expressed itself in rules. I don't object any more because, again, I see no dividing line; all I see is fallibility. I taught my children rules of conduct when what I really meant was justice, love. I meant 'other people'. And Kenny learned to pause and look at me, enquiring if what he did was right.

Enough, enough. My days lose themselves in complaint. The Mandls were a happy family.

❖

I played Tiddlywinks with my children, and Snakes and Ladders and Pick-Up-Sticks, and later on Chess, although none of us was patient enough for games that had an opening and a middle and an end. I played Blind Man's Bluff and Hunt the Slipper, games Nancy's father had played with her. She remembered another one called What's the Time, Mr Wolfie, but I did not like to hear my children screaming as they fled, even if their screams were of delight. I taught them to swim, one by one, had endless patience with them, my hand firm under throbbing belly and chest as they dogpaddled and kicked. At Paekakariki beach I taught them to dive beneath waves that might bowl them over. They were too young for that and swallowed water, and Kenny choked and vomited, but I was determined to make them safe.

I would have liked a calmer beach than Paekakariki, one with headlands and rock pools and yellow sand instead of black, but Nancy was drawn to its long sweep and raucous gulls and the piles of driftwood stripped by the sea. I said, 'It's like a charnel house,' but she only laughed and went striding off into the wind. Smaller and smaller she became as she walked barefooted at the edge of the sea, and I said, 'Your mum's gone bush again' – wondering why there should be no 'gone beach' – 'let's have a swim. Stay close to me.'

She came back after half an hour with tangled hair and rose-red cheeks and sea-water eyes; and we all swam, Kenny diving through my legs while Nancy made a stirrup of her hands and threw Elizabeth and Susan in back somersaults. The black island, Kapiti, once the stronghold, I had learned, of a chief who had murdered whole tribes of his enemies, stood mountainous, far off in the west. In the broken shallows, with me staying furthest out and Nancy back from her walk, the Mandls had nothing to be afraid of; they were close to each other, they were safe.

She slept with her sunhat over her face after our swim. The children ran about and collected shells; they made driftwood skeletons and pumice roads. Two other families approached along the beach and spread out their towels and blankets a hundred yards away, at the foot of the sandhills. While the wives sat and talked, the men and the children played rounders, using a tennis racket and ball. The children shrieked and boasted as one of the fathers, a little chap, lobbed the ball in lollipop pitches for them to hit. The big man didn't like that, he was a moralist (like me), and when his turn came to bat he slogged the ball high over the children, down to Kenny watching from the edge of the sea. Kenny picked it up, looked at me (I nodded), and ran towards the players with the ball held out straight-armed, aimed at the man who'd made the hit. A thick fellow, a slow boy, stepped up to rob him, but Kenny swerved. He had worked out where the centre of power lay. He skittered through the children, my plump cautious son just for once as quick as a terrier, and handed the ball to the big-chested man. Who spoke to him and showed him where to field, and Kenny, after only a glance at me, was in the game.

He had his turn with the racket and made a hit and almost reached first base before the thick boy tagged him. I watched with a sharp eye, and was a little breathless with my desire for him to excel. He made a catch. I had not known that Kenny could catch. I knew he could not get in the school cricket team, I knew he could not climb down from a tree. But the catch was, I recognised, made for the big man, not for me. I understood that my son had skills. Once, in a break in play, he did a neat handstand and grinned at the girl standing next to him.

Nancy stirred. She lifted her hat. 'Where are the children?'

'The girls are here. Kenny's playing rounders.'

'Who with?' She wiped her damp face with a towel and looked at the game. 'Oh God,' she said and stood up.

'What's the matter?'

'It's Neville. It's my brother. There's Val too. It's all of them.'

So, I thought, the Brisboys, the cauliflowered Brisboys at play.

'You wait here, Josef. I'll go and say hello,' Nancy said.

'I'll come.'

'No, wait here.'

I disobeyed. I followed her as she walked along the sand to the women, and then, as they met her (quick, alarmed), into the game.

'Hello, Neville,' she said.

(She had, I must record, visited her sister Valerie several times in Palmerston North and come home as though from a visit to someone terminally ill. 'She told me I should smack the children more.' Every time Elizabeth or Kenny touched a piece of furniture, Valerie swooped with a cloth and wiped it clean. She followed them with a hearth shovel and brush, sweeping up crumbs. 'I had to change Susan's nappy on the back porch. I really don't want to go again,' Nancy said.)

'What are you doing here?' Neville Brisbois said.

'I'm at the beach, same as you. Thank you for letting Kenny play.'

'It's your kid, eh? And that's your husband?' – jerking his thumb.

Nancy turned. She frowned at me, and then I saw her smile and change; she welcomed me. It was as though she'd opened her arms.

'Yes, it's Josef. This is my brother Neville, Josef, and my sister Val.'

'Pack up the things,' Brisbois said to his wife. 'We'll go somewhere else.'

'Aren't you going to say hello to me?' Nancy said. 'Isn't it time to stop all this?'

'Pack up,' Brisbois said to the women – said it to the little man too, his brother-in-law, who called his children round him and walked up to the towels.

'Please, Neville, can't we be grown up?' Nancy said.

Brisbois gave Kenny a push on the back of his head. 'Game's over, son. Go with your dad.'

202

'Don't touch him,' I said.

'Or what? You poncing kraut. We didn't ask for you in our family.'

'Josef, don't,' Nancy said, stopping me. 'Val,' she said, 'is this the way you want things to be?'

'It's for Dad,' Valerie said.

'I told you to pack up,' Neville said. He was rangier in build than his father but had slabs of muscle on his shoulders and chest, with coarse hairs growing in them like a crop. His ribs were like hands cupped around his vital parts. I don't remember his face. I can only call up the father's face – and I connect these people with Nancy in no way. There's no thread, however tenuous, linking them.

She said, 'Ah, Neville. Nev. Can't you do some thinking for yourself?'

'You made your choice. Keep out of our way.' He turned and grabbed the large boy at his side. 'I told you to get.' He cuffed him away, then followed up the beach, where his wife and sister and brother-in-law were gathering their blankets and towels. 'Keep your brat out of our game,' he said over his shoulder. 'We've got all the people we need in our family.' And cried again, further up: 'You've caused a lot of grief, Nancy.'

'There, he said my name. I didn't think he could,' Nancy said.

We walked back our own way, to the girls, with Kenny between us.

'Who were they, Mum?'

'My brother and sister.'

'Pig-people,' I said.

'Shut up, Josef.'

'You watch out who you play with,' I told Kenny.

'But Mum, it was my turn with the bat,' Kenny said.

'Too bad,' I said.

'I wanted to. I might have got it over his head.'

'You don't play games with Brizzbuggers,' I said.

Nancy turned on me and punched me hard. 'Will you shut up!' She knelt and hugged Kenny, trapping his arms, then let him go and held him by the shoulders. 'Kenny,' she said, using the diminutive we had been attempting to avoid, 'they don't like us because I married Dad. But Dad's worth all of them put together. It's not us who won't be friends with them.'

'Bad blood,' Neville Brisbois yelled from along the beach.

'We don't need them. We'll make our own friends. There's plenty of other people you can play rounders with.' She hugged him again. Her eyes were awash with tears, bright blue. I put my hand on Kenny's head, but he shrugged it off.

'I would have got a good hit. It was nearly my turn.'

Nancy left me with the girls. She went walking with Kenny along the beach and I saw how he leaned into her, and how she touched him on the neck and hair, explaining her brother and me and herself. He was groggy with tiredness when they came back. Her relatives were gone by that time: their only sign a rooting in the sand where they had played and a rounders diamond marked in shells.

Kenny slept in the car going home. I glanced at him in the mirror from time to time, frightened of seeing the mark of Brisbois there.

We came to call him 'Kenny' all the time.

Like Wilf I've had a bout of winter pneumonia. These days it's not so serious. But I wonder if I'd asked my doctor, would he have let me die?

Now I'm home, although I'm still in bed. Elizabeth nurses me, while Julie looks in once a day (prompted, no doubt), enquires how I'm feeling, puts a kiss on her fingertip and shifts it to my cheek, then goes away. It's more than I want. Like a child kissed by grandma I scrub my cheek with my hand; then apologise to Julie for thinking her unclean.

Elizabeth reports on Helen Henly's progress: that Julie's delusions reduce in extravagance each day. She (Ms Henly) won't go into detail, for which I'm glad. Glad about the reduction too. I try to believe that Julie's infection is like mine and that we'll both soon be well – and she will learn to kiss me properly and I'll no longer scrub her germs away. But she is young and I am old and it does not really matter what state my lungs are in. Her mind will carry a scar for the rest of her days.

Soon it will be spring and she will work in the garden – attack the onion weed again, and pull out the deadly nightshade growing under the hedge. For the last few days she has been playing African music that beats like a heart through the wall. I think she dances to it, for I hear muffled leaps and the swish of clothes. I don't mind as long as it doesn't go on too long. But Africa makes me think of masks. Does Helen Henly know about this? The other woman, Bonnie, was a witch-doctor of sorts and I can't help fearing a return to her.

I remember Elinor Cleghorn visiting us on one of her New Zealand tours. She confessed that she had an analyst back home (which was New York), who was as important to her as Benjamin had been when she was a girl. She compared him to a masseur, which seemed inapt to me, for she also talked, though vaguely, of dark forces working to destroy her. They were in everyone, damped down, she claimed – and Nancy was disapproving of this, and of analysts, especially for Elinor, believing that love of music ensured mental health. She grew angry when Elinor said piano playing was her job and there were all sorts of other things in her life – told me when Elinor had gone that it showed why she had stayed in the second rank and would never be one of the greats. But leaving her music aside, and whether she should be possessed by it, I believe in Elinor's dark forces and that we keep them damped down; but also that other people should not be let in where they are. Which brings me back to masks and that witch-doctor woman and whether what was loose in Julie once has now been caged. And whether, in fact, Helen Henly's is the right course. Isn't some sort of exorcism called for? It is fear that confuses me.

And now it is dinner time and her music has stopped.

And I've eaten, propped up in my bed, and drunk my glass of wine. It was white so I sent it back and asked for red. 'But it's fish,' Elizabeth said. I told her I didn't run my life by a set of rules and I'd drink what I liked with what I liked and she said, 'Ho.' I enjoyed the claret, even though she brought a thimbleful.

'What's that Julie was dancing to?'

'Oh, something of Helen's. I think it's supposed to help her get rid of stuff.'

'An exorcism?'

'Possibly.'

'Isn't that a bit dangerous?'

'Who can tell? The dangerous thing is, Kenny keeps ringing up.'

'I thought I heard the phone. Doesn't he know to keep away?'

It seems he has been ringing two or three times a day. He accuses Elizabeth of kidnapping Julie. She calms him down. Makes him reasonable for a time. She is good at it. But she looks strained. I can see I'll have to handle Kenny for her. I don't look forward to that.

I phoned him this morning. There's one good thing about having Julie here: I don't have to witness the self in Kenny's eye. He has no dignity, my son. Even Nancy had to look away from his blaze of disappointment at the smallest thing, and leave the room. It is better just to hear him on the phone.

He has, today, I admit, large things to be upset about.

'Kenny, she's under treatment. You'll set her right back if you interfere.'

'I'm her father,' he replied. 'Isn't that supposed to be the prime relationship? You always behaved as if it was.'

Not true. His 'prime relationship' was with Nancy. I made no attempt to change it because I saw she had more love than me.

'And anyway,' he said, 'she's saying all that filthy stuff about me. I've got the right to tell her doctor it's all lies. How would you like it, Dad . . .' and he went on and on until I said, 'Kenny, keep quiet and listen to me. Julie is sick. It's a question of whether you want her well. Do you? Do you want your daughter to get well?'

'Of course I do.'

'Then stay away. She's better than she was but there's no quick way –'

'I want to talk to her. I want her to admit she's made it up . . .' and off he went again until I cried, 'Kenny, shut up. You're an idiot, Kenny. The girl is sick. She's *sick*. You're not going to reason with her, or slap her around, or whatever you do. You can't cure her that way. You're what's wrong with her and I don't care whether it's fair or not, it's a fact. Do you want her well? Or do you just care about yourself?'

'I don't have to listen –'

'Yes you do. Do you love her, Kenny?'

It must have been the right question. I heard him breathing down the telephone.

'Let this doctor woman have her chance,' I said. 'She's good, she knows. Just be patient. There's no quick cure.' Before he could object I said, 'How is Priscilla taking it?' (I can't say 'Priss', which is the name she prefers. And I find it harder and harder to say 'Kenny'.)

'She won't talk about it. She doesn't want to know. She just goes to bowls. They've opened an indoor green, thank God. When she comes home she goes to bed. She's a vegetable.'

This is a not a marriage made for love. Priscilla was desperate, I believe, while Kenny was making an upward step – and perhaps an even longer outward one.

'It's hard days for everyone,' I said. 'But we'll get through.'

'That's easy for you to say, lying in bed.' He meant, perhaps, that I was like Priscilla, a vegetable; and I would have made a sharp reply, but he asked, 'How much does this head-doctor cost?'

'I'll pay.'

'How much, Dad?'

'It's eighty dollars an appointment. She goes twice a week.'

'Send the bills to me. By God, if you don't I'll come up there . . .'

'All right, I will.' But I can't let Julie know that he is paying. 'She still drives your car.'

'So she should, it cost enough.' That, I think, he said to hide his pain.

'Talking of money, Kenny . . .' I asked if Mrs Gummer was leaving him alone.

'No, she's not. She writes me letters. Listen to this, it came this morning: "Don't think you can get away with it. The law might bury its head but there are other ways of getting justice. I wouldn't feel safe if I were you." That's a threat, isn't it? I could take that to the police.'

'Leave it, Kenny. There'll only be more trouble. Telephone Gummer. He's a reasonable man.'

'He's sick, isn't he?'

'Yes, he is. He's got asbestosis.'

'Well, what's she worrying about? She'll get a decent payout for that.'

I put down the phone. I've written this to stop myself from trembling. It was a straight course when we came to this house. How can things have gone so crooked?

Julie is dancing again.

THIRTEEN

Now Willi comes back.

He was well known in Auckland and I seldom went there so I had to depend on Moser for news – Moser and *Truth*, which Willi sued for calling him a Nazi. He won his case, and was awarded damages of a shilling! He wrote and published several short stories about his love affairs in the mangroves up north. I wonder who corrected his English. He almost had a play produced. The company pulled out when he refused to moderate his language. Willi attempted revolutions years ahead of their time – a hippy in the fifties, before the word was coined, a loud four-letter man long before language was freed up. As for sexual free-doms – he published a magazine called *Flesh*, which the police closed down after one issue. He organised a nude moonlight swim at Browns Bay. There were more policemen than swimmers there. He asked a Hospital Board member at a public meeting why she didn't promote masturbation as a way of improving mental health. He was cited as co-respondent in a divorce case and lost all his money – where did he get money? – in damages.

What else was he into? Composting. Republicanism. 'Bacchan-alianism'. Carrots and parsnips for a while, then a diet of raw liver to prolong the sexual life. (It was good for the political intelligence too.) Lowering the age of consent. Federation with Australia.

It sounded to me as if Willi had broken into pieces. I wondered where his Marxism had gone, and his ambition to be boss. The most he could do, it seemed, was call himself 'the oldest teenager in Auckland'.

'Is he married?' I asked Moser.

'Only to other men's wives.'

'Is he a New Zealand citizen yet?'

'They'd deport him if he wasn't.'

'What about politics?'

'It is little games in this country. Willi likes big games.'

His activities sounded small to me. I grew disappointed in Willi and hoped I would not see him again. I had him safe, well rounded, in the past.

One night in 1962 as we sat at dinner a knock sounded on the door, no different from other knocks, and I put my knife and fork down and whispered, 'It's Willi.'

'Who?' Nancy said.

'It's Willi Gauss.'

'Shall I go?'

'No. Let me.'

'Get up from your chair then, Josef. Whoever it is won't bite.'

Kenny and Susan made a run for the door.

'No,' I said. 'Both of you sit down.'

I took a deep breath – I am taking one now – and opened the door. He grinned at me.

'Willi,' I said, reaching out my hands. He was wearing a duffel coat spotted with rain and had a woollen hat pulled over his ears.

'It is fucking frigid,' he said.

'Come in, Willi. Come out of the cold.'

'Into your mansion, Josef. You are a big man now.'

'No different,' I said, and closed the door behind him; patted him, the arms of his wet coat.

He pulled off his hat and smoothed his hair, which I saw was silver. Silver hair. I turned to Nancy (who looked at me almost with fright – tears in my eyes?) and said, 'Nancy, this is my friend Willi from Somes Island.'

'From Berlin,' he said.

'Willi Gauss. He's the one you saw in the paper.'

'How do you do?' Nancy said.

'Take your coat off. Sit down, Willi. Have you eaten yet?'

He dug in the clothes tangled in his rucksack, pulled out a bottle of wine and put it in my hands. It had no label. (Naked wine, they call it now.)

'Yours?' I said. 'You made it?'

'What I need is your toilet,' he said.

While he was gone I whispered to Nancy that we must feed him and give him a bed.

'Calm down, Josef,' she said.

'He's my friend.'

'Calm down, I didn't say no. I don't care what he looks like, I'm sure he'll be OK.'

What he looked like was fat and old. In 1962 he must have been fifty-two or -three. His ageing – middle-ageing – had gone differently from mine, and in any case I was seven years younger. His cheeks had fallen. His eyes had creased. A tooth was missing in the side of his upper jaw and another in the lower, in front. Gap-toothed Willi, who had always been so pleased with his grin. We heard the toilet flush. He cleared his throat in the bathroom and spat.

'Make room, children,' Nancy said.

The word that came to me for Willi was 'ruined'. Even with him back from the bathroom, sitting easy at the kitchen table, slicked down, warmed up, I could not get it out of my mind. All that fragmentation I had heard and read about had slackened him, decayed him, and I feared some parallel ruin in his mind.

'You look as if you've seen a ghost, Josef,' he said.

'Sixteen years is too long,' I replied.

He grinned at Nancy. 'Has he been counting? What paper did you see me in?'

I explained that she had been a schoolgirl and had seen our pictures after our escape.

'Did you write to me?'

'God, no,' Nancy said. 'Why should I do that?'

'I had letters from women. The censor cut them to bits. I had to guess what they were offering.'

'Leave the table, children. Go and do your homework,' she said.

Willi gave a crenellated grin. 'I must not corrupt the little ones, Josef, is that it?'

Nancy said, 'They've finished, Mr Gauss. They've got things to do. Go on, Kenny. Susan.'

'I'll open this wine,' I said.

It was horrible wine – creek water and sugar and vinegar – and it shocked me as much as his appearance. Uncorking the bottle, I had thought, Willi's wine, it will be good, but it tasted fat and sour, the way he looked. It had the effect of shrinking me, of disappointing me back down the years, until I came to Willi on Somes Island, walking up the hill track as I sailed out; and I thought, That's when Willi finished for me. It was hard to grasp, and I sat dumb as he laughed at me. Then I pushed my glass away and said, 'It's horse's pee, Willi. Let's have some beer.'

Nancy brought a bottle from the refrigerator. She sipped the wine I'd poured her, then left it and went to see how the children were.

'A cosy wife, Josef. You are in clover,' Willi said. He pushed his own wine away and took a glass of beer. 'It was made by a woman I was with. She plays games, they all do, women play games. Wine is a new one. And politics. It helps take their minds off the fact that all they are good for is making babies.'

'Your English has got better,' I said. 'Would you like some food?'

'I ate a pie at the pie cart.'

'I'm glad you came up here. We can find a bed for you for the night.'

'Two nights. Can you manage two?'

There was a sneer in it, and in most things that he said, but I found myself smiling; I was not affected by this Willi at all.

'Tell me what you've been doing. All I know is what I've read in *Truth*.'

'That fucking rag. They follow me like little sniffing dogs. They think I am going to start a revolution.'

'Are you still a Marxist?'

'You ask like an agent for them. For the Security.'

'No, Willi, I'm not. But I'm not a communist either.'

'How could you be? All this.' He waved his hand round the kitchen.

'I'm a socialist.'

'Yes, they all are,' he said. 'All the rich commies, socialists now. They play conscience games.'

'So what are you?'

He smiled. 'Many things' – an answer that, blindingly for a moment, brought the old Willi back. I drank some beer. I went to the fridge for another bottle.

'But I am still a Marxist. I hate Russians and Americans,' he said.

'So what do you do now?'

'Watch and listen. I sit in the back row at the Socialist Forum. It is full of ex-communists – the class of 1956. They can't get out of the habit of going to meetings. It will be good to get away from them.'

'Are you going somewhere?'

'To Berlin,' he said.

'Ah, Willi, no,' I said – talking to this one or the old?

'What would I stay here for? In a little country, little men.

213

Bakers and bed-makers and brewers of flat beer, they think they are the kings of the world.'

'But why Berlin? Why now?'

'They have built a wall there,' Willi said. 'I am going for the wall.' He smiled at me and stroked his silver hair. He looked like Buddha. 'Do you understand, Josef? Berlin is the live place in the world.'

'But what will you do? And anyway, will they let you in?'

'There are ways to get in. You can get in anywhere if you want. And I can leave this bullshit place behind, this God's Own Country, and be where there is looking other men in the face and in the end he is gone or you, and none of this "Nice day, Josef. How is little wifey and the kiddies today?"'

I said, 'You're too old. It will be too hard.'

'What do you know, Josef? You were always afraid.'

'Unless you obey the rules they'll kill you.'

The old Willi might have survived, but I saw this new one as an innocent. Twenty years in this country had made him fat and simple. Winning easy, losing easy made him forget. He would make loud noises there, and do stupid things, and he would die. Yet I understood why he thought that he must go.

'Willi,' I said, 'it's too late.'

'Pour some more of this flat beer, Josef. Smile at me and wish me luck.'

'When?' I said. 'When is it?'

'I'm booked on a ship from Auckland. It leaves next week. I'm getting off in Naples. Then I will be a tourist, and all the time heading for Berlin.'

'I see.'

'Josef, can you lend me a hundred pounds?'

'What for?'

'For travelling. For this and that. All right, give, not lend. One hundred pounds because we are friends.'

'Yes,' I said. 'I'll write you a cheque.'

'Cash will be better. Tomorrow is all right. You owe me for feeding you with eggs.'

'Yes, I do,' I said, meaning that I owed him for much more than that, things I would never pay in money. But I was pleased to give money to this man here, pay him off. I felt broken, but was just a short way from being whole.

'So,' I said, 'Berlin. What will you do for a job?'

'Josef, you are bourgeois. I have never had a job.'

'No?'

'I live my life. I do what comes next. Perhaps I will build a tunnel under this wall they have made. I will take people in or take them out, whichever they want.'

'You get scared in tunnels,' I said.

'I was saving you, Josef.'

'So it was you who told, like Moser says?'

'Of course it was me. It was going nowhere. It would have collapsed and you would have died. So, better than just give it up I made a betrayal. That is more dramatic. It is good for propaganda.'

'Especially when you can blame a Jew.'

He shrugged. 'It was Moser's role. He has centuries of practice.' He stopped me from rising with his hand. 'Sit down, Josef. All I am doing is telling the truth.'

'You can have a bed for two nights. I'll give you a hundred pounds. But when you go, this time you're gone for good.'

'Paid off?'

I jerked my head at the island. 'I'm paying you for there.' I tried to grin. 'For the eggs.'

'Ah, sentimentalism. You are a classic case. Josef, I am hungry now. Perhaps I will have something to eat.'

I fed him. I gave him more beer. I sat drinking with him after Nancy had gone to bed. We grew friendly, as two men might who do not like each other but who lose their animosity in drink. By the time I showed him where to sleep I was almost fond of him. And always, always present, connected to this man by links that I glimpsed and then lost sight of, was the Willi Gauss I loved. Several times I displayed the sentimentalism he had accused me of – talking of our escape – and he curled his lip but let me go on; and I'm not ashamed, remembering it, for it meant that I was fixing them in place – Willi then and Willi now – and doing a repair job on myself, drunkenly but with effect.

He lumbered off, belching, to the toilet, and peed a bucketful in there; and I saw Kenny in his bedroom door, wet again, and called Nancy to look after him. She washed him and changed his sheets and found him clean pyjamas (Kenny wet his bed until he was twelve). She marched up the hall in her nightie and slammed the kitchen door so that Willi, at the table, should not see.

'I think I am the lucky one, Josef,' he said.

Nancy moved away from me when I went to bed. She did not see Willi in the morning, but left for work as soon as the children had gone to school. (Nancy in the rain, umbrella up.) I wanted to go to work myself but Willi's door stayed closed; and he was a stranger, I could not leave him in my house. What if Elizabeth or Susan should come home? He would not, surely not . . . But Elizabeth was twelve, and for him perhaps old enough. No, I said, not Willi. But he was also the man with silver hair and broken teeth and a head full of half-baked ideas and perhaps he had a need to punish me for having a family and 'doing well'.

At ten o'clock I knocked on his door and gave him a cup of tea and the morning paper. 'You can have a bath or shower,' I said.

'You would like me to be clean, Josef? I will wash myself with scented soap.'

I told him it was still raining outside and I would wait for him while he had breakfast, and run him down town if he would like to go.

'You can trust me, Josef. I will not steal your silver candlesticks.'

'Yes, I trust you. All I'm doing is offering you a ride.'

He yawned. 'I think this morning I will eat and sleep. And wash myself. Your Nancy is at work, yes? Then I can relax.'

I told him to make himself at home. I told him there were bread and cereals in the pantry. And bacon if he wanted it. And eggs.

'Very good, Josef. And eggs.' He looked, I thought, older in the morning, seedier. Grey-haired not silver on his chest, grey about his jowls, yellow in his eyeballs and his teeth; but he was still confident, behaving with his old authority. I saw him, though, uncertain as I left, holding back something he wanted to say.

'It's all right, Willi, I won't forget your money,' I said.

I met Nancy for lunch and apologised for him, but said I would have had him stay even if he had been much worse. 'It's the last time. He's leaving for Berlin.'

'Did he ask for money?'

'Yes, he did.'

'Will you give him some?'

'A hundred pounds.'

'It's cheap,' she said. 'Cheap if he's going. I'm sorry, Josef. I can see how he must have been all right. But people change. Are you OK?'

'Yes.'

'I know you've got to help him. I'm glad you can.'

'I'm going up in a minute to make sure the children haven't come home.'

'Oh God,' she said.

We drove up the hill together and found the house locked. No children – and why should they come home on this one day? No Willi. The only signs a few dirty dishes in the sink, an unflushed toilet, a rumpled bed.

'Well,' Nancy said, 'I'll stay home now. What do you think he'd like for tea?'

'Make something German. Kümmelbraten,' I said.

'Go round to the butcher. Shall we open a bottle of decent wine?'

I was back in town by three o'clock so I could get his money from the bank. Just before I left the office he telephoned.

'Josef? You do not have to have me tonight.'

I experienced a moment of desolation. 'What's happened?' I said.

'I have got a bed somewhere else. So I'm off your back.'

I almost said, You can't. Nancy's cooking. I meant he could not leave me. And then he was no longer Willi and I was all right. 'Where are you? In the pub? Shall I come there?'

'It is –' he asked someone '– the St George. I will be in the private bar. We can have a drink.'

'In ten minutes, Willi. One drink. Then I'll have to go.' I rang Nancy and told her, and she laughed.

'OK,' she said. 'But I've opened the wine. You and me can drink it. And eat Kümmelbraten. And go to bed.'

She was rarely as frank as this. I saw how relieved she was to be rid of him.

I walked to the St George and looked in the private bar but there were only women and their escorts. Although the barnyard din was deafening and the beer-stink as thick as a fog, I looked into the big room at the back, the public bar, and saw his silver head above the crowd. He was with half a dozen men, none of them familiar to me, and I guessed they were chance-met and he was amusing them in return for drinks. I watched for a moment – his grinning teeth, his cheeks flushed red – and thought, Willi, how did you come to this? I wanted him out of it, I wanted him in Berlin, where it would be dangerous all right, but where he might recover himself.

I caught his eye and raised my hand, then went back to the private bar, bought two glasses of whisky – a drink I seldom touch but this, after all, was an occasion – and waited for him at a little table by the wall.

He came in, peering in the gloom, and grinned when he found me: 'Hiding, Josef? When will you come into the light?'

I saw it was to be jibes, we would end in jibes, which was a pity, for I had hoped we might exchange a word; even that we might be serious, and that I might glimpse him again.

'Have a drink, Willi. And here's your money.' I offered it over the glasses, a thick little wad of five-pound notes, but he hissed and put his hand under the table. So I passed the money there. Once it might have thrilled me, this game, but now I thought it sad and somehow in line with his ruin, his seediness. He slid the wad into his pocket, and I said, 'Where did you get the jacket, Willi? And the scarf?'

'A present from a lady,' he said.

'Anyone I know?'

He yawned. 'She'll be down soon. You can wait and say hello.'

'So, you're staying here? In the St George? It's hardly a Stundenhotel.'

'You are jealous, Josef. I can find someone for you.'

'No thanks.'

'You will go home to Nancy? Marriage is prostitution, don't you know that? You buy yourself a cosy little fuck every night.'

'Shut up, Willi.' I was tired of him. I wanted to leave before this man, this bore, began to erode the Willi I held safe – who, all the same, flashed into composite being with him and held me there, flashed on and off like a light. I drank my whisky, listening to Silver-hair boast; and learned that the lady in the room upstairs was Norma Cooksley.

'You have grown into a New Zealander, Josef, you have learned to purse your mouth.'

'She's married,' I said.

'So it is the rights of the husband now? It is the house and car and the little wife. You will be an expert on this.'

'You've got a daughter, don't you know that?'

'Who might not like her mother fucking in a hotel. Even when the man she is in bed with is her daddy.'

'You make me sick, Willi.' But even then I could not leave. I wanted a sign, I wanted a word – to peel him clean and let me see Willi Gauss again, and know that I had not been wrong. Nothing came. I listened and was bored and angry by turns; and got up at last, bought him another drink and put it on the table.

'Goodbye, Willi.'

'You are going, Josef?' He was surprised. He understood the fascination that he held for me, and would never believe I was tired of him. 'Stay and see Norma. Say hello.'

'No. Sorry. Goodbye. Be careful in Berlin.'

I left him sitting in the private bar and did not look back; and never saw Willi Gauss again – although I saw Norma Cooksley descending the stairs. A woman well set up, arrogant, majestic; but desperate and elated and in love. It flashed in her, as Willi Gauss, my Willi, had flashed in the silver-haired man. She did not see me. Her eyes glowed, then darkened; her mouth was prim, then opened, then gasped, making fine hairs shine on her upper lip. I gave no sign but went on my way, home to Nancy.

We fed the children and sent them early to bed, then ate Kümmelbraten and drank expensive, very expensive wine. Do I mention that to put Willi further in his place? I can hear him sneer that of course the thing that would impress me was the cost. But I mean wine from Bordeaux, which we paid a ridiculous price for in those days. Nancy had been willing to open it for Willi, which really meant open it for me. We drank and enjoyed it, at the table first, then sitting in our chairs by the living-room fire. I told her Somes Island stories, Willi stories, most of which she had heard before, but in words that were happy and elegiac both. We drank coffee. We showered, washing off the day – in my case washing

Willi off – and went to bed and were happy there, as Willi and Norma were happy no doubt in the St George hotel. But not once did I think of him, the silver-haired man, and have seldom thought of him since.

Willi Gauss, Willi of Somes Island, I think of him.

And now I must say what happened to Willi, and confess that I don't know which Willi it happened to. Perhaps he recovered himself in Berlin. It (the West) was surrounded by a wall as Somes Island had been by the sea. There were reasons for him to be at home, apart from growing up there. The wire of the first few weeks had been replaced by concrete – a wall one hundred miles long and twelve feet high, with watchtowers and searchlights and dogs on running wires and guards (Vopos) 'licensed to kill'. I cannot see him as the sneering man of the St George. His hair turns to blond, he loses the fat on his belly and jowls, he grins at people with all his teeth and does foolish things which succeed. But I know nothing. I know what I've read about the Berlin of the sixties, both sides of the wall, and Willi occupies it, when I'm relaxed, as the Willi Gauss of Somes Island – a person I've dreamed up, a ghost, substantial ghost, to whom I can say, 'Für immer Freunden, Willi.'

At other times, more sensibly, I say, 'He must have been lost there, he wouldn't have known what to do.' That explains his marriage. Yes, he married: news I had from Moser, whose interest in Willi matched my own. Moser had a friend in Berlin (in the West), a minor bureaucrat with a twitchy nose, and had him sniff out Willi and 'keep an eye on him'. So when I say I know nothing, it is nothing that adds up.

His wife was a woman called Renate. I never learned how old she was or whether she was fat or thin, short or tall, clever or stupid. When I try to imagine her I end up with Norma Cooksley coming down the stairs. They lived in Kreuzberg at an address

221

Moser's friend supplied him with. I sent a card there once but had no reply.

What did Willi do? Made a nuisance of himself, the bureaucrat said, and married a German national to avoid being deported. I suppose it is true. Willi would need a practical reason for taking a wife. He mixed with people 'too young for him' – students, noisy radicals, artists, anarchists, Turks. He was on the fringes of Rudi Dutschke's group, and was probably a joke there, a nuisance – or was he young Willi Gauss again? I thought I saw him in a news photograph once, throwing an egg at the Shah of Persia – an arm obscured his face but he had a Willi jaw, and there was a shine of silver hair . . .

West Berlin in the sixties was an interesting place. I imagine it pleased Willi very much. But what of East Berlin? How would he see it – outside or inside the wall? His wife had family there – another reason for him to marry her? It's all questions. I only know that he went back and forth several times on his New Zealand passport before West Germans were allowed, and that he was, in the bureaucrat's words, 'up to something'. Then one night he failed to reappear at Checkpoint Charlie. He never came back. What went wrong? Was he a victim or a criminal? Did he walk in some-where and show his Marxist credentials? In Ulbricht's Stalinist Berlin they would have been unacceptable. And Willi hated Stalinism anyway. Did he show his letter from Keith Holyoake?

In Berlin his wife made enquiries. No answer came. According to Moser's contact it meant that Willi was 'operating' there in some way. But he was 'a minor player' and everyone forgot him in short time. Except his wife, who loved him. Except Moser. Except me.

Six years went by. I tried to picture him growing old in East Berlin; could not see him 'retired', could not see him as a 'func-tionary', but only as an 'operator', which was shadowy. Nancy and I began to talk of an overseas trip – the UK of course, and France and Italy. Austria was up to me. We never mentioned Berlin.

Then one night Moser telephoned. 'I've heard from Max in Berlin. Willi's dead.'

The DDR and the FDR had exchanged information on criminals and there on the list was Willi's name, imprisoned in 1971 for illicit trading (in information, goods, money, what?); died of a brain haemorrhage in 1974. That was all; all there ever was. I suppose his wife found out where he was buried but if so the information never reached Moser's friend, who was close to retiring and had no interest left.

'So Willi is finished,' Moser said. 'I knew he must be up to no good.' Moser's English was improving. 'Josef, I can't hear you. Are you there?'

'I hope they didn't hurt him,' I said.

It silenced Moser, who for all his sharpness was a kind man. We ended by agreeing that Willi was lucky if he really had been imprisoned on criminal charges. Political would have been more dangerous. But I don't know which is more likely. Sometimes I hope it was one and sometimes the other. There's little variation in the picture I see: an old ruined man with silver hair in a prison cell. Footsteps approach in the corridor. A key turns. The door swings wide and bangs against the wall, and I see that Willi is afraid. His mouth trembles and his eyes blink. I switch off then.

After Moser's phone call I poured myself a glass of whisky and went on to the porch. I sat on the top step and looked at the harbour, where Somes Island made a black hole in the starlit water. Willi had been dead for three years. 'I'm sorry I'm late with this,' I said, and drank to him.

Nancy had heard my side of the conversation. She came out and sat with me, close against my shoulder, and took a sip of whisky from my glass. Willi resonated, back down the years, but the steadier sound, the deeper sound, came from Nancy. After a while I said, 'It's cold out here. Come inside.'

We drank coffee and talked about Kenny and Elizabeth and Susan, and only after that about Willi.

It's a different love. There's room for both.

One more thing. When we made our trip overseas in 1982 we visited West Berlin and made the tourist stop at Checkpoint Charlie. We looked with sick excitement at the Wall, and I have to confess that I found it impossible to think of Willi there; he did not fit. We walked in the Tiergarten and came out by the Brandenburg Gate, where the Wall made a great horseshoe bulge into the West, ten feet thick to stop the tanks. On top of the Gate the Goddess of Victory galloped her quadriga east, along the road doomed armies take. I managed to sense, and shiver at, history. But Willi was not there either.

I went by taxi to Kreuzberg to see where he had lived. The house was in a narrow building in a squalid street. Squalor would not have troubled him – and, knowing that, I found a ghostly Willi. But no Mrs Gauss. The Turkish woman who answered the door had never heard of her. I went back to my hotel and did not try to find Willi Gauss any more.

When I mentioned him to Nancy as we flew out of Berlin she claimed that he had started Kenny wetting his bed again.

FOURTEEN

I have been writing in these notebooks long enough. I had not intended laying everything bare. In the beginning I wished only to say that Kenny had disappointed me; or, as it seemed then, betrayed. I set out to have a moan on paper, my pen was loosened by red wine – and look where I am now. Willi is dead. And Kenny disappoints me still.

But here, in my story, Nancy is alive. When, how, did it become a story? I sip the glass of wine Elizabeth allows and wonder if I have the heart to see her die again, see Nancy die. If I say no – this sick old man (old man who recovers!) – then I must stop. But do I have the right to say, The story stops?

I'll keep on going for a while, drive on my pen (a funny language, English, demanding 'pen' although I use a biro). It is almost spring. I can see out my windows in the dawn without wiping a hole in the condensation. This morning the garden trees are standing still, resting it seems, after a night of thrashing in the wind. Now and then one of them gives a shudder, perhaps a sigh. We live in a tough place, the trees and I. It is hard to be relaxed.

Elizabeth brought the mail in a moment ago. All I got was bills. She's good about bringing them to me, although she'd like to spare me the trouble. I should have my accountant or my bank handle them and not carry on with this old-fashioned writing of cheques.

I try to explain that I enjoy paying bills, it's like feeling your pulse throb in its regularity, and the seasonal fluctuation of some puts me in touch with the patterns of life – which provoked her to her usual exclamation. I'm glad I didn't tell her that they connect me with the city down there and the world outside, for that might call in question the cosiness I'm sure she feels she has created here. I don't want cosiness, I've never liked it, although I've wanted privacy and closeness and contentment. One cannot, one mustn't, exclude the world. I need 'down there', although differently from the way I've needed 'up here'.

The tenses are interesting in that last sentence. I was not aware of choosing them and don't quite know what they mean. Is it simply that Nancy is dead? I am, in my way, contented enough.

Now there are squeals in the kitchen. What is this? Not more trouble with Julie? Three voices whinny out there.

My daughter Susan has been to visit me, and my grand-daughter Bea. (Can one really call a two-hour stop between morning and midday flights a visit?) They were on their way from Hamilton to see Susan's boy, who is studying dentistry in Dunedin. He, the boy, Jonas, wanted to be a doctor but could not make the grade and so settled for dentistry where, Susan says boldly, he'll make more money anyway. Perhaps she only says it bravely. Reading Susan is not a skill I have. I can read the other two, Elizabeth like a book, though one that shifts now and then into a language I only half know, and Kenny like the label on a packet of water crackers. But Susan has been open, closed, open again, and I only see a word here and there, or glimpse a picture: I can get nothing complete. Here she is, at forty-three, beautiful in a way that tips me off balance, forces me to bump my senses, my sensibilities, straight; for it is Nancy's beauty she has, which I'm the only one to see. (I overheard a woman whisper once that Nancy was plain.) Susan is large, round, blue-eyed, mild of countenance, and fiery, with those deep fires Nancy had. I should know her, recognising this – but read nothing in her with accuracy, and she berates me for my mistakes.

She pounced on me twice in her two hours in my house, the first time for supposing that pleasure in beauty must be a bonus in her job (she and her husband grow lilies for export to Japan), the second for mistaking her pride in Bea as less than pure. Elizabeth told her tartly to 'dry up', for flowers must bring pleasure to everyone, the grower too, or something's wrong; and Bea said that fiddle-playing was her trade and of course she hoped to make some money out of it one day and stop being a drain on her mum and dad. Susan looked as if she would cry. 'You're not a drain, you've never been a drain, we love helping you.'

'Oh, Mum,' Bea said, and gave her a hug, and I was suddenly close to tears myself, at the love these two Nancy-women poured out.

I am not mistaken in saying that it includes me. I am warm with it still, and will be, if I'm sensible, for the rest of my days.

Bea takes more after her father, the lily-grower, in temperament. She is toned down, she works things out and then performs neatly what she must do, no excess; and I wondered how, without passion, she could hope to succeed as a violinist. But I've been wrong before, over Elinor Cleghorn; and Bea has a confidence that will perhaps serve just as well. She's interested that Nancy and I knew Elinor, but not excited because, as I've said, she (Elinor) stayed in the second rank.

Susan wanted to telephone Kenny and tell him to close his office and get in his car and come on up, but Elizabeth said, 'No, don't do that', then had to explain, which she did in terms less general than I would have liked. Susan made explosions of disbelief, while Bea went round-eyed and kept quiet. 'I'd soon fix her,' Susan said, turning to anger. 'I'd give her a bloody good shake. Whatever Kenny is, he's not like that.'

'She's getting better,' Elizabeth said. 'She's with a sensible therapist now. It was all that other woman's fault.' She warned Susan that Julie would soon be home from one of her sessions and talk must be ordinary and *nothing* be even hinted at.

'Poor Julie,' Bea said, and meant it so profoundly that I thought, She'll get there because she can feel, and she can keep it in control.

She had her violin with her and I asked her to play. Susan at once said no, what Bea needed was a room for an hour's practice – which surprised me, remembering her fights with Nancy over just this sort of thing. Bea said, 'Oh, but I'd like to play for Grandpa', and I saw that although she might be dutiful, in music her mother would not tell her what to do. I grinned with pleasure at the instruction in it. The wheel turns.

We had a little concert and don't ask me the pieces. They – Elizabeth accompanied Bea on the piano – kept it popular for me. Susan frowned at first, wanting hard stuff, I suppose, so we might see how clever her daughter was, but she was smiling before long. I watched them, Bea standing, going through those motions, those intricacies, I had first admired in Benjamin Ascher, Elizabeth sure-handed, light-handed, rolling her bottom on the piano stool in Nancy's way, and Susan, the failed cellist, hearing more than I could hear; and I thought, It's enough, I'm happy now. I closed my eyes and let the melodies retreat, and dreamed of Nancy.

Julie arrived towards the end. We heard her car in the drive and her leather boots in the kitchen.

'In here, Julie,' Elizabeth called.

There were greetings then, embraces, and not what I had feared – a flow-over of Julie's aggression on to this part of Kenny's family. Her face went pink with happiness. She and Bea had not met for four or five years, when Julie had gone for a holiday in Hamilton and had helped pack lilies in the early days of Susan's and Barry's enterprise. She had flown home on the aeroplane with her arms full of blooms. She talked about it for a moment, while Susan watched too sharply.

'I love the way you're dressed,' Bea said. 'I wish I had the nerve to dress like that. I love your boots.'

I don't think she did. She was being kind, and heading off her mother.

'Can I hear you play? Can I hear how good you are?' Julie asked.

'We were just finished,' Bea said. 'I'll do one more.'

'Then I think we should ring for our taxi,' Susan said.

Bea played something fast and clever, without the piano helping her – and I've just asked Elizabeth, coming in for my cup, what it was. 'One of the Caprices. Paganini. It's music for showing off with,' she said with a smile. Julie clapped when it was over. Then the girls chattered in the lounge while mother and aunt (aunts) hissed in the kitchen, Susan wanting to know more, and boiling up more, until I, passing through, heard Elizabeth say, 'If you do you'll ruin three months' hard work. And you might even drive her mad. Ah, Dad, break up those two. I'm going to drive Susan and Bea to their plane.'

They kissed me goodbye, gave me hugs. Julie shifted her car in the drive and Elizabeth drove them off in mine. The house was suddenly so quiet it seemed a whole crowd of people had gone. I sat down to rest in my room and saw Julie at the edge of the lawn, studying it with hands on hips, as though she were planning an attack. I've bought her a new mower, an electric one, very quiet, but the wet grass has stopped her from trying it out. Later, when I went to the lounge to catch more of the winter sun, I saw her sitting halfway down the steps – saw just the top of her head, but something there, its forward slant, told me she was crying. I went out, clumping so she should not think I was sneaking up, and sat beside her and asked what was wrong – meaning, now, right this minute, for I did not want the other stuff, and we are warned off anyhow. She dried her eyes on her sleeve, which had a greasy shine in the fabric, as though she wiped everything there, her nose, her mouth. I did not touch her, knowing that man-touch of any sort was assault.

'I can never be like her,' she whimpered.

It was more than self-pity, containing something so deep – failure, loss, a kind of death – that I could do nothing but take her hand. She did not scream or pull away.

'Why can she play like that and I can't do anything?'

'You can,' I said. 'You will. You'll go back to university. You've got a good brain.'

'I can't,' she said, and with such finality that it silenced me, and we sat a while, until I said, trying for some lightness, 'What did the pair of you talk about?'

'New York. She was telling me about living there.'

'Yes? Interesting?'

'I want to go to New York. But I never can. After what my father did to me.'

We are not allowed to argue with her. Julie has her memories, and true or false – they are false – how can she ever move forward while they remain? Someone must argue with her in some way and banish them – send them howling out of her – but not me, not us, in the ways we know. We can't go there.

After a while I said that perhaps the lawns were dry enough to cut. She fetched out the new mower, ran the cord inside through the door and started work. I sat on the porch steps and watched. Once she jumped the cord over my head the way a girl in the playground whirls a skipping rope. Julie laughed. She can laugh.

Is this a way?

When Nancy's mother died I drove her to Masterton for the funeral service. (Violet Brisbois outlived her husband by nine years.) I waited in the car outside the church while she went in to say her last goodbyes to the mother she had not seen since the day we had announced our love. I tried to imagine Nancy singing hymns, kneeling to pray, and listening to words I had never heard and read in curiosity only once – words too good for Violet Brisbois. 'Vi,' I said, 'Brizzboy' – hating them for what they'd done to Nancy. When the coffin came out I saw Neville Brisbois once again – his slabs of cheek, his pouter pigeon front – and Valerie, held up in his arm. Their cheeks were wet with tears. Nancy was the one who did not cry. She spoke to her brother and sister, and they swung their heads and found me, little Jew, in my car. They turned their muscular, their Brisbois backs, and Nancy stepped away as though fended off. She crossed the road and got in the car.

'Are you all right?' I said.

'I feel sick.'

'Do you want to go to the cemetery?'

'I want to go home.'

I drove her out of Masterton, crossing streets we had taken on our first escape from her family.

'I tried to remember,' Nancy said. 'How she used to tuck me into bed. But something's gone wrong. I can't remember any more. Not even Dad.'

We drove through the Wairarapa towns and started up the Rimutaka hill. 'To be a pilgrim,' Nancy said. 'We sang that. But she never budged an inch from anywhere.'

'Are they going to the house afterwards?'

'Yes.'

'You should have gone.'

'I asked if you could come and Val said, "Mum wouldn't like it." Neville said I caused a lot of grief. He said it again.'

I could not fit 'grief' with Brisbois, even with tears on their cheeks. (And Brian Brisbois, galloping the length of the rugby field with a squealing Violet under his arm? He was, I suppose, a young man in love. It is hard to let them have that word, and 'joy', and anything good. Nancy was not theirs, she was a fluke.)

We reached the summit and saw through folding hills pieces

of our own territory. That's the end of them, no more Brisboys, I thought. It was stupid of me. Nancy rarely spoke of them again but she grieved for her lost memories: the mother who had loved her (perhaps) and the dad who played games.

They make me grit my teeth with anger still.

The child grows up, the parent becomes a child without growing down. I won't cross that out, but it needs all sorts of qualification. Did Kenny, for example, ever become a man? One thing I know, the girls became women while he remained a boy and tried to do man-things in that state. They all married early – the women and the whipper-snapper.

I liked my two sons-in-law, and like one of them still. The other is a ratbag. I say that on insufficient evidence, but evidence that will do for me. David is his name (never Dave), David Cuthbertson. How could he cast Elizabeth out? He crumpled her up in one hand like an empty fruit-juice carton and tossed her in the rub-bish, I say. She says they came to the end of their good times. Tries to make it sound as if they reached that point together. It's not true. He tossed her aside. But no, she's not empty, she's not in the rubbish, she's full and she's useful and has no need of soft language ('end of our good times') any more – so why do I go on? Because she is my daughter and he hurt her, that is why.

Does it sound now as if I've become a child? I'd better go back and cross that nonsense out. And how can one 'grow down'? I'm not as good in English as I thought.

I liked David Cuthbertson when she brought him home. I thought he was a sensitive, intelligent young man. And so he was. Too sensitive, perhaps. I thought Elizabeth would be boss; she'd make him listen while she played the piano – he cared for music no more than I – and pull him more her way than she would go his. It made me nervous that they said 'we' so easily, and that he sometimes followed it with a timid laugh.

David Cuthbertson studied economics, which Elizabeth, mistakenly, believed more important – and classier too – than Susan's Barry Macgregor's botany. He's a banker and has been a parliamentary candidate. Although his job requires him to keep quiet, in private he's an ardent Market Forces man. His eyes glow, he's passionate, he uses 'we' with a capital letter it's so large – a 'We' that leaves Elizabeth out. Kenny thinks highly of him (still). They each own a library of books by Ayn Rand; and say that libraries should be privatised, and closed down if they fail to make a profit.

One day Nancy and I went walking on the wharves with Elizabeth and David. We passed a man fishing, who pulled up a kahawai two feet long and killed it and cleaned it while we watched; and David said, 'Jesus, you're swimming along on a nice sunny day minding your own business and suddenly someone hooks you up and cuts your throat and rips out your guts.'

'Oh, David,' Elizabeth said, not liking his language.

I thought, What a gentle boy, I hope she doesn't hurt him.

Three additions to our family in one year: David and Barry and Priscilla. We liked the young men, good clever David, and Barry with his ridiculous good looks – they baffled him, he never understood, he could not see – and his devotion (and physical devotion: he shivered, his skin jumped, when Susan touched) to our naughty child. Three weddings, one fairly large, one middle-sized, one small (Susan's, on our own front lawn, with Somes Island keeping its counsel down below). I had to pay for two of them, but not for the large, in St Michael and All Angels Church in Kelburn and at the bride's father's house along the road. Priscilla was 'the daughter we gained'. I never liked her. She never liked me. I have not seen her for several years. At last she pleases me, by staying away.

Kenny became an Anglican while courting her. I don't believe he was ever taken by faith, nor is he troubled by doubt. Membership and observance make up his religious life. He still goes to church, while Priscilla stopped long ago.

She was a woman possessing physical grace, which Julie has inherited, and a conventional fine-boned prettiness, but whose mind was ugly with complaints and dissatisfactions and narrow judgements. No matter how refined her speech and sentiments were, they always had a choked quality, as though she had to force them round something tasting bad that blocked their way – as though she had a stricture in her throat. I'm sure she felt she should have done better than Kenny and could not understand why the young men she should have had quietly sloped off – my term, not hers: I imagine them leaning as they go. She was eight years older than Kenny and married him, I think, in desperation, like one of Jane Austen's secondary women. Nancy and I agreed that it was Kenny's bad luck that he happened along. He was her bad luck too.

We held a family lunch to meet her parents, and sat ten at the table – Elizabeth and David, Susan and Barry, Kenny and Priscilla, with Leighton Spence and Margaret Spence paired with Nancy and me. (Leighton was, I found out later, Ronald Leighton Spence, but he had chosen the 'better' name.) The french doors were open to the veranda. A cool breeze that I needed more as the meal went on lifted the sleeves of the summer dresses the women wore. Nancy and Margaret Spence both mentioned it – 'lovely breeze, oh, so cool on the cheeks, I love the smell of summer, don't you?' – keeping alive the talk, which threatened to die. Elizabeth, already adept, sent a little flow of deferential questions at Leighton Spence.

He was a creased man – creased and seamed and falsely jolly and direct. He had hidden folds the cool air could not reach. I am going to be unfair to him, it's my privilege. And is it so unfair to say that he, ripe with soap and after-shave, exuded also a smell of corruption, coming from behind his opacity and self-approval? It made me draw my head away and sit up straight. Here's a man, I thought, who needs an airing. He needs a bit of scrubbing round his parts.

'Do you like living by the university?' Elizabeth asked.

'When the students are away,' Leighton Spence said. 'A university without them, that'd suit me.'

'There are students and students,' David said.

'You one?'

'Not now.'

'You don't look scruffy enough. What did you do?'

'Economics and pol. sci. and history,' David said.

'History won't do you much good. All you really need to know is where your next deal is coming from and where it's going.'

'Yes,' Kenny said. 'Mr Spence is owner of the Outlook Finance Company.'

'That's all the history I need,' Leighton Spence said.

Nancy's look warned me not to start. I poured wine for Leighton Spence while Elizabeth tried again, with Mrs Spence.

'You must get a lovely view from where you live.'

'Oh we do. We see right across to the mountains,' Mrs Spence said.

'Every five degrees of that sort of view adds a thousand dollars to the value of a house. I'm talking exact figures, I've worked it out,' Leighton Spence said. He looked out the french doors. 'This is good. It's a good stroke of business, Joe, getting your mitts on this. You must have got in the market early.'

'I bought it for Somes Island. Part of my history.'

He did not hear. 'The island adds a bit. I'd have to calculate.'

'Our trouble is, we're getting blocked by trees,' Mrs Spence said.

'I'm going to cut them down,' Leighton Spence said.

'Don't do that, trim them,' Susan said. 'Barry will do it for you, won't you, Barry?'

'I trim trees as a sideline,' Barry said, blushing. 'For extra cash.'

'You a student?'

'Yes, botany.'

I saw that go round about in Leighton Spence's head and find no place where it could settle. He gave a frown, puzzled perhaps. 'I like to get professionals for a job.'

'Don't cut them down, though,' Barry managed to say.

'A good tree,' I said, 'must be worth a thousand dollars to a property. Can you calculate?'

'Barry trimmed our trees,' Nancy said. 'He made a good job.'

'I'd have a few of these out,' Leighton Spence said. He recognised no danger. 'Mind you, trees do give a place a bit of class.'

He was, plainly, puzzled by our 'class', or 'classiness'. When Elizabeth played nocturnes during coffee he smiled not at the music but the idea of it. He liked the look of my daughters and the way they dressed and spoke, although I think Susan's child, swelling her womb, offended him.

'You've both changed your name. That's clever girls.'

'What do you mean?' I said, putting down my cup.

'Foreign names are a bit of a liability.'

'Kenny's got one. Haven't you noticed?'

'Dad,' Kenny said, coming quickly from across the room, 'Mr Spence and I have been trying to sort that out.'

'What is there to sort out? Your name is your name.'

'Not necessarily,' Kenny said.

'It's a present for me,' Priscilla said. 'I don't want to be Mandl, I want Mandell.'

'A good name is important, Dad,' Kenny said.

'Oh Kenny, Kenny,' Nancy cried. (Mrs Spence went out to the veranda. I believe she was ashamed.)

'You're changing your name?' I said, and swung round on Leighton Spence, making him step back. 'This is your fault.'

'I think that immigrants should fit in,' he said. 'It's common in Europe, isn't it, all those people coming out of the East? Didn't they make a law of it somewhere, so you get all your Friedmans and so on – Greenbums, eh –' (nudging Kenny) '– instead of names no one can pronounce? And, Joe, when all's said and done, you should try to see it as adapting. You're here now, and it's a kind of compliment to us. It's like saying, "Thank you, Leighton, for letting us stay." And it smooths your path, don't forget that. I want a smooth path for my daughter. Kenny agrees.'

'Does he? Do you, Kenny?'

'I like Mandell,' Kenny said. 'So does Priss.'

'It's a painless operation, like your doggy at the vet,' Leighton Spence joked. 'Mandl today, Mandell tomorrow.'

Nancy came and took my hand.

'I'd do it myself,' he said. 'Spence into Spencer, with an "r", if it wasn't too late. For the classy sound.'

'Have you changed already?' I asked Kenny.

'I've started. I've filled in the forms.'

'Excuse me,' I said, and left the room; and found Nancy beside me, holding my hand. We went to our bedroom and lay down on the bed. I felt that without her I would float away into the dark. I felt the way I had felt when I learned that Susi had died.

I behaved badly at Priscilla and Kenneth Mandell's wedding reception. I stood dark and crooked by the wall. Explained to whoever would listen that I was Mandl not Mandell. Told Leighton Spence that it was against my religion to eat ham. And said that, on the other hand, I did not hold with usury. Outlook Finance Company?, I said to someone else, perhaps a better name would have been Look Out! Nancy took me home early – but not before Mrs Spence paraded her ancient father in a wheelchair. She dabbed with a folded handkerchief to keep his mouth dry and shouted in his ear who people were. 'Good, good,' he said to everyone, and they cried, 'You're looking well, Sir Roland. A box of birds.'

'Sir Roland who?' I said sharply to Leighton Spence.

'Sir Roland Bartram. My wife's father.'

'Used to be Secretary of Justice?' I said.

'Yes. Great man.'

When my turn came to shake the palsied hand and shout into the papery ear, I said, 'Sir Roland, we know each other. We used to write letters.'

'Good. Good.'

'I asked you to let me off Somes Island. I was locked up there. And you said no.'

'Good. Good.'

'I was a dangerous enemy alien.'

'Indeed. Oh yes.'

'And now my son has married your grand-daughter. You must have known something when you said I should be deported. Eh? Ha ha.'

'That's more than enough, Mr Mandl,' Mrs Spence said. Bless her, she pronounced it right. She rolled her father away. And Nancy led me out of there and drove me home.

'That was very silly, Josef,' she said.

'Yes, it was.'

'I doubt if we'll ever be asked back.'

'Poor Kenny.'

'Clever you.'

There's a painting by Egon Schiele called 'The Family'. He completed it in 1918 shortly before he died of the Spanish flu. (It brings a lump to my throat, thinking of his death, the way the English feel about John Keats.) I have a reproduction on my bedroom wall and sometimes, when it surprises me, I say, 'Josef' for the man who looks out unseeing, who looks in, and 'Nancy' for his wife between his knees, who has the same look, slanting away, and 'Kenny' for the child at her feet. How embarrassed Kenny would be if I showed him. It would embarrass him to hell – the nudity, the closeness – and he would say, Is it any wonder I had to get out?

238

He would not see that although the family is together it is apart. He would not see separation hanging over it.

The Outlook Finance Company belongs to him and Priscilla now. He worked for many years as an employee, a man on wages with a 'wealthy' wife, then bought in, using his patrimony, which I let him have when I sold Ascher and Mandl. (Elizabeth's and Susan's I keep in trust, with their agreement. The interest from it is how I live.) Leighton Spence fell ill and retired to a wheelchair just like his father-in-law's, and Kenny became top man at Outlook. He lends money, that is how *he* lives; he takes on borrowers the banks won't touch. The risks are high but the profits can be large. After the 1987 crash (in which he lost heavily, although he has never said how much), he added reverse annuity mortgages to his repertoire. That means he too has to borrow, while waiting for the mortgagors to die. It makes me shiver with fear for him, and with distaste. But he provides a service, Kenny says, he fills a need. So I'll keep quiet. Importing food was simple alongside what Kenny does.

Although Nancy and I went to Australia several times and once took a Pacific cruise, we did not travel properly until 1982. Proper travel meant Europe for us both. I won't name the cities we visited, or the paintings we saw and the concerts we (she) heard. I've already said we stopped in Vienna and Berlin. That will do. I did not go hunting in Vienna; I grew no lump in my throat. This perhaps signals a deficiency in me. I've read of people visiting rooms in which they grew up and finding them smaller and weeping there, but I did not set my foot in Gluckgasse, did not even glimpse our apartment there; in a sense did not set foot in Vienna but visited a city strange to me – *another* city, it made me yawn – and looked at pictures, heard music, enjoyed my wife's pleasure in all this. Just now and then I saw that Vienna had tried to scrub away what must be remembered. The Danube smelled of bathwater and soap. And once, while Nancy was resting, I walked out from our hotel and stood on the Sweden Bridge and saw grey water trickle from a drain under it; and I sensed, in the sewers, something sleeping, with an eyeball gleaming between its lids. It had no snake shape any more, it was simply a human face – and I turned away, went away fast, from what might have been revealed to me. I took Nancy on tourist outings to Mayerling and Melk; ate stale Sachertorte; sat in a Heurige in Gumpoldskirchen and drank wine that seemed to me neither good nor bad. I'm a cold fish, I thought. Nancy was pleased by my animation. I shook off a headache that had troubled me and walked in the streets with a springy step. I wasn't all there in Vienna.

There were just the two of us. No children. No ghosts. We grew very close on our European trip. It was as romantic as our early days in my Brot Werke; it was loving and erotic and meditative and practical. Our disagreements became a joke. It seemed that no one gave in, although it was me sometimes and Nancy at other times – less often. It was our trip, and her trip, and mine when it was hers. I can retrace it step by step – that's when I try. When I don't try it surprises me; an image makes me pause in my steps or in my breathing: Nancy sitting on a warm brick wall in Siena, with her arm outstretched to stop gelato dripping on her trousers; Nancy in the Österreichische Galerie, looking at the picture that hangs on my bedroom wall. 'Is it Egg-on or Ee-gon?' she says. Best though, everywhere, is Nancy listening. Operas and symphonies in London and Vienna and Stockholm and Berlin. She listens to goat bells sounding through the trees on the hill of Kronos. Listens to the Paris taxi horns. But she liked to make music as well as hear. The first thing she did when we arrived home was sit at her piano and play and play.

And then it goes on, it goes on, it seems like the next day but in fact it was almost a year and she is in hospital having the operation that comes too late, cancer cells have reached the lymph nodes under her arm, they have gone everywhere – and in another year Nancy dies.

That is all. Nancy Mandl. Sixty-one years old. I don't cry. The girls cry. Kenny walks out of the room and out of the house and away into the pine trees on Tinakori hill. I find him there when I go searching. He runs off deeper into the trees as I approach. I see his white shirt flicker in the trunks, and I turn and leave him. He is not a child, he is a man.

I do my own grieving in my own way.

We stayed three or four days in Nice and did not like that over-built coast. On our last day Nancy said, 'Let's get on a *little* train and go somewhere.' So up we went on winding tracks past villages perched on hills and got off in a town whose name I forget, where a two-mile walk by a stream would bring us to a chapel, I forget the century, but very old, decorated in fresco by an artist I forget. A mile into the country a stone bridge – elegant, Genoese, our pamphlet said – crossed the stream. We sat on it in the sun and ate our lunch of fruit and cheese and bread. A brown snake four feet long bolted – he thumped like feet on stairs – for his hole in the rocks. We lay down in the grass where he had been and snoozed for an hour, then walked on and found the chapel and admired the frescos, which told the whole story: Mary and the angel Gabriel, Christ feeding the multitude, Judas hanging on a tree with a de-mon tearing his black soul from a hole in his side, the saved in a blue heaven, the damned tormented in a red hell – no inch of wall was bare. It made us shrink and shiver, and made us laugh. A busload of tourists arrived so we explored up a track and surprised a classy-looking lady peeing on the ground. We turned our backs until she had finished and stood aside as she came down, a little slower than her urine running on the clay. ''Sieur 'dame,' she said. 'Bonjour,' we said, and carried on.

When we heard the bus leave we went back for another look at the frescos. The valley was silent, the chapel stood empty where it had been for five, six, seven hundred years. I explored along the wall by the stream where the foundations of an earlier building crumbled in the moss. Nancy appeared fifty yards up the hill, beside a spring bubbling out of rocks. (The spring was the reason the chapel had been built.) She sat down and looked into the water. She folded her hands. Nancy listened. She listened in the way she had to our babies breathing. I watched. I'm a watcher. I moved to let her see me, and climbed up and sat on the other side of the spring. She drank handfuls of cold clear water and cooled my hot cheeks with her palms.

Then we shared the apple we had saved and walked back to the station and caught our little mountain train to Nice.

Nancy Mandl. I feel her cool hands on my face again.

FIFTEEN

Kenny telephoned yesterday and asked me to go to his office at half-past two, when Mr and Mrs Gummer were coming in. I did not like the sound of that.

'Kenny, it's not my business,' I said.

'I want you here. This woman is driving me barmy. I need your help.'

I could not refuse a request like that, so I went. Now I must say what I've learned.

His office is on The Terrace, at the back of a building, three floors up. A smart young woman called Veronica sits out front. Kenny has a room overlooking the motorway. He works with his back to the window because the cars distract him, zipping by. There's a larger room through a side door, with a table and six chairs. Veronica calls it the boardroom, although there is no board. She took me through his office and ushered me in there. Kenny was at the table with his hands flat on the surface and a folder between them, neatly squared. The Gummers had not arrived, but they were close; I had seen them on the footpath as I got into the lift, and had hit the button hard, in a panic at the thought of riding up with them.

'They're on the way, Kenny. They're in the lift.'

'Veronica won't let them in until I say.'

'What do you need me for? What do they want?'

'She says she's got an ultimatum. I'm ready for them, Dad. I'm telling her exactly where she stands. And I need you as a witness, to hear what she says and back me up.'

'I can't do that. You'll have to get your girl.' I meant Veronica. Who tapped on the door and opened it: 'Mr and Mrs Gummer are here.'

'Ask them to wait a minute,' Kenny said. His fingers played piano on the table, some final chord Nancy would have known. All I could recognise was his Brisbois look, his oxblood hue. 'It won't come to court,' he said. 'But she doesn't know that. I'm going to draw up a document – my lawyer is, saying that if she doesn't stop . . . What I need you for is to say it's true. Do you know what she did? She came in here last week and stuck a card with Blu-Tack on my door: "Jewish crooks!" I don't have to stand for that.'

'No, you don't.'

'I'll scare her, that's all. Sit down, Dad. Try to look as if you're here on business.'

So I sat down and he buzzed for Veronica. She showed the Gummers in, then crossed to a cabinet by the wall and was busy there – switching on a recording machine, I found out later. Mrs Gummer had already begun: 'A thieves' kitchen.' (The recorder was too late for that.) 'Jews counting their pickings, look at them.'

'Deely, sit down and be good,' Gummer said. He pulled out a chair and she sat; opened her mouth to start again, but he said, 'Ah!', holding up his finger, 'you promised me.'

Veronica left, closing the door softly. Then for a moment we heard Gummer breathing as he lowered himself into a chair.

'I hope this is important, Mr Mandell. It's not easy for us to come in here.'

'Yes? Well I'll be brief,' Kenny said.

But I found myself impressed again by Gummer, I found myself liking him, in spite of my disgust at his wife, and I said, 'Mr

Gummer, it's good to see you. I hope you're keeping better now.'

'Me?' he said, surprised.

'And Mrs Lloyd too. How is she?'

Mrs Gummer hissed. She struck the table. 'Much you care. You want her dead.'

'Ah, Deely,' Gummer said. He looked ill and tired. He said to me, 'Don't set her off.'

'Perhaps,' Kenny said, 'I could start by outlining where Mrs Lloyd stands with Outlook as of this moment.' He opened his file but did not need to find figures there. 'We entered our agreement with her in July 1990 and made an initial payment –'

'We know all this,' Mrs Gummer cried.

'– of fifteen thousand dollars,' Kenny said, 'that being the annual sum agreed on.'

'We know.'

'Since then there have been five further payments, and now, of course, with interest added on, we've reached the valuation set on the property –'

'Your valuer was a crook.'

'So now,' Kenny said doggedly, 'it's a matter of agreeing on the rent –'

'Rent,' Mrs Gummer cried, 'we're being asked for rent in our own home. You,' she said, jutting her face at me, 'you're the one. You sucked her in. She called you because you were supposed to be her friend. And my father's friend.' She began to cry. 'How did we get in this? You and your Willy Gauss.'

'I simply referred Mrs Lloyd,' I said. 'Kenny, Mr Gummer, can't we end all this? We can't get anywhere today.'

'If you knew what he thought of you,' she said.

'Who?'

'Willy Gauss. Who's supposed to be my father. It serves you right.'

'I'm sorry, I don't know what you're talking about,' I said.

'You would, if you asked. Ask Mr Moser.'

'Deely, ah Deely,' Gummer said, 'let's go home.'

'We haven't got a home. They've got it all.'

'Quite legally,' Kenny said, 'and with your mother's full understanding. Everything is signed and notarised. So now, there's the matter of the rent. And Mrs Gummer, you had an ultimatum, I believe.'

'Oh, I do. Yes, I do. It's in here.' She scrabbled in her handbag on her knee.

'Deely,' Gummer warned; and I thought, She's going to pull a gun out of there.

Only Kenny was unalarmed. 'What?' he said, trying to keep her talking for his record.

It was not a gun, it was a knife. It had a blade three inches long and a black plastic handle. A kitchen paring knife, a Diogenes – we have one here. She might have stabbed his face with it, but he was sitting out of reach. Instead she clamped his fingers on the table and sliced the fat part of his hand like cheese. Kenny cried out and pulled away. He fell sideways off his chair and thrust his heel against the table leg, making the table slide and pin me in my chair. Gummer was pinned too but he reached out and seized his wife's wrist. There was no need. She released the knife on to the table. She panted for a moment, then blinked at him and smiled like a child who has been naughty.

'Now I've done it, Mervyn.'

'Yes, you have.'

'What made me do that?'

'Your temper, Deely.'

'It's just that I never could stand people being greedy.'

Gummer managed to push the table back. He stood up. 'No more, lovey, please.'

'No. No more. I'm finished now.' She might have meant a meal. She smiled and sighed.

'Mr Mandell,' Gummer said, 'how badly are you hurt? Let me see.'

'No,' Kenny said. He had climbed to his feet and was holding a handkerchief to his hand. He stepped close to the cabinet and bent his head to it. 'I want to record that Mrs Gummer has attacked me with a knife. I have two cuts in my hand that will require stitches. My father, Josef Mandl, will bear witness to this. Dad, your turn.'

'Yes, she did. It's true,' I said.

'That was the voice of Josef Mandl.'

'So, you've got us,' Gummer said.

'You bet I have.'

'Switch it off then, please. Will you, now?'

Kenny looked surprised. He began to look wobbly too. He turned a switch. He sat down at the far end of the table.

'The rent,' he said. 'It's three hundred dollars a week. It just went up.'

'Write to us. Put it in a letter.' Gummer was supporting himself on the table. He smiled at his wife. 'You're going to have to help me home, Deely.' He picked up the paring knife and slid it into his pocket, and she, chirping, helped him to the door. She looked – it's astonishing, for she was defenceless – she looked like Willi Gauss.

Gummer turned and spoke to me. 'Don't let him call the police.'

'No. God, no,' I said.

She opened the door and they were gone. The meeting, for it was a meeting I suppose, had taken no more than five minutes. There was blood on the table: that was the only mark that they had been. And there was Kenny, white and wounded, at the far end. He had no Brisbois cheeks any more.

'Let me see your hand,' I said.

'In there. In the cabinet. Get me a drink.'

I found a bottle of whisky and poured a glass. Kenny gulped

and fell into a coughing fit. I banged him on the back.

'Stop,' he managed to say. 'Stop that.'

'Shall I call Veronica?'

'Get some tissues from her. Wipe that blood.'

I went out, asked for some, and told her nothing was wrong, some whisky had spilled, that was all. Kenny had unwrapped the handkerchief when I came back. The wounds were ugly: two deep cuts in the meaty part of his hand between his little finger and his wrist.

'Bitch,' he said. 'I should lock her up.'

'You'll need some stitches, Kenny.'

'No. They'll heal. Get rid of that blood.'

I mopped it with tissues and found him even whiter when I'd done. 'You should go home. You've had a shock.'

'There's a bandage in the first-aid kit. And don't let dumb Veronica in here.'

I went out, not telling him that I needed attention myself: my ribs were stabbing me where the table edge had struck, and I think I too was suffering from shock. I asked Veronica for the first-aid kit, and kept her out, although she stepped one way then the other to go round me.

'He's hurt his wrist, that's all. You stay here.'

I fixed a sterile pad on Kenny's hand with sticky tape.

'You shouldn't have pushed her, Kenny. You should have seen.'

'You're blaming me?'

'You know they can't pay three hundred dollars' rent.'

'Jesus, I don't believe this. I'm to blame.'

'Listen, Kenny. Let me handle it. What I'd like to do – let them have it for, just say half, and I'll pay the rest. I'll transfer the money every week. No, listen to me –' but he would not. He swelled with rage; his cheeks came back, Brisboy red, and his eyes popped. He shouted at me, he let all his hatred out, and I won't, I can't, repeat it, for it seems to sully Nancy, who loved him – as I do, as I do – and is innocent. Veronica looked in and withdrew. I allowed him to go on until he was exhausted. My ribs hurt, my head and body hurt. I thought, He'll be better after this.

He sat and panted. I waited for his coming down, for him to shrink; and after a time he closed his eyes. Tears, a thin single tear each side, ran beside his nose.

'Now, Kenny,' I said, and I was nearly crying myself, 'tell me about Julie. What went wrong?'

'You're to blame for this fucking bad blood in our family.'

I saw that he did not keep her hidden away. She was in the front part of his mind.

'Tell me. It might help.'

'Nothing will help.'

'I know you didn't do what she says but something went on . . .'

'It's you and bloody Priscilla and everybody's fault. Not mine.'

'Please, Kenny.'

'She's got your bad blood.'

But that was no more than a defensive step. I kept at him and would not let him go, and he had to tell: exactly what was said and what was done; and more than that – I got in closer – exactly what *he* said and what *he* did.

Here's his voice: 'She was good until she was six or seven. I was a good father, I know I was –' But I can't go on. Kenny is too much there and it's not about one of them, it is all three. It is Kenny and his daughter and his wife. The time that changed their lives was less than an hour long. It hid away, and came out, and hid away again, fixing them in positions that are unnatural. Then at last it emerged in a different shape, but no more horrible than it had always been.

Julie: six. A happy child, Kenny says. An early walker and talker, able to read simple stories before she went to school . . . He went on with all this getting ready, but I can cover it by saying, she was a child the same as any other, and different from them too, with the normal differences. I'll just add that she seemed by nature dissatisfied – but I should stay out of it. Kenny wept, telling me what happened. He gulped and choked and his cheeks grew damp, and when he wiped them with his wounded hand blood squeezed through the gauze and marked him from his nose to the angle of his jaw.

The thing itself: Kenny always showered when he came home from work and Priscilla lifted Julie in with him when she hadn't given her a bath. He did not like that and asked her to stop, but 'she's a lazy bloody bitch' and once or twice a week she pulled the curtain back and sat Julie down at his feet: 'Daddy will wash you tonight.' He knelt in the falling water – rain, he and Julie had named it – and soaped her and rinsed her clean, then lifted her on to the mat and wrapped her in a towel. He stepped half out himself and opened the door: 'Run to Mummy.' Julie trotted along the hall and into the living room and Priscilla dried her by the fire. That was how it used to go.

One night as he stood up after washing her she batted his penis with her hand.

'Don't, Julie. Don't do that,' he said.

'I'm playing with your sausage. Grandpa Leighton lets me.'

For a moment he stood paralysed, then spun her round and smacked her bottom hard, four or five times, and lifted her screaming on to the mat. Priscilla ran in.

'Take her away. Get her out of here.'

He showered for a long time, trying to wash clean, but saw that he had to know everything there was. And Priscilla had to know as well: the man was her father. Then they must get rid of it and never let anything be seen.

When he went into the living room Priscilla was sitting by the fire with Julie dozing in her arms.

'What did you do to her?' Priscilla said.

Kenny knelt beside them. He woke Julie up and said to her,

'I want you to tell Mummy what you told me. I promise I won't smack you again.'

'Leave her alone, Kenny,' Priscilla said.

'No,' he said. 'There's something you've got to know. Julie, go on.'

The child would not speak. Kenny said, 'She touched me on my penis. She said Grandpa Leighton lets her play with his.'

'It's his sausage,' Julie sobbed.

'What nonsense,' Priscilla said.

'Shut up and listen.'

Slowly he got the child to talk. There were games she played with Leighton Spence. There was hunting for his sausage and making his sausage grow big, and others I'm not going to write the names of even though I can't keep them out of my head. Her mother lifted Julie off her lap and put her on the floor, where she lay shivering on her side, answering Kenny sometimes and at other times refusing. Leighton Spence had warned her something bad would happen if she told – and he wouldn't keep ice-cream dollars hidden in his pockets any more. Kenny kept on. He knelt on the floor and bent his head close to the carpet and forced her to look at him with his hand underneath her cheek. When she'd sobbed it all out, wrapped in her towel, she drifted off to sleep as though she'd been drugged. Kenny and Priscilla talked, whispering and hissing. Priscilla wept all her moisture out. At last she seemed to clear the stricture in her throat. Kenny cried too. Then they dried themselves with handkerchiefs and put blocks of wood on the fire.

They woke Julie, and Kenny told her how sick she had been. Part of being sick was nasty dreams, which she must never tell anyone or bogeymen would come and get her in the night. Priscilla said she must stay home and never go and see Grandpa and Grandma any more because they were cross about her dreams. She must never say sausage again, and try to keep only nice and pretty things in her head and say nice things about Grandpa

Leighton. If she didn't, Daddy would take her pants down and smack her very very hard. They sat on the sofa with Julie on the floor between their knees. Her mother stroked her brow, and after a while went to the kitchen and brought her back a glass of raspberryade.

That is how Kenny and Priscilla handled it.

I could not look at him. I could scarcely speak.

'What happened then?'

'We put her to bed.'

'I mean, what *happened*?'

'Nothing, Dad. We kept her out of his way as much as we could.'

'As much as you could?'

'And when she was old enough she went to boarding school. She seemed OK.'

'What about your father-in-law? Did he know she'd told you?'

'He must have, I suppose. Priscilla didn't talk to him any more. She went funny. She's as screwed up as Julie is.'

'Did you talk to him?'

'Shit, Dad, how could I? I was doing all right at Outlook. I was getting ahead. And he was my boss. Anyway, the old bugger had his stroke, he couldn't do anything any more.'

I turned away from Kenny, away from my son. And then, because I must, because of Nancy, turned back and looked at him again. He must go to Julie's therapist, I said, and tell her everything he'd just told me.

'No.'

'Write it, then. Put it all down and give it to me. I'll pass it on.'

'No. That head-shrinking stuff is hokum, Dad. It's all bloody Freud. It's bloody Jews.'

'Stop, Kenny. Shut up. Please do.' I went to the door. 'And stay away from Julie. Just keep right away.'

'I don't want her any more.' But again tears leaked from his eyes.

I walked back and gave him my handkerchief. 'Wipe your face. There's blood on it.'

He polished hard, then had a gulp of whisky.

'Now go to a doctor. You need some stitches in your hand.'

I went home by taxi. And I've had the doctor myself, to look at my ribs. They're bruised not broken. I lie up and creep about and write in my book: Kenny and Priscilla and Julie. And the other person, the creased old man whose corruption I smelled on the first day we met: I can no longer write his name. I only write 'Kenny' because he is my son. Elizabeth scolds me; she puts her arm around me and helps me here and there. I've told her what went on, in Kenny's office and that earlier time, and she has arranged to call on Helen Henly and tell her. I hope it will help Julie – help her to go back there, help her to see, if she needs to see. Kenny needs to make that journey too, just as much. But I am no longer sure he can be cured.

As for the rest of them – I mean the Gummers and Mrs Lloyd – there's nothing I can do for them any more.

I poked my nose in Julie's room while she was out. She is growing hyacinths in the sun on her window sill. There's a purple one and a cream one. They sit in jars of water and feed on pieces of charcoal trapped in their roots. The blooms are thick and beautiful, their scent fills the room.

She has already rejected caduceus and ankh so I won't attempt an explanation of these flowers to her.

SIXTEEN

I lay in bed or pottered about the house while my bruises turned from blue to yellow and faded away. It took a long time. Old men do not recover quickly; often they don't recover at all. It seemed to me that I might choose. Curiosity kept me going as much as anything else. I did not worry or brood. When I understood that I was looking forward not back I began to get well again. I want to see Julie recover, as much as she is able to, and start up her life, before I go. But I don't intend to watch too closely or expect too much. I mean to enjoy the spring that is on us now. ('On us now' – isn't that what one says about the winter?) And tomorrow morning I have arranged to visit Moser. Curiosity is my best medicine.

Because it is November we are having gales. The clouds race low over the hills, people bend as they walk and women hold their skirts down. It isn't wet and isn't cold so they look as if they enjoy the buffeting they receive. The harbour is blue flecked with white, and all the heavy colours are blown out of Somes Island, leaving it pale, leaving it pure. They don't lock people up there any more. The name change is gazetted. The island is Matiu or Somes now, as you please.

Elizabeth walks about the house jamming rubber wedges in doors that rattle. She goes into the garden, she leans into the wind, her hair blows out, silvery. It is middle-aged now that she has stopped dyeing it. She and Julie plot a new flower bed. They're like engineers. Julie's hair has grown too. It slants across her eyes in the wind. Now, this minute, she catches it in one hand and holds it on top so she can see.

In weather like this Wellington stands on the frontier between the warm north and the cold south. I can see it; I'm aware; and feel that I have earned my right to stay. My hemisphere. My city. My place.

Elizabeth and Julie are my family. It does not matter what Moser reveals. So, I take it back, my best medicine is here.

We should have been friends. His Berlin is like my Vienna. He does not want it any more but it won't go away. I advised him to write about it as I have done, and he became interested: 'What language did you use?'

He never made the efforts to learn English that I made, he just let it happen, and has done pretty well. Both of us still have a tongue that won't quite make the proper sounds. I'm a little better than him, as I deserve to be. It galls me that in finding colloquial language we're about equal. All the same, I grinned at him and he grinned back. We enjoyed competing.

He lives in an apartment on Oriental Parade and looks across the water at the Wadestown hills. I tried to see my house but the tops of Norfolk pine trees blocked my view. Somes Island (we agreed that for us it would stay Somes) was out of sight around Point Jerningham. He can watch the ferries and container ships almost at sea level. If he opens his windows, which he tells me he doesn't do because of traffic noise ('when will they learn about double glazing in this country?'), he can hear the shouts of helmsmen training dragon-boat crews.

Moser has shrunk and grown more fierce, and grown more generous and emotional. He has become scaly: his old skin flakes, it shines in concave patches here and there. He does not enjoy being ugly, he says – but likes being thin and dry better than he would like being fat and sweaty, which is what most of the men he has done business with become. They have no minds, he says, they are all belly and stuffed up with money to the gills. That's a practised speech, delivered, I think, for the metaphor.

I like his eyes, bright and blue – red-lidded though, with the lower lids collapsed. He has white eyebrows that slant down on one side, up on the other, like spear heads. Although he's seven or eight years older than me he moves as quickly, with spiky legs and a beetle roundness in his back. I am straight, and less scaly too – but I've no doubt he'd find ways to describe me that would be unflattering. He has a cold. His nose collects a dewdrop that he's quick to wipe away. He's very clean and smells of mint.

We shook hands formally, overcoming our impulse to embrace. We talked for a while about unimportant things. That's where Berlin and Vienna came in – they're interesting but of no great importance, even though they provide the base on which we stand. Take them away and we'd fall down. I feel myself begin to wail and drift on the wind at the thought. But, from day to day, they're of no importance. I asked Moser if he had worked in electronics in Berlin, but no, it was a hobby, he had liked fixing radios, he had liked to tinker. His real trade was printing. He could not work at it after the war because his English was not good enough, so he repaired toasters and irons, then went into making furniture, where he did well. I told him I could have done that too, not as a businessman but with my hands, and he acknowledged the superiority of that. He claimed that he could have baked bread. He seemed to think that he had started me off as a baker.

Often when I'm with New Zealand men, chatting away, I'm all right for a while, I can do the necessary tricks, but then I grow tired of it and I'm not with them any more, even those I like. I cannot sustain the jocular tone, or do the friendly insult, or pretend deep interest in shallow things, and cannot keep on smiling while they earbash me. So I take refuge in my foreignness, I make my courteous goodbyes; and they, understandably, are pleased to see me go. I can feel them unbutton as I slide out the door. I'm not upset by it. I'm simply relieved to have a means of retreat.

Moser and I could have talked all day if Willi Gauss had not stood between us. He told me that although he had not known Willi in Berlin he had heard his name and had probably set one or two of his articles in print.

'You were his friend, you're the one who knows him,' Moser said, 'but I am the one who knows about him.'

Willi was a gutter journalist, he said. When I challenged him on that, he agreed it was inaccurate for it was not sex and scandal Willi wrote about but politics.

Moser is less political than me. He's not able to see that market dictatorship is political and the Me-firstism that infects us now political. I find that surprising in someone who lived in Berlin during the rise of the Nazis – and I said so. He can be frightening when he glares. His eyes flash and his eyebrows work. He told me I knew nothing and I saw he had forgotten that I was, like him, a Jew. I had to get up and walk to the window and stand looking out so that he should not see from my face how upset I was. But he is quick. He's generous. He went away to his kitchen and made coffee. I looked out, seeing nothing but my parents in Vienna and Susi dying in Paris, and it came to me that Franz had loved her just as much as I. His love for her explained his life.

When Moser came back I asked him if he'd ever heard again from his friend in Berlin, if there had been more news about Willi – and Moser said yes, he had had a letter but had kept it to himself because the story in it was unconfirmed and it was better to leave Willi lying as he fell. I think he meant that to have a heroic sound and he miscued. I saw Willi dead in a gutter in East Berlin.

'It is fifteen years old. Leave it now, Josef,' Moser said.

'This is a letter that says how he died?'

'No. It is about what he was doing when he was caught.'

'Can you show me?'

'I don't keep such things. Old letters. What is the use? I keep what I need in here.' He tapped his forehead.

'What did it say?'

'If you must hear, Josef. It was not a long letter. My friend wrote because he had written before and this was the full stop, that is all. He has no interest. Nobody has any interest in Willi Gauss.'

'Only you and me.'

'Yes. Us. How can we not be interested? My friend in Berlin says Willi was trying to smuggle out a woman and her child. He had them in the boot of his car.' Moser laughed. 'He should have dug a tunnel.'

'Who were they?'

'I do not know. Perhaps it was for money, my friend says. There were such people.'

'No, not money.'

'Because he hated Stalinism? For some odd politics, you think? It could not have been because he loved the West.'

'The child might have been his. And the woman too. He might have been rescuing them.'

'His wife would have loved that,' Moser said.

'Willi wouldn't care about that. Wives,' I said. And I knew that I had it right. Some combination of arrogance and self-love had driven him. And romance too, his romantic view of himself. And love perhaps? Love at last, for the woman and her child?

'He thought he had bribed a guard,' Moser said. 'But they were waiting for him at the gate. So Willi gets captured again. He is not the best escaper in the world.'

'What happened to the woman and the child?'

'Who knows? They have no names. They are little pieces of dust that blow about. We know about such things. Do not be sad.'

'They didn't kill women, did they?'

'They would put her in prison. And take the child. They did that.'

'And hurt Willi?'

'Of course. Question him. And kill him after. Josef, it is fifteen years. It is all done.'

I saw an old man dressed in his underpants, squatting in the corner of a cell. He has silver hair and fallen cheeks. All his teeth are broken. He wipes his mouth. Footsteps sound in the corridor, a key turns in the lock. He tries to huddle deeper on the floor and hides his face. And I see Willi from Somes Island – Willi with his shirt off in the sun, curling his lip at this little city, Wellington. There is no dislocation. Both these men are Willi Gauss.

'Josef, do not imagine. Do not make a story,' Moser said.

No, I won't. What happened in Berlin is over now, although in another way it is never done. And knowing Willi has helped me see my parents again. That is strange. I see them full face – but I won't write any more, for it will make it seem that the important thing is not their pain and death but my ability to weep for them.

'How much did Willi get out of you before he left?' Moser said.

I told him one hundred pounds and he raised his eyebrows. 'You knew you would never get it back?'

'I told him it was a gift.'

'Yes. So did I. Twenty-five pounds. Getting rid of Willi was cheap at the price.'

Nothing Moser said about him would upset me now; and nothing Willi had said would cause me pain. I have moved a step: reconstituted Willi and got rid of inessential parts of myself. I'm on firm ground – which is not to say that I'm happy there. But I will not be put off balance and I will not argue. I told Moser Mrs Gummer's claim that he knew what Willi had really thought of me.

'Ach! It is nothing,' Moser said. 'The woman hurts and so she tries to hurt other people.'

'How is it that you know her?'

'The mother, Willi's concubine, she used to telephone me when she lived in Auckland. I went to see her out of curiosity. Always it was news of Willi she wanted. I wrote and told her when he died.'

'She doesn't believe it.'

'No. The daughter keeps in touch now. She pesters me. It is you and your son she wants to talk about.'

'I think that's all over.' I told Moser about her visit to Kenny in his office and that she had stabbed him with a knife, but all he answered was, 'Willi keeps on.'

'So,' I asked, 'what did he say about me?'

'It is not only you. It is all of us.'

To keep himself occupied, Moser had visited the National Archives and read the files on Aliens held there. He started with his own, which, he says, is much like mine, except that he 'exhibits low cunning'. 'We are not to be trusted because we are Jews, that is what I read between the lines.' Willi is not to be trusted because of his 'continental mentality', which is 'utterly at odds with our notions of fair play'. Also 'he is a cad where women are concerned'. But they – the Tribunal – are impressed with von Schaukel, 'an attractive type and soldierly'. They like his candour and are pleased to have captured this man who would have been a valuable fighter for Germany.

'The files are interesting,' Moser said, very dry.

I told him yes, I had read them too, Willi's and mine, and von Schaukel's and Hoch's (the enemy), but had not looked at his because I felt it should stay private.

'I have not your finer feelings,' he said.

'But there's nothing in Willi's about me.'

'Ah, you did not look far enough. There are other files. They deal with the detention camps.' He went to another room and came back with a sheaf of photocopies. 'You will not like it, Josef. I did not like it either. But I was not surprised. I thought he was up to something like this.'

The copies were from 'Secret file, part 2: Commandant's file'. The first sheet Moser showed me was a letter to the commandant: 'I have to thank you for your letter of the 15th inst. enclosing the list of German and Austrian internees prepared by Gauss. This will form an interesting record and may be of use in other ways. Would you kindly thank Gauss for what he has done.' It was signed by someone called Wilson, for the Director, Security Intelligence.

Next came a list, and I recognised the names; and of course went straight to mine: 'Mandl, Josef. Austrian Jew. 5, B.' I looked at Moser for an explanation.

'See, here I am,' he said. 'I am a German Jew. 3, C. And Willi, look at Willi, he does not leave himself out: German. 5, A.'

'What does it mean?'

'Here is the key.' He handed me another sheet, and I reproduce it from memory:

> 1 – active Nazi
> 2 – Nazi sympathiser
> 3 – opportunist
> 4 – indifferent
> 5 – anti-Nazi
> 6 – German nationalist
> A – intellectual
> B – average mentality
> C – low mentality
> D – sub-normal

'You see,' Moser said, 'you are an anti-Nazi Austrian Jew of average mentality.'

'And you,' I said, working it out.

'An opportunist German Jew of low mentality.'

'What is Willi?'

'He is an anti-Nazi German intellectual.'

We laughed. 'So,' I said, 'now I know, I'm only average.'

'And I, at least, am not sub-normal,' Moser said.

'Opportunist?' I said.

'Oh, that is not the worst. I did not know that Willi had such a vocabulary. Look here.'

He handed me the rest of the papers and I saw what he meant: fanatic, twister, double dealer, coward, liar, neurotic, cosmopolitan, religious crank, snob, sexual pervert, cheat, and more. Moser was the twister, Hoch the sexual pervert, and I the snob (among other things).

I find snob a hard word. I repudiate the charge, and I think my mentality is better than average too. I do not recognise myself in Willi's paragraphs: 'Mandl is good-natured and well-meaning but lacks intelligence and strength of will. He is easily led. Politically he is naive, mistaking the wish for the deed. In Vienna he was a member of Stalinist anti-Trotskyist youth groups, but is ruled by self-interest and will betray his so-called beliefs for personal advantage.' And so on for half a page. This is not me – but I see Willi behind the lines and I laugh at him and say, That's the stuff, Willi.

He must have worked hard at these little biographies. Someone from the commandant's office helped him with his English. I rather like his final advice that I am no danger to New Zealand's security and should not be deported after the war. 'Mandl will become a good New Zealander,' Willi says. After all the bad things he had written he must have enjoyed telling them where I belonged.

I make no judgement. All this seems of a piece with Willi. I knew that he believed he was stooping down to me. I can, if I try, find an argument for him: he was getting the Nazis – and he certainly got them, wanted deportation for the lot – and sacrificed his followers so as not to seem partisan. But I don't try. I don't need to argue for Willi. I love him, that is all. Without knowing him I would be less than I am.

Moser, who was not a follower, not a friend, comes out worse than me, but he laughs too.

'Think of it, I gave him twenty-five pounds.'

I won't start visiting the National Archives. Instead I will play bowls. I won't try to change Kenny and turn him into healthier ways. What he does is base, I believe. He has no *work*, even though he puts in long hours. I will keep on hoping that he comes to see it for himself; and that, one day, he will understand what he did to Julie and, if it's possible, know her again. I will try to stay away from down there and live up here, in the country of the natural affections, where I have been both uneasy and at home. At home with Nancy. With everyone else I've had to keep renewing my visa. How I wish it had been my native land.

Moser became restless at the end of my visit. He wanted me gone, and I found the reason when his grand-daughter came in. He did not mean to share the girl with me. She was in her school uniform and, I thought, might have been Avis Greenough, who taught me my vocabulary.

'Josef is just going,' Moser said.

'Oh,' she said, a happy girl, 'I don't mind making lunch for two.'

'No, no,' I said, 'mine is waiting for me.' I said goodbye and promised to call again, and the girl, showing me to the door, whispered, 'Please do. He's got no friends in Wellington.'

She loves him, but no more than Elizabeth loves me; and, perhaps, than Julie loves me, her Grandpa Joe.

She digs, bending her back. She digs like a navvy. Elizabeth does the fine work, planting the seedlings and the seeds. When they come inside Julie will dance to her African music, which I'm tired of now but pleased to hear – hear her feet stepping on the floor. Her hyacinths are withered, but that means nothing, they're only flowers. When she kisses me she does it properly, with no finger in between. In a little while she is running me down to bowls in her pink car. I am looking forward to that. She drives fast. We'll whip down the top road as though we're in a Ferrari and pull up at the green with a screech of tyres. That will make Clive and Dennis stare.

I won, though only just. Afterwards Clive asked us home for a glass of beer. He lives only two doors down from the club. I never knew that. It's next door to the house where I lived in the back yard in a lean-to shed. The lean-to is gone and so is Wilf White's garden. There are flats built there, two storeys high. Housewives at their dishes watch us play. Clive lives in a back yard too, in a caravan, which he keeps as neat as a matchbox, spick and span, all with one arm. His daughter waved at us from the house as we went by. He has three daughters, he told me, and a dozen grandchildren scattered here and there. A great-grandson too. We congratulated each other, although silently for Dennis's sake. He has only his faith and his cigarettes.

I telephoned Julie and told her where to find me. We drank beer from Clive's tiny fridge, and talked a bit of this and that: three old men sitting together. I've an idea, though, that when I left Clive and Dennis were on the edge of politics and religion. Perhaps I'll share those arguments next time. There's a thing or two that I can say.

Julie called and drove me home.

Elizabeth is baking bread.